MAN OF NAZARETH

Anthony Burgess is one of the major
literary figures of the twentieth century.
He is also a composer, pianist, translator,
critic, screenwriter, teacher, and lecturer.
Perhaps best known for his novel
A Clockwork Orange, he is also the author
of *1985*, *Enderby's End* and *Napoleon
Symphony*.

Man of Nazareth is Anthony Burgess's
full-length novel of his screen-play for the
Franco Zeffirelli production. It is
quintessential Burgess – allusive, cinematic,
inventive, audacious, and orchestrated with
perfect pitch. In *Man of Nazareth* Burgess
once again delights and astonishes with the
elegance of his style and the intelligence of
his narrative. He choreographs characters,
events, and dialogue to achieve his own
interpretation for modern readers of a
timeless story.

ANTHONY BURGESS

Man of Nazareth

MAGNUM BOOKS
Methuen Paperbacks Ltd

A Magnum Book

MAN OF NAZARETH
ISBN 0 417 05810 1

First published in USA 1979
by McGraw Hill Inc
Magnum edition published 1980

Copyright © 1979 by Anthony Burgess

Magnum Books are published
by Methuen Paperbacks Ltd
11 New Fetter Lane, London EC4P 4EE

Made and printed in Great Britain
by Richard Clay (The Chaucer Press) Ltd, Bungay, Suffolk

To Liana

ὃ οὖν ὁ Θεὸς
δυνεζευξεν,
ἄνθρωπος μὴ
χωριζέτω.

BOOK 1

ONE

The manner of executing a criminal in those days, as I have seen too often with my own eyes, was somewhat in the manner I shall now describe. It seems to me first, though, to be a matter of courtesy to tell the reader who I am, since I expect him to travel with me a long road and in all weathers, so I give my name, which is Azor the son of Sadoc. I am called in Greek by various names: Psilos, meaning the Tall One, since I am below the average in size; Leptos, meaning the Thin One, as I am inclined to plumpness; Makarios, meaning, among other things, fortunate. I write stories and recite them; I translate documents for the government, since I am expert in Latin, Greek and Aramaic; I write letters for petitioners. In the field of numbers, I do audits and help with the keeping of accounts for Akathartos, a large and untrustworthy wine merchant. But I come now to true and physical crucifixion.

First they would flog the man who was condemned, then make him drag the horizontal beam of his cross from the cross-yard to the place of his final punishment. At this place there would already be an upright shaft fixed as firmly as a tree in the ground, and the criminal would be nailed, with arms outstretched, by the wrists or palms of the hands to the crosspiece, which would then be attached to the upright at a distance of some ten or twelve feet above the ground. Then the feet would be nailed with a single cut nail to the upright, or vertical shaft. Sometimes a wooden wedge would be thrust in between this shaft and the bare buttocks of the crucified, to give a kind of support. The name of the criminal and the nature of his crime would be lettered in the three tongues of the province—namely, Aramaic and Latin and Greek—onto a piece of whitewashed wood. This would be tacked to the extremity of the upright—that is, above his head or, more often since it was easier and more convenient, below his feet—so that all interested could read what very quickly became his sole obituary. Death was caused by asphyxiation or by exhaustion and the failure of the muscle of the heart, but, with obdurate cases, it could be hastened through breaking the legs with an iron rod or piercing the side with a military spear.

Perhaps I should add that the criminal was stripped totally naked before being nailed to his cross, with none of his shame hidden. This made the punishment not only cruel but obscene.

Now there came a time when the ingenuity of whatever officer was in charge of crucifixions in the province of Judaea, which was then directly under the rule of Rome and not of a client monarch (like Galilee, to give one example), devised a variant mode of dispatch. In the execution ground narrow slits were dug to a considerable depth, sometimes of six or more feet, and in these slits were placed as a permanency a sort of upended box of stout wood, open at the ends, into which the upright of the cross could be slid, the whole structure then holding very firm. This meant that the malefactor would have to carry an entire cross, with upright and horizontal nailed or morticed together, from the place of whipping to the place of death, and the exhaustion thus caused would very sensibly speed his end. It meant also that he could be nailed to the cross while it lay on the ground of the hill (as it usually was) of crucifixion, in a single swift rhythm that involved three men skilled in the mystery, one for each palm or wrist and one, usually a stout man of great strength, for the feet, though he would often employ a boy as assistant to hold the feet firm for the transfixing. This act of triple nailing done, the cross would be dragged with its moaning burden to the awaiting slit in the ground, raised with much cheerful shouting, then slid in, to stand there firm and snug, though in high winds it would creak and sway like a ship's mast.

I do not approve this mode of punishing the state's offenders, and I am with Cicero in considering it a most horrible form of death, unworthy of an advanced civilisation, but I would clear the Romans of the charge, often laid against them, of originating it and perpetuating it. For it seems that the Persians, the Seleucids, the Carthaginians, and even the Jews themselves used crucifixion as a means of dispatching agitators, whether in the sphere of religion or of politics, as well as thieves, pirates and errant slaves, long before the Levant became a region for the colonising activities of Rome. It is said that Darius, king of the Persians, crucified some three thousand of his enemies in Babylon; and, less than two centuries before the time I shall be speaking of, in Jerusalem itself, the holy city, Antiochus the Fourth of Syria scourged and crucified a large number of dissident Jews; while, but eight and eighty years before the birth of Jesus Naggar (or Marangos), Alexander Jannaeus, king and high priest in Judaea, used three thousand nails and two thousand beams on one thousand Pharisees.

To see such an execution effected, to hear the groans of the dying man, to observe the shame of his bloodied nakedness, is to be made newly aware of a great principle of wrong in the world, though the moral voice in oneself will be divided, thrusting on to the shock and pity and anger with a demand to look for the primary wrong in the crucified and not in the crucifier, in his crime and not in his wholly merited punishment. His is the evil, else he would be walking in the streets, a good and honest citizen, laughing in the taverns, playing with his children, bringing them to spell out the inscriptions on the crosses in reasonable curiosity. He would certainly not be there himself. Yet the evil done by the crucified was to himself a sort of good, or he would not have pursued it to the limit of his own death; and the evil done by the agents of the crucifixion is presented as a means of protecting and preserving the commonalty and keeping it good and also happy.

It is not to my purpose to observe on good and evil, or right and wrong, since I have little skill in that kind of thinking. But I may be allowed without contradiction to state that the world is a twofold creation; indeed, I have never yet met any man who would deny it. The stability of living things, and even of man-made, seems to depend on the conflicting of opposites, which some philosphers living at the furthest stations of our camel-routes would take to be less a conflict than a kind of love of the genders, so that even God, as they see him, must have a consort to make him balanced and sane and fit to listen to prayers. In our own bodies, we see such a balance made possible by the har-mony of left and right, though some would hold, and perhaps rightly, that it is in truth a conflict, and that our stability is a kind of happy but unpurposed emanation out of a mild war whose issue is never resolved. In the universe of the spirit, at least as it appears to us in the Mediterranean lands, the twofold nature is held to be seen in the unresolved conflict between good and evil, though these are no more easily to be defined as to their true re-spective essences than are right and left, or light and darkness, since the one can only be understood in terms of the other.

When a man is drunk, he knows not his left from his right; his balance is disturbed; he is in danger of falling over; he falls over. There are times, say some, when drunkenness attacks the uni-verse of the spirit. The balance of good and evil is very notice-ably disturbed, and while some fear the end of all things, others rejoice in the belief that a new age is coming. The one party apprehends man's sinking, the other foresees his taking to the air like a bird or an angel. The times reel and babble. Omens are looked for, prophets appear, the wrath of the Eternal is much spoken of, as likewise the coming of the Kingdom of the Just. Also, since it is not easy to mark the boundaries of politics and religion, there will be many who see breaking and new beginning as coming to the realm of secular rule. There will be zealots, rebels, assassins. There will be plenty of work for the crucifiers.

The time I shall tell of was such a time, the year of the begin-ning of my story the seven hundred and fiftieth year since the founding of Rome, and the place the country called Israel, whose name signifies both a bodily location and a kingdom of the spirit (and yet how very strange that the true meaning of the name Israel should have to do with wrestling with God). This was, to the Romans, the furthermost flank of their empire, and they knew it as Palestine. They did not, at the beginning of the period I tell of, rule it directly but through a client-monarch, as he was called.

As I call myself a teller of stories, I perceive that I must now cease generalities and conjure bodies that move and voices that speak, so I will permit myself the liberty of, as it were, exercising my fingers on the harp in a brief scene before striking the chords of one more substantial and important. I will take you then to a tavern in Jerusalem with vine-leaves on the lintel, not far from a hill of crucifixion, and let you hear the words of a Roman under-officer named Sextus. He knows Palestine, having often been a humble part of the entourage of visiting Roman notables. He is seated at a rough table wet with spilled wine, and, being a man amiable enough though coarse and ignorant and contemptuous of all he calls foreigners, he has paid for a skin to be poured for a number of poor Jews about him, who are content to drink and listen and be silent. His face and body are much scarred, from tavern brawls as much as battles, and his veteranhood is proclaimed in a single eye, the left.

"And so," he says, "we stretch from kan to scham," and he scrawls a rough map on the table with a wine-dripping finger. "That is," he says, "from this stinking hot dungheap, not that I mind the heat, I can well stand it, the heat, it's the smell I can't stand, no offence meant and none I trust taken, though if taken I give not a kruvit, right up yonder through Spain and France to the very edge of the great dirty schatiach, you fall off if you go too far, Britain it's called, my little yedidim. Seen them all. The Roman nescher stretches its wings till it near splits its down that and we'll all have another. Hot here, I can well stand it, the heat. Freeze your little kadurim off, Britain would. Naked bastards with blue paint all over their thanks dear heart and how much do

I owe thee. Seem not to feel the kar or the krio, somehow, some-what. All dependent on how you are brought up, yeled. Rather have you schilschul lot any day, nice quiet lot of no offence meant and none I trust taken, though if taken I give not a morsel of stinking iltit. You there, yedid, I see you spit. I see thee spit on the ritspah, which is neither kind nor useful. There is a pot there, look, for the spitting. Now if your spitting, naar, means what I well wish I did not think it to mean, then schamah. Schamah the tramp tramp tramp of the boots outside in the stinking dust, and the raasch of the old bucina. We be around to stay, yedidim, and not all your spitting will wash it out. Not all the spit in the great meluchlach Yahudi world will lay the dust raised by one Roman toe on the tramp tramp tramp. Who is your king? I ask again: who is your melech? Herod the Big. An Arab on both sides, av and em, but a Jew too, and a friend too of the Emperor Augustus who I once saw, do you schamah, may he bless himself and keep himself, him being himself a god. So there thou hast it, yeled. Watch and have a care. Him you have and him you have and us you have, and so it will always be. Per omnia saecula saeculorum."

Now, with fingers stretched and ready, I am emboldened to take you into the presence of King Herod the Great himself, in the fine baths he had built over the hot springs at Callirhoe.

TWO

Herod was at this time in his seventy-third year, gross, indulged and big-bellied, given to mad fits of cruelty, with a rich record of murders behind him, many of them of his nearest and even dearest, his feet growing cold as stone but the pains in his calves ferocious. At the moment I am writing of, he was with L. Metellus Pediculus, on a visit from Rome, and, after the calidarium, they had both proceeded to the sudatorium to have sweat and oil cleaned off their bodies with a strigil. A slave brought wine. Metellus said that what he was now about to say he would say with deference, but Herod said: "No deference, Metellus, not between naked men. Look at that belly. Or rather, do not. It is there that the wars of my old age are waged, but I have other battlefields too." He spat out the wine onto the slave who had served it, saying: "Urine. Fetch Falernian. With deference what?"

"The Emperor says," said Metellus, "that no great ruler should let his private life become public. Especially, forgive me, in a territory where so much is made of morality."

"Show and hypocrisy," Herod said. "Hand-washing before meals and keeping the pots and pans clean. The Pharisees, greasy mean lot. Morality has nothing to do with rule. That I learned from Rome."

"The Emperor Augustus," said Metellus, "would, I think, use the term *cynical*. He believes in virtue, not only for Caesar's wife but for Caesar himself."

Relays of slaves had raced in with Falernian, which Herod now drank before saying: "You must tell me all about virtue at dinner. Let me tell you this here and now, that the ruler's one and only task is to rule. And rule begins in his own family. The Emperor Augustus does not have a mob of sons and daughters trying to wrest the crown from him. There has been some necessary *putting down,* so much I admit. I like not the smell of blood any more than dear Augustus does. I want a quiet life."

They moved to the tepidarium and then to the frigidarium. Metellus swam a little round the pool while Herod sat and panted and groaned and mumbled at some grapes, spitting the pips out at the slave who stood there with the grapes on a silver dish. Then he and his guest, dry and enrobed and anointed, moved from the baths to a small presence-chamber, Herod limping and cursing, where most of the junior seraglio sat around naked like furniture. More wine was brought, also fruit, tiny highly spiced sausages, small birds on skewers, pickled olives, gherkins, toasted cheese and other appetisers. Metellus said:

"The Palestinians are still full of their own history, are they not? They seem hard to convince that history, like the whole known world, is a Roman province."

"You are lucky to have so many teeth," Herod said, admiring. "Strong ones too, as I can see. It is a terrible thing for a man when he starts to lose his teeth. You, girl," he frowned at one of the seraglio. "A bruise on your thigh. Fighting again. By God, I'll have the whip brought for the lot of you, unruly little bitches."

"Isaac," Metellus was saying. "Abraham. Moses. I find the names hard to get the tongue round."

"The prophets go back beyond the Romans," Herod said. "Make no mistake about that. King Solomon, whose temple I'm rebuilding—he was already old in story when Romulus and Remus were sucking away."

"It is not, as you know," said Metellus, "Roman policy to wipe out indigenous religions, so long as they don't conflict overmuch with our faith in a deified emperor. The leaders of the indigenous religions have usually been helpful to the Roman power. They too seek a quiet life."

"Deified emperors have nothing to do with true religion," Herod said, squinting at a toasted sparrow he was dissecting with greasy fingers.

"You mentioned prophets," Metellus said. "We hear talk about prophets. Tell me about prophets, majesty."

"Prophets," said Herod. "A prophet is a man who prophesies that the wrath of God is coming. That God will smite sinners and that sinners had better stop sinning. He reminds them what sin is or sins are and raves at them, telling them to stop."

"By God," Metellus said, smiling, "is meant some small bearded unwashed tribal deity?"

"That," Herod said, "is unworthy, O lord Metellus, and you know it. Listen. Prophets do no harm. There have always been prophets in Palestine. Holy men who want others to be holy. Stop beating your wife. Stop eating pork. Keep your fingernails clean. No harm in it, no danger to Rome, if that's what you're thinking."

"And in what way," asked Metellus, "does a prophet differ from a what is the word *messiah?*"

"A messiah." Herod brooded a space, squinting again, on the gluteal muscle of a twelve-year-old girl from a suburb of Damascus. "A messiah is very different from a prophet. There have been prophets, but there has been no messiah. Nor will there ever be one. It's a dream, no more than that, sir."

Metellus wished to know a dream of what.

"A bad dream," Herod said. "It is this. A man has come along from nowhere. He preaches like a prophet—sin and repentance and the rest of it. But he has, so to speak, royal credentials. He's the son of a royal house, and he can prove it. He thumps out holy scripture like any priest, but he gives it a new meaning. Twists it, if you like. Adds just enough of his own to make it different, but not enough to make it *too* different. He's seen eating pork somewhere, which is totally against the Jewish dietary laws, and then he comes up with some obscure text out of the prophet Nahshon or somebody to prove that pork is in order during the time of a plague of grasshoppers when the wind is in the west and the tamarisk is in premature blossom, that sort of thing, no answer to it. He says the time has come for the building of a new kingdom, and the people believe him. They follow him to the tearing down of the old kingdom."

"And how is the tearing down done, majesty?" asked Metellus. "Where do the armies come from?"

"The armies are already there," said Herod. "The armies follow him, along with the people. They forget old allegiances, they believe in the new thing. Shall we go in to dinner? And what entertainment would the lord Metellus wish to see? We can do as well here as in Rome, I think. I have female wrestlers with very long nails. Or a cock-fight might be less noisy. We tear out their voice-boxes so they can't crow."

"Thank you," Metellus said. "Is there much talk now of a messiah?"

"No more than usual," said Herod, "and no less. Longing for the coming of the messiah is part of the Jewish way of life. A kind of family pastime. Every pregnancy may mean a son, and that son may be the messiah. And if a daughter comes—well, she has her chance, the same as her mother. It is, you could say, good for family stability."

"Which means," Metellus said, "for the stability of the state."

"Bad dreams perhaps are a small price to pay for that." Herod raised fat fingers loaded with heavy rings and, at that signal, the royal chief musician, a thin bearded Syrian, led his men into a stately and barbaric march, full of flutes, trumpets, cymbals and a single but loud sackbut. Herod was helped onto a litter. "I have to be carried to the dining-room," he said, "because of these damnable pains in the calves. If you're quit of toothache up here you have to have it down there. That is what being old means. Will you too be carried, or will you walk?" Metellus called above the sackbut that he would walk, march rather.

And so they went to dinner, which was, as you may well suppose, sumptuous enough, there being for but two eaters some twenty servers under a fat oiled though young but gelded major-domo who clapped hands discreetly for fresh napkins or cooler water or wine or another helping of calves' brains in aspic for the distinguished guest from Rome. Imagine for yourself what dishes might be served at a great banquet and be assured they were all there, with naked slave-boys serving them and bowing low. Now Herod ate very little, though he sweated much, and he also twitched and groaned and cursed and struck out with his ringed hands at a slave whose breathing was audible while he served. Metellus watched him covertly, for it was his true mission to report back to Rome on the state of Herod's health and how many years more he probably had to live. He had kept order in Palestine but after his death matters might be much different and Rome could not afford a chaos on her most easterly flank. It happened this evening that Herod the Great was visited by impressions that those who were dead, and some long dead, on his orders, including the beloved consort Doris, whose death was a cruel necessity, were alive again, many of them. They would seem to appear suddenly among the bushes beyond the terrace, or peep over the edge of the table, or stand on the very fringe of his line of vision only to dissolve on the direct challenge of his eye, or sing so clearly in his head that he sought the owner of the voice, groaning as he turned heavily about to look. He smiled in apology often at Metellus, saying he was not well tonight but would be better tomorrow, his cursed physicians were all fools, and the like. Metellus ate and smiled and nodded but said very little. It seemed to him that he should not have asked him about prophets and messiahs and so on.

THREE

It has been said that it was on the tenth day of Tishri, on the great feast of Yom Ha-Kippurim, called also Shabbat Shabbaton or the Sabbath of Solemn Rest, that the thing happened to Zacharias that rendered him dumb. This was the day of atonement for sins and mutual forgiveness of sins, since to obtain God's forgiveness one must first oneself forgive, and from one's heart too. It was a day on which there was no eating nor drinking and a putting off of physical desire. Shoes of new leather were worn and the whole of Israel smelled sweetly of the oils of ritual anointing. Zacharias was very old in years and in the service of the Lord, and he was this day to perform, to the great pride of his wife Elizabeth, who was as old as he, the duties of high priest in the Temple at Jerusalem. And so as, in his robes, he trod to music the pavement of the house of the Most High, he turned to where Elizabeth was with the women, daughters of Israel, and smiled towards her and she returned his smile. They were both very old and, to their sorrow, childless, but they had lived long together in great loving kindness.

First there came the sacrifice of a lamb, and then, this being the one day of the whole year when the high priest might do so, Zacharias moved beyond the veil to the Holy of Holies, in order that he might sprinkle the blood of the sacrifice onto the holy fire and offer also a pinch of incense. While he was doing this, and the chanting of the priests and the people proceeded on the other side of the veil, he was astonished to find a young man leaning on the altar, dressed in a simple robe whose whiteness outshone the whiteness of Zacharias's own priestly garment. The young man had golden hair which he wore short, and he was clean-shaven. He was, with what Zacharias at first took to be a manner of insolent negligence, cleaning his fingernails with a small thin sharpened stick, looking at his nails ever and anon as if he had only recently been issued with them and wondered what their function was. Zacharias spluttered and tried to speak, and the blood in the vessel shook and spilled.

"Who are you? What is this? How did you? Who let you?" Such were his words, and the young man very calmly replied, speaking pure scriptural Hebrew not merely perfectly but too perfectly, like a very well-taught foreigner:

"Zacharias, priest of the Temple, have you not often longed for a son of your loins? You and your wife Elizabeth—have you not often prayed for a son? Now perhaps you have stopped longing and praying, for she is too old, and the seed is dry within you."

The old man now felt that his heart must fail. "Is this some," he began to say, "is this some—"

"Trick?" smiled the young man. "Ah no, no trick, Zacharias. Have no fear. Put down that vessel you are carrying, you are spilling the blood in it. I do not like this sacrificing of beasts, it is filthy and barbarous, but, given time, you will change to a better and cleaner way of doing homage to the Lord. Now listen, friend. Your prayers have been heard at last, and your wife Elizabeth, though too old to bear a son, shall yet bear a son. You must call him John—do you hear me?—*John*. You shall have joy in his birth, and he shall be great in the sight of the Lord. He will be a man ungiven to the indulgences of the flesh, since it will be enough for him to be filled with the Holy Spirit—even from his mother's womb. He shall turn many of the children of Israel towards their God. He shall make ready a path for the coming of the Lord. Do you follow me? Do you understand all this?"

"I cannot," gulped and moaned Zacharias. "This cannot be

true. It is the Devil. Begone, Satan. On the day of the shedding of sins the father of all sin comes to tempt me. Out of my sight. You defile the throne of the Most High."

The young man seemed not so much angry as mildly affronted. He threw away the stick he had used for nail-cleaning and wagged a finger at the old priest. "Hear me," he said. "My name is called Gabriel. I am an archangel, and I stand in the presence of God. I was sent to tell you this thing, and I have told you this thing, and it is not seemly that you call me Satan and deny the Lord's good tidings. A punishment is, I should think, in order. You will be struck dumb till the day this thing shall come to pass. You did not believe my words, so you are to have no words of your own. And, believe me, you foolish old man, my words shall be fulfilled in their season."

Zacharias now tried to say something, but all that came out of his mouth was *hud hud hud*. The young man, archangel rather, nodded quite pleasantly and totally without rancour. Then he began to dissolve into air, his cleaned fingernails being the last part of him to dissolve, or so Zacharias was later to tell the story, and the old priest was left gasping and hudding. Then his heart seemed totally to collapse within him and he grasped at the very veil of the Temple for support. He tottered out of the inner sanctum and showed himself to the people, and the people were full of concern. *Hud hud*, he went. His fellow-priests surrounded him, frowning, and he tried, with pathetic gestures, to show what had befallen him. He even, to his shame, tried to symbolise the visitation by flapping his shaking arms like wings and using one arm to indicate great tallness. "A vision?" a priest frowned at him. "Was that what it was?" Zacharias went *hud hud hud*. The murmuring of the congregation now grew very loud. Zacharias was led out of the Temple and, in the portico, he found his wife Elizabeth awaiting him. She perceived that in his eyes there was a certain mad joy beating out the fear, and, with woman's quickness, she guessed at what the joy could be about. As she was a woman, and hence closer to the world of the true and real than most men are able to be, it did not seem to her to be impossible that, in that inner place denied even to the high priests on all days of the year but this one day, the Lord or his emissary had spoken to her husband in joyful words, and these joyful words could be about one thing only. For they had all else that they wanted. She whispered a word to him and he began to nod and hud. She started to lead him home, others following chattering at a distance, and some Syrian soldiers in Roman uniform began to guffaw and make swilling gestures. The Jews got drunk in what they called their Temple, the filthy Yahudies.

As soon as they were home, Zacharias quite calmly, and in very neat letters, began to write out what had happened to him beyond the veil. Elizabeth nodded and spoke. She said: "I had best not disbelieve. The thing that all women hope for but do not really think can ever come to them. May one say that God is a laughing God and dearly loves a jest? He chooses a woman long past child-bearing. He might just as well have chosen a virgin. And I think it may well be that the Messiah will be coming soon, for I seem to recollect that somewhere in the scriptures it says a virgin will conceive. So it is not the Messiah that is given to us, it is his herald or harbinger or whatever the word is. And, yes, I see, his name is to be John. It is a good thing you were quick to write that down or else you might have forgotten it. Our son, yes yes, our son, and now I must guard carefully what I have within me and, when the time comes for the signs to be seen, hide myself away. And during these nine months I shall have to talk enough for two. No no, you need not write down that I do that already." They clasped hands in love and joy.

On the Shabbat Shabbaton the ceremonies of atonement traditionally ended with the loading of the scapegoat with the sins of the people and the leading of it out to a clifftop not far from Jerusalem, whence it was hurled down to be shattered against the rocks and to die in pain. The name given to the beast was Sa'irla-Aza'zel, meaning the goat for the placating of the demon Aza'zel, that dwelt in the desert. You may read of this in the sixteenth chapter of the book of Leviticus. The Romans, long before the time of our story, had likewise used innocence for the taking on of guilt, though it had then been a person, not a beast, and the choice had been that of the person, choice always being important and a beast having no choice. Now on this day of the visitation to Zacharias, the scapegoat, tethered in the Temple gardens and watched over by two servants of the Temple, became unattended when these two servants went to see what all the commotion was about. It chewed through its rope and escaped. Another goat had to be found.

FOUR

We travel now north of Judaea to Ha-Galil, or Galilee, though not to the most northerly part, with its great peaks and gorges, but to what is called Lower Galilee, where the hills are gentler and there stands the city of Nazareth. In this city there lived a hale man in middle age, strong on neither imagination nor humour, but without doubt a good man, his name Joseph, his trade that of carpenter. He made, among other things of use and ornament, fine wooden ploughs, some of which are said to be in use to this day, but he would make almost anything he was asked to make: tables, stools, cupboards, lecterns, yokes for beasts, sticks for walking, even boxes for jewels and other precious objects with special secret locking devices built into the lid on a principle of ordered sliding panels which he had learned from a Persian. He had, at the time of our story, two young apprentices, James and John, and one day young James, weary of sawing and planing, said that he wished he were a great king or some other high-placed man with nothing to do but chew sweetmeats made from honey and drink sherbet from a costly goblet, whereupon Joseph turned upon him with these words:

"Now that is the way of the new kings, like Herod the Great as he is called, to do nothing but grow fat until he is too fat even for his favourite amusement, the whipping of slaves. But the true kings of Israel were not like that. They had trades to practise, they worked as we are working, or more properly as I am working, since you boys seem to me merely to play at it, but you will learn, given time. Was not King David a shepherd? Now I, as you know, am of the blood of King David and I am proud to be a carpenter. You lads have to learn this same pride. Hard hands you have to have, not like the hands of the Gentiles, which are soft as putty. To know all manner of woods and skills in the shaping of them, yes. Don't start yearning for better things, my boys, such as buying and selling in the fine shops of Jerusalem, your soft gentlemanly fingers smelling of soft soap. There is no smell better than the smell of cedar. This is to be your life and a good life too, and I ask for no change in this life, speaking for myself, that is.''

He then produced from a cupboard his timber joints, these being corners of wood jointed together for the sake of showing the kinds of joints used in carpentry, and he catechised the two boys. Foxtail wedging. Haunched mortise and tenon. Good, good. Rebated joint. No, stupid boy, those are housed joints. And this? A dowelled joint. Good.

The doorway of the shop darkened, and Joseph squinted at the shape of the visitor. "Ah, Mistress Anna," he greeted. "You look well."

"I do not look well, nor feel it," his visitor said. "You will see well enough for yourself when you're out of the light. May we for a brief time get out of the light?"

"So," he said, "you are not come then as a customer."

"No," she replied, "not as a customer." Joseph turned to his apprentices and said:

"Can I trust you two to plane gently, very gently, let the plane ride on the wood, no forcing of it?" He led his visitor to the little living quarters behind the shop, very plain and apt for a middleaged bachelor—a bedroom and a room for sitting and eating, the kitchen being in a shed in the yard where the wood was stored. He gave Anna some wine and looked at her. She was thin and she seemed now far older than her years. She was newly a widow. Joseph said:

"He was a good man."

"Joachim," she said, "was the very best of men. They spoke no less than the truth at his funeral—*a small but precious jewel of the house of David.*"

"I ask no more," Joseph said, "than that they say that of me. And of you, of course. But you, of course, have many many years to go," he added with carpenter's gallantry.

"Not long, I think," Anna said. And, now that he could see her face more clearly, with its pallor and its lines of suffering, he agreed with her within himself. "I have these fluxions which wear me down. The dysentery that wore poor Joachim to his grave. I think I must follow him soon, and that's why I come to you now. A matter of my daughter."

"You wish me to be her guardian?" Joseph asked.

"No," she replied. "I wish you to be her husband."

"Let me pour you some more wine," Joseph said after a pause. He poured her more and himself also. Then he said: "You know well enough that I can be the husband of nobody. That I was injured in this very shop when it was my father's, God rest him, and injured where it is most shameful for a man to be injured. Meaning that I cannot do a man's part, if I may say this to a lady."

"I have heard of it," she said, "but never really believed it. I have observed merely that you show no desire to be with women, in the sense that is of touching women."

"But you ask me to marry your daughter."

"Yes, because soon she must be alone and I am fearful of the future for her without a man's protection. A husband's protection is the best, in law as in life. Now, from this other viewpoint, which is the only one you have mentioned, as if it were the main thing of marriage, you have to know that she has vowed to keep her virginity."

"How old is she—thirteen—fourteen? A girl of that age cannot know her own mind."

"She knows it well enough. Virginity is a good state, pleasing to the Lord God."

"I," said Joseph, "have seen my fires go out. The fire can be a great distraction. I like the cool light, which is blessed. At least, I tell myself that. Now, with a girl of thirteen, the fires have not even been laid, let alone lighted. Let her talk of virginity being pleasing to the Lord when the fire is beginning to blaze."

"She's fourteen," Anna said, "and nearly fifteen. We have had our long talks about all this. She knows what it means, to be shut off from the hopes that go with the carnal life, the hopes of Jewish women, I mean. And the pleasure of children, whether they're chosen of the Lord or not. She's a good girl and a humble girl. Good in the house, quick and yet spotless. You need a woman, as I can see from that garment you're wearing."

"This is just an old thing for the shop."

"Yes, but it should not be torn like that. Who cooks your meals now?"

"I put on a stew in the morning," Joseph said, "and it's ready at dinner-time."

"She can do better things than stews."

"I like stews. Well, perhaps not all the time." Joseph looked at Anna, turning everything over in his mind, then he said: "Not a woman but a girl. You offer me a sort of foster-daughter."

"No," said Anna with firmness, "a wife. With a dowry, a piece of property. With the right to protection that only marriage can give. It will be a strange marriage, some will think. But there have been many such marriages in Galilee. And I think there may well be more such, with all this talk of the end of things and the kingdom of heaven coming. The coupling of men and women is for children, and there is no point in bringing more children into the world—not if the end of all things is really coming."

"I don't believe that," said Joseph, scratching his chin through his beard. "It comes and goes, that sort of talk. They talked about it once when I was a boy, a lot of excitement and agitation about nothing. Well. Anyway. A wife," he pondered, "to be loved without desire. A marriage blessed not by children but by chastity. Shall we then talk of a betrothal? Although the married state itself will be a kind of betrothal."

"Come round tonight. She'll cook you a dinner."

"You're sure she really knows her mind? That she's willing?"

"Oh, she's willing," Anna said.

The girl's name was Mary, really Miriam, the name of the sister of Moses the prophet, and she was a pretty smooth-faced girl of quick movements and sometimes of quick temper, but no harm in her at all. Her betrothal to Joseph meant mostly that, in the evenings after his work, he would come to the house of Anna and sit and talk to the sick mother, who soon could no longer rise from her bed, while the daughter sewed silently or mended or attended to matters in the kitchen. There were two servants: old Eliseba and grumbling Hezron, who looked after the garden and did such dirty man's work as he was willing to do. There was an old donkey called Malkah, a dog called Schachor, chained up in the back part most of the day and a great barker, also various cats in various phases of growth. One day, not very far from her end, as it turned out, Anna said to Joseph:

"This house, of course, is her dowry."

"You mean I'm to come and live here? I had not thought of that."

"You cannot very well take her to live in that little den full of wood shavings."

"My mother and father and I—" Then Joseph remembered that when his father died he made the shop bigger and the living quarters smaller. "Yes, yes, I see. People will talk about that. Are there no brothers of yours or cousins of hers, male ones that is, who would wish to claim the property?"

"The law of Moses is very clear on all that. On the property rights of daughters."

"Yes, I see." Mary looked up from mending an old shirt of his and smiled at Joseph a friendly smile, no more. He was aware of himself as growing into age, strong still and spare in flesh, but groaning in the mornings with pains in his legs, his hair thinning and his beard grey. She was very young, knew nothing of life, nor was he one who could teach her much about anything except foxtail wedging and dowelled joints. These, without doubt, she would show little interest in.

It was when Anna was dying, the servants and her relatives about her, that Mary, weeping as was only natural, first turned to Joseph as truly to a betrothed, seeking comfort from his presence and, indeed, from his arms. Shyly he put these arms about her, giving what comfort he could. He gently made her avert her face from the act of dying, though she had seen her father die less than six months before.

After the funeral she became the mistress of the house, and when Joseph called on her in the evenings they had to have old Eliseba sitting there with them as chaperone. He brought gifts of his own making, mostly finely wrought boxes with puzzle lids, and she baked cakes for him and his apprentices. It was a friendly courtship, with never a cross word, except from old Eliseba.

FIVE

On a fine afternoon Mary was sitting alone in the living-room carding wool. She still had mourning on, but she was cheerful and sang a Galilean song about maids at the fountain and a king coming. Birds were singing in the garden and old Schachor was barking away in the backyard. At her feet the oldest of the cats, a bitten-eared tom called Katsaf, slept in peace. But suddenly he stirred, then woke. He saw something that she could not see. He ran spitting and horrent out of the room into the garden and climbed a tree. "Silly old Katsaf," she said. "You've been dreaming again." But now she saw.

She saw a young man in a white robe, with golden hair cut short, clean-shaven, bare of feet, leaning against the sideboard that Joseph had recently made for her. He smiled at her and said:

"The greetings of God's angel to you, Mary."

"How did you, who," she choked. "What is this, where did you—"

Old Schachor was barking like mad. The young man said: "Noisy." The barking stopped. And then: "Full of grace as you are, highly favoured of the Lord. The Lord God is with you, child."

"Who are you?" she trembled.

"I am Gabriel, the archangel I stand in the presence of God. Do not be afraid, child—you have found great favour with the Lord. Believe now this unbelievable, that you shall conceive in your womb and bring forth a son, and you shall call his name

Jesus. He shall be very great, he shall be called the Son of the Most High. The Lord God shall give the throne of David to him, for being of your blood he must be of David's blood. He shall reign over the house of Jacob forever. Of his kingdom there shall be no end. Cast out unbelief as you have cast out fear. I am a messenger of God's truth."

"But," she said. "No. It cannot be. I'm an unmarried girl. I have had no no—"

"No knowledge of man," Gabriel said, "and have vowed never to have such knowledge. But to the Holy Spirit all things are possible. And the Holy Spirit shall come upon you, and the power of the Most High shall overshadow you. This you must believe. Do you believe?"

"I cannot," she said, "even think."

"Listen, Mary," Gabriel said. "You have a kinswoman, a cousin of your father—Elizabeth, wife of the priest Zacharias. Both know, though only one may speak, of the thing that has befallen her. Though old and beyond the bearing of children, she yet has conceived a son. This, in your counting, is the sixth month of her conception. You see how all things are possible to the Lord God. Rather, see you will. Go to her. She may talk to you of a wonder, as you to her, but to no other."

"But," she said, "there is the matter of—I must tell—"

"The worker in wood?" Gabriel said. He patted the sideboard briskly, then tried to make it rock. It stood very firm on the stone floor. "Time for that," he said. "No hurry for that." Then he turned to look at the garden, where Katsaf had come down from the tree and was crouching in the grass, wide eyes on the archangel. Gabriel must, she was to think later, have made himself exude a strong odour of catnip or some other catherb, for now Katsaf came running in, though very low-slung, to sniff at the stranger. Soon his purr filled the room, and he rubbed and rubbed against the archangelic ankles, eyes shut and tail stiff and high. Gabriel smiled at Mary and said: "All things are possible to the Lord."

Mary, who had not so far found courage to move from her

chair, now stood and said: "Here I stand," and then: "Here I kneel." But Gabriel would have none of this. He said:

"Ah, no. If there is kneeling to be done, it is I, your humble messenger, who should do the kneeling." But she would not have that. "Very well," said Gabriel, "neither of us shall kneel." But it seemed that there was something else she should say, perhaps for him to bear back and tell, for he waited while Katsaf continued his ecstasy. She found the words and spoke them. She said:

"Behold the handmaiden of the Lord. May it be done unto me according to your word."

Gabriel nodded smiling, then set the dog barking again, as a sign that the visit was over. A second later he was no longer there, and Katsaf, that ankle gone, nearly fell clumsily onto his side. But he went on purring for a long time. His purring helped Mary to believe that what had seemed to happen had in fact happened.

She told Joseph, who came that evening to a meal of mutton chunks and onions roasted on skewers, with stewed fruit to follow, that she must go to visit her kinswoman Elizabeth in Judaea. She had had, she said, a dream in which Elizabeth was asking for her (this was true, but it was a dream of some years back, and she had not then acted on the dream). There might be nothing in dreams, of course, though the scriptures, so she understood, not knowing the scriptures at all well, seemed to assert otherwise, didn't they? However, the dream could at least be taken as a reminder that she had a duty to tell her kinswoman about her coming marriage and so on. Invite her and her husband Zacharias to the wedding and so on. "I must go with you," Joseph said, "as a protection. In fact, I insist on coming with you." They were not yet married, she reminded him, and so he had no right to *insist*. He must stay in the shop and carry on with his work, worker in wood as he was (she saw Gabriel's lips on the phrase and nearly cried aloud); she would go to Judaea, just outside Jerusalem, with grumbling Hezron. She would ride on Malkah the donkey and Hezron would walk beside her. It was no great distance, and they would travel with the caravan that left Nazareth next Yom Rischon, yes, why not next Yom Rischon? Very well, but let her not stay away too long, since he would be bound to worry.

And so she made the journey south, in fine spring weather, and arriving at the house of Zacharias, not much changed since she was a very little girl except that the trees in the garden were taller, she was surprised when a chewing servant came to the door and said: "My master is indisposed. He is seeing no one."

"Meaning," said Mary with a new sharpness, "that I interrupt you at your meal and you are annoyed."

"My orders. Seeing no one."

"Say it is Mary daughter of Joachim. From the town of Nazareth in Galilee. Say also it is your mistress I am come to visit."

"She is seeing no one either."

"Enough of this," Mary said. "Let me in." And with an authority she was astonished at finding herself possessing, she pushed her way in, and the servant swallowed his mouthful and, though doubtful, let her pass.

The living-room was empty but she called, and soon her kinswoman Elizabeth peeped out from a curtain. Then, smiling with pleasure to see Mary, she came out, arms out, and Mary saw she was in a loose robe. She said: "I know what you carry under the loose robe. It is true, then. Blessed, blessed and again blessed be the Lord."

"How do you know?" Elizabeth asked. "Who told you?"

"The angel of God," Mary said, as though angels were her regular acquaintances. "And he told me another thing. A thing as wonderful."

"A thing," Elizabeth said, "more wonderful." She knew at once what the thing more wonderful was, and it was as if the child in her belly knew too, for it leapt. She put her hands there, pressing as if she thought the child would burst through the very skin and alleluia to the living air. "The one wonderful thing. You shall be blessed among women. And blessed shall be the fruit of your womb. And I am blessed too, that the mother of the Lord should come to me. And this child is blessed, he who shall prepare the coming of the Lord."

It is believed that it was during this time, the time of her stay with Elizabeth, that Mary made a song or a prayer or both. One morning, while she was feeding the chickens, words came to her: "My soul speaks of the greatness of the Lord. My spirit rejoices in God my saviour. For he has looked kindly upon the most humble of his handmaidens. And he has told me that all generations shall call me blessed. He who is mighty has done unto me a mighty thing." Then there was no more of the song or prayer, as though time had to be granted to her to learn by heart what had already been given, that it might be transmitted through Zacharias, who had become a vigorous writer during his dumbness, on a tablet that was found dusty in the house when he and his wife, already now near enough to death, were no more. Fondling one of the two donkeys that grazed on the land behind the house, Mary found herself, a day or two after, saying this continuation: "His name is holy. And his mercy shall be shown in generation after generation of those who fear him. His arm is an arm of strength. He has scattered the proud of heart. He has put down princes from their thrones and has exalted those of low degree. He has filled the hungry with good things, and the rich he has sent empty away." Gathering flowers a few days later still, she felt the end of the song or prayer come to her: "He will bring help to Israel. He will fulfil the promise he made to our fathers, and to the seed of Abraham be merciful for ever. Alleluia. Alleluia."

Zacharias, though dumb, was hale and ate well. At dinner one evening he paid close attention to what his wife and her kinswoman were saying, interjecting nods and grunts and whistles at every statement that seemed to require his priestly confirmation.

"You think he will believe?" Elizabeth said, having swallowed a mouthful of broiled fish.

"God's angel will come to him." Zacharias made a comical little mime of the terror of that kind of visitation.

"In God's good time," Elizabeth said. "First he must suffer

the test of doubt. It is God's humour that his son and the prophet of his son should be conceived where conception is impossible. Not out of the lusty embraces of carnal love, but from a womb untouched and a womb long barren. You would express it so, I think, Zacharias." Zacharias nodded and nodded and then seemed about to speak, starting a word with a guttural letter, but it was only a fishbone. "Has your Joseph," Elizabeth said to Mary, having thumped Zacharias on the back for the bone's dislodgement, "any of God's laughter in him?"

"He's a good man and a holy man. But he's a carpenter, not a prophet or a poet."

"Does he know why you are here?"

"I said I was coming for your blessing. On my marriage. My nearest kinswoman, after all. I said I would stay some little time."

"Yes," said Elizabeth, "the little time left. You must be here—for the event. And when you go back, the news will have preceded you. He will be the more ready to believe what you tell him."

"But not entirely ready," Mary said with young calm. "He must have his hour of rage and disappointment. But I pray God's angel may—"

"Yes, child?"

"Make it a brief hour."

Zacharias nodded and nodded at that.

The news, in truth, of Elizabeth's conception was already in Nazareth. Joseph was sanding smooth an ox-yoke he had finished outside his shop one fine morning, talking about it. There was a sour middleaged man, a baker, called Jotham, sceptical about most things and certainly sceptical about this. "A lot of nonsense," he said, "comes in on the caravan from Ain-Karim. That you know."

"A lot of truth too," Joseph said. "And I'll tell you another thing. I think Mary knew about it already."

"How?" another man, Ishmael, said. "Did she get it in a dream?"

"Why not? A lot of things come in dreams. This you know."

"It's all madness," Jotham said. "This is the Elizabeth married to who-is-it, the priest, the one that was struck dumb, so they say, that one?"

"That's right," Joseph said. "Mary's second cousin."

"The Lord comes on his left side," Jotham said, "and strikes him dumb. The Lord comes on his right side, and he's going to be a father already."

"No guarantee of a son, though," Ishmael said. "Puffing themselves up, no doubt, on the Lord's favour—and then, lo, a daughter."

"The Lord wouldn't take that trouble for a daughter," Jotham said. "Anyway, how could he let her know—him, the priest, I mean—her, I mean, his wife? Being dumb, that is."

"She can read," Joseph said. "I'm sure she can read. A matter of his writing it down. They're a well-connected family, hers. Well off too, not too badly. Related by marriage, distant, yes, but still related to—well, to royalty, you might say. The royal house."

"No recommendation," Jotham said. And then: "When do we get our invitations to the wedding?"

"Plenty of time," Joseph said. "We've not long signed the contract."

"Joseph the betrothed," Jotham said solemnly, "and his beloved has already left him."

"Careful," Joseph said, lifting the polished ox-yoke. "Careful, Jotham. There's limits."

Ishmael, who was old and weak-chested, began to cough. Jotham said: "A reminder of mortality. 'Remember, O man, when thou coughest, it is the rasp of the saw through the trunk of the tree of thy life.'"

"I don't seem to recall that text," Ishmael said when he had finished coughing.

"I just made it up. The prophet Jotham." Then he went across the street back to his ovens.

SIX

There were far more midwives than Elizabeth needed when the time for her delivery came. All the midwives for many miles around were there, anxious to assist at or merely witness the prodigy of a birth their experience knew to be impossible or improbable or certainly unlikely. There might, true, be something in books about such a thing having happened to other women well past the life change, so, as they knew nothing of books, they held their peace. Zacharias the priest, a man of books, expected the prodigy to happen, but he was dumb and, for all the midwives knew, newly in the madness of dotage. But the signs were there in the sweating and straining Eizabeth, swelling certainly not brought on by the mind, as sometimes happened, and the labour pains as real as any they had ever seen.

Then, with very little true difficulty, Elizabeth loosed the child, a boy, and when the boy, very sturdy, had been cut loose and slapped, he yelled at the light very lustily. A big child, as big as any they had ever seen.

I think it must be made clear at this point that, despite the legends put about after his death, this child was not a giant. We have all heard the stories of the severed head preserved in a huge wine-jar, how this head was the size of a bull's and so on, and of the heaviness (this tale was put about by a Gaul) that required two or three men to lift it, but none can say where the head is. The child was a big child who grew into a man of a stature uncommon among the Israelites, who are a small people, but he was no Goliath nor, to keep within the bounds of the faithful, even a Samson. Of Jesus Naggar (or Marangos), who was of course his kinsman, similar stories of gigantism have been told, and I think there is truth in them, though only of the grown man, but let me not anticipate. Of this newborn child let it be said that he was strong and loud, and when the day came for his circumcision he howled pitiably at the loss of his foreskin, as though that were the most precious thing in the world. The priest who officiated said:

"This child offers to the God of Abraham this flesh of the body that the body will not miss, this blood that scarce films the lip of the cup that receives it. And he shall be called by the name of his father—Zacharias."

Zacharias grew very agitated at that, but it was left to his wife Elizabeth to say: "No. His name is John."

There was surprise among the company assembled for the rite, but the priest was not merely surprised but ready, despite the *hud hud* and shaking of a fellow and senior priest, to deliver reproof, saying: "John? There is none of your family or of the family of his father so called. This is irregular." Elizabeth said:

"In the temple when my husband was vouchsafed the vision and the prophecy this name was given to him. And this name is John."

"We must," the priest said, "have the word from his father's mouth, and in his father's mouth there is no word."

But Zacharias made pathetic noises and gestures showing that he wished a tablet and a stylus to be brought, and it was Elizabeth herself who brought them. There is no credence at all to be attached to the pretty story that the child began to howl out his own name while she was fetching them. There would have been no point in God's making him so howl, since almost at once, in the act of beginning to write, Zacharias found that his tongue was, after nine months' silence, loosed. Zacharias said, firmly and quietly:

"His name is John."

There was general astonishment and some went down on their knees. Zacharias, as if to make up for the long enforced dumbness, became voluble and prophetic. His son howled, and the father shouted him down. Zacharias was most articulate and his sentences were beautifully woven, and one may not doubt that what he now said he had rehearsed long though in silence. He said:

"Blessed be the Lord, the God of Israel. For he has visited us and wrought redemption for his people. He has raised for us a horn of salvation in the house of his servant David." John was so loud that it was as if he were blowing a horn of a different kind. His mother rocked and hushed him, but he only bellowed the louder. "And what he spoke through the mouths of the holy prophets shall be fulfilled—salvation from our enemies, and from the hand of all that hate us—mercy to his people, who shall serve him without fear, in holiness and righteousness before him all our days."

Zacharias seemed to many to be going on too long, but the only voice of protest was the child's, and Zacharias had almost to bellow himself to say:

"And you, my child, whose voice is already great and shall be greater still in the Lord's service—" Many smiled at this, but not Zacharias. "—You shall be called the Prophet of the Most High, for you shall go before the face of the Lord to make ready his path, to give knowledge of salvation to his people, in the remission of their sins, because of the tender mercy of our God."

His final words on this holy and indeed miraculous occasion are said by some to have been sung by him in a fine priestly voice, and indeed there is a quality of song about them:

"Whereby the dayspring from on high shall visit us, to shine upon them that sit in darkness and the shadow of death, to guide our feet into the way of peace." He hung his head, eyes closed, and prayed silently. The infant John was given the breast.

Mary, riding back with the caravan to Nazareth, had that

phrase—"dayspring from on high"—ringing in her head like the very bells of the camels. She was calm and very confident, but those words helped her be so. "The dayspring from on high." In her it would dawn, so it had been promised, but who would believe it? Better to be ravished now on this journey by highway thieves and scoundrels or soldiers marching through from Damascus or somewhere. They would believe that, Joseph would believe. God's rape, though, was a blasphemous conceit.

Back home she sat quietly with the cat Katsaf on her lap, stroking him under the chin with two fingers. He purred loudly. Joseph was saying:

"Cunning, cunning, your mother had that cunning, knowing where she could impose, knowing me to be the biggest and most credulous fool in all Nazareth." He stamped his way all about the table he had made, groaning, shaking weak fists. Mary said, patiently trying to ease his way into belief:

"What has happened to my kinswoman is true. You may go and see that for yourself."

"I do not doubt that is true," he shouted, "and I am not talking of that. I am speaking of your cunning—using talk of a second miracle in the family to cover your your your. But I have no right to rave at you. I am merely glad I have found out in time. I will go to Rabbi Gomer first thing in the morning and cancel cancel all, I will cancel all, thank God I have found out."

"You have found out nothing," Mary said. "It will be some time before you see the truth with your own eyes. As for now, you are to believe what I tell you, and remember that I tell you, and know that you have found out nothing."

"Why should I believe?" he cried. "If I believe, then any man has to believe a mad fairy tale told by a faithless woman to cover her faithlessness. I am sorry for you, I will say as much—it is no pleasant thing to live alone with a child born out of fornication—but there is such a thing as a man's honour—"

"Soon," Mary said boldly, "you will use the word *cuckold*."

"No, thank God," Joseph said, "that's a state reserved for married men. Well, that dream is over, and again I say thank God. I go back to my lonely shop and my faithful apprentices—"

"Faithful? James, I know, makes children's toys behind your back with your own wood and tools and sells them."

"So like a woman, never on the point. Faithless and never on the point. Joseph the unmarried man, I say, but no longer Joseph the fool."

"You talked of love once," Mary said, "and not so long ago either. Can you throw out love so easily? Love should be a lasting thing, and faith and love should go together. You told me you love God, and you have never seen God. There your faith and your love dance one dance. Why can they not do so now?"

He mumbled then. "Because," he mumbled, "it is easier to believe in God than to believe—"

She was quick. "That you are betrothed to one who shall be—"

"Do not say it," he almost howled. "Do not speak the blasphemy." Then, quieter (she was only a girl and a girl in trouble, she did not know the meaning of the word *blasphemy*): "That is too much for any man to believe."

"But you are not any man," Mary said, "any more than I am any woman. You too are chosen. You will see. But it is a great pity that God must exert himself to make you see." Joseph mumbled again, waved his arms, did another sad turn, this time not stamping, about the table he had made for her, them. "Go in peace, Joseph," she said. "Put off bitterness if you will not put off disbelief. Tomorrow you will come back to me. And you will have something different to say. This I promise."

"You promise?" he said. *"You?"*

"I have the right to promise."

He looked at her in terrible pain which twisted his very body, then left. She continued to caress her cat, who purred as though his heart would break, serene, faintly smiling.

That night Joseph lay groaning, fretful, sleepless, bruised, guilty. He caught a very clear image of this faithless girl Mary punished for her fornication, big-bellied, running away from stones hurled by grinning louts, sobbing. How far did the law permit compassion to go? Then there was the matter of his own impotence, the crushing of the testicles in his far youth when an iron vice had fallen on him. True, there were few now in Nazareth who knew of this or, if they had heard the story, were disposed to believe it. In early manhood he had taken up with a very cleanly sect of people who believed only in the spirit, condemning the body and the things of the body as evil, eating and drinking with groans and dunging in horror. He flirted still in public with this sect and thus gave the Nazarenes a credible ground for accepting his long indifference to women. If he accepted another man's child as his own, abetting an act of which she seemed no whit ashamed, proud rather, at least it would be a proclamation of an aspect of manliness that might draw him closer to the town's saner citizenry. This over-clean sect, though uncondemned by the synagogue, was not, when all was said, truly sane. The body was not evil. Food was pleasant and dunging was a healthy ritual of the morning.

But God, God, the treachery, the simpering unrepentant unholiness, the cunning that was not, after all, so cunning. Still, to reject, to throw her to the throwers of stones—could he live with that? He did something now unwonted. He took the wine jug from the dresser and swigged surlily. He wanted sleep. It was heavy wine, very drowsy stuff. He hoped, though with little faith in the chance of hope's fulfilment, that the wine, of its charity, would throw him into a sleep heavy enough to breed dreams that would enlighten him as to the way he should go in this terrible matter. So he slept, and things were resolved for him.

"Joseph. Joseph."

"Who calls me? Who?"

"God's messenger, Joseph. Listen."

"Let me see you. Show yourself. I have had too much of this nonsense about God's messenger and God's new pretty tricks in the way of making children without fleshly coupling. Come on, show yourself."

"No, Joseph. It is enough for you to listen. And to believe."

"Why should I believe? I'm already asked to believe too much. The things I'm asked to believe are all to do with the turning of Joseph the woodworker into a fool. Well, I'm already fool enough, thank you, but not such a fool as to believe just because someone says he's God's angel. Show yourself or go away."

"I will not go away until I know that you believe now and will believe when you wake at cockcrow. As for showing myself, I am, on this visitation, not empowered to take on a show of flesh for a surly carpenter. At least listen. One thing at a time."

"Very well, then. I'm listening."

"Good. Now, let me tell me you of your betrothed, Mary, daughter of Joachim and Anna, of this town of Nazareth, in this land of Galilee."

"I'm listening."

The wedding feast was decorously jolly. There was unwonted rain, which some took as a good omen, so the cakes and wine and roasted mutton were consumed indoors. A couple of foolish gossips gossiped about how she could have done better for herself, not marry an old dribbler frosty in the blood, and so on. *Had to marry*, somebody whispered, as at all wedding feasts. Ben-oni and Caleb, a couple of elderly and pious Galileans, admired the house and even stroked the walls.

"There's not much money passing over, I think. How much is the dowry?"

"This piece of property. The house was left to her."

"Irregular, surely? Shouldn't it be entailed on some male of the family?"

"Come, come, do I have to teach you the law of Moses? The daughters may inherit."

"A girl under age?"

"Well, it's Joseph's house now."

"Unseemly, somehow. The bride takes the bridegroom

home. Something Gentile about it. You know—matriarchal."

"It's Joseph's house now."

There were, among the guests, members of that sect of clean-liness with whose doctrines Joseph had professed sympathy, but they were sour now in their white robes, refusing the roast meat and raising shocked very clean hands at the proffered wine. One, called merely Head of the Brethren, as though his true name were an aspect of uncleanliness, spoke his disappointment frankly to the bridegroom. The bridegroom said:

"I always told you I could never go all the way. I always said that you take purity too far."

"Can one," almost sneered the man known among the brethren as Dawn Light, "take purity too far?"

"I know the argument by heart," Joseph said. "God is the ul-timate purity, pure spirit. But God made man's flesh. You can-not deny the flesh—not altogether. A man needs a dish of meat and a cup of wine after a day's work."

"Agh, you sound like a soldier. You will be saying next that a man needs" (and he shuddered) "a woman after a day's work."

"A man does not *need* a woman in that sense, nor a woman a man. But there is another kind of need between the two —a need of the spirit."

"Spiritual wife and spiritual husband. You will be talking next of spiritual parenthood."

"Forgive me," Joseph said. "I must speak to, well, some of my lowlier guests."

So he went off to talk to an ill-dressed rather laughing kind of group, making the most of the food and wine. Head of the Brethren said to Dawn Light:

"You have to remember what he is. A woodworker. Rather a dirty occupation."

These two left early, to nobody's regret.

Now much of what I have recounted you will not be ready to believe, and so for much of what is to come. But you will readily believe, I think, that Joseph and Mary were happy together and, whether you believe in the great wonder or not, they lived in the light of a great wonder. One evening, as they ate dinner together, Joseph said:

"I was speaking with Rabbi Gomer this morning. He talked of the usual thing."

"John, you mean? Elizabeth, Zacharias?"

"The usual thing. How that he could not be the Messiah. He quoted scripture. Strange, I'd always taken scripture to be just, well, scripture. I never took it to be, well, like a book about what really happened. Or is going to happen. Prophecy, that is."

"What did he *say*?" She tapped with her knife on the table, sharply. Joseph was rather clumsily serving out the stew.

"I kept my mouth shut, of course, as I always do when the prophecy comes up about a young girl shall conceive. Rabbi Gomer this morning was very strong, though, on the young girl really being a virgin."

"Ah."

"That made me, you know, shiver. Then there was the big crying out on that as nonsense, by Jotham and the others. How it was impossible because God always works through things as they are. When he can, that is. You know, it's God's creation and it's there and having made it God leaves it alone. But Gomer said how about Elizabeth and Zacharias, there was God *not* leaving things alone. A woman past childbearing bears a child. This is a kind of warning, portent the word is. The next time the strange birth idea comes into God's head it will be a virgin. Too late for children, too early for children—you see? Not a young girl, said Rabbi Gomer, not just that, but a young girl who's never—Well, I kept my mouth shut as I said, but I shivered a bit, and Jotham, a very quick man in some ways, invented some scripture-sounding thing about it is the shiver of the tree that expecteth the axe. In joke, of course."

"Go on." Hungry, feeding two, Mary cut herself more bread and soaked it in stew-juice.

"The real point is this, and Gomer showed us the text and thumped on it with his scaly fishmonger's thumb, this, that the Messiah has to be born in Bethlehem. The house of David produces him, and Bethlehem is David's town. Then my heart dropped, I can tell you. There it was, I saw it, and something about thou O Bethlehem art not the least of cities. It's not a city, of course, it's a kind of rubbishy small town outside Jerusalem. But he has to be born in Bethlehem."

Mary chewed and swallowed. "*In* Bethlehem or *of* Bethlehem? It's *of* Bethlehem. It must be that. He'll be born here, in this house. Nazareth, Galilee. *Of* Bethlehem."

"He said it was definitely *in*. Nobody argued much about that, it didn't seem a very interesting point to most of them. Then we all got back to work."

"So you said nothing, gave no sign?"

"Of course not. Joseph the mad, Joseph the betrayed? In all the others I see myself as I was. No capacity for faith in them, most of them. Jotham, for instance. Jotham believes only that things have always been bad and things always will be, unless they get worse. No, I go silent, just as you stay unseen. I need no striking dumb, like Zacharias. *In* Bethlehem, he said, it says. He struck his finger so often on the text you could see the mark of the nail. This knife needs sharpening. *In* Bethlehem."

"*Of* Bethlehem. He shall be born in his own house, where Gabriel came to me. God leaves all things now to nature. In Nazareth."

"In Bethlehem, he says."

"*Of* Bethlehem. Pass me the bread. Why does this table wobble so? It didn't wobble before."

"You must have shifted it. The floor isn't all that even. It was all right when I first brought it."

"It was all right till just now."

"You must have pushed it without knowing. Heavy," he grinned. "You're a heavy girl."

SEVEN

In Jerusalem, that very evening, in the great palace of Herod, Rabbi Gomer's finger-struck text, redolent of his fishy trade, was preparing itself for fulfilment. Herod, sicker than he was, more bloated, was being visited by two high men from Rome, one the L. Metellus Pediculus you have already met, the other a snorting man named P. Sentius Naso. They were in Palestine on imperial business. Sentius was saying:

"Despite the legalistic argument that Palestine is not strictly a dependency of the Empire, nevertheless the divine Augustus considers himself entitled to regard it as such for the purposes of taxation. And, as I said at dinner, before taxes can be gathered a census must be taken."

"I don't like it," Herod said. He was sipping some foul brew for his stomach. A bolus of gas behind his breastbone refused to come up and be released. He sipped. "This is an independent kingdom. Why should Augustus tax us when he gives us nothing for our taxes?"

"You have a great deal already from the divine Augustus," Metellus said, "The protection of Roman arms. A resident military cadre made up of the cream of Syria."

"Protection from what? I need no protection from anything or anybody except my own family. Augustus presumes on our friendship. It is I who keep his eastern flank secure, and I need no Syrian cadre for that or for anything else." The ball of wind pushed harder at his sternum. The two

Romans looked at him kindly, seeing pain but no true protest; they knew well how well he knew his true position in relation to Rome: a big-bodied king but very small. They waited. Herod said: "A census. Within my territories. Carried out by Roman functionaries. This is bound to meet with suspicion and, indeed, hostility. Augustus has been ill-advised, very."

"We are merely," Sentius snorted, "here to carry out orders. I am not empowered to offer those orders as material for leisurely discussion. Majesty," he added.

The wind blessedly rushed up. A small aromatic gale blew out of Herod and made a near-by torch flicker. "Better," he said. And then: "Perhaps I had better go to Rome myself. The divine Augustus needs to be told certain things. If he requires peace in these territories—"

"I fear there is no time," Metellus said. "For my part, I fail to understand your majesty's disquiet. After all, our troops will be here to protect you."

"You fail to understand something else," Herod said. "The mode in which it is proposed to implement your census—it totally flouts local tradition."

"In what way?" Sentius asked.

"Yes," Metellus said. "The honourable consul is not well informed as to the tradition to which your majesty refers. He does, with respect, not know this territory. It is a question of *residence*. For such official purposes as the taking of a census, every Palestinian—"

"Let's say," said Herod, "every Israelite."

"Every person living in this country considers himself as belonging not to the place where he actually resides but to the place of origin of his family group. His tribe. May I say tribe?"

"You may say tribe," said Herod. "Just about."

"A census entails the movement of every single inhabitant of this territory back to what he considers to be his native township—ancestral capital, to dignify what is usually no more than a stinking dungheap—"

"You choose your terms exquisitely, sir," Herod said.

"I was given one example," said Metellus. "The tribe of David, meaning all who consider themselves descended from that legendary tribal leader—a king, they call him. To them the ancestral capital is Bethlehem—that er dungheap er township south of Jerusalem—we passed through it on the way here—"

"Handkerchiefs shielding your exquisite noses, I doubt not."

Sentius snorted (and the snort, I may explain, had no so to speak attitudinal signification; it had something to do with an inherited inability to separate mouth-air from nose-air, a matter for the physiologues to explicate learnedly and not such as myself, a mere story-teller): "Would a census conducted according to—local tradition be acceptable to your subjects?"

"A census of our own?" Herod puffed. "There will be a disruption of the economy, the roads will be jammed—"

"A census of your own, majesty—but conducted for our purposes," said Metellus.

"Here, I think, we have a solution," Sentius said. "Give the temporary disruption a comfortable name—call it a national festival. All the tribes return to—"

"Their dungheaps of origin?" Herod put in.

"The joy of reunion," Metellus nodded. "Drinking, feasting, tales of old times. And as for the census—why, the census practically takes itself."

"Automatic," Sentius said, snorting hard in the middle of the word. "An automatic census."

"These Greek words, master consul," Herod said. "When I hear Greek I smell danger."

The spreading of the news of the census, which was to be taken between the ides of December and the calends of January, was effected through a crisp-worded letter which the Religious Council in Jerusalem grudgingly agreed to send to local religious leaders, as men who had most authority in the Palestinian townships, that it might be read out after the Sabbath synagogue meeting, this giving it a whiff of divine sanction not inappropriate considering its divine provenance. After Rabbi Gomer had read it out and released his congregation, there was

loud agitation among the Nazarenes outside the synagogue.
Jotham cried:

"It's a trick, you see, just to raise taxes. Well, why should we
pay taxes? What will the Romans give us for the taxes?" Ben-oni
said to Joseph:

"You're of the tribe of David, right? And you have to trudge
off to Bethlehem, isn't that so? Leaving your wife behind, and
her in her condition." For Nazareth knew of this condition and
was pleased with it for Joseph's sake: it gave the lie to certain
malicious rumours about his inability to perform a man's part.
Joseph was, meanwhile, hardly taking in any word that was
spoken, shaken to the root as he was by the impending fulfilment
of prophecy. "Is that fair?" Ben-oni said. "Do you consider that
fair?"

Ishmael pointed out that the women had to go too; had Ben-
oni not been listening, then?

"Suppose we say no?" said Jotham. "How about if we say
no?"

"Orders are orders and duty is duty," Joseph said slowly.
"There's no getting out of anything. Now if the taxes turn out to
be unfair—that will be different, that will be the time for saying
no."

A small twisted man called Isaac said: "You know how the
old saying goes? Take one step and you find yourself jumping
over a ditch."

Another man said: "No choice. What's the point in talking
about it? And I'll say this: those that shout loudest give in
soonest."

"I'm not going," Jotham said. They all looked at him. "I've
things to do here. Work. Bread to be baked."

"Nobody here to eat it," Ben-oni said.

"I'm not going," Jotham said. They all looked at him.

As was to be expected, when the day arrived for departure to
the various places of tribal origin, Jotham was among the earliest
to assemble at the place outside Nazareth whence the southern
caravan was to leave. He naturally told all who would listen that
his true purpose in going was to register protest at the highest

available level. It was a fine blue day, not over-warm, and the scene was lively and bustling. There was a kind of excitement about, even elation, since any mode of change is, however proleptically resented, always in the end somehow acceptable to people who live dull lives. Camels, their bells playing. Donkeys. Baggage. Children chasing each other. The caravan-master waving his stick, shouting, herding his charges together. Rabbi Gomer led all in a travellers' prayer:

"Blessed be the Eternal Lord, king of the earth and the heavens, in whose hands we voyagers entrust our safety."

Mary, with Joseph's tender help and some difficulty, heaved her heaviness up onto the donkey they had hired (old Malkah was dead; so was old Hezron). Eliseba, their servant, her mother's formerly, was unsure of her tribal origin but insisted that it belonged to Nazareth. There she would stay, looking after the house and animals. If the census scoundrels wanted her they would know where to find her. The women nearest Mary commented on her condition:

"She'll come back from Bethlehem a few pounds lighter."

"From her shape I'd say it was going to be a girl. I know shapes. I've never been wrong yet."

"There's always a first time, missus."

The horn blasted, the laggards rushed to take their places in the long file of travellers, and the southbound caravan began to move towards the Galilean border. At the day's end, with the sun sinking on their left hand, the Bethlehem-bound were weary but they sang a song to the dying light which had been made many years before by a shepherd long dead named Nathan. The words said something to the effect that the singers were the descendants of David, a shepherd who became king, and that they wished the spirit of David to watch over them. Somewhat after this manner:

> David's people we,
> Seeking David's town.
> A simple shepherd he
> Who acquired a crown.
> David, king of Israel,
> Wish us well.

There was a prayer of thanksgiving for the safe completion of that day's journey and a prayer humbly begging the Lord to watch over his people during the night to come, to keep away robbers, murderers, wild beasts, chills in the belly, wandering malign spirits. Fires were lighted by the roadside. Joseph and Mary set their donkey to grazing and ate their simple victuals of cheese and hard bread, washing these down with a draught of wine mixed with water. Joseph said:

"How is it, girl?"

"Well, but heavy."

"Not long to go. Two more days and we reach Jerusalem."

"Not many more days before he comes. I think. But don't worry. I shall be well." Joseph said, his horny carpenter's hand round her small delicate one, his eyes closed the better to remember the text he was quoting:

"'For thou, O Bethlehem, art in no wise the least of cities. For from thee shall come forth a chief, a shepherd of my people, Israel.' And we said no, the scripture's wrong. And here we are, two days off. Another of the Lord's jokes. That the scriptures may be fulfilled. The Romans order him to be born there, not Gabriel, not God."

"God can use anyone," Mary said. "Even the Emperor Augustus."

"Will you sleep now?"

"You sleep," she said. "I'll sit a little while longer, looking at the pictures in the fire."

So he kissed her tenderly and settled himself for sleep, well-wrapped in his woollen cloak. Mary sat and saw in the fire pictures that gave her no pleasure. She saw one picture that made her catch her breath with fear; there was a pain in her midriff, as if a sword had struck.

EIGHT

You will have heard of the three wise men, or magi, or astrologers, who are also held by most to have been kings of small lands as yet untouched by the Roman Empire, the wise men, I mean, who also travelled to Bethlehem, having discovered in the changed map of the heavens that a redeemer or messiah or great monarch of the soul was to be born there or had already been born there. You will know also that it was not uncommon in the ancient days for a king to be an astrologer or an astrologer to be a king. Knowledge of the heavens, which to the uninstructed meant power over the heavens, was a greater qualification for kingship in those old small realms than mere ability to adjudge cases like Solomon or, like David, kill giants. It all had much to do, of course, with knowing about the mysteries of the seasons, which could be read in the heavens by a man skilled in scrying, since the seasons mean everything to planters of crops and crops sustain life.

The king or magus named, by tradition, Balthazar seems to have been a black man who ruled a small Berber country. We will, if you please, see him now, handsome, intellectual, muscular, in the prime of life, taking wine in his bare throne-room with its rough stone floor, mutton-fat-fed torches smelling all about him, and hear him talk to his ministers. He said:

"Two words—two Roman words, and they contradict each other. The words are *protection* and *expansion*. How much longer can the small kingdoms last? Already we receive offers of protection, though protection from what is never made clear—vague hosts in the East, mostly. It all truly means no more than the aggrandisement of Rome. How much longer can we stay outside that iron family?"

"The new philosophy," said his first minister, "teaches the virtue of the imperial dream—the rational empire of which all men can be free citizens, whatever their nation, whatever their colour."

"Whatever their colour," Balthazar repeated. In those days it was commonly held that some colours were better than others, and that the blackness of a man's skin denoted evil or stupidity, sometimes—impossibly—both. "We must accept the dominion of Rome, then—not as the necessity to which the weak must yield, but as the desirable thing which reason tells even the strong to choose. And what can Rome give us?"

"Law," said his second minister, who had studied law. "The strength of her arms. A kind of athletic philosophy of physical toughness, ascetic self-denial. Honour. Military virtue. Order. Above all, order."

"Anything else?"

"Oh, poetry, oratory. They have many books."

"But they have little imagination," Balthazar said. "What little literature they have they stole, I am told, from the Greeks. The Romans offer us a safe life, protected by the greatest army and navy the world has ever seen. They build fine roads that lead nowhere. Or, if you will, from Rome to nowhere and from nowhere to Rome. And what is their faith? Our religion is a dying one, true. To worship the sun is not enough. But at least the sun is a great fiery mystery and the source of all life. The Romans, I am told, worship the head of a man on a silver coin."

"With respect, majesty," said the first minister, "however much you may disparage the Romans, we still have to belong to their Empire—all of us in the world, sooner or later. We have little choice in the matter."

"There may well be a choice," the king said. "There may

well be an alternative to the dead metal of Roman domination. What, for instance, do you know of Israel? Have you read any of their books?"

"The people of Israel," said the second minister, "are in a worse state than ourselves. We await Roman domination—they already suffer it. Their King Herod rules as a client monarch, they pay taxes like any whipped colony. They were once the slaves of the Egyptians, the Babylonians. Slaves again, they write a history of slavery and a poetry of bondage."

"And yet," Balthazar said, "they hope, while the Romans bask in fancied achievement. They write and sing of an empire of the imagination, and of a more subtly human kind of justice than the Romans know. They talk of the coming of a new leader, whose dominion shall be of the spirit—"

"No dominion of the spirit," said the first minister, "can prevail against a dominion of steel and stone."

"And what," cried Balthazar, "if the spirit fire an enslaved people to find freedom? It happened before to the Israelites, with the man Moishe in Egypt. What if the spirit fire the enslavers and burn out their harshness and inhumanity?"

"That will be a long time coming," the first minister thought and the second minister said.

"But there are signs," Balthazar said, "that their new king will not be a long time coming. Signs that his hour is upon us."

"Signs, majesty?"

"Yes, and you know where the signs are, though you leave it to me to look for them. We must some day free the monarchy from this burden—looking at the stars, planning the planting and the sowing, fixing time and season."

"It is a king's burden, majesty."

"A star king. A king should keep his eyes on what is around him, not what is above him."

"You spoke of a sign, sir," the second minister said.

"Forgive me, I wander. The calculations point to a place and time. I will not weary you with the details. My investigations of the rhythm of the heavens lead me to this knowledge. And, I should think, not me alone. There must be others, many. If, gentlemen, you look out tonight into the eastern heavens, in that segment of the sky we call the Den of the Lynx, you will see a new star. But no, being untrained in stellar observation, you will not. To you all stars are the same, and their number could be augmented or diminished every hour of the night and you would fail to notice. Take it from me, however, that a new star is added to the multitude of the heavens."

The first minister said: "This is of considerable interest, no doubt, to a trained astronomer such as yourself, your majesty, but for my part I scarcely see—"

"The stars, gentlemen," said Balthazar loudly, "are not cold unpassionate bodies cut off from the lives of men. The stars are not, shall we say, Roman sentries. The rising of a new star entails an immense labour of the heavens. This has its counterpart on earth. History is bringing forth a prodigy. I am going forth to seek it."

"And where," said the second minister, "will your majesty look?"

Balthazar smiled and said simply: "I will follow that star."

I should think that a similar decision was made by the other two kings or magi or astrologers at about the same time and after a similar conversation with their ministers. Of the convergence of their several journeys I will speak later. Meanwhile, long before them, we must ourselves arrive at Bethlehem.

Imagine the bustle in the sunset, fresh caravans ever arriving, lost children crying and children not lost in danger of being trodden on by camels, thieves at work, sellers of kebabs and sherbet charging exorbitant prices, carts overturned, the desperate search for lodgings on the part of those without hospitable kinfolk in the town. Mary was already feeling premonitory pains, Joseph was desperate as any in his looking for a place to stay. He fought his way through knots of wealthy with servants carrying baggage into the courtyard of the solitary inn, seeking and at last finding a disdainful host, obsequious however to the arriving rich with his "Your rooms are ready, sir and madam" and "Sup-

per will be served as soon as you are ready for it, your lordship"
and so on. Joseph spoke his needs, his desperate worry over
his wife, in labour, her pains starting. The landlord said:

"It cannot be done, friend. Nothing's available."

"If," said Joseph, fumbling in his little leather moneybag,
"it's a matter of paying a little something extra—"

"Oh, more than that, friend, much more," the landlord said,
peering. And then: "Ah, good day, your august benignity, if you
would be good enough to follow the boy here."

Joseph went back, deeply troubled, to his wife who sat by the
roadside with their bundles and donkey. "Nothing," he said,
"nothing." But at that moment a very fat woman, employed by
the inn, ox-strong, the guests' baggage she handled nothing
to her, came by and saw Mary writhe and give a gasp. She
said kindly:

"Poor girl, so that's the way of it. Looking for lodgings? You'll
find nothing in this town, I can tell you. That one I work for is
charging four times more than he does when Bethlehem's just a
mudheap nobody wants to visit. But if you just cross that bit of a
field there, see, you'll come to some stables. There's an old ox
there but he won't do you no harm, bless you. Nor your donkey
neither. Not much, I know, but it'll be clean and dry and warm
enough. Plenty of fresh straw. If I can manage it I'll be along later to help. My married sister's had six, all living, and I helped
her with every one. Go that way, see, by that men's jakes, you
can turn your eyes away, missus, quicker that way. If anybody
tries to throw you out, just say you was sent by Anastasia. Big
name for a big girl. Anastasia, remember it."

"I'll remember it," said Joseph. And he led Mary and their
donkey the way Anastasia pointed. How far one has to believe
the stories told of the landlord and of this fat kind woman in later
years and, indeed, in their ghost life after death, I do not know.
But our hunger for punishment and reward is such that we will
not too readily reject the tale of the host's perishing, some twen-
ty-five years later, in a fire that consumed his inn and of his ap-
pearing yearly round about the calends of January on the spot

where it stood, screaming *Plenty of room, plenty, clean and cheap, you are heartily welcome.* Anastasia, they say, married a very rich though blind man when she was thirty-seven years old and had a fine house and servants. To women of goodwill, they say, who are in childbirth's throes she appears now as a sort of smiling shining moonface murmuring comfort. There must be very few women of goodwill in my part of the world.

We come now to the shepherds watching their flocks in a field adjacent to the inn and its stabling. Mary and her burden, Joseph and the ass were now, and the word is apt, installed, and Joseph had bought for a high price some slices of cold broiled mutton, a loaf, and a scoop of mixed sweet pickle. Mary ate little of this supper and groaned much. Joseph bit his nails. It was full night now, and their only light was their small mutton-fat lantern, whose charred wick Joseph had trimmed with dithering fingers and lighted, cursed much the while and told to clear out, with a spill from the fire of the inn kitchen. Meanwhile, under the immense cold sky, the shepherds watched.

We must give them names, and Adam, Abel and Enoch (whom the Arabs call Idris) will do, old names to match an old profession. They sat in their woollen cloaks under the stars, guarding the sheepfold, and Adam said:

"So then he coughs all up in one go and says that's the way of it, lads. Never could manage to take it, something in his stomach they say what fights its going down. Then out like a light on the floor."

"Did he pay that time?" Abel asked. "Not that time, the other time?"

"Him?" Enoch said. "You know him. Wears his little moneybag like it was a mitten. There was that time—you was there, Adam, no, I'm telling a lie, it was just me and whatsisname—he calls a pail of red for the lads, I'm paying he says, then he snakes off when the skin's near the dregs and we has to dip in and schilam."

"Mean scut," said Adam. "Give him a fistful of water and it won't drip. Stars is bright tonight. My old father used to say it's a book to read when you're out watching. Never get tired with the watching, he'd say, when you've the old rakia to look at. See that one there, that big one? Don't reckon to have seen that one afore."

There is a question to be asked here, I think, if I may interrupt this pastoral colloquy, whose content, you will admit, is not of the most compelling. How is it that these uninstructed shepherds should be able to see a new star, when apparently only three astrologer kings, by dint of constant and professional watching, had observed it? The answer is, I think, that these shepherds were accustomed to looking every night at a particular segment of the heavens and no other, such was their conservatism, and that this was the segment into which the chimney of the inn stubbily thrust. They would become accustomed, though without conscious awareness, of a particular configuration about and above this chimney, and a stellar newcomer would, sooner or later, make a firm registration on their eyes. Add to this, perhaps fancifully, that stars in the field of heaven are a kind of flock, and the shepherds' long inbred ability to note changes of number in their woolly constellations, and you have reason enough for believing that they would notice the fateful star if it was above the inn chimney, and above the inn chimney it was. Abel said:

"Big it is too." And then: "Talk of the devil. It's the mean old bastard hisself." For he had observed someone walking over the field towards them, still some way off.

"Naw," said Enoch, "that's not his walk. Stranger by the look of him. How about giving him the knock? You know, the old schalom. Lot of mamon around tonight. Lot of strangers in town."

But the stranger was upon them sooner than, by his distance and leisurely gait, they had expected him to be. It was Gabriel, human and cheerful, wearing a white cloak. He said:

"Fine starry night." And he sat down on the ground.

"We was just saying that," Abel said cautiously. "And that one there looks like it was practically sitting on top of the Grapes."

"Grapes?"

"Bunch of Grapes. That's the inn there, like, but you wouldn't know perhaps, being a stranger in these parts." Adam looked very curiously at the cheerful smooth boyish face, the powerful neck and massive shoulders. Wouldn't care to tackle this bugger, he thought. "Come far, have you?"

"It depends what you mean by *far*," Gabriel said. "There are different ways of looking at distance." And then, urgently: "What kind of men are you?"

"What kind of a question's that meant to be?" asked Enoch, somewhat truculent. "You see what we are—shepherds. Them things there with wool on them, that go baaaah if you kick them in the arse, them's sheep. Heard of them, have you?"

"While questions is being asked," said Adam, "what kind of man are you, then?"

"A question harder to answer than mine," Gabriel said cheerfully. "Call me a sort of messenger. *Aggelos*, if you know Greek."

"Greeks?" Abel said. "Wouldn't trust the bastards from here to there. My sister got tied up with a Greek once."

"High up, from the look of you," said Enoch. "What sort of wool's that then? His cloak here, Abel. Have a feel."

"Shepherds," Gabriel said. "They say that Israel is a scattered flock without a shepherd. Do you believe that?"

"Not a Roman, are you?" Enoch asked with great suspicion.

"No, not a Roman. I'm one of you. In a way, in a way. And if I were to tell you the meaning of that star—if I were to tell you that tonight the shepherd is born—what would you say?"

"A messenger, you said," said Adam. "What would the likes of us want with messengers?"

"And what's your message?" Enoch said.

At that moment Gabriel felt a kind of painful tug in his nonexistent guts—he was an appearance, after all, no more—and he knew that he himself was receiving a message. So he smiled and gave these shepherds the message.

A short distance away the flesh-and-blood message was thrusting its way into the world, meaning a stable with an ass and an ox whose ears Joseph was absently tugging in rhythm, in rhythm. The fat woman Anastasia was, God bless her, at work there, saying soothingly: "Easy, my love, easy. Hold on tight to this bit of rag here. Come on now, it'll soon be over. You there," she said sharply to Joseph, "you started all this, all said and done, don't stand there doing nothing. Clean water, clean. There's a bucket there and a well just behind the rowan tree outside. Go on—*stir*."

Joseph stirred.

The shepherds listened open-mouthed. "You'll be the first," Gabriel was saying. "The first—do you see that? This will be something to tell your grandchildren."

"I'll not marry," Enoch said. "Made up my mind to that. I'll have no grandchildren."

"That you were the *first*," Gabriel said.

"Why us?" Adam said.

"Why not you?" Gabriel told him. "It's for you he comes." And then he stood in what seemed to be starlight of his own. His head was high up there, his hair wearing Arcturus. The shepherds lumbered to their feet, felt somehow they had to, stood awkwardly about him, gawping. Gabriel said, and they were almost damned sure they heard trumpets: "Glory be to God in the highest, and on earth peace to men of good will. It has happened. It is true. Go. Worship. *Go now*."

The shepherds looked towards the chimney, on whose squat top the star seemed to dance, unobscured by the smoke. It seemed improbable, somehow. Enoch said:

"Oughtn't we to take something? A present or something?"

"A lamb," Abel said. "We could give him a lamb."

"He has enough animals there already," Gabriel said.

In the stable, meanly but warmly wrapped, the newborn howled loudly. He was a large baby and well-formed, but it is not, I think, true that he was born with a thatch of golden hair and all his milk-teeth. Anastasia, wiping her hands on the bit of old rag that Mary had used for bearing down, said: "Well, I've got my work to do in the scullery. I'll be back to see how you are. Lovely fat little boy he is. You'll have to start thinking of a name for him."

"That," Joseph said, "has already been taken care of."

Leaving, Anastasia met the shepherds shyly coming in. "No place for you, this," she said. "Go on, off, off. Can't you see what's just been happening?"

"That's what we came for, missus," Adam said. "We was told to come."

She did not understand, so she turned to Joseph, the responsible one here, all said and done, and Joseph nodded. The shepherds shuffled forward, pushing each other so as not to be first.

"You were told?" Joseph said.

"That's right, mister, by this haggler or whatever he is. In the fields out there it was, and we mustn't be long because there's sheep to be watched and there's plenty as will take advantage," Enoch said. "Lovely fat little boy," he said to Mary, "he is that, missus. You feeling all right then?" Mary smiled.

Adam, rightly, was the first to kneel. The old Adam, his Adam's apple working away, no lover of Adam's ale. The others awkwardly knelt too. Then it seemed right to Joseph that he kneel. There was the sound of music, whether of the heavenly host singing *Holy holy holy* or of drunken men in the tavern I do not know, but all the legends concur in saying that there was music.

We must speak now of another concurrence, that of the caravans of our three magi or astrologer-kings. It would be tedious to attempt to recount their journeys, long and over sand but joyful enough, since all believed, separately and severally, that they would end in a joyful revelation or, as it is sometimes termed, epiphany. As it was, all three journeys ended for the moment in the frustration of a night or two in a khan, where Balthazar met Melchior and Gaspar, lighter-coloured kings though still swarthy, and had many things to discuss. The khan was not far from the eastern gates of Jerusalem and, you can be quite sure, the appearance of these potentates in the territory of Herod was noticed and reported to the great monarch himself. The three were uneasily aware that, coming so and undoubtedly noticed, they had the duty of paying their respects to Herod, a brother-king though immeasurably more powerful, friendly moreover to the Roman power, who might not be happy to learn that a new leader was to be born, or had already been, in his territory. Balthazar might have been even more uneasy than he already was had he been informed of a particular incident outside the khan. Two of his servants were drawing water from a well. In this well they saw, drowned, a single great shining star, and they raised their heads to look for its counterpart in the heavens. At this moment they were seized by four armed men. They screamed and were hit unconscious by bludgeons. One was hit too hard and his body was thrown into the well, disturbing the starlight, and the other, alive though moaning in his coma, was thrown over a horse and tied to it. Then the intruders galloped away.

Inside a tent, over supper, the three kings talked. Gaspar said:

"A rough location only. To establish the *exact* location—difficult. I've already sent out two discreet messengers."

"We're under surveillance, I'm quite sure," Melchior said. "Herod's frontiers are very efficiently policed. Perhaps we ought to make ourselves known."

"And how do we answer his questions?" Balthazar gloomed. "What are three kings of small territories doing, creeping around his kingdom?"

And then there was a pulling aside of the tent-flap. "A visitor," Melchior said. "This is perhaps a relief. The matter is, I think, to be taken out of our hands."

And indeed an officer, a Syrian speaking a Semitic dialect they could understand well enough, came in, smiled cordially and saluted. Outside was an armed escort: the clank and shuffle could clearly be heard. The officer said:

"Pardon me—I fear I do not know the collective term—your majesties?"

"You know who we are, I take it," Melchior said.

"We know," said the officer. "King Herod knows. He has asked me to bid you welcome. He is overjoyed that you have come to visit him. He has prepared accommodation for you. Rather," he added, looking around, "more sumptuous than this."

The three kings glanced sardonically at each other, then got up from the sandy carpet. The officer held open the tent-flap for them.

NINE

While they were still riding towards the palace, Herod was already at work on possible reasons for their visit. There was a cellar deep in the building that housed the seraglio, and here Herod sat, well wrapped up against the stony earthy chill, winecup in fist, watching torture proceeding. He had two expert torturers, both Berbers, and they had no apparent objection to twisting the bones of a fellow countryman. Their victim was, in fact, the servant of Balthazar, stolen away from that starry well. Behind Herod stood the man he called his theological adviser, a sort of unfrocked priest. Herod could not abide real priests, whose very eyes were sermons against his way of life and who were in no wise mollified by his rebuilding of the Temple of Solomon. Herod said, as the victim howled, all tears and blood and sweat:

"Break the fingers in the other hand now."

"No no no no no no no—"

"Very well," Herod said, smacking his lips after a draught, "what were the exact words you heard them say?"

"They said. They would. Follow the. Star. Rising over. The place of place of place of."

"Birth of the new prophet. Prophet. Are you sure it was prophet they said?"

"Prophet. Yes. Prophet."

"Break the thumb first," Herod said.

"No no no no no no. It was not prophet."

"Ah, not prophet then. Messiah? Saviour of the people? A new ruler in Israel?"

"One said said said it was was like Ristos. The others said Mashiah. Oh no no no no no I cannot."

"Christos," Herod said. "Messiah. Anointed. King." To his theological adviser he said: "Have you found the reference?"

"Majesty. Shall I read it out?"

"Of course, you fool."

"Majesty. 'And thou, Bethlehem, land of Judah—'"

"*Bethlehem,*" Herod growled.

"'. . . Art in no wise least among the princes of Judah. For out of thee shall come forth a governor, which shall be the shepherd of my people Israel.'"

"So," Herod nodded and nodded. He drained his gold cup and threw it at the more portly of the torturers. It rolled and clanked on the stone flags. "You'd best kill this one here," he said. "He must not report back to his black master *mutilated*. He must not report back at all."

"Kill him, your grace? How, your grace?"

"Anyway you like. Slow or quick, as you like. We can always say he ran away or something. No. Knifed in a tavern brawl. So. Bethlehem. Go on, now. I want to see it done. Hand me back that cup first. Bring me that wineflask. You," he said to the theological adviser, "read that again."

The passage was read again, somewhat more loudly than before. The victim was noisy. He was on the point of death when a messenger came to say that Herod's guests had arrived.

"Serve supper. I shall be along directly."

"Majesty."

When Herod rolled into the dining-room his guests were already seated, though as yet eating nothing, playing with bread, twirling winecups by the stem, saying little to each other except odd comments expressive of conventional admiration of the appointments of the palace. Guards stood about, discreetly shrunk into mere furniture. Herod was drunk more on cruelty than on wine, affable though, greeting, asking about their journey, the economic situations obtaining in their kingdoms, at last, when the spitted fowls were wheeled in, coming to his point.

"Astronomical observations, eh? A clearer view of a certain stellar concurrence in my kingdom, eh? Interesting, very. You should have written. I could have put the latest, Roman, astronomical equipment at your disposal. Still, you are welcome, heartily, and I trust your rooms are to your liking. Astronomical—astrological. Where do you draw the line, eh? We have our own, as I implied, star-gazers. And this new star—naturally, supernaturally—has not escaped their, er, gaze. And we also have experts in holy writ, who will quote the ancient Hebrew prophets at you, and they say this, this: if you seek a new governor of the people—ah, your majesties, I see you looking at each other with surprise—no monopoly or tripoly, this collation of an astronomical phenomenon with an earthly-divine, divine-earthly er one, eh?—you must go to Bethlehem—a little suburb south of Jerusalem. Dunghill, those Romans called it, but cocks crow in the dawn from dunghills. So what I say to your majesties is this: go to Bethlehem, with my blessing, for what it's worth. And it's evident to me that destiny, supernature, eh?—has chosen you to find him. Find him then. And then bring him to me. I too can then bow down and adore him. But here, on my throne. My throne shall be his throne, eh?"

"Bring him here, you say?" said Balthazar.

"Yes," said Herod. "True, a little early for putting him on a throne, best to leave him with his mother wherever he is, true, but my need to see him is great. And I'm too old, too ill, as you see, to go myself. Bring him. Go to Bethlehem—you, blessed strangers to whom, in the mystery of God's eternal workings, the sign has been given. Go and bring joy to the people of Israel, who have waited so long for the good news." He now, after this chilling holy afflatus, sank to a sharp practicality: "I'll give you an armed escort."

"We have our own escorts, majesty," Melchior said. "But thank you for the offer. We will go then at once, late as it is. Find him. And bring him to," he said, "his people."

"I'll give you an armed escort."

"Again, majesty, our thanks, as also for your hospitality, but we can manage very well with the three entourages we have between us," Gaspar said. "We wish not to seem ungrateful, but it would surely be a waste to—"

"I'll give you an armed escort."

This conversation took place on the evening of the day on which Joseph and Mary took the child to be circumcised, so you may observe how tardy the astrologers were in coming to the blessed lowly place of the messiah's birth. The circumcision took place not in the Temple at Jerusalem, as has too often been asserted, but in the synagogue at Bethlehem. The rabbi snipped off the prepuce and the child howled.

"By this act he enters the family of Israel. He gains a name and his name shall be—" The rabbi looked at Joseph.

"Jesus."

"Jesus. Bar-Joseph."

Bar-Joseph? Was this really true? Joseph hesitated and then nodded. "Bar-Joseph."

"The blessing of the Most High. There. The pain will soon go."

Now as the Holy Family, as it is convenient to call them, were leaving the synagogue, an old man, almost blind, doddered up to them and, as it were, smelt out who they were. With a faint cry he got down on his knees and spoke very clearly where they had the right to expect a tremulous babble. "Now let your servant depart, O Lord—in peace, according to your word. For my eyes have seen the salvation you have prepared before the face of all the peoples, a light of revelation to the Gentiles, and the glory of your people Israel." Then he got up, peered at them and said: "Praise be to God, my eyes have truly seen and still see, for a little while longer, a little while. You look at me as if I am mad. But holy knowledge from the Lord is ofttimes called madness. I am Simeon, an old man who has waited long to see his salvation. And now I see a child who is set for the falling and rising up of many in Israel, and for a sign which is spoken against." Mary shuddered at that, and this Simeon said to her: "Yes, and a sword shall pierce your own heart. Your own heart." She clutched her crying child and drew closer to Joseph, who put his arm about her. "And now I may gladly die," Simeon said, "in the knowledge that I have seen him. Let your servant depart, O God, in peace, according to your word, according to your word."

Joseph shyly sketched a blessing on behalf of his son, yes you could say son, had to say son, while the rabbi shook his head sadly at this poor old Simeon. Then the Holy Family went back to the stable, which was beginning to feel like home.

Meanwhile some of Herod's men were having a quiet, or noisy, word with the census officials, the Syrian officer saying:

"We want all the names. Even those of the newborn."

"The newborn?"

"Yes. If you must know, it's the newborn we're chiefly interested in."

"Any request you care to make," said a thin bald census official, "with regard to the whole process of enrolment—well, we'll naturally be glad to do what we can—"

"We don't deal in requests," the Syrian officer said loudly. "Orders. And I'm ordering you to keep us informed."

"Yes yes, an order. Children, you say. And especially the newborn. I quite understand."

It was after midnight that Joseph was wakened by a creaking open of the stable door. Mary and the child did not wake. The mutton-fat lamp was burning with a low wick, but greater light came in at the door, also an apologetic voice. Outside there was the noise of feet and clank of metal. The owner of the apologetic voice was revealed to Joseph, who was on his feet now, in his cloak. Mary had awakened, but the child slept. To both of them it was revealed that the owner of the voice was a man, large and very dark of complexion. He saw a child and a mother and father. He said:

"You may understand our shock—holiest of women, most blessed of men. We had not expected to find him here. But we see the justice of it. There could be no other place. Not in glory but in humility. And the burden of the filth of the world shall be laid upon him." Two other men came in, doubtful. They all, to Joseph's eyes now they were used to the light, seemed high-placed men, important, foreign. Gentiles, not Israelites. Strange. The black man looked at Mary and said:

"And a sword shall pierce your heart, yours also."

She started terribly at that. One of the other men said, taking small bundles from beneath his cape: "We bring gifts—you cannot well see them in this lack of light, but you will have leisure to see them on your journey."

"Journey?" Joseph said. "What journey?"

"Gold, for kingly rule. Frankincense, for divinity. Myrrh, the bitterest of herbs, for the bitterness of the cup he must drink—"

"What journey?"

"Yes," the black stranger said. "After the gifts, a warning. You must leave Bethlehem at once. Leave Palestine. You must leave the kingdom of Herod without delay. Herod knows of the birth of a new governor, a new shepherd of the people. He will not suffer him to live—"

"It comes early," Mary moaned. "The cup. Its bitterness."

"Egypt. Go into Egypt. Make for Gaza to the south-west, keep to the coast. Do you need money?"

"Something we've always needed," sighed Joseph. "But you say you've given us gold."

"Wait till the streets are clear. Then leave. Egypt. It will not be for ever. Herod's remaining days are few."

The eyes of the wife and husband were large in the light of their own lantern when the three strangers had knelt a moment in fealty to the sleeping child, then taken their own light out with them. Outside the stable, none of the magi would deign to address the officers of Herod. A higher servant of Melchior told the Syrian:

"This is not the one. How could it be? A stinking stable full of the dung of oxen. We must continue our search, so says my master. He orders me to tell you that he fears we shall find nothing. The world has waited long for its messiah. It may have to wait longer still. Tell King Herod, he says, they say, that their majesties are returning to their kingdoms."

The Syrian officer shrugged and, with a weary over-arm gesture, pointed to his underlings the dark road back to Jerusalem. So it was to a still and sleeping street that the Holy Family stole out, Mary with the child warm-wrapped, seated on the donkey, Joseph holding the bridle, furtive, looking all about him. The child inopportunely woke and cried bitterly. Mary hushed him. The new star still rode above the inn chimney. They turned their backs to it and took the road to Hebron, where, when the time came, they could turn their backs on the greater star of the day and move towards Gaza.

In Herod's palace the Syrian officer gave his negative report. Herod was up and pacing, had taken much wine but was terribly sober. He swung his heavy-footed winecup at the officer's face and struck him a blow on the temple. Blood gushed but the officer still stood to attention, trembling.

"Tricked. You benighted fool. Idiot. You're not worthy to bear the rank of—" And he tore at the officer's insignia with sharp fingernails. "Tricked. And now they're over the border, out of my jurisdiction. Clever. But the child is still there, we can be sure of that."

"But, your majesty, which child? We were taken to see all the newborn."

"And now," Herod calmly said, "you can kill all the newborn. Do you hear me? Kill them all—all the boy-children. No, the girls as well, it will take too long to sort out the sexes. Be on the safe side, if I can trust you to be on any side, safe or unsafe, you fool. All those up to a year old. Two years, for that matter. The safe side. Those damned charlatans may have got their calculations wrong. Better all the innocent suffer than the one guilty get away."

"Guilty, your majesty?" said the theological adviser. "A child guilty?"

"Yes. Guilty of being destined to the throne of this land.

Born to the guilt of usurpation. Go on, you—take your men and let your men take their swords. Make sure they're sharp. To Bethlehem. Hack. Lunge. Chop. Kill."

He was by now, without doubt, mad. A mad king's orders must, however, still be obeyed. Told of their mission, some of the men refused. They were hacked first. Practice. "Easier, lad, with these soft small bodies," a kindly sergeant said to one soldier who vomited after killing a comrade. "Nothing to it. They're just soft squashy things. Take a stiff mouthful of red and then we'll march."

This, they say, was foretold by Jeremiah the prophet. Something about a voice heard in Ramah, weeping and great mourning, Rachel weeping for her children. And she would not be comforted, for her children were no more. One story they tell is how the little hacked bones of the slaughtered rose like birds into the air and tapped on the gates of heaven very feebly and were not heard. Such tales of bitterness were bound to be told by those who remembered the screams and the steel-swish. The first of the prices that had to be paid for having a new shepherd of the people.

BOOK 2

One day, a year or so later, Joseph was fitting a mortice and tenon joint together, using a very light hammer. The man who employed him looked on, approving and disapproving, saying:

"How often must I tell you that that's not the Egyptian way? Beautifully done, yes, but the customer won't thank us for it. A couple of light nails is enough."

"That's the way we do it in Galilee."

"That's the way you *did* it in Galilee. Forget Galilee, Galilee's all over."

"I'm not going to unlearn it now," Joseph said.

"Well," said his employer, sitting heavily on a work-stool. "To tell you the truth, that's the way my grandfather did it back in Damascus. Immigrants. Egypt's all immigrants. The Egyptians never learned to do anything for themselves. Immigrant slaves, then free immigrants. And what's Egypt now? A piece of mud with slave monuments and a lot of ancient junk in the desert. Romans, Greeks, Syrians. And now the Israelites back again, eh?"

"If by that you mean me, no. A change of rule in Palestine, then back home to Galilee."

"Change of rule? There's no change of rule. It's all Romans, man. Wherever you go it's Romans. I've a proposition for you."

"No propositions.

"A partnership. What do you say to that?"

"I've no money to put into a partnership."

"You've skill, and that's as good as money."

"I'm not staying."

"You'll stay. This place, you know, well, it sort of grows on you. Especially in the evenings."

This was the fifth position Joseph had taken since the coming of the Holy Family into Egypt. He was a man by nature given to settling in one place, asking nothing more than a chance to work at his trade, a quiet life. But he had been made aware of the long arm of King Herod—the occasional appearance of Romans travelling on business not clearly defined, questions asked in inns (any from Palestine moved here at all?). He was also aware of the need to be restless, not to wish the quiet life. But Herod would not die, travellers spoke of a mad and tyrannous and desperately sick Herod but not of a dying Herod: he was staying alive, they said, to spite his sons. So Joseph and Mary and the child stayed in Egypt, changing from town to town, village to village, moving ever farther away from the frontier with Palestine and farther towards the Great Bitter Lake.

"I'm not staying," Joseph stubbornly said.

"You'll stay. And you'll stay with me, if you know what's good for you. Big opportunities here. The town's growing."

Outside the mean lodgings where they owned not even a waterpot (possessions were dangerous, possessions imposed an obligation to stay with the possessions), Joseph said to Mary:

"He said we'd stay. Will we stay?"

"Will we?" Mary said, looking up from her mending. "That sounds as if you think I can see the future. I can't see the future. But I know we're not staying."

And yet, that evening, it seemed that this was a good place to stay. There was a smell of hot oil and garlic all down the street, children played round the well, a woman unseen sang a song, a love-song that seemed a mere wail of intricate sadness. The air was cool, the wind spicy. At their feet the child Jesus played with wooden blocks that Joseph brought home, building a little town for himself. He was a sturdy child and likely to grow big. He seemed to possess no very special gifts, proper for a son of

God. He did not make birds out of mud and bid them fly off. He seemed sometimes to listen to voices that were not there, but this meant merely that he was unusually sharp-eared—a matter of hearing voices afar before others heard them. He had seen Egyptian magic, watching it gravely, not easily astonished. Magicians often travelled from town to town, putting on their shows in the open air, collecting coins after. One popular trick was to turn a rod into a snake, a trick that Moses had learnt. The serpent was fed with a potion that induced sleep and stiffness; held by its head, it looked sufficiently like a rod; thrown to the ground it woke from its trance and wriggled. He had seen Egyptian physicians cure sick men and blind men through the power of suggestion accompanied by the laying on of hands or the application to the sick part of the physician's spittle. He was, however, not at all excited by such wonders. He learned early to speak, and to speak sensibly, gravely. He rarely smiled. Sometimes he would turn a glance on his parents that seemed to ask the question: who are you and what are you doing here? If he had special God-given knowledge he did not impart it, he kept it locked within.

"He knows we're not staying," Mary said.

Whether he knew it or not, the time for their leaving Egypt could, had the news whistled in on the wind from the east that evening, have been that evening, or certainly the following morning. The news, I mean, of Herod's loud, spectacular, violent end. The circumstance leading directly to this had been the monarch's unexpected, even by himself, attempt at self-slaughter. Lying on his couch in great pain and depression, his belly swollen with a liquid whose fierce bubbling could be heard ten yards off, his legs lacking all feeling, his head in a perpetual ache, he said, to his own surprise: "An apple. Bring me an apple. I wish an apple." A servant ran off and brought him an apple ready peeled and sliced. "No, fool, fool," he screeched, hitting out though harmlessly, "an apple with its red skin on and a knife to peel it." The servant ran off again and brought a polished red apple on a silver dish and a steel knife to cut it. Herod took the knife, felt its edge with his thumb and then, to his, as I say, own surprise, plunged the knife into his belly. Blood came, an oily water, a stench as of rotting meat overlaid with herbs. He lay there, breathing heavily, eyes closed, smiling villainously, growling: "It is done, done." But it, or he, was not done. Servants ran, ministers too, crying; the seraglio girls screamed. Physicians came. They shook their heads. But Herod had life in him still.

Now the Crown Prince, Archilaus, was at that time in prison. His father had screamed of his treachery, his plotting, for weeks and months and at length, after a sneering insult to the king at the dinner-table and the king's roaring and impotent lashing out, Archilaus had, on the king's lip-lathered bellowing orders, been thrust behind bars. Archilaus, this night of the apple-knife, heard voices crying "Dead, dead, the king is dead" and asked the captain of the guard, with great excitement, if this was true. The captain himself ran off to find out, returned, said the king was certainly dying, would be dead before the night was done. Well then, said Archilaus, release me. On whose authority, sir? On mine, you fool. I am the Crown Prince and in a short while I must be addressed as your majesty. So the captain turned the great key in the lock and, five minutes after, Archilaus went boldly to his father's bedroom, where the bandaged and moaning monarch lay surrounded by physicians and ministers, eyes shut. Some instinct told him to open these eyes as soon as his son padded in. He saw Archilaus and cried, with all his old vigour:

"Who let you out? Who let this plotting swine go free? Well, sir, you may now join those others who have been put to silence." Saying this, he grasped the sword from the sheath of the nearest minister and, with incredible agility but an inefficacy only to be expected, he struck at his son but succeeded only in ripping his son's right sleeve. Then Herod went over, making the room rumble, dislodging mobile objects from tables with the force of his fall. He rolled, groaning terribly, his whole body convulsed two or three times, he heaved a feeble fist to heaven, he kicked violently, then he died, loosing a nauseous flood from his bladder and bowels. The heart, the physicians knew and soon said aloud, the heart had cracked. The death of Herod. Herod the Great is dead. Archilaus spoke loud words, smirking and at the same time trying to look kingly.

"I am your monarch now. Make proper obeisance, my lords." Ten slaves carried the body away. "Chief minister, announce to the people the accession to the throne of the realm of his majesty King Archilaus."

"Not yet, sir," the chief minister said firmly. "Rome must first be consulted."

"Rome? Rome? Rome has nothing to do with it. Make the announcement at once."

"I must certainly announce the demise of his late majesty. But I may do no more till Rome has been consulted. In the meantime, I am empowered, in pursuance of his late majesty's provisional enactment, to place government in the hands of a regency council whose members have already been nominated, with yourself and your brothers as titular heads of the executive." Archilaus raged at that, but it was impotent rage.

Rome indeed had to be consulted, and I must take you back in time to a conference held in the private quarters of the Emperor Augustus in Rome, out of which a plan for the government of Palestine in the event of the death of Herod, daily expected, was drawn up by the divine personage himself. A burly adviser on the affairs of the Levant named Saturninus said:

"I concur with your divine imperial majesty on the very marginal strategic importance of Palestine in the present phase of the *Pax*, but I would certainly recommend the installation of a Roman presence in Jerusalem."

"A waste, Saturninus," Augustus said. "A mass of squabbling Jews—our legions have worthier tasks to perform than to hold them down. Let us not break the succession. These Jews may loathe the family of Herod, but they know them to be of the land and of the faith, such as it is. The Herodian tyranny will go on, but they will prefer it to the efficiency and justice of aliens."

"And which," Saturninus said, "of the Herodian tyrants has your divine imperial majesty in mind?"

"None," said Augustus, "is fit to rule the entire territory. And if one were, in fact, to be placed on the Palestinian throne, he would not last long. Fratricide, Saturninus. No, I have another idea. Valerius, bring me the map."

Valerius, a quick nervous secretary, had a map ready. He unrolled it on the divine imperial marble table and secured its corners with heavy marble corner-securers.

"You see here, Saturninus," Augustus said, pointing. "I propose a fourfold division. The correct technical term is, I believe, tetrarchy. Four tetrarchs, and each of the blood of the soon to be late lamented Herod."

"Lamented, your divine imperial majesty?"

"He kept order, he loved Rome, he understood the Jews. But look. Iturea and Trachonitis—sounds like a disease, does it not?—they go to Philip. Herod Antipater rules Galilee. Lysanias has this region here—Abilene. And Judea—Judea goes to Archilaus. You know Archilaus?"

"Unfortunately, yes. A grinning sort of man. Very unstable. So. He gets Judea."

"Provisional, Saturninus. Let us keep the term *provisional* very much in mind."

"The tetrarchy of Palestine. It sounds impressive."

It was some two weeks after the death of Herod that Joseph heard the news. A small caravan with asses and camels had come from Judea into Egypt, and Joseph was quick to go to the inn and talk with these men. One of the travellers exaggerated the tale of Herod's end in the manner of travellers:

"Burst like a blown frog. Belly cracked wide open and the palace was near awash with what spewed out. Had to shut up the palace, even the gardens, while they cleaned it out and burnt thyme and marjoram and the rest of the sweet herbs. They say the stench is still coming from his grave."

"And who rules now?" asked Joseph, not yet willing to feel the elation proper to the end of an exile, feeling rather the promise of pain at leaving what was now the known, having to return to what had become all the more the unknown for its once having been the known.

"It's split up into four, like a cake. One man for Jerusalem, one man for Trachonitis—sounds a bit like a disease, doesn't it?—and another one for Galilee—"

"Who rules Galilee?"

"Herod. Herod Antipater, which means I think that he'll be the dead opposite of his father. Decent quiet lad he seems to be. Only a child, surrounded by what they call regents. Romans, some of them. King of Galilee anyway, another Herod. You know the place, then?"

"I know it," Joseph said.

"The place to keep out of," said another traveller, "is Jerusalem. They have a mad one there. Great for the fire and slaughter."

This was all too true. Archilaus made the mistake, among other mistakes, of saying that he was greater than God, since God was only an idea in men's minds and he, Archilaus, was very much flesh and blood. The rule of Archilaus, Archilaus insisted, was above such sodden antiquities as the law of Moses and, as for the temple which his father Herod had restored, that was a costly superstition full of air. One small tyranny—arrest of an old blind man who spat, all unknowing naturally, on the sandals of the captain of the royal guard, his torture and execution without trial—led to another—Archilaus demanding a fourteen-year-old bride, seen from the royal litter in a marriage procession, as his concubine. Stones were thrown at the troops of Archilaus, the troops responded with swords and javelins, women and children as well as men went down. Slaughter and unjust executions were proceeding in Jerusalem while Mary, Joseph and the child slowly made their way across the desert.

Resting under palms one evening, Joseph said: "Man is strangely made. I'm homesick for Egypt. Especially in the evenings, as now. You remember what the Israelites said when Moses led them to freedom?"

"I don't know the scriptures," Mary said. "I was never a very good reader. Nor listener either."

"They said: 'Where are the onions and garlic and leeks we knew in Egypt?' That's what they thought of, onions, not freedom. And when I think of what it will be like in Nazareth— well, my heart sinks lower with every step towards it. Gossip. Mockery. Perhaps fear. They'll have heard everything by now."

"They will have heard," said Mary, eating very hard bread and hence somewhat indistinctly, "of a mad king and a lucky escape. They are not yet ready for for—"

"Belief?"

"Belief. They will take us as a family that went to Egypt and then came home again. With a child no different from other children."

But that quiet grave child with the sharp ears seemed to be listening to what proceeded in Jerusalem, two hundred miles away, where the cavalry and infantry of the Roman Twelfth Legion were restoring order to a tyrannously misruled province.

In Rome, Saturninus deferentially told the divine Augustus that he had always said Archilaus was unstable, unfit to rule even the fourth part of a province. Augustus said yes yes testily and said there was only one solution.

"Judea then comes under the direct rule of Rome, your divine imperial majesty?"

"Against my will, Saturninus, totally against my will. It is the waste I cannot tolerate. We need the Twelfth Legion elsewhere. As for rule—better if our governor control Judea from Cesarea—remote, not in the midst of things. The occasional show of strength in Jerusalem, of course. As now. Archilaus—a stupid man, a very bad strain in Herod's family. I always said so, you will admit as much."

"If you please, your divine imperial majesty." And then, with the same tact: "Your majesty knows the Jews."

"I know that *you* know them, Saturninus. You expect resentment, riots, a growth of let us call it nationalistic fanaticism?"

"Much depends on the governor."

"Procurator, procurator. Judea is hardly important enough to merit a governor. So now we must choose a procurator. Valerius," he said to his secretary, "bring me that list of names."

The list was brought.

The return of the Holy Family to Nazareth had not been unexpected there. When the three arrived, shy and travel-worn, they were given loud greetings and warm embraces and Rabbi Gomer cried a prayer to the heavens: "God be praised, for they that were lost are found, they that were dead rise again before us." This, Joseph thought, went too far. For the rest, things could well be worse. Eliseba, bent and complaining but vigorous still, had lived in the house and kept it clean, so that it smelled of life and not the mould and dust of a tomb. James and John had kept the shop going, but James had put out some story that the business was now rightfully his and that Joseph, before departing for Bethlehem, had said: "If I die on the journey, all this is yours, though I expect you to make provision for my relicts. If we all die, it is yours and yours and only yours." What is death? (so James had asked). It is a prolonged absence. Therefore Joseph and his relicts were dead. Joseph now put all that right. James went away from Nazareth to start a shop of his own. Everyone knew where the money had come from, but Joseph made no murmur. He would, for the time being, make do with one assistant. When the time came, there would be another one all ready in the family.

Already the major problem of this story-teller beckons— namely, how to deal with a life hidden, and not a short one either, for Jesus enters the world we call great or public when no longer strictly a young man, and thirty years of quiet Nazareth life cannot well be ignored, for all my reader's conceivable interest in the career of the preacher and redeemer and probable eagerness to reach it without overmuch delay. I will, then, be as quick as I can with the facts of the Galilee life before Jesus's baptism (and the scantiness of those facts will conduce to speed. Of course, also, as I see now, I shall have the problem of John's premissionary life to consider: there is no end to the pains of story-telling.)

Jesus was a sturdy and quiet child and, at the age of seven, already bigger and brawnier than many of the ten-year-olds of Nazareth. Though quiet, he was quick to take offence and hit out at his offender, even if the offender were much older and bigger. He had firm muscles and did not seem very specially to be a child of God, meaning one of the puny who trust God to look after them. He had a large appetite up to the age of fourteen and was especially a great eater of fish. If there had been more mutton in the house he would have been a great eater of that too, for he was not backward in asking for second helpings of his mother's mutton stew, which he liked well-salted and pungent with herbs. He had, in matters of diet, something of the heretic in him, for he could not see what was wrong in taking a cup of goat's milk to wash down his meat.

"It is against the law, son," Joseph said, "as you have been told a thousand times."

"I know it is against the law, but I do not see why."

"It is in Leviticus. It was laid down by Moses. It is to do with the body's health and the soul's sanctity, and that is an end of it."

"Why?"

"You must not be asking why all the time."

This was unjust; he rarely asked why. At school he accepted the doctrines of Moses and was good at his catechism, especially the number questions.

"Who knows what four is? You, Jesus, what is four?"

"Four is the mothers—Sara, Reba, Leah, Rachel. Three is the patriarchs—Abraham, Isaac, Jacob. Two is the tables of the law. One is the Lord our God, who made the heavens and the earth."

"Good boy."

The day came when Rabbi Gomer said to the boys at his school: "Now you have learned the letters. The time has come for you to see what they look like when they are kneaded into those loaves we call words. Here, see, is one of the holy psalms

of the blessed King David." And he handed round a scroll for
reverent handling. Jesus, to his surprise, was able to read it right
away, and with fair speed:

"The Lord is my shepherd, I shall not lack anything, he leads
me to fine grazing fields and feeds me beside comfortable
waters."

"Very good boy."

It is said, though we do not have to believe it, that Joseph
gave his foster-child homely lessons of his own, which were
based on the things of wood that he made:

"I'm no rabbi, but I think I have something to teach. Not just
the trade but the meaning of the trade, the trade in God's eye, so
to speak. So, as we use this rule for marking the straight line on
the wood we must cut, so we make rules of right conduct. But
perhaps right conduct is not enough. You see this new plough
I've just finished—for cutting straight furrows that will take the
seed: that may stand for the good but lowly life, head to the
earth, the muscles struggling forward. But a man must also learn
to rise above the earth. See this ladder—it is a thing that our
great great great great great-grandfather Adam did not even
dream of. It is something his children, with God's help, have
learned to make, so that they may rise into the treetops and take
the high-growing fruit and see the eggs lying snug in their nests,
so that we may rise to the high shelf where the secret books lie
gathering dust. Step by step, as in music. Step by step: the low-
est rung is our senses—smell, taste, touch and the others; then
comes speech, which raises us above the animals; then thought;
then fancy; then imagination; then the vision—and at the top of
the ladder the reality, which is another word for nearness to
God."

At the age of ten Jesus was already earning the name of Jesus
Naggar (which is Hebrew for carpenter, Marangos in Greek).
He liked the heavy work of sawing and the lighter work of planing. He was careless sometimes at measuring, trusting too much
in his eye and not enough in the rule, but at fourteen he was as
skilful in making ploughs as his foster-father (whom, of course,

he called father), and this was as well, for Joseph was growing old and weak in the muscles. At fourteen Jesus became a man in more than his ability to practise a trade, for this is the age of the bar-mitzvah, whereby a boy enters fully into the life of his faith and his community.

Rabbi Gomer, himself now old, was wavering final words to the boys who had just become men—"Passover is coming, prepare yourselves for Passover, for the first time you will be spending it in Jerusalem, you will see the great glory of the Holy Temple of the Lord our God"—when his voice was wholly drowned by the thud and rattle of armed horsemen riding past the synagogue. The rabbi ended the humble man-making ceremony at once, since all eyes were turned towards the noise, gave his blessing, then led the way out. Blinking in the bright light, coughing and sneezing at the hoof-raised dust, Jesus and his fellows saw Roman troops galloping along the main street, truly the only street. Jotham the baker saw them too, but saw them closer. The sergeant and a couple of his men dismounted and strode into Jotham's shop without, as we say, either a good day or a kiss my arse.

"Bread, lads, Jewish bread, but it'll do you no lasting harm."

"What is this?" Jotham said. "What do you want?"

The sergeant spoke bad Aramaic. "Requisition, call it. An army's got to be fed. It's a long long way from Damascus to Jerusalem."

"This is Nazareth," Jotham said, "in Galilee. This is not Roman territory."

"Isn't it, isn't it? Well, we could argue that out over a quart of wine if there was time enough. Talking of wine, any good wine about? All right, all right, thanks for the provender."

A young Nazarene named Nahum cursed as they came out. "God's malediction on you, Romans. The God of Israel that is the God of the world strike you down. And he will. Roman bones rotting on our sacred soil. Curses on you, Roman filth." Then he spat.

"Didn't quite understand all that," said a loaf-laden soldier good-humouredly, "but it sounded bad."

"I understood the spit all right," said one of his fellows, looking ugly.

"Leave him, ignore him," said the sergeant, a man of twenty
years' service. "You'll meet plenty of these in Jerusalem.
Zealots, they're called. Mad bastards." And, nodding pleasantly
at Jotham, he led his men back to their mounts. Jotham
grinned nastily at Nahum and said:

"Want to fight, do you? Well, it won't do you any good.
They're everywhere now, the Romans. And the kingdom of
Israel shall be as dust upon the wind."

The wind blew the Roman dust away, the troops were no
longer to be heard, riding towards Jerusalem. There was, it
seemed, need of them in Jerusalem. Because of a reign just
ended in Rome and a reign just begun.

Augustus died. He lay on his death-bed, surrounded by the
men he called friends, by physicians, senators, consuls, also the
friends of the man who was to succeed him, Tiberius. Tiberius, of
course, was also there and, for that matter, the procurator of
Roman Judea, on leave at the time. Augustus spoke his last
words with a kind of ghost of the crisp articulation of an actor:

"Ei de ti
Echoi kalos, to paignio dote kroton
Kai pantes emas meta charas propempsate."

Saturninus understood the words and nodded, then shook his
head. Tiberius whispered loudly:

"What did he say?"

"Greek."

"I know, but what does it mean?"

"The comedy of his life is over. If we at all enjoyed it, we
ought to applaud the actor as he takes his leave of us."

"Does he mean *really* applaud?" Tiberius was not the brightest of men. "He jests at the end," he then said, not too sure of
the propriety of this; indeed, not too sure, as his career was to
show, of the propriety of anything. But that it was the end was
certain. Augustus gave a little sigh and then was silent. A

physician looked closely at him and then gently shut the once imperial eyes. The god had turned truly into a god. All turned to Tiberius. They muttered "Hail, Tiberius Caesar" and made a sketch of a salute of fealty, though the hearts of many sank into their boots. Tiberius smirked and spoke thanks that were first too soft and then too loud.

Tiberius was, shortly after, crowned, and his smirking image was to be seen everywhere throughout the Empire. It appeared, on the orders of the procurator (who had always got on better with Tiberius than with Augustus), in Jerusalem. None seriously objected to the silly jowls smirking in public offices or from the walls of taverns (where games of spitting into the imperial eye could safely be indulged in), but when it was decided to carry a most ornate icon of Tiberius into the temple, that the Jews might be reminded who was truly their god, then the people of Jerusalem very naturally revolted. There was a sect or party of most fervent believers in independence from the Roman yoke, zealous men who read the scriptures together and reminded each other of former slaveries and of the breaking of the chains on God's own orders, and these men were rightly called Zealots. It was the Zealots, under the leadership of a man called Abbas, who removed the image of Tiberius from the temple while it was still in procession towards the Holy of Holies and fought fiercely, though to no avail, with the Roman troops who had brought it in. Many arrests were made and a mass execution was arranged. The procurator of Judea, whose name was Pontius Pilate, sat sternly on the terrace of his palace (formerly Herod's) as the malefactors were ranged before him. A couple of headsmen with sharp axes flashing in the sun stood waiting, smirking like their own divine imperial ultimate employer. Sternly Pilate addressed the condemned, saying:

"When will you Jews realise what you are? When will you understand that the personage of the Emperor is literally divine, and that the defacement of his image is a gross act of blasphemy?"

The sturdy Abbas, by trade a butcher, spoke out. "This, master procurator," he said, "we do not and cannot accept. The introduction of the image of a mere temporal ruler into the sanctuary of the Most High is a blasphemy that shakes the very heavens. As to *what we are,* we know what we are—the people chosen of God. And we know what you Romans are—infidel intruders, defilers of the Holy City, an unjust scourge and a foul abomination."

"You will not speak so," Pilate cried, trembling. He was, at this time, neither old nor experienced in the art of managing dissident natives. "You pile crime on crime."

"But you cannot pile death on death," Abbas grinned. "A man can die once only."

Pilate was very angry. "To your work," he told the headsmen. "I have heard enough."

To his surprise, the Jews broke loudly into a patriotic hymn, led off by Abbas, and, at his signal, they all knelt in a single body and bared their necks to the axe. Pilate was astonished. He strode forward to where Abbas knelt and shrieked:

"You wish to die? You," he shrieked, "wish to," he shrieked, "die?"

"Rather than submit," bellowed Abbas, "to the shame of an enforced blasphemy, yes and yes again. Wait, Pontius Pilate. Soon you may have to rule over a graveyard." And he calmly awaited the axe. In Pilate's head the word *clemency* leered. But all he could do for the moment was to shout:

"The execution is postponed. Back to jail with them." To his deputy L. Vitellius Flavicomus, a dark man with hair the colour of soot, he muttered: "I ought really to take advice."

"From whom, sir?"

"That is the problem, Vitellius. I am much on my own. I ask nothing but tranquillity."

"And a measure of popularity, sir?" He watched the Jews, still singing lustily about Zion and the Lord's love, marching back to the jailhouse.

"If we just quietly execute the man Abbas and let the rest go free? Imperial clemency and so forth?"

"Certainly cut off Abbas's head, certainly do that."

And so Abbas was, without trumpets, executed and the rest allowed to return to life, though severely warned. Still, there was no further attempt to instal the smirking imperial jowls in the Holy of Holies. The son of Abbas, a young man of eighteen, brooded revolution but decided that the time to strike at the imperial power was not yet. There was need of some great poetic leader, filled full with the magic substance known in those days as *charisma*.

The Jerusalem to which Jesus and his parents proceeded, along with a great number of Nazarenes, for the celebration of Passover, was tranquil enough though full of barelegged Roman soldiers. The boy's first view of the city was from the crown of a hill; there it lay in its valley, bone-white and dung-coloured, sun-washed. The entire party of Nazareth pilgrims, at Rabbi Gomer's instigation, went down on its knees and intoned the psalm that begins "I was glad when they said unto me: lo, let us go into the house of the Everlasting." Seeing the city, the boy was not overwhelmed with filial love as one might have expected him to be. A city was made out of people, when all was said and done, and he did not expect the citizens of Jerusalem to shine with any especial grace. They would, he thought, mostly be a bad lot, anxious to make money out of Passover pilgrims. Besides, he had vague images rising into his brain of other cities, bigger—Rome, say, and Alexandria—which he had heard of but never seen.

There were untrustworthy men with insincere smiles and quick hands for money, anxious to show the visitors around the tombs of the prophets. There were drunken Roman soldiers and a great number of prostitutes. His young blood was roused by the sight of proffered bosoms and lascivious teeth. He saw frank embraces in dark alleyways. Swift robbers, their near-naked bodies greased against the grasp of pursuers, grabbed at purses. It was a city, he thought, of hands, hands ready to take money, to slither over the glowing shoulders of the street-girls, to bunch in fight outside taverns. And, in the Temple, priestly hands kniving the shrieking sacrifice, hands red with goat-blood and the thinner blood of pigeons, hands unclean with the entrails of lambs, hands deft at splaying the cleansed carcase of lamb or kid and holding it flat, a kind of pathetic sacrificial banner, with transverse laths of wood.

Hands grasped at his mother Mary in the courtyard of the temple, down onto which the armed sentries looked from their watch-tower. They were gnarled, brown, old hands, those of an old woman.

"Elizabeth?"

"The same. You're hardly a day older, God's grace blooms in you, most blessed of women. And this is—"

"This is he."

"John is somewhere. John is about some boy's business of his own. Well, we'll take the Passover meal together. They are much of a size, God bless them both, his father must be proud, ah, poor Zacharias."

They ate their meal in an upper room, John and Jesus eyeing each other warily as the rabbi intoned the ancient words over the symbolic victuals: "This is the bread baked in haste, with no time for the leavening, such as our fathers ate the night before their exile in Egypt ended. These are the bitter herbs. This is the roasted lamb whose blood had smeared their lintels, that the Angel of Death might read the sign and pass over their houses without touching a hair of the head of the first-born. Roast lamb-flesh, bread baked in haste, herbs whose bitterness should remind their mouths of the bitterness of exile . . ."

John and Jesus, big tough youths both, walked together through the streets bright with windowed Passover lamps, not fearful of the drunken bravos, of the Syrian soldiers jeering *Yahudi Yahudi.*

"What do you do?"

"Work in the shop. Sawing wood mostly, I read a lot."

"I read all the time. I'm to be a priest. Like my father."

"Do you believe in fathers?"

"What do you mean, believe?"

"Fathers, fathers, the plurality. We all have one father, source of life. The men we call father are his instruments. Whence comes the potency of the seed? Not from men. There is only one creator."

"You speak strangely."

"I fear I do."

"Fear?"

"I fear I may speak more strangely still. But not yet."

"Do you believe the stories—about you and me, I mean?"

"I cannot see much of the future. Wherever we arrive, we must travel slowly."

"You've arrived." A girl sprang out of the shadows of a doorway.

"I speak too loudly," Jesus grinned.

"There's two of us," said the girl, big-eyed, loose-garmented, smelling of sandalwood. "But there's only the one room. Would you mind that?"

"Forgive us," Jesus said courteously. "Moved as we are by your kind invitation, charmed as we are by your youth and beauty, we must plead another engagement, for which we are already late."

"Nice," the girl said, "you speak nice. All right, darling, off to your whatever it is." And she patted Jesus on the crupper, mouth-clicking at him as though he were a horse. Jesus grinned affectionately.

"You should," John said, as they walked, "by rights have rebuked her. It is a sinful profession."

"You could have rebuked her yourself if you considered rebuking so necessary."

"I was rebuking her with my eyes and the sternness of my countenance. Unfortunately you distracted her attention away from me with your little courtly speech."

"Sinful, yes," Jesus said. "She hires out her body, which is a walking temple of the Lord, and she encourages men to use their seed for mere pleasure and not for the thickening of the ranks of Israel. She makes her living out of the sin of Onan. Very sinful."

"And yet you smile."

"I liked the girl. She was not respectable. It is respectability I hate, and yet respectability is not put among the sins. The Perishayya and the followers of Zadok the righteous are very respectable and, on their own proud admission, very holy. I find sinners more interesting than the righteous."

"You speak very very strangely."

"If you and I have any big work to do in the future, it is among the sinners we must go. We had better start learning to like sinners."

"To like sinners is to like sin."

"Ah no, not at all. It is as much as to say that to cherish the sick is to cherish their sickness. Let me not say *like* either. *Love* is the needful word."

Walking in daylight near the execution hill which is shaped like a man's skull, they saw what they would have been willing not even to hear of, namely the whipping of two howling men to their crucifixion. The men, so said a portly merchant to them in satisfaction at the fact of justice being seen to be done, were thieves. "Well," said Jesus to John, shaking with rage as he spoke, "it is laid down in the law of Moses that thou shalt not steal, but I had rather be stolen from and say amen to the crime than have my thief rent and nailed. Thou shalt not steal, and why not? So that thou shalt not be crucified. Look at them all, look at smirking respectability in its laundered robes." His loud words made many look curiously at him, a large boy with the voice of a man. "Let us go from here," John said. Jesus was all too willing to go, shaking with anger.

When the time came for the Passover pilgrims to leave Jerusalem, Mary and Joseph sought their son in vain. "He'll be in the middle," said the caravan master, vaguely pointing to the midst of the forming train of camels and asses and folk. "The young people are together in the middle there, singing their new Jerusalem songs and twanging their two-string fiddles. He'll be there all right." But he was not there. "Wait," Joseph said, "we must look." The caravan master said: "When the sun touches the tip of the tower, we leave. No waiting for anybody." They went off looking, very agitated. Thieves, pugnacious Syrian soldiers, dangers.

Now Jesus had gone alone to the Temple, knowing it would be empty now of money chinking, doves whirring, lambs baaing, all the brisk trade of tribute and sacrifice. In the forecourt he stood, not alone, for speared troops watched from their tower, a legacy of that image of Tiberius business. He wiped them from his eye, as from his ear their rough pleasantries in bad Aramaic: "Bit late, aren't you, yeled?" and so on. He stood in that forecourt, making the presence of God in the hidden shrine ray out at him stronger than the sun. He stood, one could say, entranced. Then a venerable doctor of the Temple came by, saw him, said kindly:

"What are you doing here, my son, all alone?"

"Hardly alone," the boy said with a half-smile. "God is here."

"Out of the mouths," the doctor quoted.

"I am neither a babe nor a suckling—though I should have thought, now I hear the words on my own lips, a babe and a suckling were one and the same. The faith says I am now a man, your reverence."

Another learned bearded one came along, ignoring the boy, telling his fellow-doctor that So-and-so had been along and reported that the arrangement concerning old What's-his-name had been satisfactorily concluded. "Ah, good, good," said the first. "A very ant, that man, all the work he does. Go to the ant, thou sluggard. There, my boy," he smiled at Jesus, "Holy Writ has a word for everything."

The boy smiled back. "The Proverbs of Solomon are sensible rather than holy. We must distinguish, must we not, between the secular jottings of a king, who is a sort of man of business, and those truly holy pronouncements of the book which rise above the daily world."

"It seems you read," said the first doctor, "and also think about what you read. But take some well-meant advice, my boy, and do not think overmuch. To think is to split, to divide, to put into categories, and this must not be done with God's word. You must not say that this is secular and this holy, for you will end up by refusing to swallow Holy Writ whole, and therein lies the danger of heresy."

"Dogs swallow whole," Jesus said, "but man chews and spits out what is not worth chewing. There, would not that do for the Wisdom that is Solomon's?"

Neither holy doctor could well take offence at what might be interpreted as a boy's pertness, since Jesus spoke with a modest smile and used the gestures of deference. Also they were, almost against their will, fascinated by the maturity of this mere youngster, big-bodied but almost beardless, his fine grey eyes all innocence. Another wise man came to join his colleagues, very dry and humourless, and he very stupidly said:

"Boy, what are you doing here, boy?"

"Learning wisdom, learning holiness, taking warmth from the presence of the Lord in the Lord's high place. Sir."

"Where are you from? You're a Galilee boy by your way of speaking."

"I am from two places, like all men. That should be enough for you. My dust is from earth and my spirit is from God. That is in Ecclesiastes."

The first doctor, smiling still, said: "'The voice said, Cry And he said, What shall I cry?' Can you continue?"

Very readily Jesus continued, looking the third doctor, the sour dry one, humorously in the eyes: "'All flesh is grass, and all the goodliness thereof is as the flower of the field—'"

"And where is that from?" asked the dry sour one.

"Isaiah, eleven. Think sometime, gentlemen, reverend sirs, of what comes before. Of the exalting of valleys and the making low of every mountain and hill. A time is coming." They all now uncomfortably felt that they were taught, not teachers. And it was now that Jesus, with the warmth of the presence radiating at him from the Holy of Holies, knew his destiny. But he knew it would be a long time waiting for the fulfilment.

His father and mother found him at last, heard him saying to a listening group of four or five doctors words from the ninetieth psalm of David: "Let thy work appear unto thy servants, and thy glory unto their children . . ."

"Why did you do this to us, son?" Joseph said, in sorrow, not anger. "Forgive me, reverend sirs—we have been looking everywhere for him. We've already missed the caravan back to Nazareth. It was not kind. Your mother, see, has been weeping."

Jesus's brow furrowed in true astonishment. At the same time he looked at his parents for a moment as though he had never seen them before. "But you knew," he said, "you *must* have known where I would be. Where else would I be except in the house of my father?" This was unfair, for he had made no regular habit of visiting the Temple on this pilgrimage. Still, Joseph said no more except, "Come, son. We may yet catch up with the caravan."

They did not, despite the brisk pace they and their donkey kept, catch up with it. Twenty miles outside Jerusalem, robbers burst upon them, though they had nothing except the donkey worth the stealing. But, seeing this strange boy and his bigness, watching his hands fist and his muscles tauten, finding an amused smile on his face and no fear, they said: "On your way, paupers. If you had been rich, it would have gone badly for you." This, I suppose, could be accounted a kind of miracle.

Jesus worked harder as his foster-father grew older and weaker, sitting more and more on the stool outside the shop, gossiping, comparing pains and aches with the rest of the ageing, leaving the acceptance, fulfilment and invoicing of orders more and more to the young man. There were but the two of them, since the assistant John had long followed the example of the other, James, married and set up shop of his own elsewhere. Despite the hardness of the work, Jesus found time in the cool of the evening to engage in the tough sports of young men—wrestling, race-running, stone-hurling—as also, and let none be shocked to hear this, in the softer games of wooing, speaking flattering language to the dark-eyed girls, even singing songs to a two-string fiddle accompaniment:

Thy mouth a fig, thy teeth
Troops in ivory array.
Of the treasures ranged beneath
I may yet nothing say.
Must I wait till the nuptial day?

The courting was not serious, as all knew: it was but practice. But all knew that wooing in earnest would come in time, when the wooer was ready for leaving his parents and setting up house on his own.

One morning Joseph called Jesus to his bedside and said: "I don't think I'll get up today. I shall lie here, I think."

"You're not well?"

"I have this pain to the left side of the belly which yields only to my lying down."

TWO

"Is there anything I can do?"

Joseph knew what he meant. Joseph had picked up in Egypt various curative devices for easing pain—modes of rubbing and kneading the afflicted part of the body, herbal tisanes which soothed a sick stomach—and he had taught these to Jesus. Jesus also, on his own account, was skilful at curing ailments of no great gravity—stiffness of the joints, headaches, toothache (the cantrip *kera kera fantoloth* written thrice with charcoal on a thin shive of wood, the wood burnt, the ashes applied to the tooth). But there had been a notable occasion when an old man shrieked that he had been struck blind—a time of sorrow for him, his wife recently and suddenly dead and his son, according to a letter from a cousin in Jerusalem, taken to such evil ways that he had been thrown into prison—and Jesus, using the spittle of his mouth, stroking hands, gentle words and yet an authoritative manner, had persuaded him that he was not truly blind, only stricken to his soul by calamity, and he had seen again, shouting praise to God and spreading, to the embarrassment of Jesus, words about a young worker of miracles.

"I don't think there's anything you can do," Joseph said. "I'm old and must expect this kind of thing. I've no great desire to go on living, having done my share of the world's work and being, I truly believe, not unloved of God, since he honoured me with a great trust, the greatest in the world I truly believe. There was an old man called Simeon I may have mentioned—"

"Several times."

"Yes, my memory goes too. I remember my childhood clearly enough but not the time of my vigour and failing vigour. I have done better than that Simeon, who merely witnessed the dawning of the redemption. I have seen the redeemer grow to manhood and had him, moreover, in my fatherly charge. I regret only that I shall not live to see the work of redemption begin."

"It will be some time yet. There will be a long time of preparation. There will be the problem of the disbelief of the many. But first I must grow to proper manhood. I must do my work. I'm already late for the opening of the shop." He laid a cool hand on Joseph's hot forehead and said: "Rest."

Joseph lived two more months after this, not getting up from his bed again, except to totter, helped by his wife or wife and son together, to the privy for his body's always painful cleansing. One morning he said:

"I think it must be today."

"Will you have the rabbi come in with prayers?"

"He may pray over me when I am dead. Perhaps you had better shut up the shop. Though there is that order for that man on the three-acre farm out by—I forget where."

"Long fulfilled. Long done. I will shut up the shop."

The people of Nazareth knew what the shutting meant, and throughout the day the dying Joseph had visitors. But it was at nightfall, alone with Jesus and Mary, that he spoke his last words, saying:

"Look after your mother. She is the most blessed of all women."

"That I know. And you have been the best of fathers. In the earthly dispensation, I should say. You have had a son's love, and you will always have it, for, since love is an aspect of our heavenly father and cannot die, so the loved and lover must also live forever."

Joseph understood little of this. Jesus spoke certain words from memory, remembering that time when they had been in his mind in the Temple forecourt, when the sun of his mission had put forth its first rays from the Holy of Holies:

"'Because man goeth to his long home, and the mourners go about the streets: or ever the silver cord be loosed, or the golden bowl be broken, or the pitcher be broken at the fountain, or the wheel broken at the cistern. Then shall the dust return to the earth as it was: and the spirit shall return unto God who gave it. . . .'"

Joseph heard little of it. He put out a feeble hand towards his wife, who, he knew, stood at the right side of his bed. She took it and wept. Jesus stood dry-eyed. Joseph died in peace on the brink of morning, with the first cock crowing. The watchers were weary, but they made arrangements for the burial and nodded with weak smiles at the formulae of condolence. And so, for a time, Jesus and his mother lived together alone.

For a time only. Jesus said more than once, seeing a woman still in the flower of beauty: "Will you marry again?"

"True bodily marriage? With children begotten not of God but of the coupling of husband and wife?"

"All children are begotten of God, mother. Men are the mere channels of God's creation. Will you marry again?"

"If I am asked, I may think about it. I may say yes, or no, as the whim comes. Is that frivolous?"

"A woman's whims are Godly enough. Some say that it was but a whim of God to create earth and sea and men to inherit them."

He was often, these days, saying *some say*. He had been learning things other than the journeys of Moses and the enactments of the kings and judges of Israel. He had, she knew, learnt to wrestle with the outlandish scripts of Greek and Latin, had conversed with visiting Greeks and the members of entourages of great men visiting Herod Antipater from Jerusalem and even from Rome. He knew of Roman poets and one great ancient poet of Greece. He kept the faith, heathen beliefs of many gods did not touch him. He had enquired into the religion of the strange clean people who had founded their flesh-denying doctrines near the Dead Sea, but he would not deny the flesh. The flesh was important, he said. His mother said:

"You ask me if I will marry. I ask that question now of you."

He blushed. "I have been thinking about it. Would you be unhappy if there were another woman in the house—other, I mean, than our dear old, very old, I fear, Eliseba?"

"That depends on the woman. Do you have some particular girl in mind?"

"The girl at Cana."

"Ah. Dikla the date-palm. The tall girl who talks little."

"That is her pet-name only. Her true name is Sara."

"A name of ill omen, I would say. But is it fatherhood you have more in mind than the love of a woman? For—" She found the words hard to put together. "You were begotten in the way you know, the way you believe— Do you truly believe?"

"Of course I believe. And I say again there is only one father, and if I have children they deserve no special love. I am to be a shepherd with the whole of Israel as my flock."

"Now you talk like what you are, a very young man. I wonder whether it is right for you to think of marriage. Your cousin John does not think of marriage."

"My cousin John goes his own way. The way of preparation. I must teach fulfilment—though I do not properly know yet what the word means—and I must be myself fulfilled. I mean, I must know the whole life of a man."

"Marriage out of a kind of duty, not for companionship or fatherhood?"

"When will you learn that fatherhood is for our father in heaven only? I have told you often enough."

"I do not like your tone, my son. I do not think that a boy should speak so to his mother. I suppose you will admit that motherhood is something only for women, and that our father in heaven is content to leave that state to us creatures of female flesh? Very well, then. I do not cry out for special respect from my son, but I think my son should be sensible enough to know that he should give it."

"I'm sorry, mother," and he kissed her.

"You are set on marriage, then?"

He nodded gravely several times, as if it were indeed a duty on which he had to embark and not a joyful entry into what can be the most joyous of states.

The marriage, as my readers will know, was solemnised at Cana, and the wedding feast took place in the gardens of the inn of which the father of the bride, Nathan, was landlord. Sara was a girl of fifteen, five years younger than her groom, and pretty enough, also tall for the daughters of Israel, who may be hymned in love-songs as date-palms but are more often than not squat sturdy girls, bushes not trees, though, if I may say so without offence, burning bushes. From the point of view of size, the two were well-matched, for Jesus was taller than most of the sons of Galilee—some three and a half cubits—as well as great-chested and hard-muscled. He was also, but this needs no special mention as it was the bodily basis of his power as a preacher, loud-voiced when he wished to be, a very bull, though usually he spoke softly if rapidly, over-ready with words. The two, then, made a tall and handsome couple standing in the garden, toasted by the guests, sometimes with good-hearted ribaldry, dressed in simple but brightly clean white apparel.

Now it happened that one of the guests at the wedding—though neither family could remember inviting him—was the old man who had become blind with grief and been brought back to the conviction that he could see again if he tried, helped by firmness and harmless magic. In his cups he told a group, including Nathan, of Sara's remarkable good fortune in gaining such a husband as Jesus, since he was a hard worker, careful with money, and had great healing gifts beyond the ordinary. He went further, he said that Jesus had remarkable powers in other fields than healing, and that with his own recovered eyes he had observed the young man start a fire in wood shavings by merely calling upon the sun to exert its strength. More, he had heard from another man that Jesus had once walked through the rain from the shop to his home and, on arrival, had been as dry as a bone.

"Dry as a bone," said one of the wedding guests. "That will serve to describe my condition at this moment. Fill, friend Nathan, for I've a thirst on me I wouldn't sell for ten Roman sesterces, as they call them."

It is said that the cobbler's child is always the worst shod, and one should not be surprised that the supply of wine in this inn garden ran out sooner than was seemly. The sun was still high in the sky, and new late guests were arriving (some not really guests at all: that is often the way at weddings, when an interloper will pose to the bride's family as a friend of the groom's family and the other way about), but Nathan's butts were empty. The truth was that deliveries from the vintner were due the next day, and he had thought what was in stock would be sufficient. A party-host not an innkeeper would certainly have been more provident. Discovering the sudden drouth, one hearty drinker who had heard these tales of magical Jesus cried out jocularly: "Let him give us some of his Egyptian sorcery. Make him turn water into wine."

"He could do it," said the old man who had been blind. "I vow he could do it as easily as the rest of us turn wine into water." It must be admitted that the old man was more eager to give out this coarse joke than he was to claim further thauma-turgical power for the bridegroom. Still, in their drunkenness, in the envy of the strong, handsome and clever that drunkenness will often bring to the surface (like a dead fish or a bad egg to the surface of water) in the usually timid or those who generally do not care one way or the other, some of the more faceless and anonymous of the guests began to cry out: "Eh, Jesus, eh, happy bridegroom, turn water into wine for us and be smart about it."

"What are they shouting?" Jesus said to his mother.

His mother, who had no great head for wine, smiled rather sillily and said, her lips moist from the cup she had been tasting: "They're asking you to work a miracle. To turn water into wine."

Jesus frowned very terribly at that. "Who has been talking to them? Who has been putting mad stories about?"

"Oh, they guess, I think. Some of them guess what you are, I think."

"Father has let us run out of wine," said Sara. "I told him there would not be enough, but he would not listen."

"Well," Jesus said, "if the wine is finished the celebration is finished, and we may all go home."

"Ah, come," said his mother, "you can do it. Come, do it for me."

Jesus stared at her in disbelief. "Are you serious? Are you, God forbid, drunk? You, of all people?"

A group of young men, to whose heads the drink had long

gone, were jocularly filling an empty butt with water, bucket after bucket, from the well, yelling with joy as they splashed it over each other. Some turned to Jesus: "Hey—all ready for the Egyptian magic." I ought to mention here that to some, because of his childhood exile, Jesus was known as Jesus the Egyptian. "Come on, Jesus of Egypt, show us your tricks."

Jesus looked more softly on his mother. This was not the happiest of days for her, having to welcome a woman she hardly knew to her home, having to resign her place as its mistress. She had eaten nothing, a little wine had flushed her, she was proud of her son, the son she was yielding up to another, a mere chit of a tall girl. She meant no harm. Still, he said: "Woman, you know my hour is not yet come." That sobered her; she flushed, this time not with wine. With a kind of bent smile on his face though not in his eyes, he walked over to the brimming butt and laid his hands over it. There was a hush among the revellers. The village magician was going to perform. Jesus said, in his great voice, apter for five thousand auditors than a mere fifty: "Behold, friends, here is water—sweet, fresh, cool, straight from the well. Behold, in the time of an eye-blink or a finger-flick, I make a secret pass, murmuring to myself a secret word, and—ah, I see it—the water is changed to wine. Such perfume." He dipped in his hand and supped a scoop dripping silver in the sun. "Ah, the taste. Come, all, drink. But—" he held up a stern finger—"a warning first. The nature of the transformation is such that to sinners—men who owe money, women who gossip about their neighbours, fornicators, adulterers and blasphemers—the wine will look like water, taste like water, go to the head like water. For the pure and godly the appearance will be as of sunshot rubies, the taste of what the Greeks call *nektar*, the effect as of sweet bells and harmonious singing. Come, who will be first to taste? Who better than your host and my father-in-law?" So Nathan, grinning, was pushed forward, filled himself a sparkling cup and drank deep. He said:

"Never have I tasted such wine. Served I such wine in my tavern I would make a fortune. Look at the bloody colour of it."

All roared except his wife, for it was well-known that he had an eye for the pertness of young breasts and a hand for a well-turned buttock. And so, in the best of humours, some voting this a great game for a wedding, all filled cups and quaffed. One silly youth said, "Why, this is only water" and was at once booed and slapped as a great sinner, of course to his guffawing pleasure. There was a man whose name, but I refuse to believe it to have been really so, has been handed down to me as Rechab, who said grandiloquently:

"Most unusual. At most feasts, and believe me, friends, I have attended many, the best is served first and the least best last, taking natural advantage of the dulling of the palate. But at this, O best of hosts, you have reserved your cream of wines till the end, and this shall ever be accounted an honour to you. Such heavenly colour, such sparkling coolness, how it rings like a silver coin on the palate. It elevates but inebriates not," and much of the same heavy jesting kind.

This so-called miracle has passed down into our annals, so that it appears that Jesus was establishing a precedent for the converting of other fluids to wine, but some remember the true tale and call water wine of Cana. I certainly believe that this feast ended soberly.

Jesus Naggar was now a married man, and we may suppose that he savoured the bodily joys as much as any of us who have entered the blessed state, though I do not doubt that he suffered from woman's foolishness, capriciousness and loquacity like the rest of us and, on occasion, felt the burden of the contention of mother and wife: my son likes it done this way, he may be your son but he is also my husband, I do not call this washing well-done, while we are on the subject of things well-done I wish you had taught *your son* not to throw his newly washed garments on the floor when he takes them off for that makes more work, doubtless since there is always plenty of dust there you are no great hand with the broom, and so on. But all went well enough.

Sara, though named for Abraham's barren wife, did not herself prove barren though she bore children only to lose them. I mean bearing within her, for she suffered two miscarriages. Jesus's mother thought much of the meaning of this but kept her own counsel, wondering no doubt about the propriety of the destined Messiah's begetting sons and daughters like other men. Indeed, the very propriety of his marriage remained in doubt with her, and she had strange presentiments about the future of it. One morning, at cock-crow, she had a vivid dream in which Sara melted like wax before her very eyes, while cooking the evening meal in the kitchen. There was the kitchen, there was Sara with the stirring spoon in her hand, then the spoon fell from an arm turning swiftly to honey-coloured wax, along with the rest of her body. A pool of wax lay on the stone floor and then it dissolved into a fine steam that dispersed in a sudden wind. The bubbling pot was still on the fire but its tender was no more. Jesus came home and said: Where is Sara? She is no more, no more. Ah, no more you say, I expected this. Who then has cooked the dinner?

A terrible dream and she woke trembling from it. Sara was already up, solid enough, making a thin pottage for her husband's breakfast, she heard their voices in morning gentleness. She had to wait five years for the fulfilment of the dream.

The story of the death of Sara, a good wife though the mother of three miscarriages, is not one I care to recount, but the storyteller has his duty not to flinch at unhappy elements in his story. When Jesus and his wife and his mother went, according to the custom which they never broke, to Jerusalem for the Passover, they found the city in a great turmoil. Some drunken Syrian soldiers had ostentatiously pissed on the walls of the Temple in full view of some members of the sect called the Zealots, and this had led to a fight in which the soldiers, who were quick to whistle and call for reinforcements, had things very much their own way. The procurator shrugged away warnings of great coming disorder and did not, as was his duty, issue special orders about the inviolability of the Temple, nor did he punish the violators, who admitted grinning to what they had done. During the time of the Passover visit in the sixth year of the marriage of Jesus and

Sara, there was, true, a much augmented police force in the city, especially in the precincts of the Temple, but it seemed to be there to protect ill-behaving Imperial troops against Hebrew resentment of their brutality and bad manners.

One day there was arranged, in the Temple portico, a meeting for Jewish wives and mothers, presided over by one of the doctors of religion, at which matters of familial conduct (the emphasis being mostly, I fear, on the wife's duties to the husband rather than the other way) were discussed and the basic holy principles propounded. The doctor of theology did not find it as easy as he had expected to impose on these fiery Hebrew women (burning bushes, as I have said) an acceptance of woman's submissive part, her status in relation to the man a merely, so to speak, costal one, and he found plenty of bold-eyed and clear-voiced matrons ready to throw common sense and practical experience at his theoretical exhortations and text-jabbings. The women left the meeting in high excitement, while the doctor of the faith left with hands raised in the air at the horror of what things were coming to, young girls brought up to be pert and disobedient, the daughters of Eve no credit to their mother. No, when you came to think of it, every credit to that old beldam who had sold us into slavery for the sake of a bit of fruit. Ah, woman, woman.

The women walked into a riot. Some drunken Syrians were at it again, pulling the beard of an old bewildered Hebrew, and a number of the women were on fire enough to rush in with claws and teeth, their only weapons if you except spitting and words of vituperation which the Syrians did not understand. Most of the troops took this as a great joke, grinning and saying give us a kiss dear one and do Hebrew bints have between their legs what our women have and so on. But a phalanx of women can be terrible enough, and when one Syrian escaped from the melee with a bloodied face and torn uniform, yelling murder moreover, the police, seeing, rushed in with clubs. What first met their sight was a circle of male spectators who hid the angry women from view, and they began thudding away at these. In the urge to get away from the police, there was crushing of delicate bodies under foot, and among these was the body of Sara. She was, as I have said, a tall girl, also sturdy and no pale flower of meekness, but she went under when she tripped on the hem of her own garment and then, screaming to no avail, was heavily trampled.

She was one of five Hebrew women who died on this occasion. Mary, Jesus's mother, who had intended to go to the Temple meeting with her daughter-in-law, had providentially (and I feel one may use the term very advisedly, as they say) been visited by a most profound headache that paralysed her and made her moan. Jesus was not happy about letting his wife go to the Temple without male accompaniment, but there was a big enough party of women leaving from the inn where they lodged to ensure safety from the molestation of the Gentile, so he stayed with his mother and exerted his healing powers. It appears that Mary's headache vanished at the very moment of Sara's brutal death, but one need not take the tale too seriously nor draw dangerous conclusions from it. That Jesus was first heart-stricken and later angry we make take for granted. His anger was such, we are told, that he sought an interview with the procurator but was not granted one, as on a later occasion that is a long way off in our story he undoubtedly was. He tried to lodge protest with the chief of police but was waved away by underlings as a Hebrew nuisance. That one's wife should die wretchedly in fear and pain a few steps away from the Temple of the Most High in the Holy City—this was a tangible and terrible example of the putrid cauldron of sin that was the world. We are told that he was bitter with God and addressed him with the bitterness of a son to a father who has failed in paternal love. In words such as these, and I guess at the replies, if replies there were:

"My beloved is snatched away in the flower of her youth. You, who know all, knew from the beginning of time that this would happen. Why did you let it happen? Why, cursed father, did you not prevent it?"

Do not curse, son, though I take the word as but the

purulence of human grief. I gave men free will, which means power to choose between good and evil. If they could not choose evil they could not also choose good. If they were always good they would still be in Eden. But there is no Eden, since Adam and Eve chose, in their God-given freedom, that that blessed garden be denied to them, and hence to their children.

"But you, the all-knowing, know what men will do. You know they will do evil. If you know this, they cannot be free, since all their acts are pre-ordained. Therefore you will the evil they do. I cannot call you a God in love with justice."

Call me a God in love with man. Do not ask why. My passions are not to be explained. To ensure that man is truly free—and this gift is the measure of the greatness of my love—I choose not to foreknow his actions. I choose, remember, I discard omniscience. But when man's acts are once performed, then I have, as it were, a sudden memory of my own foreknowledge. For man, I render myself less than perfect.

"For man," Jesus said, "you become man."

You have hit it. And now, though it may be small comfort in your tribulation, take your scriptures and read the Book of Job.

There was not in Jerusalem at that time a burial-ground for strangers since, so it was officially said, there was insufficient money in the civic fisc for such an amenity. But certain prominent citizens of Jerusalem were quick with offers of family burial space for the poor women who were to be accounted a kind of martyrs (I take the liberty of coining this word out of the Greek stem *martur*, meaning a witness, as for a faith or cause. The nominative should properly be *martus*, but this form seems not to be found in any Greek writings.) The heat and the length of the journeys home forbade the transporting of the bodies for interment in their own towns, so, that their poor corpses be not visited with the further outrage of putrescence, certain beloved women had to rest in the tombs of strangers. But could one properly talk of strangers? Was not Israel one suffering family? The Sanhedrin, or Supreme Religious Council, had nothing to say about the outrage of the women's deaths, though it sent a small priest to the burial service (at which cautious Roman spears were much in evidence). The prayers were intoned by the very theological doctor who had summoned the women to that meeting, and he unashamedly wept. Jesus, head and shoulders grimly above the crowd, was dry-eyed but grim of countenance. Those who stood by him noticed that his fists were clenched tight.

So, for the five years that remained before the beginning of his mission, we must think now of Jesus the widower. He did not seek marriage again. He worked hard in his shop, abating nothing of his conscientious devotion to the skill or art of the trade, and he spent the evenings quietly with his mother. They said little to each other of her that was gone, though her ghost flitted from time to time through the house, dislodging kitchen utensils, and the cat seemed to see her, his fur bristling with fear. Old Eliseba died peacefully and in her sleep, and her ghost joined the other. Then both ghosts faded, and Sara did not even appear to Jesus in dreams. He grew thin for a time, eating little, reading much, talking hardly at all, then he filled out again and came to the peak of his man's strength and beauty. The day came when he was able to speak again of Sara, though without personal sorrow. He spoke gratefully.

"The three kinds of love," he said to his mother, "that I have known already must now teach me the way to another kind. I mean love of all created beings, friend and enemy alike. I think the love of husband for wife has taught me most. For the love of a parent is, as it were, the very marrow of the bone, while the love of husband for wife entails a discipline. One holds oneself back from railing or counter-railing, one learns not to utter the bitter word of resentment, one learns to be grateful for the proffered pleasure, the companionship. Despite the marriage vow, one is free not to love, yet one chooses to love. I have to teach love as choice, as the one weapon against evil. I must, I think, start to get myself ready."

"You will be leaving me then," said his mother. "What will you do about the shop?"

"Yes, the shop. I had a visit today from a young man looking for work. Ephraim is his name, he comes from Gaza, he says. No Samson, but he is well-muscled, having worked at stone-breaking for roads. He had done some carpentry and seemed familiar with the tools. He is about twenty, I think he is honest. He claims distant relationship with the baker Jotham, but Jotham says he has enough relatives coming for free loaves without needing another. For all that, he is staying the night with Jotham. Jotham is a good man, one of God's chosen."

"Jotham? You think that?"

"Oh, yes. Jotham spills all sourness into his speech. We expect the sourness now as his own kind of honey. Under the roughness there is gold enough. He is so soft that he must make himself a shell, like a snail. I will work with his distant kinsman for the next six months or so and see how he gets on. He is likeable, the customers will like him. It means, though, mother, that you must become a nominal kind of carpenter. I am thinking of accounts, the handling of money."

Mary sighed at that. "I wonder if I should marry again. I see none I fancy."

"We will see," Jesus said, "how we get on. That is comfortable doctrine. Not to worry overmuch about the future. Sufficient unto the day is what the day sends. I promise you, you will not starve."

"Six months you say. You are thinking of the future. Are you worrying about it?"

Jesus did not answer that. Instead he said: "Our cousin John has started his work. Preparing the way, as he terms it."

THREE

It is time now to say something of this John, the preparer of the way. He had grown strong and tall, like Jesus himself, and had filled his mind with reading and rendered it lively with converse and debate. It had soon become evident that he was not truly suited to the office of priest as the make and duty of priest were then understood, or defined, or delimited. He was impatient with ritual and all the surface aspects of the faith and had no time for the Pharisees and the Sadducees. He lived alone in the house that had been first his father's and then his widowed mother's, eating little, drinking no wine, praying much, asking for guidance. He was already, by the standards of the time, a man far gone into maturity when the light came to him. He had a dream in which he saw himself very clearly as he must be—shorn of house and possessions, even of the garments suitable to a man of the town, of learning, of position, a wild creature shorn indeed of all except locks and beard unshorn, wandering in the desert, meditating, conversing with the Lord, living on the food provided by lonely places not altogether desert—honey garnered from tree-trunks where bees had nested, grasshoppers raw or fried on his little night fire, water from spring or river. The water of the river Jordan appeared to him in this dream as a strange image of salvation. Men and women had to be cleansed of sin before they could become worthy of following the Messiah, and the outward sign of their cleansing must be immersion in that sacred river. They would, remembering the shock of wetness, the damp garments clinging to their limbs, remember also the day of the shedding of their sins and their solemn undertaking to sin no more.

We use the word *baptise* to describe the fusion of bodily immersion in water, or aspersion with water, and the solemn undertaking to cleanse the soul at the moment of this ritual cleansing of the body. There is a Greek word *baptein,* meaning to dip, from which *baptise* derives, and the priest who is responsible for the dipping we call a baptist. The term *sacrament,* which properly in its Latin form signifies the solemn oath taken by a soldier, takes on a wholly new and original meaning when it is applied to such a function as baptism. For the outward sign, the dipping or sprinkling, is of huge importance, and the silent or private oath, or even public if confined solely to a form of words, is to be regarded as insufficient in this new order of faith. There are religions, such as that of the Dead Sea people, that scorn the stuff of earth and of bodily life as of no account in comparison with the soul; there are others that assign to matter an origin and a purpose wholly diabolical, against which the soul, whose substance is divine, must do unremitting battle. But John, and Jesus after him, saw clearly that soul on the one hand, and flesh and earthly substance on the other, were both of God's making. Wine and bread and water and spittle were holy, and as God himself did not scorn to take on human flesh, so the divine spirit itself, the mysterious link between the godhead and the word made flesh, was content to appear to men's eyes as a lowly pigeon, the crumb-pecker, treader and cooer of our roofs. But I anticipate.

John read a passage in Isaiah over and over, perceived its prophetic intent, and identified himself with the figure shadowed within it. It was a passage that had been in Jesus's mind that day in Jerusalem, when he had confronted the holy doctors of the Temple and missed the home-going caravan:

"Comfort ye, comfort ye my people, saith your God. Speak ye comfortably to Jerusalem, and cry unto her that her warfare is accomplished, that her iniquity is pardoned: for she hath received of the Lord's hand double for all her sins.

"The voice of him that crieth in the wilderness, Prepare ye the way of the Lord, make straight in the desert a highway for our God. Every valley shall be exalted, and every mountain and hill shall be made low: and the crooked shall be made straight, and the rough places plain: and the glory of the Lord shall be revealed, and all flesh shall see it together: for the mouth of the Lord hath spoken it."

John at first took the identification very literally, truly retiring to the wilderness and crying to the empty air the words "Repent, for the Lord is coming" while his mane and beard grew shaggier, himself thinner and dirtier, his stomach sicker with the harsh provender of the scrubland. The time came though when his belly shrugged at what came its way and surrendered to the only nutriment it seemed likely henceforth to receive. His body, clad in a couple of old stinking goatskins, grew harder. He coughed much at first and his nose was stopped up with the rheum that was a gift of the harsh nights, and he did not at first shelter from the rain, striding though it and crying "Repent" to nobody. But he learned to accommodate himself to the wilderness and the time came for him to appear, waving in the air a dry branch that served him as both walking-rod and staff of prophetic vocation, on the outskirts of small villages, bidding the inhabitants, who were gratified by his uncouth gauntness and apparent madness, to repent of their sins and to make an appointment with him to be immersed in the Jordan's waters and washed into a new life. The older ones laughed, the younger threw stones. Dogs barked at him and sometimes tried to bite him. He would go sadly away, crying "Repent, for the Lord is coming."

But, as we know well, he was not rejected of all. Those who discovered who he was, the son of a miraculous pregnancy, believed him to be the promised Messiah. There were not many of these, but there were some. Others, close to the Zealot persuasion that was surreptitiously flourishing not only in Jerusalem but in other towns, and even villages, of Palestine, believed that he was the destined charismatic leader who would give the word for the revolt against Roman tyranny. Certainly he began to attract interest, especially when he began his baptising mission on the Jordan's banks. But how gaunt, how ill-clad, how huge those staring eyes, how manically urgent the words of his mouth. A madman, one would say; I reject totally the possibility of messiahship. But the scriptures do not tell us in what guise the Messiah is to come; do you expect someone fat and pharasaic? Listen.

"The word," John was saying to a group sitting by Jordan's stream, "is baptism. It is a simple ceremony. You must cleanse yourselves of sin, and the sign of the cleansing of the soul is the cleansing of the body in this, our river. You may say: is the water necessary? The answer is yes, because our minds will always cling to a ceremony while they are quick to forget a resolution of the lips. Step with me then into this water."

"What happens?" a man said. "After we wash and repent, what happens then?"

"Then," said John, "you will be fit to receive him who comes after me, him who will teach the new kingdom."

Kingdom—you note the word. How is it to be taken—as metaphor, as in *kingdom of the spirit,* or in literal signification of change in the state, with all that that implies—rebellion against Rome, the setting up of a new essentially sacred monarchy? There was a measure of ambiguity at the very start, at the very precursion of the mission, liable to lead the simple-minded, which includes the politically minded, well astray.

"And what is this new kingdom?"

"It will be all that the kingdom of Caesar is not. Love, not fear. No slavery, no tyranny, no getting and hoarding. The kingdom of free souls under God."

Dangerous words. The penitents lined up, and the lines grew daily longer.

"I baptise you in the name of the all-highest. May the water of the spirit cleanse you of the will to sin and absolve you of all past sins."

But, one would say, to be cleansed of the will to sin is also to be cleansed of the will to do good. Hard words, difficult doctrine. We must abide the coming of the explicator, the clarifier.

Sins. "I cheated—I gave short measure when I served in the shop. I stole five talents from the man next door and let his son take the blame. I I I felt strong desire for the woman next door, though I did nothing about it. I shouted at my wife, rest her soul, and many times I struck her. I did not observe the feast of the Passover last year. I I I I I I. Committed the sin of Onan."

The long day of confessing and absolving. The cold night under a tree or in a cave, the breakfast of Jordan water and honey from the comb and locusts roasted on the fire. The morning resumption of the office of confessor, baptiser, exhorter to virtue, prophet of the coming of him who is to come.

"I hated my daughter-in-law and told my son false stories of her infidelity. I ate forbidden meat and drank goat-milk with it. I committed the sin of adultery. I lay brooding on the ways and means to find the time and opportunity and place to commit the sin again and again, loathing the husband who snored by my side."

One day John addressed a large crowd, full of carpers and doubters, well-seasoned with evident Pharisees and, perhaps, small tools of the rule in Jerusalem, paid to provoke treasonable words.

"What do you seek from me?" cried John. "The beginning of the end of the rule of the stranger in our holy places—the deliverance of Jerusalem from what is termed by some her Roman bondage? It is not this that is promised. It is not this that will be preached by him who is to come. For the bondage a man suffers is the bondage he fashions for himself."

A Pharisee called: "Why do you teach a new way? Is the way of our fathers not enough for you?"

"I hear," cried John, "the voice of a Pharisee. I see among you many Pharisees, who are content with hand-washing before meals and the empty forms of the faith. I see among you also Sadducees, who find God's grace in the wealth they have hoarded. To both Pharisees and Sadducees I say: *Offspring of vipers.*" There was an echo: *ipers ipers.*

Dangerous, very. A sure way to make enemies.

"*Vipers, vipers.* If you come to me, bring fruits worthy of repentance. Do not say within your hearts: We have Abraham as our father, and let that suffice for our salvation. I say this to you: God could take, if he chose, these stones at my feet and turn each one into a son of Abraham. If you bring no fruit of repentance, fear the axe, which is already laid to the roots of the trees that are barren. Fear the axe and the hewing down and the casting into the fire."

When John spoke again in such terms he was accosted courteously by two officers of the Sanhedrin and taken to a kind of provincial court where a kind of circuit priests were anxious to see him and question him. Their eyes opened wide when they saw him, who had come meekly enough but was evidently impatient to get all this over, whatever it was to be, and resume his preaching and baptising. They saw a big-boned gaunt man dressed in camel-skin (the goat's pelts had long since fallen to pieces), very unkempt. They hid their smiles and the president of the little court questioned him, hitting flies away the while with an ivory-spoked fan (gift of a Roman, ultimately from Egypt).

"Now, sir, who is it you say you are?"

"First I will say who I am not. I am not the Messiah. The Messiah is yet to come."

"Do you say you are Elijah the prophet come back again?"

"I do not."

"Who are you, then?"

"The voice of one crying in the wilderness these words: Make straight the way of the Lord. I am not Elijah come back, but I fulfil the words that were spoken by Elijah."

"By what authority do you perform this ceremony you term baptism?"

"By the authority of him who shall come. One whose shoes I am unworthy to unloose. I baptise with water, but he will baptise with the fire of the holy spirit. His fan is in his hand, and with it he will cleanse the threshing-floor. He will gather the wheat into the garner, but the chaff he will burn up with fire that may not be quenched."

"You mean the Messiah?"

John said nothing but bowed his head.

"Leave us a little while. We must confer about you."

He left, head high now; they conferred.

"Harmless enough, I think. Mad, of course."

"He's saying hard things against the pillars and rocks of the secular faithful. Talking of hypocrisy and hand-washing and so on. Using terms like *viper* and *foul abomination before the Lord*."

"We know that, but do any of you smell heresy?"

"Heresy" (a fan-wave) "is always hard to prove. Remember he's been a priest. He will not willingly walk into heresy. Nor can we condemn a man for his appearance. A *prophetic* appearance, one might say. A nuisance, but hardly a *religious* nuisance."

"A civil nuisance, then?"

"You could say that, at least potentially. He has already been saying things, but carefully swathed in generalities, about the, well, the presence of a certain marital irregularity, call it, in the state of Galilee."

"Ah, you mean—?"

"I do indeed mean. Leave him, then, to the civil authorities."

"Shall we then call him in and tell him he may go?"

"He seems to have gone already."

Now it happened that John's dead mother Elizabeth was related to the family of Herod the Great, being a second cousin of the beloved consort Doris, who so regrettably had to be put to silence. John, as a boy, had met Herod the Great's son Herod Antipater in Jerusalem and been overfed by the young prince, potential tetrarch, with candied fruits and very sweet sticky sherbet. They were men now, a big-bellied flesh-loving quarter-king (third-king really) the one, a stark starveling and doom-preacher the other, but when John heard of Herod Antipater's intention to marry the wife of his own living brother, the tetrarch Philip of Iturea, the man of water and repentance vomited again, combining the new sin with a memory of an old surfeit. To tell the truth, Herodias, the queen of Philip, had contrived the marriage herself, in defiance of Mosaic law, flouting priests and pious plebeians alike. She wanted to be Herod Antipater's consort because she desired power, and Philip had been unwilling to give her much of that, stingy in everything, including the pleasures of the bed. He had condoned his queen's desertion and sin, being glad enough to be rid of her, and he knew that his brother's weak and pleasure-loving nature (an easy man, really, no tyrant but also no wise and moderate ruler either) would, through insouciance, grant her what she desired: power in the state, a ruthless voice in the council chamber, the exercise of a natural gift for cruelty that would serve as a substitute for amorous purgations which Herod Antipater was even less well-qualified than his brother to supply in the ordinary commerce of the marriage-bed.

I find it somewhat embarrassing to discuss the amorous propensities of monarchs, even, for that matter, of their subjects. Herod Antipater had in youth worn out the possibilities of normal sensual gratification and, in maturity, had to exploit such fantastic variations on the basic theme of coition as a fevered imagination could suggest to him. Herodias, to whom Philip had surprisingly given a daughter named Salome, did not at first realise, so hot was she on fulfilling her ambition to gain power, that the main attraction for Herod Antipater in the legally incestuous marriage was the hope of piling, as it were, incest on incest. For he had reached a stage in his libidinous odyssey when he could only attain erotic purgation through contact with very young flesh of either sex, and the flesh of Salome was very young, though undoubtedly female, flesh. Herod Antipater did not demand coition at this phase of his anabasis towards eventuall impotence: it was enough that his eyes be excited by the sight of a young body unclothed, half-clothed, progressively and somewhat slowly divested of its clothes with, if possible, an accompaniment of precociously wanton writhings, leers, poutings, pantings, the movements of simulated rut. This would procure in the tetrarch at least an ithyphallic engorgement and, if certain gods unrelated to the God of Israel smiled upon him, an accession of spontaneous pollution. As I say, I find the exposition of such matters very embarrassing to myself and do not doubt that they are also distasteful to the reader, but, as I have said before, it is the duty of the story-teller to confront the unpleasant squarely and without flinching in the interests of presenting life as it truly is.

Herodias herself was a handsome woman, and never did she look more handsome than when, sinfully attired as a bride, she went in procession after the incestuous ceremony on the arm of her tetrarch husband. They were both magnificently arrayed in silk and cloth of gold and a scintillant myriad of precious stones. Flutes and trumpets played, drums thudded, cymbals tinkled, and handmaidens threw flowers of the season in the path of the abominable pair. The subjects of the tetrarch watched, bedazzled, and some of them, indeed most of them, cheered. Standing head and shoulders above the crowd was a grim-eyed man who did not cheer but called sternly:

"Herod. King Herod. King Herod Antipater."

Soldiers tried to push him away, but he seemed intent on addressing the tetrarch seriously and urgently. Herod said to his bride:

"That rather remote kinsman of mine, my dear. I had heard that John bar-Zacharias had turned himself into an intinerant prophet but had not expected him here. All right," he said to the soldiers, "let him through. It is John, is it? The miracle child of aged loins? I thought I could not be mistaken. I do not approve your wedding garment, but you're free to speak."

"Herod of Galilee," John said, "it is laid down in the sacred tablets of the law that a man may not marry the wife of his living brother. Your queen Herodias is the—"

"Wife of my brother Philip. I know, I know, I know. Don't you think my ears buzz already with the tut-tuttings and downright denunciations of the professionally holy? A word in your ear, John: consider the word *consummation*." He spoke indeed in John's ear; his bride was thunder-faced and her jewels were shimmering lightning, but she did not hear what her husband said. John cried aloud, that all might hear:

"The man you call your king is a sinner and a foul sinner. The woman he calls his wife is an adulteress and an incestuous fornicator. The sin is upon you all who abet the sin."

The soldiers tried to seize John then and hurry him away to jail, but Herod Antipater said: "Interesting, but hardly the words appropriate to a happy occasion. No, no, captain—let him go free. We are disposed to be clement on our wedding day."

So John was let go free to howl "Sin sin foul sin" among the crowd which, not wishing to hear of dreary sin on this heart-warming day of celebration and ceremony (rendered, indeed, the more poignantly tasty by the spicy odour of sin that ascended heavenwards with the smoke of the torches), buffeted him and jeered and thrust him on his way. But there were men who did not join in the rejoicing, who looked as stern-eyed on the glitter of the abomination as had John himself, though they held their peace out of prudence. One thrust out a hand at John's arm and said, urgently gripping him:

"Say quickly: does a monarch have authority over his subjects if he is in a state of sin?"

"If," said John, "you seek to draw me into the plotting of treason you will be disappointed. I denounce sin where I see it and I call on the sinner to repent. No more than that."

"Are you not he who was promised to us, the one who shall drive out the stranger and unify the people under God's law?"

"I am not he. I am but the unworthy precursor of him who shall come. Plot no treason. Repent of your sins. Seek the waters of new life. Be baptised in the name of the imminent saviour."

"You are the one. Craftily you hide the truth of what you are. When is the time of the harvest?"

"You speak riddles. Let me go."

On the bank of Jordan, as may well be imagined, the crowds

would now increase. In the palace of the tetrarch, as may well also be imagined, the consort of Herod Antipater spent much of the rest of her wedding day railing and screeching against the baptist. "Treason, I call it treason."

"Yes, my dear," Herod said, lying on a long chair well-cushioned, his shoes off, a tray of sweetmeats ever-ready in the hands of an Ethiopian servant. "Let us both call it a kind of treason, if by treason we mean a kind of speaking of the truth. What a pretty necklace, my sweet little Salome. What a pretty neck for that matter." Salome, a well-shaped precocious little minx of twelve and a half years, still in her festive clothes, honey-coloured arms and neck warm under the ice-flash of her jewels, sat near the tetrarch's feet (their ache was easing), finding her ranting mother a bore, finding her sort of stepfather rather pleasant and amusing and charmingly ready with the sort of compliment that made her feel herself already to be a woman.

"High treason," cried Herodias. "I demand his arrest."

"Demand? A strong word, beloved. Now let us consider the matter calmly, as princes should. You, little princess, do you not think that matters should always be considered calmly? Of course you do, bless you, delicious creature that you are. We today, dearest queen, concluded a ceremony at which certain things were solemnly vowed. To love and cherish each other and so on, to afford each other what is euphemistically termed bodily comfort—"

"Salome," her mother said, "go away. Go and feed the peacocks."

"Too young to hear of these sacred things, is she? To hear of what husbands and wives vow to each other? I would say not. A royal princess is never too young to learn about the *essential* things."

"Go, Salome."

"But, mother—"

"Go, child."

The child pouted, got up from her cushions as slowly as she dared, and walked out with an insolent wag of her crupper, tight-clad in rippling flame-coloured silk. "Charming, charming," Herod Antipater said, lazily smiling. Then he said to his bride: "I take it you did not seek marriage with me for the sake of bodily comfort?"

"There are duties, pleasures—"

"Which, if deferred, render our marriage a mere form, a phantom, a smoke. I find it rather pleasant to be informed that I am sinning when I know perfectly well that I am not."

"You're a fool," she said. "You close your eyes to the reality of the problems of rule and engage in mystical stupidities like like like that trouble-maker himself."

"Something in the blood perhaps, dearest. The true realities that lie behind crass appearances—they've always interested me."

"And while metaphysical stupidities interest you you will find the whole of Galilee seething with unrest because of that scarecrow. They will try to have me put away, they will have you deposed, they will have the Romans imposing direct rule as they did in Judea. Something in the blood, yes, but not in your father's blood."

"Oh, he was by way of being a mystic too. Only a mystic who truly believed in the coming of the Messiah would have had all those poor children massacred. *Put away,* you said. They won't have me *put away* if I repent and send you back to my brother Philip. Remember that, my love. And in the meantime let John curse and screech about sin and repentance. People will take it as a free show, a dramatic entertainment. They certainly won't act on what he shouts about."

"I demand that he be arrested. I demand that he pay the penalty for high treason."

"Demand, demand, always demanding. Well, I'm disposed to meet you half-way, my beloved. I'm disposed to have John here in the palace—free to come and go within its halls and gardens but, if he seeks the front door, he will find sharp daggers and long spears and hard muscles getting in his way."

"In prison, in the palace cells, till he's forgotten by the mob, and then—quietly, without fuss, as one kills an insolent servant—"

"You like killing, don't you, my love? A very bloodthirsty lady, decked like a bride as you are, brooding on summary executions. Now listen," and he spoke with unwonted and uncharacteristic sharpness. "I do things my own way, do you understand? One thing I learned from my father was that killing solves no problems. He, the great killer, saw on his deathbed that killing had done him no good. The ghosts of the killed, many thousands of them, all put to silence by his order and sometimes by his own hand, their ghosts, I say, glided before him in a long long line while he lay dying and shook their heads sadly at him. You see, when you start killing you never know when to stop. You end up by killing everybody. I've no desire to rule over a kingdom of dry bones. So we won't rush at anything, will we, my beloved? I'll send some men to find John and have them, in the most courteous manner imaginable, invite him here. He will reject the invitation, so, with all the gentleness in the world, he will be *made* to come here."

"And thrown into prison."

"One thing at a time." And then: "Oh, go away, you weary me."

She nodded, smiling viciously. "Shall I send in my daughter? She, I notice, never wearies you."

"Perhaps we share a common innocence, which you, without doubt, would term a common frivolity. No, don't send her, don't send anyone. I want to be alone. I want to meditate on the realities that lie behind the shifting phantasmagoric shadows of the world. And later, perhaps Salome and I can talk nonsense together."

"If you touch that child," Herodias said, "if you lay one finger on that child—"

"Blood, blood, blood. Oh, leave me. That's a royal order."

There were now a number of men who stayed close to John, believing him to be the destined leader of the people despite his disavowal of that vocation, waiting for him to throw off the cloak (a very inept metaphor to apply to one so naked) and appear as the head of the Zealots, ready to drive out the Romans and unify Israel from a holy throne. But there were other men who believed every word he spoke, looking for the coming of a Messiah who would seek change within before change without. They clung to him. One, whose name was Philip, gave diffident warning:

"They will not forget. That woman will not forgive. This means that your mission is in jeopardy. What happens if they come for you and take you?"

John nodded several times. He was seated at the mouth of a cave with Philip and with another follower, Andrew. They had a fire going and had finished a meal not of roasted locusts but of broiled fish and bread, provender which Philip had acquired in some way there is no need for us to pursue. John said: "I expect two things any day now. I expect the coming of the one you must follow, for, as you say, my time is short. He too must be baptised. He knows this. He will know too of the other thing. I think—nay, I know—he will come to the river before the armed men of the sinning Herod. Any day now. Perhaps tomorrow."

The prophet had prophesied truly. The next day, in cloudy weather, he stood on Jordan's banks baptising. There was a long line of penitents. A woman was mumbling:

"I dreamed of committing adultery with my daughter's own husband, and I think the dream was as bad as the doing of it. I cursed my neighbour in the market-place—"

John smiled gently and gently gave the sinner to the waters, which, under that sky of boiling clouds, was of the dull colour of a military shield. Then he looked up and saw. He saw his cousin Jesus on the opposed bank. He took off his sandals and waded into the water, with gravity, no smile of acquaintanceship or greeting for John. At this point of the river the water was shallow. He walked through the rippling metal towards the end of the line of the repentant. Hands joined, head lowered, he awaited his turn.

"I washed clothes on the Sabbath," a woman was saying. "And I told my daughter to gather wood for the fire on the same day. Are you listening?" For John's eyes were not on her.

"Yes, I heard you. Have you more to say?"

"Only that I'm sorry."

John baptised her.

What happened now has been, I fear, obscured by superstitious tales, which will ever please the multitude more than the truth. Jesus is said to have looked up at the heavens and seen a white dove pursued by vultures. The dove settled above his head, about five cubits up, and the vultures, as frightened, winged off. The sun suddenly pierced a hole in the clouds and there was a great radiance. Jesus's turn for baptism had almost come. There was an old and toothless man in front of him, confessing sturdily:

"I stole, sir. I lied. I fornicated, sir."

"Anything more?"

"Isn't that enough, sir?"

John baptised him. The man raised his dripping head, his mouth opened, and the following words seemed to be spoken:

"This is my beloved son, in whom I am well pleased."

"What," said John, "did you say then?"

"I said," said the man, "that it didn't take long."

And now John and Jesus confronted each other, and each permitted himself a smile of greeting. John said: "It is not for *me* to baptise *you*."

"Nevertheless," Jesus replied, "let us fulfil all righteousness. Do it." So John baptised him and then clumsily tried to kneel to him in the water, but Jesus raised him gently, embraced him briefly, then waded back to the bank where his sandals lay. One old woman said to an old man:

"Big, isn't he?"

"He didn't confess his sins," said the old man. "Did you notice?"

"Yes," the old woman said. "He's very big."

John nodded to Philip and Andrew. They came to him splashing. "The town is Nazareth," John said. "It will begin in Nazareth."

"That is he?"

"He will return to Nazareth, and in Nazareth it will all begin."

"We must follow him?"

"You will see him in Nazareth."

The next day John preached in the square of a small riverside town. He was saying: "Is the baptism by water needful?—so you may ask. And the answer is yes, for what new thing happens in the world within us—that is, the soul—must find a companion in the world without us—for we are two things, not one."

Somebody in the small knot of listeners called: "Has Herod the tetrarch been baptised yet?"

"It is my most earnest wish," said John, "that he set his subjects an example in this matter. Alas, he has sinned gravely and seems to rejoice in his sins. I pray daily that the spirit of the Lord may work in him and bring him to the humility of repentance."

"You mean," said the man, "that he must put away his wife?"

"I mean that. We are all subject to the law of Moses."

"Doesn't what you're saying amount to a treasonable statement?"

"In the world of the spirit the only treason is defiance of God's law."

"Is not the king above the law?"

"You heard my words. No man is above the law."

"John bar-Zacharias," said the man "will you come to the king with myself and my companions here?" He pointed out two cloaked men who stood near him. "We are of the king's household and have been deputed to fetch you to the palace that you may speak to the king."

"But," said John, "the blessed river Jordan does not flow through the palace of the king. Take this message to Herod Antipater—that John the precursor awaits him, and there will be rejoicing in the land and in heaven when he comes to repent and be purified with the water of the spirit."

"I have no authority to bear such a message," said the man. He flung his cloak back from his shoulders to disclose the chainmail and the sword of a kind of military or police officer. The two other men followed him in this. Most of the crowd, no lovers of authority, gasped and began to disperse. "If you will not come freely then you must come under duress, though we are ordered to do you no bodily harm." He cleared his throat and announced: "In that you have spoken against our lord King Herod Antipater, alleging him to be guilty of crimes whereof, by reason of his very rank, birth and office, he can in no wise be guilty—"

"Say no more," John smiled grimly. "I am under arrest."

They took him away.

They took him not to the king but to the palace prison. He was placed in a cell that was a sort of cistern, damp and slimy, where toads hopped. There was an iron grille on top of it, a lid that was lifted for the literal throwing of him in, and this formed part of the floor of the passage-way that led from the quarters of the palace guard to a door that opened onto the public street. Light entered the corridor by way of further vertical grilles three cubits up from the stone paving. John saw over his head, day and night, the traversing feet and legs of soldiers, rattling the grille as they went over it. Bread and bones were thrown down to him by the guard—three men lifting the heavy iron while a fourth thrust the fodder through the space thus temporarily opened. The guard had the grace to lower a crock of water to him by means of a string attached to its neck, but much of the water was lost in the rough passage downwards. For the lowlier functions of the body, John had to use a dark corner and cover his mess with straw; straw was thrown down to him when the guard remembered to get it. John did not resign himself to the end of his mission. His great voice came out of the depths and escaped through the wall-grilles to the street outside:

"Repent. Seek baptism of the spirit. The Christ is abroad. The one whose shoe none is worthy to unloose. He will cleanse you and grant remission of your sins. Repent, for the kingdom of heaven is upon us!"

John's followers, as well as a shifting population of the curious, stood outside on the street and listened. Buffeted and kicked away by the outside guard, they still came back to hear. The soldiers inside naturally jeered and mocked and tried to drown the prophetic voice with sword-clangs and step-dances on the grille or else sang in chorus dirty soldier's songs, but John's voice rose above them and never tired. In the palace he was not audible, but Herodias was aware of his presence every hour of the day and night.

"His followers are there all the time. They grow in number. The soldiers cannot keep them away. You must be done with him."

"Oh, do be quiet, heart of my heart. Let John shout himself hoarse. And you, for heaven's sake, put your mind to something useful. Embroidery or something."

"I shall give the order for his execution if you will not. Tetrarch, not even half a king. You're as bad as your brother."

"Listen, beloved," Herod Antipater said in a voice all ice. "Orders in this palace are given by me and me only. And my order shall be for John's release. Not now, no. Later. When there is some occasion that calls for special clemency. My birthday perhaps. But John is not to be killed. Do you understand, O my heart's blood?"

"I understand that you are a weakling and a fool."

"Oh, this is such a nuisance," Herod Antipater murmured, getting up from the table where he was reading Frenosius on Body and Spirit and soiling the parchment sheets with sweet-meat-sticky fingers. He got up, approached her and, with a sweetmeat-sticky hand, struck her a damned hard slap on the cheek. "There," he said.

"A fool and a bully and a coward," she said, and she flounced out.

"Add," he told her departing back, "that I am a burker of my marital duties and lack altogether the lusty sap of a man. Stupid woman."

Salome, being only a girl and finding palace life, except for an occasional whipping of a servant, somewhat boring, took to stealing to the passage whence John's voice boomed and, fascinated, all wide eyes, listened to him crying "Repent" and threaten the coming of the burner of chaff. The soldiers said, kindly: "Keep away from here, your royal highness, no place for you, begging your royal pardon, dirty and full of disease he is and his fleas jump. Naked he is too, miss, your highness that is, and it's not decent you should see him."

"Naked?"

"Holofernes and all," grinned a soldier, thinking that she might not know the cant term.

"Holofernes? That was the man that had his head cut off by Judith. What do you mean?"

"Oh, we use the word in a different sense, no harm meant." She was a plump desirable little thing in her rustling silk and her skirt slit to above her knees, nice little knees, and there was not one man there who would not have—but, she was a princess, you had to be careful, like most well-grown girls of that age she probably knew less than she seemed to know. Her body knew more than her mind, so to speak.

"Keep away, miss, madam, is our advice."

Despite this advice, Salome sometimes stole from her bedchamber in the middle of the night, when the guards defied discipline and dozed off and the prisoner himself lay in an uneasy sleep. She would sit on the grille and look down, seeing little in the light of the dim corridor lamp but still obscurely excited. Sometimes she would lie down on her belly on the cold rusty iron bars and John would awaken to see two small breasts pressed against the roof of his prison, arms spread, a girl's silent body in a posture of swimming. They looked at each other and neither spoke a word. Holofernes. What did they mean?

In Nazareth Jesus prepared for the first phase of his mission. As he came from the carpenter's shop, satisfied that it was in good hands and would provide a sufficient income for his mother, Jotham accosted him and said:

"A good business like that, and you leave it to that lout in there. I know the family, I tell you. There's no good in them."

"You'll keep an eye on him, no doubt?"

"Both eyes, I'll count the bits of sawdust. Can't trust one of that family, and your mother's no businesswoman. I've short-changed her for years and she's never noticed."

"Liar. Jotham, Jotham, I must do what I have to do."

"Following this John the Baptiser, as they call him?"

"You may say that. I follow him, yes."

"To prison? To death?"

"If need be."

Jotham sighed deeply. "You're mad, of course. You join the world's madness. The world needs respectable men, who follow a trade, who see the badness of the times and hold off the badness. But you go wandering off—pah. It's a good thing in a way that decent old man your father is dead. At least he can't see the shame of it. It's mad, I tell you, it's wicked."

Jesus smiled. At home, to his mother he said: "Forty days and forty nights."

"Why? Why?" And, in a kind of anger, she heaped more stewed mutton and herbed gravy on his dish and thrust the Jotham-loaf towards him. "Eat. Eat all you can, child." And again: "*Why*?"

"I must test my strength against evil. At the lower limit of my strength I must test it."

"In the desert? There's no evil in the desert. Evil's in the world, made by man, you don't need me to tell you that. You'll kill yourself and that's the only evil that will come out of the desert, you'll swoon and dry up and be eaten by the vultures."

"I think not. I'm strong. You've fed me well for the last thirty years. I shall drink water when I can find it."

"When you can find it."

"Evil," he said. "You, mother, have no evil in you, but in myself I can sometimes hear the demons growling. There are two kinds of evil in the world, one springing from man's own will, the other burrowing into him against his will by the agency of the fiend. I must lay myself open to the father of evil and prevail. I shall be tempted to ally my own will with his, to my destruction. But I shall not be destroyed. Then, after forty days and nights, I can go forth and fight the evil that man makes. And," he added, wiping his trencher clean with bread, "the devils too, the evil from out there, the innocent struck with evil from the great fount of evil." He chewed his bread and said indistinctly: "You are not to worry."

"I am not to what?"

"Worry."

He slept deeply that night and woke at the first cock. In the cool morning, not disturbing his mother, he took a great draught of well water and walked out on to the empty street. The sky was reddening. He moved east towards the desert. The cocks trumpeted like the very challenge of the fiend.

BOOK 3

After ten days Jesus found a clear spring and, lapping from it in full sunlight, he saw a sick and haggard face coming to the surface to touch tongues. He smiled and his image smiled back haggardly.

The forms and faces and voices that oppressed his uneasy sleep and his deliria of the noontime were, he knew, made out of his own sick fancies. One voice only, that of his mother, nearly drove him back to what the world of Jotham would call sanity:

"I am not well, son, and there is none to look after me. Come back at once. By the Lord's grace I am able to talk to you over this vast distance and I know you hear me. Come back, son. I have pain in my right side, as of a sword going in. I can hardly breathe. I cannot bear the agony. Oh come back."

He heard the voice in full daylight and it seemed not to come from his own head but from a cluster of small rocks littered with dry white bird-bones.

"No, mother, you know I cannot."

"The sword pierces my heart, son. The prophecy comes true that I heard in Bethlehem. Return at once to your mother. Let me be healed and let us live happily again together."

"I am to forget my undertaking and live the life of other men?"

"Oh, my dear son, we will talk of this some other time when I am well. You know your duty. The pain is intense. Come back to me. I will have Jotham's wife prepare you a hot mutton stew with herbs and fresh bread from his bakery. You're hungry, you're ill. I die with the thought of your death in the desert."

Jesus grinned bitterly. "So at last you appear. A voice only, but I smell your presence. Away, father of evil."

"Son, son, you ramble, you talk no sense. This is your mother who loves you. Oh, I am in such pain."

"I shut my ears to your voice. It is a good imitation of the voice of my mother but it rises where her voice falls. Talk on if you wish but you will talk in vain."

There was a silence then. Then, an hour later, came a piercing wail of agony. "Cure me, cure me, son, relieve the pain. I cannot stand the pain."

"No, I am not coming home."

"You who seek evil need look no further than your own heart. You are a wicked boy. Oh, the agony like a fire."

He hesitated. The moan of pain was authentic and made him shudder. He looked west towards the way home. A sick mother and he himself sick. He was doing no good here. Evil was in the world and must at once be engaged in the fulness of his strength. Vultures wheeled, one, two, three, very high above him. They always knew when the gift of dry meat was coming, the impatient rending of the wrapping of the filthy garment, the first hammer-stroke of the beak, the engaging of the first strip of dry but tasty flesh, the moister banquet to follow.

"Oh, thank God, thank God you are coming home. I need your soothing hands, the comfort of your voice."

"No!" He prayed aloud and the voice tried to prevail against him. "Father in heaven, give me strength to close my ears to the counsels of wickedness."

"Oh, my son, you too are sick, you are being driven mad."

"*Mad, mad,*" he cried. "That is not my mother's voice. The sound of the word is close but not close enough. You must try harder, father of evil."

He then heard, from the same cluster of rocks, a throaty chuckle. "We have her," came a male voice he did not know. "In her weakness we have laid claws upon her. A good son, a very good son."

He smiled with relief. "At last," he said, "you come into the open. Shall I see you soon? In the form of the light-bringer, the most beautiful of all the angels?"

There was silence. There was a silence of many days, so many he could not compute them. He wandered far from this spot, knowing it to be no more unclean than any other that the presence of evil would touch but knowing it too to be marked with the shame of a temptation to which he had nearly yielded. At sunset one day he rested near a rock that had the shape of a giant rotting dog-tooth. The jagged upper surface melted and writhed and set into a face, long-nosed with a torn mouth. Fireflies settled into the eye-crevices. Jesus spoke first.

"Why do you not come in your own form?"

"Ah," and the voice came from the moving mouth in the very tone and pitch of Jesus himself, "you mean as the light-bringer, the most beautiful of all the angels." And then the voice clanged like a fall of piled Roman javelins. "But fallen, fallen—so it is written. You know or should know that the story is told upside down. It is God who fell. How do you take me—as a vision spun out of your own starved guts?"

"Ah, no. I've waited for you. It's satisfying somehow to be at last in the presence of the first and final evil."

"Final, eh? You admit the finality? That all shall end with me and the old fellow melt moaning away yielding the victory?"

"You know well what I mean. The evil that stood before man himself learned evil. The last enemy. The putridity that lies at the centre of all others."

"You have the makings of an orator. But don't talk of putridity. If evil stinks, does good smell of rose petals? Soon you will end by saying that God is good as the taste of a pomegranate is good. Beware words. There are bigger things in the world than words. Peace is wordless, love is wordless."

"The word *love* sounds strange coming from you."

"Why strange? The coupling of man and woman, the cock at

work in the cunt, the seed coming and then the seed comes, the honeyed spurt and the great crying out—ah, you know it, and it is all my province."

"Love was the word I used, love."

"I used it first, little one. And Adam knew his wife. Knowledge, knowledge. The fruit of the tree, and what juicier? See." Jesus saw. He saw himself with his dead wife Sara, live again and lively in bed. Pumping away, his face mindless, lips parted, then parted further as the cry came and the seed flooded.

"Sanctified by the all highest," Jesus said. "The means of begetting human souls."

"You begot no human souls. No, no, don't say it was not for lack of trying. And remember that *love* does not think of human souls, it thinks only of itself."

"That is God's purpose. The creation is God's, and God's mind alone is on the creation."

"Good, so we keep God's mind out of it. Room, then, for your humble servant."

"A servant who said he would not serve."

"You are distressingly literal, young man. Humourless too, I should think. For my part, I like laughter. Watch and listen." The desert came alive with lights. Girls, plump and slender, yielded naked to their takers, moaning with delight, takers polished with sweat with spread hairy paws on squirming haunches. "Pleasure," the voice said. "No thought of good and evil here. Wearisome terms, anyway. Ah, I can tell your own flesh is stirring. You're a human being after all. And look, there you are among them, big and naked. What you're doing, see, has little to do with peopling God's kingdom with souls. Things you dreamed of doing with Sara but were too bashful to seek out of the dream. Now—see where your seed spurts. That will create no souls. But why worry? Where is the harm? See how happy you both are, you and that woman, whoever she is, no matter. Hear the joy. They laugh, they're happy. What dismal propositions have *you* to give to the world?"

"If," Jesus said, "you would be good enough to dispel this

empty vision, you could contrive more solid temptations. This is very childish."

Obediently the force unseen dispersed the vision. But then there was nothing except cold night. Jesus sought sleep in a rock-fissure, but he shivered. It was with a kind of relief that he saw a lantern swinging towards him and, carrying the lantern, a middleaged man in a white garment, cleanly bald, clean-shaven. The man said:

"Ah, two night-wanderers meet. May God be thanked that I have found one with whom to outwatch this night, with its chill and noises and nasty visions spun out of hunger. Do you travel far?" As he talked he built a fire with great speed, sure hands finding twigs and dry branchlets in the lantern's small light, a fistful or two of straw, flints to strike from some recess of his garment. "I am come a great distance, from the Greek islands." Jesus said nothing, merely watched, very wary. "You do not ask what I seek here in Palestine?"

"I do not ask."

"Ah, but you at least speak. You find my Aramaic adequate?" The fire blazed, the man heaped more sapless wood on it. "It is not the best of instruments for probing into the heart of the truth. Aramaic, I mean. Terms like *God, law*—these in Aramaic, or Hebrew too for that matter, are all encrusted with convention and superstition. and prejudices of the tribe. Do you follow me? Do I go too fast for you? Or would you say this is neither the place nor the hour for such talk?"

"You know who I am?" asked Jesus.

"Neither of us need speak his name. From the look of you and the desert habitation you have chosen, I would say you are some holy hermit come to contemplate the eternal mysteries of God and good and evil. Am I right?"

"Leave me," Jesus said. "Stamp out your fire if you will. Build another elsewhere. You may be Greek but you are still the father of lies."

The man chuckled. "You do me too much honour. I am the father of nothing. If I knew what a lie was I would know what the truth is. Perhaps you know the truth. Perhaps God, if there is a God, has sent me to you. Then, think, armed with the truth I speed back to the Greek isles and sow its dragon teeth, if you know the image. Do you deny me an hour of talk?"

"It is written—"

"Ah, no, ah, no." The Greek was very quick. "I was not brought up, please remember, on the sacred writings of the Jews. Confirmation, confutation, confounding, confusing—ah no, your texts can do nothing to me. I come that my reason be enlightened. Perhaps I am come to the wrong place. You are silent now. Perhaps you fear the naked blade of reason. You prefer instead the weary game of text-dealing. It will not do for me, my friend. And even if, absurdity of absurdities, I were this father of lies you called me, reason would still be reason. Reason stands apart from God and devil and the thunderings or blandishments of either."

"What," Jesus now said, "do you wish to know?"

"Better, much. I wish to know if evil is needful to the world and, indeed, the universe. You yourself must sometimes use the term *a necessary evil*. Our ordinary sayings often enshrine profound truths. Is evil then necessary?"

"God's goodness may be said to shine the more clearly for the existence of evil. And if God's creatures were made free to choose, then there must be good and some other thing to choose between."

"So evil is necessary?"

"It is not necessary. It is the consequence of free will. But free will is necessary."

"How confused you are without the mud walls of your texts to lean on."

"In no wise confused, Greek or father of lies or whatever you are. God lets man choose good or not choose good. If man does not choose good he chooses not-good. It does not have to be evil. But, thanks to the depravity of man's will as acted upon by the father of lies, it is most frequently evil."

"An evil that God is not great enough to expunge from the world?"

"God would first have to destroy man's power of free choice. This he will not do."

"You speak as though you are privy to God's mind."

"God is in me. I am in God."

"Perhaps you *are* God?"

"I am *of* God. God is not a creature of flesh."

"*Of* God? You claim some special relationship to God? God's son, perhaps?" Jesus said nothing. "Strange chimera, if you know the word. Flesh proceeding from pure spirit." Despite the warmth of the fire, Jesus began to shiver. The Greek was quick to notice. "Very human flesh."

"In the flesh," Jesus shivered, "born of woman, but not of man and woman. In the spirit, of the substance of God who is God the Father. In both, he who was to come and has come and whose presence will be made manifest in the world. The Messiah."

"Made manifest," smiled the Greek, beginning to melt like tallow. "If, that is, you come through this desert ordeal. And if you do, the Messiah of a small and disregarded nation. There is a world outside Palestine. And, even among those unwashed and enslaved speakers of a dull dialect that cannot cope with the utterances of reason, how are you to be made manifest as God's word made flesh? Through the speaking of God's word. And how will the unwashed know it is God's word? Through the things you shall do to open their mouths with wonder. Turning water to wine. Healing hysterical blindness and palsy. Do you know that word *hysterical*? You will prevail through trickery, not God's word, whatever God's word is. Love one another, children. Love God, whom you have never seen. Cease to do evil, or the big fire will bite you. All this has been heard before. So you must sauce it with miracles, if you know the word. You disgust me."

The tallow mouth dissolved into the tallow chin. The lantern became tallow. The blob of tallow that had been the father of lies tipped over into the fire, which flared an instant and then went out. Laughter came out of the moon that was just rising.

Days went by with no further visitation. Then, as he was

delirious from his empty belly, Jesus went round a rock to be met by a table laden with dainties. It was wearisomely like what a man would expect to dream of in the faintness of hunger— warm barley water, golden custards, not wine but grape juice, chickens shredding in broth still bubbling. He turned from it towards a stagnant pool in which faint moonlight feebly danced. The pool said to him: "A Messiah? A king? And in rags?" Jesus drank and then said at his leisure:

"You know I do not seek an earthly kingdom."

"Leave the earth, then. Die," said the dissolving table. "Seek the other one."

"In God's good time."

"Hungry, yes? Like other things made of the earth? Starved, tortured, your belly writhing with the anguish of it all? The Son of God should be above all that. If you *are* the Son of God."

Son of God? What did the phrase mean? Jesus yearned towards the dissolving ghost of custard. Son of God? What was it all about? He passed, on the pool's edge, into what he half-willed to be his final sleep, *seek the other one*. And yet he woke as ever at dawn to hear the voice coming from a rock tinted the most delicate rose:

"If you *are* the Son of God, why not turn these stones into bread? Not a sumptuous breakfast but an adequate one. Go on, do it."

"You know scripture," he answered with almost no voice. "It is written: man shall not live by bread alone, but by every word that proceeds from the mouth of God."

"The relevance is not clear. Come. A vision. Dawn is a good time for visions."

Jesus turned his heavy head with a creak of tendons he could hear like the tearing of branch from tree and found himself on an unexpected summit, looking down a great distance, hearing the voice proceeding from out of the rising sun:

"If you *are* the Son of God, throw yourself down. I seem to remember some lines from one of the psalms of your revered ancestor—the ninety-first, I think."

"You know scripture," Jesus said faintly. "I know you know scripture."

"'He shall give his angels charge concerning thee. And on their hands they shall bear thee up, lest haply thou dash thy foot against a stone.'"

"Well quoted, father father—" The phrase would not complete itself. *Of lies* would not come forth.

"So do it—leap. And down the angels will come to stop you breaking your holy neck."

Jesus said carefully: "In the Book of the Second Law it is written: thou shalt not tempt the Lord thy God."

"The eighth chapter, the third verse. Good."

He turned away from the sun but found that his only path led him to a higher summit still. Below, far below, lay the city of Jerusalem basking in the dawn. A thorn bush spoke to him, saying:

"There—Jerusalem. I promised you a vision, did I not? The holy city, as they call it. But it could as well be Rome, Athens, Alexandria. Or some city not yet born. We all know what you really want. Power."

Jesus tried to turn from the shimmering vision, which indeed began to change its towers and the configuration of its streets and squares to become another city, one he had never seen. But he found his path blocked by great stones. A jagged rock spoke to him from a fissure like a twisted mouth:

"Even this fasting in the desert. You are testing the power of your own flesh. For your power must be of the flesh, and in the flesh you must rule. Forget all that nonsense about being the Son of God. How can a mess of flesh and blood and nerve be the offspring of a spirit? Ah, I can tell you're unsure now. I can see it in your eyes. Power is real, temporal but solid. Gain the power first, then impose your visions, but first gain the power. You can have it. A simple matter. Very simple."

A new strength was trickling into Jesus. It seemed to him that the temptation was coming to an end, that it would soon be time for him to break the long fast and trudge home. He scrambled over rock and rock and found himself again in bare scrubland. But a huge high stone faced him, and it spoke:

"Get down on your knees before me. A mere formality, a courtesy call it. And then it is all yours—mastery of the world of men. See." And Jesus saw. He saw himself crowned in gold amid huge pillars of marble, purple silk flowing over his limbs. Crowds acclaimed him and went down on their knees. The trumpets blared.

"Come," said the rock. "Do it. Take it."

"You weary me," said Jesus. "It is written in the Book of the Second Law—"

"The sixth chapter, the thirteenth verse—"

"Thou shalt worship the Lord thy God and him only shalt thou serve."

There was no reply except a stony chuckle. Jesus smiled very faintly and turned to see a pastoral landscape with a river ahead. He walked to the river and drank. There was a bush filled with black shining berries. Cautiously he plucked and began to eat. He found he had no appetite. He saw a flock of sheep with a shepherd. He heard a ram's bell and the thin gurgle of a flute. He took more berries and had an intimation of the return of hunger. Soon his mouth flooded with saliva.

t is said that Jesus arrived back in Nazareth on the morning of a Sabbath, and that he did not go home to rest and feed but went at once to the synagogue. An unnatural son, Jotham told Mary, unnatural. And Mary nodded. Jotham spoke better than he knew.

In the synagogue he sat, thin, eyes huge, a stranger among the congregation that looked on him with fear and something of hostility. They all knew of his forty days in the desert; they did not like it. But the rabbi, though fearful for reasons he could not bring to the surface of his brain, yet felt forced to say to him:

"Will you now read from the scriptures?"

Jesus got up, went in his thinness to the rough lectern and faced them all. Thin with great eyes, but still very tall and muscular. He lacked flesh, it was only flesh he lacked. In the congregation he saw two faces, young men, very attentive, who did not seem hostile. He had not, he thought, seen those faces before. Jesus opened the scroll, looked fearlessly at the coldness and fear and hostility of his fellow townsmen, then spoke.

"The Book of the Prophet Esaias. In which it is written: 'The Spirit of the Lord is upon me, because he has anointed me to preach the gospel to the poor. He has sent me to heal the broken-hearted, to preach deliverance to the captive, to give sight to the blind, to set at liberty those that are bruised and broken. To preach the kingdom

TWO

of the Lord God.'" He closed up the scroll, then carefully said: "This day is this scripture fulfilled. In your ears." There was silence, then murmuring. He walked back to his seat. An old man stood and cried:

"He's the son of Joseph the carpenter. What do you mean, the scripture's fulfilled? Who are you to talk about giving sight to the blind?"

Encouraged, other voices started up: that's right, a carpenter laying down the law, and so on. Who does he think he is? What right has he to talk of preaching the gospel to the poor? And much more in the same vein. Jesus stood again and said, loudly, noting scum on the shouting mouth of a man who dabbled in money-lending:

"Let me tell you an ancient truth. No prophet is accepted in his own country. And let me tell you another thing that is written in the scriptures here. There were many lepers in Israel in the time of Eliseus the prophet. And none of them was cleansed, not one son or daughter of Israel. For the only one to be healed of his leprosy was Naaman—and Naaman was not of Israel but of Syria."

The anger was growing. The rabbi, old Gomer, came anxiously up to Jesus and said:

"Say no more. This is the house of the Lord. It is not right that it should be a place of noise and brawling. Go."

Jesus nodded, looked up towards the women's gallery, and saw his mother there. He nodded, more slowly, but made no further sign of recognition, regret, affection. He strode out, hearing words like: disgraceful, blasphemous, the carpenter's son making himself out to be a prophet, who in the name of God does he think he is, and so forth. Out in the sun, three yards away from the synagogue door, he looked back and waited. The two young men he had noted within, attentive strangers, came out and up to him. One was big and swarthy and had a slight limp. The other was more delicately made. The big one said:

"We were told to make ourselves known to you. I'm Andrew, by trade a fisherman, but now your follower, if you will so have it. This is Philip." Philip said:

"I follow a less useful trade, or did. You must now give me a new one." Jesus said:

"What trade?"

"I'm a singer and maker of songs."

"And who said you must make yourselves known to me?"

Rabbi Gomer was ahead of the emerging tide of the angry. He said: "They're ready to drive you out of town. Leave and leave quickly." And then: "I am sorry it should turn out so." His look seemed to mean that he was sorry his congregation had not had the courtesy, imagination, decency and also that Jesus should seem to be opening a door which perhaps had to be opened but now, here, well, it was perhaps not—

"We were sent by John," Andrew said. "John the prophet, the baptist."

The rabbi heard that and showed distress. Things happening, new things beginning when he was old, needed a quiet life. He turned back with his arms feebly out to stem the stream of the stone-throwers. One threw, then another, another.

"You see," Jesus said, "that there is no work for us here in Nazareth." Meanwhile the crowd yelled about his not showing his face there again, blasphemer, get out, and the rest of it. Philip caught a sharp flint on his left cheek and began to bleed. He smiled. Jesus said: "So we take the road." But he did not at once turn his back on the Nazarenes. He strode towards them, and it was some of them who retreated. But there were still plenty to throw stones.

"To the lake," Andrew said. "Isn't that right—to the lake? To Capernaum, where my brother is. Simon, you must meet Simon."

"Capernaum, yes," Jesus said. "Your brother later." And they took the road. Andrew limped along, grim. Philip, at the request of Jesus, sang some of his songs, one of which began:

> When shall the trees cry love?
>   Not in the spring,
> But a season of
>   God's making.

Some were about girls, others about wine. They were simple songs, and Philip's voice was sweet though not strong. When they arrived at Capernaum, a fresh wind blowing from the lake, Jesus said:

"To the synagogue."

"Of course," Andrew replied.

In the synagogue here Jesus had no hostile reception. The congregation was used to the to-and-fro of debate. They listened and they shouted back. If they agreed, they agreed very audibly. They were not like the Nazarenes. Jesus said:

"You must not think I am come to destroy the law, or strangle the prophets. I come not to destroy, but to fulfil. The commandments of the Lord, given to Moses in the old time, are not however to remain dead stone for the reverence of unthinking minds—"

"Dead stone?" cried a wiry hairy little man. "Dead? The tablets of the law dead stone?"

"The stone," said Jesus, "is what the law is written on, but the law itself is living as flesh is living—flesh and blood. A man is made of flesh and blood, and he changes—yet he remains the same man. Isn't that true?"

Some shrugged agreement, others pulled their beards as if to indicate that they would like to think there was sense in denying that it was true. Jesus said:

"Now let's take one of the commandments—thou shalt not kill. And whosoever, so we're told, shall kill shall be in danger of the judgment. I accept that, we all accept that. But I ask you to think on this question: why does a man kill?"

A young man, well set-up, with fine flowing hair, at once said: "Because he hates."

"You're quick with your answer," Jesus said, "and your answer is the right one. So we should add to that old commandment a further commandment, new-seeming but not really new, since its substance is implied in the old. Thou shalt not hate. For to hate is to kill in the heart. And so, if you hate your brother, if you're angry with your brother, you should be in danger of the judgment—"

A placid-looking elder said mildly: "That goes too far. Anger is a natural thing in a man. We all get angry."

"Human nature," said the wiry hairy little man. Jesus said:

"Well, we must learn not to be angry, as we learn not to kill. We are not quick to kill, since we are aware of the law. We must set up in our hearts a law that tells us to avoid hate and anger as if hate and anger were acts of murder. And I go further. I say this: if you call your brother a fool, saying 'Damn you, you fool,' then you are as much in danger of hell-fire as if you took a knife to him."

Jesus smiled at the babble of protest: oh no, that goes too far, and so on. We're not allowed to do anything, then. I mean, it's human nature. *You fool*—why we say that ten times a day, and the rest of it. "All right," he smiled. "I seem to exaggerate. But all I mean to stress is our need to love. A loveless heart carries its own hell-fire. Isn't that true, isn't it?"

Well, perhaps, something in that perhaps, goes too far perhaps but perhaps something in it perhaps. The young man with fine flowing hair smiled and smiled broadly.

"Something in it, something?" cried Jesus. "There's *everything* in it. It's not the things that the world sees and the world judges that are important. It is the things within. Hell and judgment are in the human heart, as is the kingdom of heaven itself—for hate and love are in the human heart. Let me now take another of the commandments of Moses. 'Thou shalt not commit adultery.' Now what follows from what I have already said?"

There were, as was to be expected, many grins and smirks at this, as at a notion totally untenable. Even Andrew grinned for three seconds. A man in strong early middle age with a large but well-moulded wet red mouth said: "What follows, in your way of thought, is that if you feel unlawful desire for another man's wife you're already committing adultery. Well, if you see a handsome woman in the street, desire often stirs, since that is the way God made us. You can't always tell whether she's married or not, though. You'd turn all natural desire into a sin. The desire can be harmful, yes, but only if it's acted upon. You speak nonsense, sir."

Jesus smiled very good-humouredly where, so both Philip and Andrew thought, their master John would have thundered. "Oh," he said, "we may admire, we may admit lust's first stirring, but it is hardly fair to our wives if we nourish the desire and brood upon it. You still do not seem to understand the drift of my general argument—that sin is not a matter of fleshly enactment, sin is here, in here." And he crashed his own breast with his large fist. The little wiry hairy man cried:

"Well, master, there's a pleasure to be gained from the acting out of the lust of the flesh which is not to be found in brooding on it. If the thought's as bad as the act I'll still take the act any time." There was some laughter at this. Jesus said:

"It is not in the pleasure that the sin lies, though the prospect of pleasure, of course, is what leads to the sin." A loud though wavering voice now called from the door:

"Get away from us, Jesus. Leave us alone. We don't want you here." It was a man of about sixty, almost naked, much scarred with torn skin hanging from him. He crawled into the synagogue on hands and knees but now reared like a beast at the sight of Jesus. Many of the synagogue congregation seemed to know him; some went pale and tried to leave; others pushed to the walls. Jesus smiled as though in recognition, though with no joy in the smile.

"We know you, Jesus, all of us in here. Raccaba golafokh, son of the god who's a butcher, go back to your sawing of wood and leave us."

"Quiet!" called Jesus very loudly.

"Take your big godrod in your hand and frot it, bastard Jesus."

"Be silent!" yelled Jesus. "I command you, unclean spirits from the pit of hell—leave him. *Leave him!*"

Strange words came from the mouth which seemed to be many mouths all opening in silly joy: "Domuz chiros chanzir chasir nguruwe." The body went into powerful convulsions, threshing and jumping, so that those by the walls tried to burrow into the walls. Then there was a rending paroxysm and a variety of foul reeks like monstrous farts.

"There is a tree outside," Jesus said almost conversationally to the departing devils. "Nest there." And, to two men who bent over the body now still but desperately snoring: "Take him. Home to his bed. He'll be well by sunset."

And then, while the limp snoring body was being carried off, Jesus went on with his discourse as though nothing had happened, though it was noticed that he did not seem to wish to pursue further for the moment the theme of adultery in the head. "You have heard it was spoken in the old time that an eye should be rendered for an eye, a tooth for a tooth. Well, I say to you this: do not resist evil. Whoever strikes you on the right cheek—turn to him the other cheek also. Prepare your laughter if you wish, but consider that what I say may be based on some knowledge of the world. If you strike a man, the pleasure lies not in the striking but in the exciting of resentment and anger. How if these be not excited? Where then is the point of your violence? I ask not more than a willingness to learn control of the feelings. If evil is not met by evil but by love, then there is some hope of our building the kingdom of heaven."

A burly man with a squint lumbered to his feet and rumbled: "Now see here, master. I spy a certain danger in all this. Because you have a kind of power which none of us here has seen before—"

"I did not," said Jesus almost humbly, "contrive this showing of the power you talk of. It was not my wish to impress. The matter was forced upon me—"

"Be that as it may, we must now be expected to take all you say as the authentic voice of, well—I think everybody here knows what I mean—"

"You must take nothing," said Jesus firmly, "that your heart rejects. And what heart will reject the law of love? Yet love is slow to be learned. You must first drive out demons more vicious than those that tormented that poor man. The demons of custom, chiefly. The demons of the easy road. The demons of what you call human nature. It is not easy to love, but you must learn the way of it."

"Must? Must?"

"Oh, I do not give any orders. Cherish your gift of freedom of choice. But if you want the kingdom of heaven, then you *must* choose the way of love. If you want the hell of the heart, continue with the demons of custom. Man is a free creature."

The well-set young man with the flowing hair joined Jesus and Philip and Andrew on their walk shorewards. His name, he said, was John. He said:

"All fishermen in our family. Andrew there knows us well. But I was sent off to study."

"All you were fit for perhaps," Andrew grinned. "You were never much good with the nets."

"And what have you learned?" asked Jesus.

"Oh, that two and two make four. Sometimes. That people are here chiefly to be knocked down. That getting on in the world is a fine thing. That birth is the beginning of death. The term *love* did not seem to be in any of my books."

Jesus smiled. Andrew pointed, saying:

"There he is. Simon. You stay in his house tonight."

By the shore of the lake a gnarled frowning burly man was knotting two broken strands of a fishing-net. There was another fisherman with him, young, a little older than this John, with something of his eyes and nose and mouth but coarser, wind-lashed and sunburnt. Andrew said:

"Simon, James. James is John's brother. Simon, James, this is the man. The one John spoke of. The other John."

Simon looked at Jesus with little welcoming in his look. "A lot of talk these days," he said, "about big changes. All I want is big catches."

"How are your catches?" asked Jesus.

"Bad, bad, and again bad. Nothing coming in, and then the taxman coming round. Catch your own taxes, I tell him. Take my net and my boat and go out into that lake. Fish is what I earn, when I'm lucky. I'm not lucky just now, I tell him, them. If you want me to pay my taxes, tell those fish to bite."

"Always going on about taxes," James said. "He's right, though. Seen the light, John, have you? Let your studying go and come back to the lake?"

"I'll come out with you," said John.

"For the trip only it'll be," said Simon. "Fish won't bite. Bad yesterday and bad the day before. And bad tomorrow."

"May I come too?" said Jesus.

"Tell the fishes all about it," Simon growled. "About the great changes coming. Perhaps they'll gather round and listen."

Simon's boat was big enough to accommodate not only its owner but also Jesus, Andrew and Philip. James and John were together in James's boat, which was almost half the size. It was a calm sunset as they rowed off. Philip sang:

> "My love lay across the waters,
>   Twenty leagues away,
> Fairest of fifteen daughters,
>   So they used to say.
>   I'll go back to her some day."

But James and John drowned him easily with their more practical song:

> "Fish grey, fish brown,
> Will you come up, or must we go down?
> Fish silver, fish white,
> Will you permit us to eat you tonight?"

"They have good loud voices," said Jesus.

"They could yell down any gale," Simon admitted. "Pity that John left the fishing to become a scholar. No, not really. No future in fishing."

"I think," Jesus said quietly, "you are going to be fishers of men."

"Eh?" said Simon. "I didn't quite—"

"James and John," said Jesus, "the sons of thunder. We shall need their loud voices when the time comes." The sons of thunder were thundering:

> "Fish green, fish red,
> How on earth can the people be fed?
> Fish dull, fish bright,
> Will you permit us to catch you tonight?"

They were some fifty yards from shore. Jesus said: "Now. Let down your nets."

"Eh?" said Simon. "What good will it do?"

"Let them down," Jesus said. "Look, the fish are swarming."

"By God," said Simon. "It's unnatural." There was no more singing now. Jesus joined the others in hauling. The nets were crammed with writhing bodies, silver, black, grey, red, golden. "They'll swamp the boat," cried Simon, never satisfied. "Too many of them."

"Take what you can," said Jesus.

"Who are you?" Simon said accusingly. "Who in the devil's name?"

"This is no time," said Jesus, "for such fundamental enquiries. Do your work."

"I know who you are, I think," Simon said. "You're *him*. Well, I tell you straight—we're not worth it. We're nothing. Get away from us. We're only ordinary people. Leave us."

"You ask me," said Jesus, hauling, "to leave you," as the boat sank with the weight of the catch almost to the oarlocks, "at a very inconvenient moment."

Capernaum was full that evening of the smell of fish frying in oil with garlic. The next morning the basket-weavers were busy early; there were not enough baskets around to take home the catch that still lay on the strand. Two basketmen, Nahum and Malachi, were of the Pharisee persuasion, suspicious of the new.

They wove busily as a woman stood waiting for her new basket. She said:

"He has a way with the fish all right."

"Who is he, what is he?" frowned Nahum. "I don't like it, I tell you. It upsets the established order. It smacks of magic or something."

"Magic's right," said the woman happily. "Shore's crammed with them. What's wrong with magic?"

"Magic is of the devil," Malachi said. "We heard all about this casting out of devils he did in the synagogue. It takes the devil to know his own."

"Where is he now?" asked Nahum of the woman.

"At Simon's house. He spent the night there. He cured Simon's mother of the fever. He has a way with that too."

At that moment the crowds outside Simon's small house were considerable. There were men with cataract, women with mortified wombs, lame children, paralytics, epileptics, all clamouring to get in. There was trouble because a group of men and boys were trying to pull Simon's roof off, so that they could lower straight into the house an elderly man on a four-handed bed or stretcher. Simon was out there, shaking away at their ladder.

"God, hasn't a man a right to a damned roof over his head, damn you? Get him away there, damn the lot of you. God almighty, the damned insolence."

"Got a right to be cured, hasn't he? As much as that lot out there, hasn't he?"

"Get him down, let him wait his turn like the others, damn you. My roof, that is, get that damned roof back on again."

Inside the house Jesus spoke as he cured:

"You've heard it said in the old time: thou shalt love thy neighbour and hate thine enemy. But what I say to you is this: love your enemies and pray for those who persecute you. Only in this way can you become the true children of your father in heaven. For he makes the rain fall on the good and evil alike, and he bids the sun shine equally on the just and the unjust."

Simon's mother fussed round him. "Some wine, sir? You'll be thirsty with all this talking. Some cake, see—see—made with my own hands this morning. Look, steady as a rock they are. And when he came to me," she told everybody for the twelfth time or more, "I was all of a tremble and a dither with the fever when he came here last night, and look at me now. Why, somebody's trying to take the roof off. Stop that, you there." An old man on a stretcher was being carefully lowered by means of ropes into the crammed room. "Watch your heads there," came a voice from the sky.

"Let me," Jesus said loudly some little time after, "tell you all a fear that I have. That some who come to me, through doorway or by some other less orthodox entrance, will not come to hear my words but in the hope of cures and miracles. See how this leg loses its running sore and is healed of its lameness. How can I do this thing, James?"

"It's the great power," James said, "God's power."

"Let us talk rather of the power of love. Perfect love casts out fear, but it also casts out evil. The evil of the heart as much as of the body. Love, love," he cried fiercely. "Do you all hear this word?"

Many, including the newly cured, were more intent on looking at a large man whose way had been shouldered in for him by a pair of low-browed louts carrying sticks. The large man was decked in good linen and had a finely woven woollen cloak. Some of the crowd shied away from him, affording him and Jesus a good look at each other. Nahum the basket-weaver said:

"Come to gather taxes, have you? Got them all nicely bottled up in here for you. Nobody can get away."

Jesus was now saying: "If you love those who love you, what reward can you expect? Even publicans and sinners do that." He grinned at the newcomer, guessing what he was. "Is that not true?"

"What do you address me as?" said the big man. "As a publican or as a sinner?"

"Both," Simon growled. "Grinding the faces of the poor

—isn't that sin enough? Go on, out of my house, I owe you nothing."

"I hear stories of sudden prosperity, Simon. The lake spewing up all its fish into your nets."

"Go on, out," cried Simon. "I won't have you and your strong-arm men defiling my little bit of property."

"So," said the publican. "I am not allowed to see the new teacher or preacher or magician or whatever he is. I would have been glad, like others, to have seen him in the synagogue, but publicans are not allowed in the synagogue."

"You seem not to be welcome anywhere," Jesus said. "I do not know your name, but I know your unfortunate office."

"Levi," said the publican. "Or Matthew. I'm known by both names."

"He's called other names too," said, inevitably, someone.

"And," Jesus said, "if, as you say, he's a sinner, he is also called to repentance. And if he is an enemy, he demands your love."

There were some titters at this and, among those furthest from Jesus, even loud laughs. The man who had descended on his bed and now sat on its edge, whole and healthy, munching some of Simon's mother's cake, spluttered forth crumbs in his amusement. "Very well," cried Jesus in anger, "let us know your minds or common mind or common stupidity in the matter. If you hate him, kill him and make an end." There was uncomfortable silence then. Simon said:

"He may be kind to children and to his servants. We don't know. We know nothing about him. All we know is that he gathers taxes."

"It is the paying of the taxes you hate then?"

"All men hate paying taxes." Simon then shouted: "Look at him, with his two big dogs that tear at people. Don't ask me to love, because I won't."

"You will, Simon," Jesus said quietly. "Sooner than you think."

Matthew Levi said: "I have called on you and, it seems, caused an eruption of bad feeling where there should be, and let

none regard the word as strange coming from these lips, gratitude. Master, or whatever I'm to call you, I ask an impossible
thing. Come to my house. Be defiled by setting foot in the
dwelling of a tax-gatherer." There was renewed tittering and
some tsk tsks of disgust. Jesus said:

"There is no defilement possible to man, except of the heart.
I see two Pharisees among us, who show by their sourness that
they do not agree. I will come to your house, Matthew. Will you
invite me to supper?"

"This very night," smiled Matthew.

"Well," said Malachi the basketman, "now we know what
manner of man you are. It is of the essence of the faith to keep
clean."

"Yes," said Jesus, "but not in the way of you Pharisees. For
you are great washers of your hands and watchers of what goes
into your bellies. A man is not judged clean by what goes into
him, but by what comes out."

Somebody in a corner was muttering the word *propriety propriety*. Simon and James and Philip said nothing but seemed
most uncomfortable. But John smiled and said to Matthew Levi:
"Would you invite also a friend of him you have rightly called
master?"

"Friend or friends, all are welcome. His friends shall meet
mine."

Already Simon's house was clearing. The blind walked out
seeing and the halt on firm legs. The man who had come on a bed
said he would send for it later in the day. Jesus said to Philip:
"Come. You must make a song for us."

"A song, a song?"

"A ballad call it. A story in song. You will sing it this evening."

"At the house of—" Philip looked very doubtful.

"No, no, you need not defile yourself. Not yet. Your lessons
must be slow and easy. Self-defilement is an art even more difficult than the song-maker's. The song is not to be sung in the
house of the tax-gatherer, fear not."

Simon grumbled: "I'd come too, but there's the question of

the neighbours and and and. I smell of fish, I have nothing to wear."

"Better," Jesus said, "much better. The self-righteousness is beginning to scale off. You will all learn in time."

As was to be expected, the whole of Capernaum turned out that evening to watch Jesus and John proceed, washed and combed, to the fine house of the tax-gatherer. There was murmuring but no very audible cries of *propriety* and *defilement* startled the sleeping birds. No stones were thrown, except at two well-known local prostitutes and a notorious bugger and his pair of ganymedes, all friends of Matthew Levi. Within the fine house Jesus admired taste and beauty and felt pity for the pert and defiant rejected of the temple. The meal was sumptuous and the wine, through Roman connections, was the finest that the vineyards of Campania could produce. John was uncomfortable, could not bring himself to eat much of the meat unblessed by the rabbi, nor even of the fresh legumes and the purple grapes. Moreover, the notorious bugger kept stroking his arm, to the resentment of the two ganymedes, saying "Sweet flesh and the most *exquisite* hair." Jesus was altogether at his ease, far more so than his host, who was both proud and nervous.

"Taxes," said Matthew Levi at one point during the leisurely wine-drinking at the meal's end, "taxes have to be gathered. Do you accept that?"

"Everything," Jesus said, "depends on the use to which the taxes are put. A state may not impose taxes and then spend the money as it wills. It may demand taxes for great public works that help the people, for almshouses and lazarhouses, but it may not say: I rule you and demand your money as a right. Then men may justly sew up their pockets and hide their purses and say no."

"And abide," said Matthew Levi, "the clanking entrance of the armed officers of the law? Herod of Galilee imposes the taxes. He is the head of the state and has the immemorial right to do with the money as he thinks fit. Do we oppose that and submit to the lawful slaughter of our wives and children? No, taxes are a fact of existence, and it follows that there must be men who gather the taxes."

"If there were no tax-gatherers, then there would be no taxes. And King Herod would have to eat bread and cheese instead of the brains of peacocks. But true—there will always be tax-gatherers, Matthew. Nobody forced you into the trade. And you do yourself well enough, it seems, out of your tax-gathering."

"Well, yes," said Matthew Levi, "an unpopular trade, not one that anybody would willingly take up. It has to be well rewarded."

"Treasure on earth, where moth and rust eat and destroy, and where thieves break in and steal. Is that good enough?"

"Treasure on earth is the only treasure there is."

"No," said Jesus strongly. "Lay up rather treasure in heaven, where moth and rust do not consume, and where no thieves break in. You cannot serve God and Mammon."

"Heaven, eh?" smiled Matthew Levi. "And what is heaven?"

"Peace and freedom under God," said Jesus promptly. "With God, in God, of God. The peace of love, the freedom to love. Possessions get in the way." He drained his winecup and rose. "Shall we take the air, you and I, Matthew? Alone, without your armed men? A stroll in the cool of the evening, one of the treasures of heaven which none can steal?"

"I would rather," said Matthew Levi, "we stayed here."

"The evening air is free to all men but you, Matthew. The evening breeze, so you fancy, whispers curses at you. Still, rejoice, for you have your treasures on earth."

"We will go," said Matthew, as we may now—following a good example—begin to call him. And he motioned to his armed men to stay behind and eat and not to follow. So Jesus and John and Matthew left the house and stood awhile on the fenced lawn, seeing beyond nearly the whole town gathered. "Come," said Jesus, "let's go among the curious. Let us, if you dare, embrace before them in token of new friendship."

"You dare?" said Matthew. "*You* dare?"

There were murmurs among the crowd, and Jesus called gaily: "We've eaten supper together, my friend Matthew and I. It was perhaps a little too rich for my taste, but it will be my stomach that will suffer, not my soul."

Malachi the basketman called: "Defilement, you've defiled yourself, no amount of washing can make you clean."

"If, as you believe," said Jesus, "Matthew is a sinner, then my place is with him. I can't help the good men, can I? They're already beyond my help, so let them glory in it and let me leave them alone. But I can help sinners, and it is my chief task to call sinners to repentance."

"He called you to his house," cried Nahum, "and you went."

"I called to him to call me. Enough of this. Earlier this evening I told Matthew a little story. He has not thought of the story yet or of its meaning, but perhaps tonight, tossing on his fine bed, he will. My friend Philip there has made a song of the story, brand-new. Let him sing it to us."

"Songs, songs," growled Malachi. "Profanity and wickedness."

"Listen before you pronounce," smiled Jesus. "Sing for us, Philip."

And Philip, in his clear voice, sang:

> "There was a man who had two sons,
> And he loved them both in equal measure.
> He put aside, so the story runs,
> Gold for both from his ample treasure.
> Oh, the prodigal son.
>
> "'Father, father, the time is come,'
> So said the younger son one day,
> 'To give to me my promised sum.
> Thank you, father.' And he went away.
> Oh, the prodigal son.
>
> "He wasted his gold on whores and wine,
> And very soon the gold was gone.

A famine came to Palestine
And it did not spare this spendthrift one.
Oh, the prodigal son.

"So he became, against his will,
A swineherd, far from Galilee.
He would have eaten of the porkers' swill,
Had he not been something of a Pharisee.
Oh, the prodigal son.

"'My father's men have bellies full
With bread and wine and roasts to carve.
They are snug and warm in leather and wool,
While I must shiver and I must starve.'
Oh, the prodigal son.

"'I will arise and go to my father,
Saying: I've sinned against heaven and thee.
I'm unworthy to be your son, so rather
Make me a servant of low degree.'
Oh, the prodigal son.

"He has left the swine, he has left the trough,
He has left the foul hut wherein he slept.
His father saw him a good way off
And ran to him, kissed him, laughed and wept.
Oh, the prodigal son.

"'Father, I'm but a worthless thing,
I am not fit to be your son.'
But his father gave him a costly ring
And the finest robe that was ever spun.
Oh, the prodigal son.

"'Bring out the fatted calf,' he cried.
'Let us eat and drink and stamp the ground,
For he is alive that I deemed had died.
Rejoice, for he that was lost is found.'
Oh, the prodigal son.

"The elder son was an angry one,
He would have no part in feast or song.
'All these years I have been a good son,
Asking no favour, doing no wrong,
Never a prodigal son.

"'Yet never even a kid did you slay
That my friends and I might eat and laugh.
But my brother, who's thrown his wealth away,
For him you kill the fatted calf.
For that prodigal son.'

"'Son, son, you are always with me,
What I have is yours,' said his father then.
'But it is right that we shout with glee,
For he that was dead is alive again.
It is right that we dance in a joyous round,
For he that was lost, my son, is found.
Oh, my prodigal son.'"

"Matthew," said Jesus quietly. "I promise you that I will show you heaven. You may not be less hated than now, but at least you will deserve men's love. You were lost, and now you are found."

Jesus now had six disciples. Simon and the others were surprised to find that Matthew, no longer clean-shaven in the Roman manner but sprouting a thin beard, no longer well-dressed but clad in a single belted garment, no longer rich and no longer a man in office, was no longer hatable. Indeed, Simon grumbled far more about giving up his boat and his net and his house (though it was his mother's house really) than did Matthew about the loss of his pictures and statues and coffers. The poor of Capernaum did well out of the dissolution of Matthew's property, and Matthew's servants joined the poor. There were more poor in Capernaum than the town had ever seen before, as also more sick and blind and dying. One day on the lake shore, seeing, as the sun rose, the big crowd coming from sleep and a dream of hope which, they hoped, would now be fulfilled, Jesus shook his head in sadness and said:

"I cannot. You know I cannot. There are far too many. And I am not come merely to mend sick bodies. We must go across the lake."

There was a ferryboat some yards away and they began to run towards it. A young man appeared from nowhere and ran too, though faster, a handsome young man who practically threw himself at Jesus.

"Let me join you. Let me be one of your followers. Where do you go now? Where do I find you?"

"You find me here," said Jesus, "hastening to the ferry. From here on you follow me."

"But it can't be just now," said the young man in distress. "My father died yesterday. I must go first and bury my father. A son's duty. Greater than all others."

Jesus said, somewhat harshly: "Let the dead bury the dead. Follow me."

He said this as he waded towards the boat, turning round, holding his garment up away from the wet, to say it. From the boat he saw the young man, standing desperate, almost dancing with desperation, his hands turned into shaking impotent claws, saw his mouth open howling. He disappeared then among the crowd of the sick and the lame, wading in, setting up a great animal yell as they saw the ferry move towards the other shore, taking the magician away.

The ferryman was old and ill-tempered. "Pay me now," he growled. "I want my money now. Running away, are you? That crowd after you. Tax-men. One of you's a tax-man, I know you, you bastard. Dressed all low and humble to get into people's houses, pretending to faint for a cup of cold water. Then out it comes: taxes, taxes. Let's see the colour of your money. You're a bad lot, whoever you are."

"Here," said Matthew. "All I have." And he handed over a couple of battered coins.

"Don't trust you, don't like the look of any of you."

"Be quiet," called Jesus. "Do your work and be quiet."

"I *work,* anyway. I do a useful job. Not like some as I could mention."

"You're a sour man," said Simon, straight. "You're even turning the sky sour." The sky, indeed, was now full of dirty coiling clouds. The wind was blowing their hair horizontal. "Dirty big storm coming up, by the look of it."

"Prayer," said Jesus suddenly. "Let me say a word about prayer."

"You mean," James said, "we ought to start praying? Now?"

"Prayer," said Jesus. "Don't pray loudly as hypocrites do—in the synagogues and at street corners. Pray quietly and secretly, for your heavenly father is not hard of hearing."

"What words should we use?" asked John.

"Words that ask simply for the things you need." He had to raise his voice now against the wind. Simon was saying to the ferryman: "Here, I'll take the other oar." Jesus said: "Like this. Our father in heaven—may your name be blessed, may you grant that we see your kingdom. May your will be done on earth, as we know it is done in heaven. Give us this day the bread we need for today. Forgive the wrongs we do, as we hope to forgive the wrongs that are done to us. Do not put us too much to the test, for we are frail and feeble. And keep us from the clutches of the evil one. Something like that. And with those words warming, I hope, your cold ears, I will now sleep a little."

"Sleep, master?" said Andrew. "With this storm blowing up?"

Jesus laid his great length in the well of the boat and smiled and said: "You must learn the art of sleeping anywhere and at any time."

"Rest, then," said John. "We'll wake you."

"I know you will," said Jesus, and he at once sank into a slumber that the wind and the raging waters did nothing to prick or puncture.

"Well," James said, loudly over the gale, his arms firm on the gunwale, "it's a strange strange business. Here we are and there he is and we don't know what we're letting ourselves in for."

"One thing at a time," said Matthew. "We seem to have let ourselves in for the father and the mother of a buffeting." The boat hove and bobbed like a toy. Lightning wrote curt messages on the clouds and the thunder made speech of them. The rain teemed.

"Knew I'd done wrong," said the ferryman, gasping. "Got a Jonah on board, that's how it is."

"Leave it," snarled Simon. "My brother there will take over. Go and take a sleep like him there. Shouldn't do the job if you can't do it properly."

"Our father in heaven," said James. "What comes next?"

"May your name be blessed," said Matthew. "May your kingdom be seen by us, but not just yet, O Lord."

"Do not put us too much to the test the test the test the—"

"And keep us from the clutches of the ugh," said Simon, and he swallowed a quart of the lake.

"We'd best wake him," said John. "We must." And he shook Jesus. Jesus ascended through layer after layer of sleep. "Master, we'll drown. Lord, sir, wake up. Please. Save us."

Jesus awoke calmly, yawned, stretched, surveyed the boiling waves and the seething lake, nodded to the lightning as to a brother, then said: "Why are you afraid—you of so little faith?"

"It's human nature to be afraid," said Philip, no waterman, "when the boat's filling and—" He was bailing out with a bucket or trying to. Green-faced, he had vomit at the corner of his mouth.

"I've warned you already about using terms like *human nature*," said Jesus. "I'd say that this storm is about to blow itself out."

"That," said the cowering ferryman, "is what I'd call a good joke. Ha ha ha ha. Blowing itself out, very good." He stared up at a sudden patch of blue as at an affront, his mouth open.

"You're a good," gulped Matthew, "weatherman."

The wind had quietened, the water was settling as though to the pouring on of whole oil-vats. The shore of the country of the Gadarenes loomed glum and lovely. The ferryman said: "I've never seen that happen afore. Who is he? Influence, influence, that's the way of it."

Philip, whose stomach was not strong, was retching still, already having given his breakfast bread to the waters.

"Well," said Matthew, "we came through."

"Never seen that happen afore."

It was chilly ashore. The seven squelched on damp earth

near sedge, with a prospect of gravestones. "This is where they do their burying," Simon said. "Cheerful sort of a place."

"A question none of us have yet thought of," said Matthew. "Where do we stay tonight? Damp earth, damp twigs. What do we eat?"

"You're not going to starve," grinned Andrew, limping along. "You've provender enough in your belly from the years back. You'll do as well as a camel." Jesus said:

"Foxes have holes, and the birds of the air have nests. But I, but we— Come, there's dryness under those trees there. Who has flints? As for food, John has bread for the day."

"Soaked," said John.

"It will dry. We can scorch it and make it doubly tasty. There are wild boar, I should think, in the wood there. Surely there's a hunter among us."

"Boar?" said Simon. "Pigs? We can't eat pig-flesh."

"No," said Jesus. "A man can starve, but the law remains the law. Wait. You will see that the new law will fit the starving as well as the fed. For now, no hunting, then. But there's fish in the lake."

"I brought lines and hooks," said James.

In less than half an hour they had a fire blazing. They undressed and dried their garments, looking shyly at each other's bodies. Jesus was gaunt still, though the flesh was returning. Matthew had a tax-collector's paunch. John's skin was white and like velvet. Philip was very thin, and his ribs showed. Simon was tough and gnarled. James was small but with firmly rounded muscles. Andrew's left leg, as he demonstrated, lying straight with his toes to the fire, was a thumb-length shorter than his right. In just over an hour they were eating broiled fish and toasted bread and drinking lake water from the leather bottle Simon carried on a strap.

"Well," said Jesus, "you see how life must be led. Were any of you ever happier than now?"

Philip let out a high scream and pointed, dithering. A naked man, very hairy, clanking chains that were affixed to a metal belt, the ends of the chains broken, suddenly leaped out from behind a tombstone. He snarled, and voices, voices, more than one, came out of a mouth that opened only to snarl. The voices said:

"We know you know you Jesus Jesus Jejejesusus son of the most most low. Bad power they say they know we know you have have." Philip and John and Matthew sat as frozen. The others stumbled, fell, found shelter behind trees. Philip, though frozen, still screamed.

"Let one of you speak," said Jesus. "One speak for all. If you have something to say to me, let it be said clearly." He poked calmly at the fire with a stick.

"We have only this body," said a heavy somehow greasy voice. "We ask only to be left in peace. They said you were coming through the storm to look for us. Don't torment us. We must have somewhere to be."

"What is your name?"

"We are a gathering, many, legion. Manymanymanymany." The single voice was not permitted to prevail for long. "Driiiiive usususus out and we will will seekseek go look find otherother homes. Torment many. Leave us us us us leave."

Jesus looked calmly towards his men, frozen by the fire or peering fearfully from behind trees. "It grieves me to do what I must do. Beasts have a right to the innocence that my father in heaven gave them. But it is better that I do what I do than have human souls defiled." He suddenly raised his voice in a penetrating scream. *"Out, unclean spirits. Leave. I command you."*

The hairy naked possessed writhed and clanked, fell into the fire, thrust out again, howled with open mouth. Voices sped from the mouth speaking nonsense—*ververikandarahkrofemadam-damdamu*—and blew the fire like a great wind, so that Philip jumped to his feet with the hem of his garment burning, rubbing it out with his hands, gurgling. Then the possessed lay still, seen in his firelit stillness to be terribly torn and scarred. Open-mouthed, the disciples saw a strange thing—braying and hooting and roaring wild boar, their tusks glowing as with an inner light, stampeding down a hillside and into the lake, splashing, threshing.

"It grieves me," said Jesus again.

Matthew covered the naked man with his cloak. He slept long and honked in his sleep. He woke like a healthy man, despite his scars and wounds and the degradation of his chains. His neighbours had, then, driven him out of the town or village where he had lived, driven him perhaps many times, finally ordered strong chainwork from the blacksmith and had him fastened to a tree among the gravestones. This they divined. This the man could not confirm, since he remembered so little. His first words on waking related to his shame at being among strangers naked, and whence these bruises and sores, and why these chains? He knew nothing of being the home of devils, but he remembered well being married to a fair wife and having fathered three fine children. How long had he been wandering away from home, and why?

"Well," said Jesus, "since you talk of home we had best take you back there. If you return to your town crying that you were sick of something that made you wander but are now cured, there is a chance that none will be willing to believe you. You've been the sin-eater of your community, and while you were the home of devils no doubt all felt that they were safe from becoming a like habitation. The fact is, you had best go in our company. You will be safer that way."

"What are you, who are you, you, sir, and all of you?" asked the man.

"We're healers of sick minds and preachers of a new faith," Jesus said. "It is a very simple faith, a matter of love. It grows late now, and perhaps we can find shelter for the night in your town. Tomorrow, if any will listen, I have things to say to the people."

"My house," said the man, "is small, but I can find room for seven with no trouble." He looked on Jesus with a sort of awe. "It was you, sir, who cured me? You drove out, God help us, devils?"

"Let us go," said Jesus, and they took the road, the town being some two miles off. The man, whose chains still clanked and who needed a contrary service from the blacksmith than had previously been forced on him, kept to Jesus's side like a dog. Evening had not yet become night, and some were taking the air in the main street of the town as the eight entered it. There was an elder with an embroidered cap and a stick, one who seemed to have authority, drinking outside a tavern with other people of importance. None seemed pleased to see the exorcised, none greeted him.

"Do you not know me any more?" the man cried. "I was, I know now, possessed, but, praise God, the foul things have departed. Praise too to him who drove out the evil."

The elder said to Jesus: "We are not used to seeing strangers here. May I ask who you are?"

"I think I know who," said the man who had been possessed. "I think it is the Son of the Most High. Praise him, praise him."

The elder waved away the extravagance of this nomination. "Cured, are you?" he said. "But how was it done? That's what I'd like to know." Jesus at once broke into fierce words:

"Your meaning is plain, and you are a fool. Can a man use devils for the driving out of devils? Will Beelzebub, king of the flies, drive out his own? But I see that where there is no understanding there will be no faith." And he spat on the ground.

Another elder, more reasonable, said: "Pardon. You see how it is. We're not much used to strangers coming here. We prefer things to go on as they always have gone on. If you want lodging for the night—well, we're not much used to strangers, as I say."

"You stay in my house," said the dispossessed. "It is the least I can do."

"No," Jesus said firmly. "You do not want strangers tonight. You must be alone with those you love. And tomorrow start to serve the kingdom of heaven. Declare the great thing God has done. Try to love your neighbours." And he looked these neighbours coldly in the eye.

That night Jesus and his followers slept outside the town, under the stars, John having flinted another fire into being against the cold of the small hours. Now Jesus, with a prudence that he did not always show, went to sleep some time before the others were ready and, first having said that he would be warm enough, some way from the fire. He knew that his six disciples must get to know each other freely and without the constraints imposed by his presence. Getting to know each other must, he knew, necessarily entail fearless discussion of himself.

Simon said to Matthew: "I think you ought to take over the money side of things."

"Money?" said Matthew. "What money? I thought we'd all renounced money."

"We have to do a bit of begging," Simon said. "We have to eat. We can't live off fish and berries, that's a fine way to get diarrhea. We need bread, daily bread, like the prayer says. There'll be some, mark my words, as will follow us and won't go away. They have to be fed. Alms for the poor, for that matter, that sort of thing."

"We're the poor," said James.

"Oh, there'll always be poorer," Simon said. "You be what they call treasurer, Matthew. You're an educated man. You can keep accounts, as they're called."

"Young John's educated too," said Matthew.

"John's a fool with money," said James.

"Hell, hell, danger of hell," grinned John. "You called me a fool."

"I don't like doing it," Matthew said. "I don't like the handling of money any more. But I'll take it on, give it a try."

"Good," Simon said. "So there we are, lads, beggars that used to be skilled men with crafts, and there's the prospect before us."

"I wonder sometimes," Philip said, "about the prospect. When he's not here, as now, I wonder if I'm a fool, and there's no hell, I think, if you call yourself a fool. It was the same with John—the other John, the real John, begging your pardon, John. I'd believe anything he said till he turned his back. I mean, is this life from now on? For the next thirty or forty years?"

"You're not supposed to think of the future," Andrew said. "Sufficient unto the day, he says. That makes sense, you have to admit."

"Yes," said Philip, "but every man plans. Marriage, say,

children, a house. And there's a big point. There's something un-natural about all this. We're all single men, and he sort of as-sumes that none of us will ever think of marrying. Or of women at all, for that matter."

"I'm a widower," Simon said, "the only real single man among you. I don't think of marrying."

"He's a widower too," said Andrew. "You all know that?"

"I didn't know," said Matthew. "Did he tell you?"

"John told us," Philip said. "Big John, the Baptist."

"Well, I never knew. I thought he was, well, sort of all for celibacy."

"For what?" said Simon. "I don't know these big words."

"Learning," said Matthew, "to get the better of natural in-stincts. *Love* has two meanings, but we seem to be concerned with only one of them."

Simon grunted. "Shall I tell you what I think, lads? I think that this business won't go on too long. Give it a year, two at most. And why won't it be long? Because he almost sets out to make enemies. The Pharisees, I mean, the hand-washers. The Pharisees are big people with a lot of influence. Imagine what would happen if he went to Jerusalem and started on about the Pharisees being a bad lot. They'd eat him alive, man. Us too."

"Are we supposed to be going to Jerusalem?" said James. "I hadn't thought of that, Jerusalem."

"We'll hear in time," said Andrew. "One thing at a time."

There was silence, enough for a near owl to twit a few measures. Then John asked shyly, of no one in particular: "What do you really think of him?"

"Oh, he's special all right," said Simon. "I mean, we've all seen what he can do. He's one of the special ones, what they call the Sons of God. Like Moses and King David and Samson. A man would be a damned fool to say no to following him. I mean, apart from what he does, what he says makes sense. It's a, you know, an adventure," he said, stretching. "Do you young ones no harm at all. John, better get some wood on that fire, it's get-ting chilly, and then me and Matthew here will watch for two hours, then it'll be Andrew and Philip. Got to make it a bit military. Enemies, like I said. I've been in these parts before, there's some funny buggers in these parts."

At dawn, while John and James were sitting over the dying fire and considering the gentle waking of the others, they saw a man coming towards them, well wrapped against the morning chill in a coloured cloak, alone, middleaged, grave of countenance. Seeing John and James, he waved his hand, stumbled, recovered, then came up to them and spoke, looking at first one then the other.

"Is it you, sir? Are you the one, or is it you?"

"The one you most likely want is still asleep," said James, pointing behind him with his thumb. "But you can tell us what you want him for."

"My name is Jairus. I'm ruler of the synagogue in these parts. Is it true that he can heal the sick, cast out devils? Is it true that he can raise the dead?"

Both John and James were, against their will, shocked at the notion of anyone raising the dead. It had never crossed their minds before. They had been brought up to believe, very sensibly, that the dead once dead stayed dead. Then they found Jesus with them, wide awake, clean-looking, warming his hands at the near-dead fire. Jesus said, as though he had expected the man and, indeed, already knew him: "What is it, Jairus?"

"It's you, sir, is it? Oh, master, I heard of what you—"

"What is it, Jairus?"

"I have a daughter, only twelve. Very sick, dying. I think indeed she may now already—" Jairus began to weep.

"Is it far?" asked Jesus.

"Under a mile. To the south, by the main road. Oh, master, if you could. Could at least—"

"See if there's hope. Yes, yes. Call the others, John, James." He seemed eager to work. Perhaps Simon was right and time was short.

Matthew said to Simon, as they approached the fine garden of the fine house of Jairus: "They're certain to give us some breakfast. I could eat some breakfast, and not fish either. A piece of grilled meat and some new bread still smoking."

"There doesn't seem to be anybody in the mood for cooking breakfast," Simon said. "Look at them." The garden was full of lament: family lamenting near the door of the house, servants lamenting away from it. The wailing rose over the funeral music of flute and drum. A kind of major-domo approached Jairus, tears rilling down his fat cheeks, hands awring, wailing: "She's sinking, sir. She's past help."

Jesus very firmly raised a hand. "Stop this noise," he cried. "The child is not dead. She is only sleeping." A grey-bearded, beetle-browed servant in a green smock, probably a gardener, was as firm in coming up to Jesus and saying:

"Who are ye to come hither with your sour jokes? We've seen and ye have not. Away with ye."

Jesus smiled and said: "What's your name?"

"What's that to do with you? Away with ye and your impertinence, smiler."

"This is Thomas," said Jairus. "But, with respect, come in, if what you say is, can it possibly be, I can hardly—"

"I am glad to meet you, Thomas," said Jesus, still smiling, bowing very courteously to the angry greybeard in green. Then, taking his time, he went into the house with Jairus. Outside an open door a couple of men in the black gowns of physicians shook their heads very sadly. Jesus went into a darkened bedroom full of the scent of spicy ointments, shot with the bitter odour of medicines. On the bed lay a girl, pretty, white, motionless. A woman who was evidently the girl's mother flew to the comfort of her husband and sobbed. Jesus took the girl's hand and said:

"*Talitha cumi.* Rise up, my girl."

The girl did not rise up, not at once. But she opened her eyes and looked round, frowning, as wondering where she was.

"Come on, rise. These silly people thought you were dead. Show them how you can stand and walk."

She stood, but, trying to walk, she fell. But she laughed at her clumsiness. She tried to say something but only noises came from her mouth. She kept to laughing, as this was a kind of articulate or meaningful noise. The parents did not know what to do—to fall on their knees in thanksgiving or to seize their awakened daughter. They compromised by standing, gaping. Then the mother enfolded the girl and the father tried to kiss Jesus's garment. Jesus said:

"She's hungry, probably. I should think everybody is hungry. I most certainly am."

"Good, good," said Matthew quietly.

Over the noise of rejoicing Thomas's voice could be clearly heard: "Ye have to admit that I put it to ye all that there was the possibility that it was no more than a trance, aye. It was a kind of a very deep sleep of a healing nature. And now, ye may see, it's come to an end."

They all sat down to a cold though joyful meal—roast joints of beef and mutton, yesterday's bread, fruit-cake, jams and sweet pickles, wine red and white. Thomas, though a gardener, waited on the guests with apparent reluctance, though his master had not ordered him to do so. He kept frowning and beetling at Jesus, hostile yet fascinated. The flute-player, a slight young man with dreaming eyes not unlike Philip's, played joyful music. The awakened girl took a little bread and jam and some goat-milk. Her parents seemed to think that she should be helpless; they tried to feed her—a mother's hand and a father's, each laden with a scrap of bread well jammed going to her mouth at the same time—but she fed herself firmly, asking: "What was the matter? Where was I? What was going on?" Philip said to the flute-player:

"Forgive me—you told me your name and I've forgotten it already."

"Thaddeus."

"Thaddeus, yes. Thaddeus, do you know a tune which I believe comes from these parts, called 'The Brown-eyed Girl at the Well'?"

"I think so, yes." He played a measure. "Is it that?"

"Yes, yes, that's it." Thaddeus played. Jesus beckoned with a finger at Thomas. Thomas came, frowning.

"What is it ye want more of? It's all here on the table. Emptied the larder they have for the lot of ye."

"Thomas," said Jesus, "you must come with me. I think you know that."

"I know nothing of the sort. Come with ye, indeed. And come where? I've obligations here, haven't I? Even if I wanted, I could not walk out just like that. Where's your sense, man?"

"Your master," said Jesus, "would very willingly give you to me as a present. This I know, this you must know."

"Aye, very funny. I'm not something given away like a nanny-goat. I'm a free man, a man of independent ways and independent thinking. I'm a man that speaks his own mind, ye'd best know that. No bowing and scraping with me, I can tell ye."

"I don't want you as a servant, Thomas. I want you as a friend."

"Oh aye? Well, I mun think on it. No putting things over on me, I can tell ye. I'm a man that knows what's what. Have ye done with me now? All's on the table, as I told ye."

So it was that Jesus left the house of Jairus with eight disciples, for Thaddeus the flute-player, to Philip's especial pleasure, came along as well as Thomas. Thomas said: "Well, one of the main reasons I was willing to leave was the wailing and skriking of that wooden pipe all day long, and now observe what the Lord God would no doubt call his sense of humour. That's right, laugh. At least when ye laugh ye don't blow yon contraption." Matthew the treasurer was given a leather bag with some silver coins in it. Jairus would gladly have filled it with gold, but Matthew said:

"Moderation, moderation, sir. Sufficient to the day."

They purposed now to take the ferry back to the other shore, but first Jesus spoke to a large crowd on the town's outskirts. His fame had already spread wide, and the crowd was attentive. Jesus spoke clear and loud and simple words:

"I say this to you, then: don't be anxious for your life, what you shall eat and what you shall drink—nor for your body, what you shall put on. For surely life is more than food and the body more than raiment. Consider the lilies of the field, how they grow. They toil not, neither do they spin, but I say this to you—that not even Solomon in all his glory was arrayed like one of these. Now if God so clothes the grass of the field, which lives today and tomorrow is thrown into the fire, how much more is he likely to concern himself with *your* needs? Don't be anxious, then, about food and drink—for your father in heaven knows you have need of these things. Seek first his kingdom and his justice, and all these things will be added unto you. Do not worry about tomorrow, for tomorrow will take care of itself. Sufficient unto the day is the evil thereof."

Thomas had his reservations about this philosophy. He told his new friends that there was, perhaps, a lot in what Jesus said. "But," said Thomas, "I'd question that very deeply—about God feeding the hungry and so on. I've seen many a case of starvation in my time. And what did God do about it?"

FIVE

Jesus and his eight arrived back on the shore of Capernaum before dawn (the ferryman, noticeably less sour than before, said: "Grown a bit, haven't you? Twice as many as you was before, way I reckon it") to find two men waiting. Philip and Andrew knew them, greeted them as James and Bartholomew, disciples of John the Baptist. This James recognised Jesus at once and said:

"Sir, you know whence we come."

"He is still in prison, is he not?" said Jesus. "A prisoner, but alive?"

"Also strong and full of fire," said Bartholomew. Bartholomew had a bowed and studious look, a worried man in his thirties. James on the other hand was about twenty and only an inch or so shorter than Jesus himself, very muscular, and his speech, even when its content was mild, was most aggressive. James said:

"But he fears his time is not long. We are to join you now, he says."

"So you are James," Jesus said. "We already have a James—our small friend there. What do I call you?"

"I'm sometimes called Little James," aggressively frowning, "but that one is properly the little one."

"You shall be Little James," Jesus said. "What has your work been?"

"Before going with John? I have wrestled at country fairs. For a time, and to my shame, I was strong man for a publican." Matthew nodded at that, smiling. "Bartholomew here is a cut above all that kind of thing. Educated, clever."

Bartholomew shrugged his thin shoulders. "Neither, not much. I know about herbs and potions. Call me a small country healer. I have had some success, a little. Before we join you, if you will have us, we must report back to John and give him what news there is to give."

"You mean," said Jesus, "news of the kingdom. Well, tell him that the blind receive their sight, the lepers are cleansed, the deaf hear, the dead are raised up, and the poor have the good news preached to them. And tell him this also: whatever happens to him, his name rings and rings throughout the kingdom. Among those born of women there has not arisen a greater than John the Baptist. Let him know this. And then return to me here. You will have no difficulty finding me."

"Master," frowned Little James, "there is something." He scraped his feet on the sand and looked embarrassed. "If such great works have been done—well, angels came to the prophets of old, you know what I mean, when they were cast into prison, and they lifted them out. Can it not be made possible—you see, sir, what I'm trying to ask. Nor me only. Bartholomew and I have talked of this."

Jesus shook his head. "No. He bears his burden as I must bear mine, when the time comes. It is the measure of his greatness in heaven that the cup shall not be made to pass. A cup of exceeding bitterness. Go then and tell him. Then return here to me."

"You do not, I hope, we, that is to say—" mumbled Bartholomew.

"He means perhaps we presumed," said Little James, frowning on Jesus as though about to strike him down.

"You love him," Jesus said. "Let us not have any talk of presumption. Go now, God speed."

Before they could deliver their news, John the Baptist, now thin and sore and filthy, was one day let out of his cell by means of a ladder inserted in the floor-grating under which he had long lain, worse tended than a beast. "Up, you, out," cried the guards, but John could scarce raise his wasted limbs to mount the rungs. When, hands dragging him on the final pitch, he reached the corridor which led to the guard-room, he was roughly sluiced with water from a bucket, dried on old sacking, then draped in a fine cloak. Thus attired, otherwise naked, he was butted and spear-pricked towards the gold and perfumed palace, met by a high officer, then escorted to a private room where Herod Antipater awaited him, lounging in a deep chair. There was a brass table with delicacies on it, also a silver pitcher of wine and another of fresh well-water. John stood upright, though in much pain, and suffered Herod to survey him, bruised, broken, emaciated, shamefully soiled. Herod said:

"They, we, have not treated you well, I can see that. Well, all that can change. Sit, eat something, take some wine. Be at ease, if you can. Have no fear of imminent execution. This is no viaticum. Be at ease, damn you, John. We know each other. We used to be friends." John stood saying nothing, taking nothing. His eyes burned. "What *do* you want, John?" asked Herod petulantly. "Is it just a matter of my violating the marriage laws? Because I've a mind to repent of that and put the matter right. Will that satisfy you?"

"Can you," said John, "then wipe out sin with more sin? For it is new sin that infests your mind. I know you, Herod."

"Yes," pouted the king, "I know you know me. As for my knowing you—there was a time when we knew each other. We were only children then. You're of the family, John, of the blood. How do you think I feel, having you there rotting away in prison, and that howling gang outside the bars? Why don't you see reason? Why don't you remember what you are?"

"And what am I, Herod?"

"A man I could use." Herod took wine for himself and swallowed a pint of it in three greedy gulps. "There's work for you in this wretched kingdom," he gasped. "If it's power you want, you can have power—power to build, not break—"

"To build corruption on corruption."

"I see," Herod said. "Delegated power would not be enough. Look, John, I know what you've been preaching. You've been preaching a new kingdom. You're of the royal blood and the crowd knows it. Is it the crown you want?"

"My task," John said, "has been to prepare the way for the one who shall wear the crown. But it is not the sort of crown that the goldsmiths fashion and the priests bless."

"Oh, you and your cheap mob rhetoric. Balanced phrases and portentous negatives. You mean the new preacher who's been going around. Is he good? Is he worth worrying about? Shall I have him sent for to do a little preaching to the court? We need novelties, John. We grow so tired of wine and dancing and games with straws. Where is he now?"

"You're a fox, Herod. But you won't trap him into treason and have him put away. You needn't fear the toppling of your throne. There will be no usurpations, no wresting of the gold-smith's work from your head. Men must change before king-doms change."

Herod was silent. He played with his beard, new-dyed with the murex. Then he said: "If I set you free, what would you do with your freedom?"

"I would follow him," said John, "whose way I have prepared. But you will not set me free."

"Sure of that, are you? Always a little too sure of things, John—that was always your trouble. It was your trouble when we were boys together. The names of flowers and the kings of Babylon, all that rubbish. You always knew, didn't you? All right, back to your filth. Bang that gong there for me, would you? I want the guard."

"When," John said, "are you going to execute me?"

"Never, never, never," Herod said. "If only to spite that bitch of a queen of mine I'd never do it. You're going to rot. Bang that gong. You're nearer to it than I. Oh, very well, don't then. I don't suppose I can expect favours from somebody who's going to rot." He came over and petulantly crashed the brass gong with its iron beater. He went over to the brass table then and proffered a sweetmeat in his fingers. "You're sure you won't take a little something before you go back to your bread and water? Try this—exquisite—made out of locusts and wild honey." The guard came in, led by a captain. John was taken away. Little Salome watched from the shadows, eyes and mouth wide.

When Herod sat down to dinner with his queen and niece-stepdaughter, his appetite was ruined by Herodias's loud laments:

"... Cannot set foot outside the palace, *my* palace, without a mob yelling adulteress adulteress. Have I to be a prisoner, I, the Queen? Queen of Galilee, if you've forgotten. I say this: get it over now."

"The mob," said Herod, carving a slice of veal into a tetrarchy, "will still cry adulteress adulteress. And murderess murderess as well." Salome looked properly horrified, sweet child. "Sweet child," smiled Herod. "You're eating nothing, sweet child."

"They'll forget when he's dead," said Herodias. "Mobs are like that."

"Far from falling in with your bloodthirsty desires, my dear, I've a mind to release him. On my birthday, you know. It's the expected thing—to show unexpected clemency. Do you like that, Salome, my sweetness? That is what's known as a paradox or anomaly or something."

"And then," said Herodias, "let him go into Judea? Where he can cry adulteress adulteress in the ear of Pontius Pilate? And have Pilate go to Tiberius Caesar and recommend that the Romans march into Galilee, since the tetrarch Herod Antipater cannot keep order. Kill him."

Herod stood up. "I'll have some of that meat there cold before I go to bed. No appetite now, and no wonder. I have a council meeting."

"Or," said Herodias, "send him into Egypt. He can do no

harm in Egypt. Release him and send him into Egypt. I accept his release on that condition."

"What a strange woman you are. But, of course, that's as much as to say: you're a woman. Quick to change devices. But I see through you. Once he steps outside that prison he may meet, may he not, with an unfortunate accident. Better than an execution. Very clever. Not clever enough, is it, little Salome?"

"It is you, my dear lord, who have the woman's mind, meaning a man's notion of what a woman's mind is," said Herodias. "I thought not at all of accidents, as you term them, only of being rid of the man by the least troublesome of ways. I am persuaded now that to kill him would be dangerous for you. Send him to Egypt and in my book he is stone dead."

"When," said Herod, "and I truly mean when and not if, John leaves that prison and this kingdom, he will be given an armed escort as far as the border. I'm having none of your one-eyed and squinting hirelings jumping in with their itchy daggers. And one further thing, my love. If harm, between now and my birthday, should come to John despite all my precautions, I shall fix the blame in one place only, and in great pain of spirit, grieving myself to death, I shall bid the axe fall. There, dear little Salome, strong language, is it not? And what will you give me for my birthday, eh? No, no, tell me not, let it be a surprise. And now I leave both you lovely ladies."

Bartholomew and James, John's James, soon to be Jesus's James or Little James, were able to deliver their message to their master only when drums and trumpets blasted Herod's birthday in and the prophet, cleansed and clad, against his will though the alternative was a total nakedness, in a fine tunic and cloak from the tetrarch's own wardrobe, stood outside his former prison blinking in the light, armed guards close to him, other guards kicking and buffeting the shouting mob. James did his own buffeting and took little notice of the lance-pricks and sword-swipes. He yelled: "John, master—James and Bartholomew are here, look." John looked, "Listen, master—we saw him face to face. The work goes well, your prophecies start to be fulfilled. This news and his blessing we got from his own lips."

"Tell," said John, "all my friends and followers that they may now go to him. My work is done here. I am thrust out of the kingdom. I expected death, but this is like to a death. God bless you." And he was marched on his way.

The followers of Jesus now made up a decemvirate, a body that was too big to possess the first quality of a loose bundle of friends come together casually and had to take on of necessity the properties of a dedicated maniple. The disciples, even when as many as eight in number, had rarely used the term *messiah* or thought of the urgent task, foretold in the scriptures and confirmed thunderingly by John, of saving all Israel from sin and building the holy kingdom. Encouraged by the doctrine of their master, with its emphasis on the sufficiency of quotidian bread and evil, they had conceived of their life vaguely as to be devoted to travelling through Galilee and helping Jesus to preach his new philosophy to such crowds as they could persuade to gather, persuasion in truth being needful only in such places as had not yet heard of Jesus's healing powers. Their work became rather a matter of holding off mobs that wanted miracles and did not care much to pay the price of listening to the new doctrine. Now, with the coming of Little James and Bartholomew, they began to be schooled in the bigger purpose. James was blunt with a country wrestler's bluntness, Bartholomew more subtle and qualificatory, but their speech added up to the same essence: that Israel was to saved, that tough Jerusalem, the Roman occupation one mailed fist and the Sanhedrin the other, had sooner or later to be engaged, and that the kingdom was not a poetic term apt for a song from Philip but an impending reality. Jesus was the Messiah, the Chosen one, the Christ or Anointed if they wanted it in Greek, and all that was laid down in Isaiah and the other ancient prophets was to be fulfilled by him, and not in forty or fifty years either but in a matter of months—ten, twenty, thirty. Simon, who had once said that this whole business of wandering and healing and preaching could not go on very long, had shown himself to be right in his instincts, though he had believed that the Pharisees would put a stop to it. The Pharisees were, he now learned, to be overcome through the force of a public opinion hammered and burnished out of the new doctrine. The Romans? There was nothing in the scriptures about the Romans. The Romans, said Bartholomew, were a temporary occupying force, weed and driftwood on the great river of the life of Israel. Jewish faith was not their concern. The Messiah's work was to be done first in the world of the spirit. The world of buying and selling, building roads, repairing streets, policing alleys, trying men for civil crimes, levying taxes, this was not the Messiah's world.

These ten men were a group of dedicated companions, united in a great loyalty, but within the total group there was room for the smaller patterns of friendship. Thus, Philip and Thaddeus, who delighted in blending voice and flute into a thin and pleasing harmony, were drawn together by art, by the dreamy and gentle temperament that chooses art rather than hog-slaughtering. Simon and Matthew, once the sorely taxed and the sorely taxing, possessed in common the phlegmatic resignation to unrightable wrongs that is a doubtful blessing of middle age. Thomas was drawn to this pair, but was truly the friend of no one, being quarrelsome, hard to please, so pessimistic that he would frown if, at day's end, the rain he had prognosticated from the colour of the dawn had not come to soak them all. It was somewhat of a joke that the two Jameses should become quickly friends, usually together, easing the problem of name-calling: so that phrases like "I did not mean you, James, but the other one" generally had little application. Bartholomew, a somewhat melancholy and contemplative man, liked to spend free time gathering herbs and testing odd mixtures for the soothing of his stomach, which was none of the strongest, and, at the request of Thomas, for the easing of aches in the limbs occasioned by sleeping in the open and being the prey of little sharp knife winds before dawn. Bartholomew was not adept at the lighting of fires, whereas Andrew, who had more or less appointed himself cook to the undecemvirate, could make one blaze quickly (John was helpful in the provision of flints and kindling). Often Bartholomew would have his simples bubbling when Andrew needed the whole stretch of flame for his skewered or leaf-wrapped fish. They would quarrel, though not much. The group usually had their main meal of the day at nightfall—fish, herbs, olives, figs, bread, water to drink—and a bit of dry bread with water at daybreak. Much of the day, given over to travel on foot, gained sustension from distracted nibbling of fruit on trees and hedges, corn-ears, succulent leaves. Sometimes the family of a man or woman or child healed would joyfully donate cold hunks of mutton, loaves, crocks of wine. More rarely they would be bidden dine at table, with servants waiting on.

John, the loud-voiced (when loudness was in order) but somewhat delicate of body and feature, was, if not the closest friend of Jesus, yet his nearest walking companion, the loving washer of his garments, the solicitous in moments of gloom, the soother of anger. But Jesus, with cool justice, showed him no special favours. Yet one night, in sleep, he called his name several times, powerfully, and as if in agony. He awoke not only John, who slept near him, but also several others, though not Little James, who slept like the dead, nor Bartholomew, who was sipping a thin cold brew for a stomach quarrelling with the broiled mud-fish they had had for supper. John went over to Jesus and said:

"Master, what is the trouble? John is here, master."

Jesus looked at him as though he had never seen him before, then sighed profoundly and said: "The other, the other. Not you. Get back to sleep. I must pray."

SIX

The birthday feast of the tetrarch Herod was properly sumptuous with larks' tongues in cassia honey, raw peacocks' brains seasoned with mint and saffron, sheep roasted on hot stones to a softness that would yield easily to a prying thumb and finger and served on beds of dates and quinces and raisins, flawns and fruit-cakes, fruit soups, doves seethed in syrup and egg-yolk, wine, wine. Herod sat gorging and swilling, grinning sillily at the display of fire-swallowing, the Egyptian wrestling, the acrobatic dancers. Herodias sat next to him, very queenly, and little Salome came and nuzzled up to him. Herod was touched and felt, as it were, a kind of memory of the stirring of his loins. The child was beautifully dressed in silk and reeked of her mother's Arab perfume. He said:

"Such a positively frightening accession of affection, my dear girl. I wish I had a birthday every day."

"And if I danced for you," said Salome, "the dance you are always asking me to dance?"

"No king," sighed Herod, "could ask for a more, shall I say, delirium-inducing gift. But you don't mean it, my sweetness."

"What will you give me if I do?" asked the child. Some of the guests guffawed, and one said:

"Women, your grace, women. Nothing for nothing." Wine rilled from his blue beard.

"Anything for something," Herod said,

wondering then what the phrase meant. "Anything you wish, dear child. Within reason, of course."

Another guest said: "You said *anything,* majesty. We hold you to it, ha ha."

"Music," Herod called. "The princess will dance."

The music was discoursed by three flutes of different sizes, a droning bagpipe, a shawm, six little bells variously tuned, a big gong and a small one, a crass but soft thumping drum, a twelve-stringed harp, and two pairs of finger-clackers. The piece was performed expertly, as though it had been carefully rehearsed, and it consisted of a two-part tune, announced by the flutes first, then the shawm and the gongs, then seven variations on the tune for different combinations of the instruments, each faster than the preceding one, ending with a very fast and somewhat fantastic variation for the whole ensemble. When the tune had its first soft playing, Salome merely stood and swayed like a sapling in a gale, weaving her thin bare arms. Then, with the first variation, she began to use her feet, though languidly. At the end of it she shed an outer silken garment.

"Ah," said the blue-bearded guest, "one can, I think, foretell the pattern."

"I saw this," said another, "in Alexandria."

"Be quiet," Herod said, "quiet, all of you." And his breathing was visibly and audibly quicker, at least to the attentive Herodias. At the end of the second variation, Salome removed her second silk wrap, leaving bare her pouting navel and her lower limbs from knee to toe. After the third, with its roll on gongs and drums prolonged till she should be ready for the fourth, she was naked from the thighs downwards. Not only was Herodias now watching the king but others started to swivel their heads almost to the beat of the music from dancer to royal viewer, much struck by his sweaty pallor, his eyes widening almost to dementia, his rasping asthma and wet teeth. At the end of the fourth variation the girl threw off a silk veil that revealed other silk veils promising the ultimate revelation of her breasts and her shame, the nipples of those and the dark mane of that already beginning, as it were, their rise to the surface through the remaining waves of silk. At the end of the fifth Herod was thrusting in his royal chair, at the end of the sixth he was close to a rare ecstatic death. And Salome paused in her dance and fixed her great black eyes on him, her lower lip like a blob of blood, panting. She said:

"You said *anything*."

"Yes yes, child—"

"My mother will tell you what I want." And she went back into the dance. The last variation was prolonged, with much ornamentation on the flutes and shawm, and the girl did a mime, in the last veil that interposed only a film of mist between eyes and the revelation, of frank rutting. Herodias whispered to Herod and Herod cried:

"No no." But, on the point of spending, he cried: "Yes yes." So the girl dropped the final veil, Herod shuddered and then was still though panting hard. The guests clapped and cried her name. Herod called it too. The girl's mother went out, kissed her daughter, then wrapped her wet bareness in a purple cloak. Then Herod said: "I must qualify that *yes*." There was a murmur among the guests, though subdued. "I released him, as you should know. A birthday act of clemency. He's out of our hands now, a free man." And to Herodias, who came close with burning eyes: "Clever, cunning, my dear. Out of *your* hands, should I say—"

"You promised, my lord the king," cried Herodias. "A king's promise. Let the trumpets bray and the drums beat, and let it be known that the king does not keep his promises."

"It was a theoretical *yes*," said Herod, calmed and cool. "I stand by it. The practical fulfilment of the *yes* depends on— Very well, do it if you can. I depute you to do it. There, that must serve."

"I have," Herodias said, "the royal order already engrossed. It needs only the royal signature and the royal seal."

"And, I suppose," said Herod, shivering but in no ecstasy, "you have undoubtedly horsemen ready waiting, one of them with a sharp axe in a bag. You will be too late, however hard they ride."

But John's progress to the Galilean border had been much slowed by the crowds of joyful followers, by the insistence of the faithful that he speak to them, even by some who called for baptism at his hands. He and his escort were trudging in sunlight over a rocky plain when the captain of the escort, a man who admired John more than he durst show, observed dust approaching them the way they had come, and a horseman reining a frothing horse in dust. He carried a ribboned scroll which he handed to the captain. The captain unrolled the scroll and read it. He would not believe what the scroll contained. He looked up at the horseman and said: "Not possible. Some error."

"No error," the horseman said. "The signature is that of the king, as is the seal." He took a black bundle from a saddlebag and began to unroll the cloth. The axe he showed was clean and bright in the sun. John said:

"You gentlemen are, I see, more shocked than I. How is the execution to be carried out? There is a suitable flat stone over there that will serve as a block." And he began to stride towards it.

The severing of John's head was accomplished in three strokes. As it rolled into the dust the lips were observed to part but none could tell if a last word was uttered or not. "I brought a bag for it," the horseman said. "If you'll be good enough to help me stow it. Lift it carefully by the hair. Yes, heavier than you'd think. I don't want to report back with my hands bloody. Good, that's right. Thank you." So he galloped back towards the palace, while the escort looked down on the headless trunk and the glisten of flies already fretful round the bloody tubes of the neck. They would have to leave the body. The ravening creatures of plain and air would see to the body. They began their slow march back, ready with lies for such of John's followers as they were likely to meet again. They had nothing to say to each other.

When, in Herod's banqueting hall, a huge covered silver dish was borne in by two servants, some said jocularly: "Ha, we start again. Too late, alas, for the vomitorium. I'm already in the digesting stage." Herodias supervised the placing of the dish was borne in by two servants, some said jocularly: "Ha, cover. Salome screamed and screamed and the king said: "Take it away, take that thing away," in a voice strangely uncompelling. "You, throw it away, take it," he ordered his butler, and the butler hurled it into one of the fires. The birthday banquet did not last much longer.

BOOK 4

ONE

ow there were certain men of Israel, and no small number either, who considered themselves followers of John but were never properly acknowledged as such by John, since they persisted in misinterpreting both his doctrine and his purpose. These men have been called Zealots because of their zeal for freeing Israel from the foreign yoke, and, for some reason, they assumed that John's cries about clearing the way for him who should come and his fervent baptismal ministrations were a gesture of defiance to the State. In so far as Herod the tetrarch was himself the Galilean State and John had inveighed against his incestuous adultery, the Zealots may be seen, in a tortuous way, as being justified in equating John's mission with a political movement, but, like all political men, they over-simplified, understanding in truth very little about human priorities and, for that matter, human nature itself.

Five of these Zealots stood among more genuine followers of the Baptist when, on the spot where he had been beheaded, what was left of his trunk was interred. Their names were Joel, Simon, Amos, Daniel and Saul and they were all stern men in trade, and, had they cared to probe, they might have found that their zeal for a free and holy Israel had something pharisaic about it. Joel growled, using prophetic words:

"His head shorn off like a rabbit's. Wrapped in a wrapping of blood scarce dry. Then given to a dancing girl as a present.

So it should be now we act, now we do it." The logic of the conclusion was somewhat subtle. Amos said:

"We seek to avenge our leader. But we lack a leader to lead us to revenge."

"Revenge," said Daniel, "makes bad politics. Nor did John ever say he was our leader. He said he was there to prepare the way for our leader."

"The assassination of Herod of Galilee," Joel growled again. "There needs no council of war. We can go to it now, while the people of Galilee and beyond have the blood of John in their nostrils. Even his own people in the palace wash themselves ten times daily. To be rid of the smell of the blood on their own skin."

"So we kill Herod the tetrarch," said Daniel, "and who goes in his place in lack of an immediate leader? I'll tell you who. Some faceless man sent by Tiberius Caesar. It will be the story of Judea all over again. A procurator, as they call them."

"Whatever you do," Simon said, "it will be a declaration of war on the whole Roman Empire."

"No," yelped Joel. "Merely on a few hundred Roman soldiers yawning away in a disregarded province. But Simon here is partly right. It's not Galilee alone or even first that has to be freed from tyranny. It's the whole of Israel. It's a matter of the whole people rising, and rising together."

"Councils of war, then," said Saul. "Arsenals. Strategies. Leadership. The great kingdom. A free Israel. The unity of a people with its chains broken. Under its Messiah."

They all made a kind of truculent obeisance to the buried body, then they started to walk away towards Melach, which was the nearest town. The morning air was cool and, after their vicarious engagement with flies and decay and dried blood, they relished its sweetness. Joel said: "You believe this other one to be the Messiah? He preaches about goodness and love and the rest of it, but he says nothing about the breaking of the chains."

"So," said Saul, "you'd have it that John the Baptist—rest, John, rest," he said suddenly in anguish, turning back to look his last at the nameless burial mound. "Though your blood cries out for revenge, may your soul rest." To his companions he continued: "You'd have it, would you, that John was mistaken?"

"Unclear, say," said Joel. "John was unclear, and rightly, too. He didn't want to expose him—the one to come, that is—expose him to Herod's foxiness and the vindictiveness of that adulterous bitch of a queen of his."

There was a pause. They walked many paces. Then Simon said: "Ask him. Go to him, somebody, and put the blunt question. Say to him: Is it you, then?"

"He'll be wary," said Saul. "And can you blame him? He has to keep his secret, if he has one, till the day the fruit's ready to drop. He'll go on being the preacher of love and goodness."

"Ask him," said Simon. "There's no harm in asking."

"You lie in peace, John," cried Saul with renewed anguish, "above the noise of the battle."

"There's no battle," said Joel. "Not yet."

Jesus was, at that moment, preaching goodness and love in tones not usually associated with those essences. In the public square of the town of Nachasch, he was seeking quiet from a knot of Pharisee sneerers with words like: "You washers and scourers neglect your ears however you scrub your hands. Do wax and dirt and hypocrisy forbid entrance to the voice of reason? Very well, very well, Little James, cease to scowl and clench your fists. Neither force nor common sense will prevail against them. But there are others here, thank God, less stiff with the law's letter and more open to its spirit. These I bid listen again. What commandment is the greatest of all the commandments? The answer is well known, even to the Pharisees here. You shall love the Lord with all your heart, and with all your soul, and with all your mind, and with all your strength. But—listen now carefully—to this we must add something new but something that follows in nature and reason, for to love the creator you must love his creation too. And so I say: you shall love your neighbour as you love yourself."

There was, among the sneerers and carpers, one young

Pharisee who was disinclined to dismiss this burly preacher as a fool. He found good sense and what the Greeks call logic in his preaching. The question he now asked was no carping question: "And who is my neighbour, then? King Herod of Galilee? Tiberius the Emperor of Rome? Those who hate us in Syria? Those we hate in Samaria?" The young man's name was Judas Iscariot.

"Well asked," Jesus smiled. "And the answer expected is this: he is my neighbour who is of my blood and kin and language and faith and custom. But the true answer I could tell you best in a story. Nay, the story may be sweeter to your honourable sournesses if told in song. You spoke of hateful Samaria. You could not have said anything better." He nodded at Philip, and, while Thaddeus played a symphony of a few measures, Philip felt for the right pitch and at length began to sing:

"There was a man of Israel,
    A brother of our faith and blood.
He bought and sold and his work went well.
    Like us, he was neither bad nor good.

"He travelled one day from Jerusalem
    To do some business in Jericho.
He fell among thieves and was stripped by them
    And beaten with many a savage blow.

"He lay at the side of the road near dead.
    A priest of the temple came riding by,
A dying man, to himself he said.
    What can I do but let him die?

"A man of the Levites rode on his way,
    Yea, one of Moses' and Aaron's race.
His horse said nothing but he said nay,
    And they cantered on at a merry pace.

"Now who should come next but a foreign man,
    A son of a race that the Jews despise,
Yes, as you guess, a Samaritan,
    But he halted and pity flooded his eyes.

"He cared for this wretch all blood and rags,
  He washed his wounds in wine and oil,
He tore white linen from his saddlebags,
  He did not scorn the surgeon's toil.

"He set him tenderly on his steed,
  Rode to a nearby inn, and then
His only care was to tend and feed
  And bring that wretch to life again.

"'Landlord, landlord, I must go away.
  Care for this poor sick man, I pray,
Whatever the cost I will gladly pay.
  I will be back in a week and a day.'

"Now who was the kindly neighbour here
  In the eyes of that robbed and wretched man—
The Levite, to the Lord most dear,
  The priest he had been taught to revere,
  Or the despised Samaritan?"

"What more need I say?" said Jesus. "I will say, less melodiously than my friend Philip, that we do not judge men by race or creed or rank, but by their inner hearts. And if their inner hearts are set against us, then we must seek to change them by the power of love. Yes, you may laugh"—though in fact only a couple of silly youths were giggling—"but I say it again and again: love your enemies. Do good to those who do evil to you. It is not easy, but we must strive to learn. And the beginning of love, remember, is forgiveness."

"So," said Judas Iscariot, "a man robs me of all I have, and I must forgive. And a man cuts the throat of my youngest son, and I must forgive. And as I too lie exposed to his dagger, I must forgive."

"You preach the doctrine eloquently," said Jesus. "But I will go further. I will ask this question: how often must I forgive? You have heard it said: up to seven times. But I say to you: unto seventy times seven. And if you do not learn to forgive from your hearts, your heavenly father shall deliver you to the tormentors and cast you into the outer darkness." He spoke with a mildness that his disciples considered inappropriate. Judas Iscariot said:

"You speak with the voice of the old law when it suits you."

Jesus smiled faintly and said: "I use language most of you understand. But those hard words mean this: he who does not love shall not be loved by our father in heaven. Is not the lack of his love the worst of torments and the blackest of nights?"

There was no visible change of heart in the greater number of the Pharisees present, but one man who had heard part of Jesus's discourse—not properly a Pharisee, not properly anything but a rather self-satisfied small man of business—spoke of Jesus himself, and approvingly, in a place where Jesus would have been glad to know he was spoken of with approval, namely a small house of ill fame in this same town of Nachasch. The man's name was Elihu, and he had been shaking his fat belly in the act of lust with a girl of Magdala called Mary. He said, as he lay in convalescence beside her:

"You have a friend in town today."

"I know of no friends," Mary said.

"The preacher Jesus has been around," Elihu said, "talking of forgiveness of sins. Fornication? somebody said. Yes, he said, forgive it. The sins of the flesh are terrible, one of these Pharisees said. The sins of the flesh are nothing, he said, compared with the sins of the soul. Don't you find that encouraging, kitten?"

"A man will always forgive a man," Mary said. "A woman's sins of the flesh are a different story."

"Oh, not with him. Adultery? he said. Nothing. Forgive it. No putting away of wives and all that nonsense, he said. Man and wife stay together. Man and wife are one flesh. They didn't like all this. They went off growling. He's always full of surprises."

"Always?" said Mary. "You've seen him often?"

"He's very hard not to see," Elihu said, now putting on his robe, "if your business takes you round the towns and villages, like mine does. He sits there in the open, eating and drinking away with thieves and rogues and, if you'll pardon the word, prostitutes and tax-collectors. And if anyone comes whining about it, he rounds on them strong and loud. The righteous, he says, have no need of him. It's the sinners he wants. So, you see, sweetheart, you ought to feel encouraged."

"Encouraged to end all this?" said Mary.

"Ah," said Elihu, "I see your meaning." He patted himself, looked around to be sure he had left nothing behind, then said: "Well, must go. The wife will be waiting up for me. Man and wife are one flesh. Hm. Not too sure that I like that."

"Does he have a wife?" said Mary.

"Him? He's put off the flesh for the sake of the kingdom of heaven. As I say, he's full of surprises. The same time same day next week?" He kissed her with a loud final smack and went off jauntily. Mary lay tired and dispirited. The Sabbath had already begun. She would obey the law of Moses and refrain from work on it, whatever the fat madam downstairs said.

In the Sabbath noontime Jesus and his disciples were walking through a cornfield. The corn was ripe, and Jesus was happy to pluck ears of corn and eat them, as the disciples were happy to follow his example. As they came through the field and found themselves on a dirt road leading to the town of Marad, they found also a pair of Pharisees, dressed up elaborately for the Sabbath, frowning at them. One of them, whose name was Ezekiel, said harshly:

"Have you lost track of the days of the week? This is the Sabbath. You pluck corn as the sinners in the time of Moses plucked the manna of the desert. He stoned them to death for profaning the Sabbath. Read the scriptures, you, all of you."

"*You* read the scriptures," responded Jesus with like rudeness. "Did you never read what David did when he was hungry? He went into the house of God and ate the holy bread on the altar, which it was lawful only for the priests to eat. Yet God did not strike him down. Remember this, you snakes: the

Sabbath was made for man, not man for the Sabbath." And so he passed, bowing ironically, on, and his disciples followed, some of them unable to resist making faces of triumph at the silenced Pharisees. Thomas said:

"Answer that, then, ye flibbertigibbets. Ye can't, can ye, eh?"

Ezekiel looked very sourly at the group which, he knew, was making for the synagogue, and he said: "This is where he will fall down. Blasphemy. If ever he gets to Jerusalem they'll eat him alive."

"He's going to Jerusalem?"

"There's talk of it. Of course, we could do for him here. Have him stoned as a blasphemer. It's been done before."

"There's never enough witnesses. Those men of his will perjure their souls black. Wait. How about Nathan?"

"What about Nathan?"

"Nathan. Nathan." And he made a mime of being bent double with deformity.

"Ah, Nathan. I think I see what you might be driving at."

Now Mary the Magdalene girl had walked to Marad, hearing that Jesus would be preaching in the synagogue. She went into the women's gallery veiled. She listened with close attention to the words of Jesus, who said, among other things:

"Judge not, that ye be not judged. For with the kind of judgment you judge with you yourselves shall be judged. With whatever measure you deal out, with that same measure shall it be dealt out to you. Measure for measure. Some of you are quick to see a speck of sawdust in the eye of your neighbour, but you miss entirely the big plank in your own."

Judas Iscariot was there. He grinned appreciatively.

"Let such hypocrites deal first with that great hunk of wood, then they'll be able to see well enough to pull out the speck of sawdust. And now I say this to you: ask, and it shall be given you. Seek, and you'll surely find. Knock, and the door will be opened. And if you say *when will this be so?* I answer: *now*."

At this moment, well judged, the deformed Nathan was pushed forward by the sly Pharisees of the cornfield, and Nathan, very quick, cried:

"Now, master, I ask now."

Everyone stirred to look at him, standing in the middle of the congregation. His deformities were manifold. His back was bent double, his right leg was fixed at an angle which made walking almost impossible, one arm was thrust permanently out in a Roman salute, his nose was covered in great warts, on his left cheek was a sickening wen. Jesus looked on him without too much pity, since the man had not learnt compensatory virtues for his deformities: the eyes were sly and the voice had a whine in it. Jesus said:

"This, as I have been reminded, is the Sabbath day, when no man may work. When the physician locks up his physic, and the healer's art is forced to wait till the working week begins again. But I ask you this: is it lawful on the Sabbath day to do good, or is it not lawful? I see that none of you Pharisees deigns to answer. Listen, then. Suppose one of you here has an ass or an ox that falls into a well on the Sabbath. What will you do—leave the beast to drown? No, there is not one among you who would not hasten to draw him out, even though it be the Sabbath day. How much more valuable than the life of a beast is the life of a man. If you will not let a beast suffer, nor shall you let a man suffer. And so to you there I say: stand straight in the presence of God and of man. Be clean, be whole." And the deformed man Nathan found his limbs mobile and supple, his trunk straightening, the wen on his face dissolving, even the warts vanishing. He was not, as Jesus knew, wholly happy about this, since he had become accustomed to self-pity. The Pharisees looked black and baffled. Jesus yelled at them, a huge man with a huge voice:

"I see you there, you vipers. You are already wondering how best to encompass my destruction. You hear the word, but you cling to the letter. Because John the Baptist came neither eating nor drinking, you said he had a devil inside him. Because I came eating and drinking, you said: behold—a glutton and a wine-bibber. You have seen God's work, and you whine about washing before meals and keeping the Sabbath. What are you, any of you, but whited sepulchres—fair and clean without, but within full of dirt and dust and dead men's bones? Serpents, offspring of vipers, how shall you escape the judgment of hell? God sends prophets to you, and these you are ready to scourge in your synagogues, to kill and crucify without the city's walls. You were happy when the head of John the Baptist was shorn off like the head of a rabbit. Upon you comes all the righteous blood shed on earth, from the blood of Abel, whom Cain slew, even unto the son of Zachariah—"

And then Jesus strode out of the synagogue, his disciples behind him, and all stood waiting, about four or five yards before the entrance of the synagogue, all ready for open-air anger, shouting, stones. When the first stone came, Little James was quick to hurl one back. Unfortunately, or not so, it struck the newly healed Nathan in the chest, giving him cause to whine again. Jesus said:

"Don't trouble to fight them. The judgment will come in its own time. The wheat and the weeds will be separated out in the time of the harvest."

Ezekiel the Pharisee heard this very clearly. He cried: "And is it only we who obey the law who are to be thrown into the fire? Are the thieves and prostitutes to be gathered in with the wheat?"

He pointed at the prostitute Mary, whom he seemed to know better than so upright and God-fearing a Pharisee ought to, and another man, grinning, pulled the girl's veil off.

"Like her?" called Ezekiel. "Like this filth here?"

Mary was bewildered and fearful. Those hostile to Jesus but too wary now to attack him were happy to find in the poor girl an easier target. The women were as bad as the men, if not worse. But, at a nod from Jesus, Philip and Thaddeus went over to Mary and brought her to the safety of Jesus's huge shadow. Jesus said loudly to her, for the crowd's benefit:

"Have no fear, daughter. For the sins of the body are quickly purged. But the fire is a strong one that will burn out the sin in the soul."

And then he turned his back on the mob and its stones and marched off, Mary clinging to him, the others following (not too sure, especially Thomas, about the propriety of having a whore in their company: "Shot our bolt now, properly, no going back now, one with the riff-raff now"), the two Jameses forming a pugnacious rearguard. Simon agreed with Thomas about there being no going back now. No more respectability. A fiery dangerous lot, just like the Zealots. That's what they were.

They camped that evening by a small stream, and Mary the Magdalene wished to camp with them. Jesus talked to her very kindly. When Andrew passed near them, gathering wood for the cooking-fire, he heard Jesus saying:

"So you see, daughter, it's not enough to weep because the Pharisees spit in your path—"

"They're ready enough to come to me in the darkness," she said, "with their money and the word *love* on their lips."

"What the voices of prejudice and hypocrisy say, and even the eyes of jealousy —for you are, to be poetical, one of the fairer daughters of Eve—such, I say, are of no account. But, if you must weep, you must weep because you sell what is sacred. It's as if the vessels of the holy temple were filled with offal for the dogs to eat. God smiles on the embraces of love, though he turns his eyes decently away, since not even our heavenly father may intrude upon lovers—but he weeps when the embraces are turned into a mockery. And now you may weep too."

She did not weep, not for the moment. Instead she said: "They say you know nothing of the embraces of women."

"Well," he smiled, "they say wrong. But as for now—what wife would stand for this life of wandering and preaching?"

"I can speak of one," she said boldly, "who would find it no hardship. And all your men are ragged and eat fish they think is

TWO

cooked when it is really still raw. And even your garments are dirty and need stitching."

"God bless you, daughter," said Jesus, "but you know it cannot be. What would the world say? We know the world is foolish, but we must abide some of its foolishness that the seed of the kingdom may be sown."

"I may not follow you?"

"You may take the same road. But you may not travel with us. My men are but men, after all. And every day they pray," he smiled, "that they be not led into temptation."

Temptation. Judas Iscariot heard that word, approaching, then saw the two talking. He hesitated to show himself. He waited behind a tree, listening.

"And is the money too defiled money," asked the girl, "the money I've saved?"

"Money is neither clean nor defiled," Jesus said, "Gold and silver have no conscience. If you wish to give it to the poor, don't hesitate."

"I did not think of giving it to the poor. I had in mind another—" She saw a flash of white garments behind a tree and cried in distress: "Some one has been listening." And when Judas Iscariot apologetically appeared, she shouted: "This is one of the Pharisees, one of those who curse me in the sun—"

"And bless you in the dark," said Judas Iscariot. "You needn't say it. I don't think you have to call me a Pharisee any more."

"Go now, daughter," Jesus said. "We'll meet soon." She kissed his hands and left, giving Iscariot a baleful look. Jesus said to him: "I'm not hearing your voice for the first time, am I?"

"May I sit?" He sat, a clean-looking sinewy man of about thirty, with keen eyes and the voice of a Jerusalem education. "The voice you are hearing now," he said, "you are certainly hearing for the first time. I am not here now to ask questions. All my life I've been what you termed me and the rest of my hypocritical brethren—a whited sepulchre (a good phrase, if I may say so), a washer of hands before eating—"

"There is nothing wrong with that," said Jesus. "Don't give up that custom for my sake, but remember that God is not especially impressed by water and towels."

"I use the term figuratively, and you know I do, I think. Tease me by all means. I mean an observer of outward forms, a scourer of the pot, a man loud with formal prayers in the synagogue but indifferent to the meaning of word and gesture. I ask you now to believe that I am—no longer satisfied with myself. Will you believe that?"

"Yes. But beware of being satisfied with yourself for no longer being satisfied with yourself. What's your trade, my son?"

"Call me a scholar the State finds useful. I read and write Hebrew, Greek, Latin. I translate documents. This has become a country of many tongues. I have, you see, the hands of a lady. I have never carved wood nor caught fish—tasks your men have done, for I know about your men. My father was a prosperous builder who said: my son must never have callouses on his hands nor brick-dust in his hair. My money, he said, must go to making him a scholar. So—behold the scholar. May a scholar serve you? But first—I must be washed free of the past—forgiven—"

"It is not for me to forgive," Jesus said. "Ask forgiveness of your father in heaven. Though I may ask: forgiveness of what?"

"I wish to be clean. Wholly clean." And he moved his shoulders with distaste, as though foul clothes had been forced upon him.

"If you mean clean of past hypocrisy, past lack of charity, past sins of the flesh or the spirit—then, if you're truly sorry, you may say that forgiveness has been granted. The future must take care of itself."

"There is the sense of a past before my own past—of my being part of a general dirtiness—"

"You mean Adam's sin, you mean you feel yourself to be born into sin because you were born into humanity. All men must carry the guilt of that, but the guilt may be tempered by the justice and love of a man's own life."

"But, being human, being born sinful, I feel guilty about the future too."

"You're too scrupulous," said Jesus, shaking his head. "You seem to be carrying a burden for all the unregenerate Pharisees. See, over there supper seems to be ready. The bread of charity and fish caught by— You must come and eat and make yourself known to your new brothers."

THREE

Some of the Zealots, made bold by the death of John the Baptist, struck out at the Galilean State, in the persons of odd harmless officials, poor soldiers, a scullion of the royal scullery. The cries of the Zealots on arrest always added up to the same thing: "Down with tyranny, down with oppression, murder the murderers of the messenger of liberty. Herod is a tyrant and a lackey of Rome. Arise, O Israel." The maturer Zealots did not approve. At a meeting in the house of Joel, Joel said:

"Who ordered that foolishness?" He referred to a recent bungling attempt at poisoning the wine supply of the lower servants of the royal palace.

"Nobody orders," said Saul, "since there is nobody to give orders. All we have are spontaneous demonstrations, daggers in the dark, so to speak."

"Daggers mostly in the light," said Joel. "Foolish men dragged off to jail in sunlight, shouting their foolishness to the world."

"Terrorism," said Simon, tasting the word. "Slow attrition." He made a sour mouth. "Yes, it all adds up to foolishness."

"So," said Joel, "we go straight to him and *ask*."

"Always my counsel. As you know," said Simon.

"If we can fight our way through the crowds," said Saul.

"Crowds, yes," said Amos. "He's no lonely voice crying in the wilderness. He unites the crowds, he works spells on them."

"Miracles too," said Daniel. "The miracles draw the crowds. Egyptian tricks really. He was in Egypt, as we know. The miracles will be a great help."

"I'll believe in the miracles when I see them," said Joel. "We don't require miracles anyway. We require hard work, leadership, control at the centre. We can't wait for ever. Amos, you go to him. You too, Simon."

"But where is he?" asked Simon.

"Pretty well everywhere," Joel said. "Where you see a crowd, there you will find him. The time is come, then. *Ask him.*"

There was a great crowd assembling to hear Jesus in the vale or bowl called Nekev, from which gentle hillocks rose all around. He was to speak from the slope of the hill named Schen or Sin, because of its resemblance to a tooth. The number of the crowd has been variously computed: some say it was a thousand strong, others as many as ten. One thing is certain, and that is that there was never too great a crowd for Jesus, whose immense voice, fed by the huge jars of air that were his immense lungs, could, it was said, have addressed the entire nation without strain and with complete audibility at the remotest corners. Even the deaf heard. While he was mounting the hill Schen or Sin, he was followed by many suppliants, all of whom were thrust away by his disciples, though Jesus himself could, had he wished, have sent them all off with some immense rebuke from his immense voice. But he suffered the buzzing of the horse-flies, as Thomas called them, and sometimes he would stop, lend an ear, his eyes humorous or compassionate, and give blunt counsel or deliver a curse or a blessing. It happened that, ascending to the middle of the slope of Schen or Sin, he was much struck by a young man, rather richly dressed, who was fighting against Little James's restraining muscles and calling: "Master, master, a word."

"You," said Jesus, "are not of our people. You do not speak like a man of Palestine. Where are you from, my son?"

"I'm a Greek," the young man said, "the son of a Greek merchant."

Jesus smiled at his disciples. "So you see, my children, the word spreads now among the Gentiles. What word do you wish from me, my son?"

"Master," said the young man, "what must I do to be of the kingdom?"

Jesus said promptly, with a hint of the weariness of the rote: "You must love the Lord your God with all your mind, heart, strength. You must love your neighbour as you love yourself."

"All this I try to do," said the young man. "But what more must I do?"

"You must sell all you have," said Jesus. "Land, houses, horses, gold and silver ornaments, gorgeous raiment. And then you must give the money to the poor."

The raiment of the young man glittered in the afternoon sun. He looked very doubtful. He said: "It is easy to say that, very easy to say. But— You cannot understand the— It is all too easy for a poor man to say things like that, it is—"

"My son," said Jesus firmly. "As you are Greek, I will say something to you in your own language. Listen." And he said: "Eukopoteron estin kam?lon dia trupematos rhaphidos eiselthein i plousion eis tin basileian tou Theou."

The young man looked as though he had been violently struck in the face. All the disciples except Judas Iscariot looked puzzled. Simon said: "We don't understand these foreign tongues. What did you say, master?"

"Tell him, my son," said Jesus to Judas Iscariot. "Tell them all."

So Judas Iscariot translated as best he could. "It is easier for a—I could not tell whether the word you used was *kamilon* or *kamiilon,* master. It is easier for a rope—or was it a camel?"

Jesus merely smiled and shrugged his great shoulders.

"Easier for whatever it is to pass through the eye of a needle than for a rich man to get to the kingdom of God."

And so they went up, Matthew unabashedly shaking his moneybag at the rich young man, whose tears now glittered more than his raiment, with "Spare a penny or two, my lord. For the poor." The young man did not seem to hear. There was a clump of young date-trees on the hillside, and in its shade three women were waiting. One was Mary the Magdalene, the others were prim unmarried ladies named, so Mary said, introducing them, Rachel and Eliseba. They had a gift for Jesus—a garment, evidently costly, priestly. Rachel said:

"Sir, we've done this for you. We feared you might already have gone to Jerusalem before it was finished—"

"Who told you I was going to Jerusalem?" said Jesus, not unkindly.

"It must be so," Eliseba said. "You must bring all Jerusalem to the glory of the kingdom. And this is the proper garment for you. See, it is without seams."

"That," said Thomas, looking at it closely, "is what they call a seamless garment. Worth a pretty penny they are, when you can buy them. A deal of work in it, ladies, I'll say that."

"Yes," said Eliseba. "For preaching the kingdom in."

"The priest," said Jesus, "is not the vestment. Still, I thank you for your love and your kindness. It must have been a costly business. The fineness of it." And he felt it gently with his fingertips.

"We were put to the doing of it—" Rachel began, and then Mary the Magdalene gave her a hard and warning look. "Glad of the money," Rachel mumbled. "We're poor women, sir."

Everybody looked at everybody. A priestly garment made out of prostitute's money, well. The end of respectability, they had already reached that. Now blasphemy or something was creeping into things. Ah well, it was to be expected, had to be. Simon said:

"There's a great multitude down there, master. Best look your best for them. See, your present garment's hardly decent, a great rent, see, and near there too, embarrassing if it tore more. Get behind that tree there and put this one on." Jesus good-humouredly gave in and soon stood before them the very model of respectability. "A bit too clean perhaps," Simon said. "A couple of days should put that to rights. A bit small at the shoulders. Still."

Before addressing the crowd Jesus had a word with his disciples, a word they did not well understand. "God's holy numbers," he said. "What are the great sacred numbers? Some say three, some say seven, some say ten. None ever says eight. And yet eight is woven into God's creation more deeply than men can yet know. In the miracle of the creation of the waters of the earth, two spirits of the air conjoined and became a new being, and they are caught forever in a dance of eight—" They all looked at him in devoted incomprehension, even Judas Iscariot and John the scholars. "Never mind," Jesus sighed. "You may forget that. But it is the number eight that is to come into my discourse, such as it is." And he went to preach to the multitude.

At the first ring of his great voice, Amos and Simon, whom we must call, for clarity's sake, Simon the Zealot, nodded at each other with approval. Here was strength, here was authority. Jesus said:

"I wish to speak to you of those who are blessed, that is to say—those who are of the kingdom. The blessed, like some great army, are made up of eight brigades or battalions or companies. *Company* is the best word, since it smacks of companionship. Blessed, then, are the poor in spirit—theirs is the kingdom. Blessed are they that mourn, for they shall be comforted. Blessed are the meek, for they shall inherit the earth. Blessed are they who hunger and thirst after justice, for they shall have their fill. Blessed are the merciful, for they shall obtain mercy. Blessed are the pure in heart, for they shall see God. Blessed are the peacemakers, for they shall be called the children of God. Blessed are they who, being righteous, are persecuted because they are righteous—theirs too is the kingdom. Blessed are you, all of you, any of you, when great and powerful men shall revile you, and persecute you, and say all kinds of evil about you and against you—falsely, falsely, for if you are of the kingdom the evil words must of need be false. Rejoice, be glad. The prophets before you were so persecuted and traduced and reviled—"

There was a great murmur running round the bowl or vale called Nekev, and the Zealots present nodded grimly at each other. They all believed that Jesus spoke of one prophet and one only and him most recently persecuted, traduced, reviled, killed. "And killed," called some. "Remember that—killed. His head shorn off like a rabbit's."

"Rejoice, I say again," cried Jesus. "Great is your reward in the kingdom." He spoke more, but not too much, for there is always a limit to what the uninstructed ear can absorb, but not once did the immense voice flag or the command of words grow weak, and, while he spoke of the reward that must come to the patient and unaggressive, none could say that he was making virtue out of his own weakness, for never had so powerful a voice hurled among those hills, never so powerful a body raised arms that were both muscular and loving. Here was a man who could eat whole sheep and wrestle with lions, a very Samson with none of Samson's stupidity, and he spoke of meekness and love. He said at one point: "I do not expect love to gush unbidden from your heart to enfold them that are, in truth, most unloveable. I call love rather a craft a man or woman must learn as I, in my youth, learned the craft of carpentry. Love is the tool, we may say, that shapes the hard rough dull knotty splintery wood of the hearts of our enemies into the smoothness of friendship. Anger feeds anger always. If a man is angry and he strikes you in his anger, do not strike him in return. Turn the other cheek, baffle him. He will learn from you what to do when he himself is assailed and struck. So we spread love and extend the kingdom." He told stories, he spoke parables, he delivered tough enigmas, he was harsh, he was smooth. At the end of his discourse his disciples made a circle about him, that he might be protected from those who would have torn his seamless garment off him out of love. The Zealots were not among the criers and clutchers and adorers. They waited.

The Zealots Simon and Amos waited a whole day. They were zealous to know where Jesus and his followers made their camp and they discovered it was in a bosky clearing near the small river Bimhirut, not far from the village called by everyone Meluchlach, though that was not its true name. Simon and Amos came at nightfall, when the company was eating its fish and bread and olives. Simon said:

"We are called Zealots. You will know the word. You will also know what we are trying to do."

"Must do," Amos added.

"Yes," said Jesus. He picked a fish-spine clean, wiped his fingers on his costly seamless garment, and then said: "You are zealous in seeking to end the enslavement of the people, to rid all Israel of corrupt rulers, to expel the stranger, to build again a strong free land under the dominion of the king of heaven."

"You put it well," said Simon the Zealot, "as we expected you to. Except that you should say: under the dominion of the Messiah. Now here comes our question: are you the Messiah?"

"I preach a kingdom," Jesus said, "but I know it is not the kingdom you and your fellows seek. For you would overcome and overthrow in swift strokes of the axe. You wish for the autumn now which shall also be the spring. But it is not given to men to speed the pattern of the sowing and reaping."

"You don't," said Amos, "make yourself clear." Simon the Zealot said:

"He makes himself all too clear, I'd say. But, sir, you're mistaken if you think we mean that the forces of Israel should strike for justice now, at once, at this moment. We know there has to be a time of preparation."

"Listen to me," said Jesus. "If I ascend the throne of Israel, I do so after slaying my enemies. Yes?" The two Zealots nodded with vigour. "But I teach that we must love our enemies. I cannot love and kill at the same time. You may say—very well, overcome your enemies with love. But, from your faces, I would not think you inclined ever to say that—"

"We had taken it," said Simon the Zealot, "that you did not mean all this business about loving very literally."

"Oh, very literally," said Jesus. "Most literally. And I say another disappointing thing to you—that the overcoming of an enemy through love is as slow a business as the growing of a tree from a seed. More of that later, perhaps, if you will listen. Let us talk about earthly rule for the moment. Earthly rule is but earthly rule, and who shall rule in the earthly dispensation is the smallest of man's concerns. You slay the tyrant, and you put a good man in his place, but the good man is very likely himself to turn into a tyrant. It is in the nature of earthly power for this to happen. It is not through change in the governing of men that men themselves are changed. For the change must come from within."

"Men do not change," said Simon the Zealot stoutly. "Men are men and camels are camels and dogs are dogs. And if camels and dogs may be slaves to men, men must not be slaves to each other. Men must be free."

"Yes," said Jesus. "Free. But free of the inner tyrants—lust, hate, self-seeking. Men do change. Men must change. It is the free kingdom within that I teach, whose name is the kingdom of heaven. Let me go back to my similitude of the seed and the tree. Take a seed, a grain of mustard, say, that being the smallest of all the seeds. Plant it. The time will come when it shall grow into a tree, and the birds of the air shall dwell in its branches. That seed is my word, which I scatter. Often enough the birds will eat it, or the stony ground will fail to nourish it. But here and there it will take root and grow. But the growing is not done overnight."

Simon, not the Zealot, Jesus's Simon, said, in some distress: "Look, master, you mean this? For my part, I hadn't thought—I mean, it seemed to me—that is, we were led to believe— Well, it's a very long time to wait between the time of the seed and the tree. Sometimes it's a man's whole life."

"So you too, Simon," said Jesus, "dream of the spring and the harvest as one thing. Did I ever speak of an earthly kingdom?"

"You spoke of a kingdom, though," said this Simon, "and a kingdom has to have a king. I'm a simple man, I know, and I may have heard wrong and misunderstood, but I thought we were moving on with the new teaching to fill all Israel with it, and establish—what was it, Andrew?"

"The kingdom of the righteous," said Andrew.

Little James said: "My old master John spoke against the

sins of Herod of Galilee. For this Herod imprisoned him and slew him. But we went on believing in the kingdom of righteousness that was going to take the place of Herod's kingdom and the kingdom of Caesar, empire I should say. It was to you he sent us."

"Sent you to me," said Jesus, "to build an army of seekers after righteousness—an army to hammer at the gates of kingly corruption and shout: Away—we will crown righteousness and put righteousness on your throne? Was that it?"

"Something like that," said Bartholomew slowly and diffidently. "We certainly understood that the baptising and the preaching and the, well, the urgency were directed to—well, I would not speak of hammering and shouting exactly—"

"Listen," said Jesus fiercely, "you deaf ones, deafer even than the Pharisees. First we must learn righteousness in ourselves, along with forbearance and love. And the learning is very slow, as the growth of the seed is very slow. You, Philip, who dream when you're not singing songs—what do you dream of?"

"I dream," said Philip. "I dream—well, of what the old law taught us to dream—the Messiah burning out evil, as the fire burns the forest, and then the establishing of the kingdom."

"Heaven's king in Jerusalem," said Jesus, "and the swords and breastplates of Israel flashing in the sun. No, children. A false false dream."

"It was written," said Amos, "that the government shall be upon his shoulders. But it was not *your* shoulders that were meant, big and strong though they seem to be. I must go back with the bad news."

"Amos is your name, isn't it?" said Jesus. "Well, go back rather with the *good* news, Amos. News of the kingdom of heaven." Jesus saw woebegone faces around him. First he laughed and then, with utmost earnestness, said: "Understand what I say. I am here to begin the spreading of the word of the kingdom. Begin, I say, begin. Who knows when the kingdom will be fulfilled? If I said ten thousand years for the making of the tree, I might well be falling woefully short of the truth. But, in the eye of God, ten thousand years is nothing. He can wait, and I can wait with him, for the fulfilment. Now, as for this life of ours, this mission, it will take us to Jerusalem soon, the place where the throne of rule is occupied by the usurper and the rulers of men's souls teach a Pharisee perversion of God's truth. In Jerusalem, make no mistake of this, some will listen to our word but many will not, and if there is to be a triumph it will have nothing to do with eagles and trumpets. In Jerusalem there will be suffering, humiliation, disaster. Make no mistake of it. Know the worst now." None would look him in the eye, except John and Judas Iscariot. "No, you cannot know the worst now. You are all too innocent to conceive of what the worst can be."

Amos was the first to say something, and all he could find to say was a disappointed "Yes, yes, yes." And then: "Are you coming, Simon?"

Simon, Jesus's Simon, Simon the fisherman, said: "Why me? Why should I? Oh yes, there's this other Simon." The other Simon said:

"One of us is enough to bear the message. I'll follow. I've much on my mind."

"So have I," said Amos, getting up, apparently in pain, from the ground. "All bitter, very bitter." And he made a vague obeisance to Jesus, then he left, walking alone, head bent, under the half-moon.

"Well," Jesus said almost cheerfully, "you see there is a road there, with the moon obligingly lighting it, and it leads to a world of sanity and safety. Go back to your trades, start building families, dream of the coming man who will knock the kings off their thrones and stab Tiberius Caesar in his bath. Go on. Man must be free, said the other Simon."

"I am not *the other Simon*," said the other Simon. "I am Simon."

"Man is indeed free," said Jesus, "for so God made him. Free to take whatever road he will."

Thomas said: "I always had my doubts, and ye all know that—I never minced matters. Doubts, aye, of the whole venture being worthwhile. Oh, it has been an education to me, that I will say without grudge. But, as I see it and as I've said often enough, a man has a right to see—well, a kind of fulfilment in his own lifetime ye could call it. It was never my intention to sit by a tree and watch it grow. I've other things to do."

"Well said, Thomas," said Jesus. "But I promise you that you will see a kind of fulfilment. The men of politics will hate me now as much as the men of the synagogue hate me. Love is a dangerous word, you see. At first, and for a long time, it provokes hatred. This hatred will surely bear fruit. There will be much of interest to see if you stay with me. But you are not bound to stay."

"I mean," said Simon, not the Zealot, "you've thousands of followers, thousands. I keep on puzzling it over. Is all this to be wasted?"

Thaddeus, who usually spoke little, now spoke most uncharacteristically. "We could march into Jerusalem—thousands, as he says—and force them to accept the kingdom of righteousness."

"Force them to accept righteousness," said Jesus. "I must remember that, Thaddeus. Perhaps now you would play us a little tune on your flute."

Thaddeus had his flute on his lap. He put it inside his robe. He looked at Philip, but Philip was looking into the fire. The fire would die soon unless somebody put wood on it. Nobody put wood on it. Bartholomew rubbed his stomach, wincing softly. Matthew took a deep breath, then began to swing his moneybag. He said:

"There's a little in here—a few bits of silver. I give this back to you, then."

"I stay," said Judas Iscariot. "I will be the treasurer of those who stay with me. With him, that is."

"Matthew," said Jesus. "The prodigal son." Matthew looked very unhappy. Simon the Zealot looked at them all and cried:

"By the living God of Israel, I would not have such men as you in my party. How is any kingdom to be built by men who are so quick to be disappointed? How is any party to be maintained by men so ready to desert their leader?"

"We're not deserting him," said the other Simon. "We're just—"

"Getting ready to desert him, yes. You're Simon, are you? You make me ashamed to share the name with you. Let me say this—I've met leaders before, many—roaring out big empty words, belching forth big empty promises. I've never yet met a leader whose trade was honesty—not before now. Choose me as your leader, they all yell, and the tree of justice will grow overnight. He talks of the planting of the seed and the slow growth of the seed. Who are we to talk of the planting of justice in the world when we have no justice in ourselves? He speaks sense, he speaks God's truth. If you won't follow him, then I will."

"My other name," said the other Simon, "is Peter. You're welcome to be Simon. I'll be Peter. My father sometimes called me that, poor man." Then he began to weep like a child.

"Good," said Jesus. "I think it's over."

"I'll have the bag back," said Matthew. "I don't quite know what came over me."

"No," said Judas Iscariot. "I'm the treasurer." And then: "If you'll permit me to be, that is."

"Well, perhaps it might be better if—I don't really like handling money. Good, you're treasurer."

"I'm sorry, sorry, sorry," howled Simon who was now Simon Peter. Simon the Zealot said:

"All right, you're sorry. Look, if you've a bit of cold fish and a hunk of bread left over I wouldn't say no. Not eaten since daybreak."

"Aye," Thomas said. "When I said what I said just then, ye understand, about having other things to do, I meant I was impatient to be working myself at the promoting of this love and so forth. Twelve of us now, to my counting, and it's time to start thinking, correct my supposition if I'm supposing wrong as I sometimes do, what was I saying, yes, to be on the road ourselves, in twos or ones, spreading the message. I mean, we've stood too long behind ye, master, like flower-pots, letting you do the spouting, if ye'll forgive the word. It's time we did some work and stopped standing there watching the tree grow, so to speak, that's all I meant."

"You're a liar, Thomas," growled Little James. "Trying to get out of it, that's what you are. See right through you, I can, we all can."

"Who're ye calling a liar? Big as ye are, I could eat two like ye at a breakfast."

"A bit of cold fish," said Simon the Zealot, "if you can spare it."

Jesus said: "Liar or not, Thomas speaks for me. It's time you went around Galilee and even beyond, telling the good news." He grinned at Simon, who was now eating fish. "Go in fours, then turn the fours to twos, then the two to ones. Learn to be alone, but not too quickly. Start tomorrow—why not?" And he told them what they must do and what not do. He said:

"Don't speak much of miracles, healings, giving sight to the blind. For miracles join all the acts of man's history in becoming matter for doubt to those who have not witnessed them. But the truth that is spoken remains truth for all eternity."

Simon Peter said, mumbling, his eyes down: "I think we must all know what's in your mind, master. That we will all go briskly enough, and that some of us will not come back. But we will come back."

"If and when you come back," said Jesus, "you will know where to find me. I must do my own teaching and I myself must hold back the importunate. You will know where I am." Then he said: "If love has power to sustain you and then to draw you home to me—you must know that you have that love. We must sleep soon, so I will say little more. Teach simply, for they will be simple people. Tell the parables I taught you. Above all, let them learn love by example."

Excitement and fear kept most of them awake, listening to the owls. Simon, formerly Simon the Zealot, dropped off at once, snoring like a woodsaw.

It is not necessary to show you all the disciples at work, but I will give brief glimples to show that they did well. Thus, Peter, as we had better now call him, preached in the town of Matateh in this wise:

"The way I see it is this: it's not just a matter of the Jews and the Romans. Or the Syrians or the Samaritans or the blue-arsed barbarians out there in Britain, wherever that is. It's a matter of human beings. Now you don't put things right in this country or that country until you've put things right inside yourself, in here, here, do you get that? Do you see that now? You've got to stop hating, for one thing. It's no good hating the Romans or your mother-in-law or your wife's second cousin once removed. You've got to learn how to tolerate. You've got to learn how to love."

A loud man shouted from among the small knot that listened near the fish-market: "Love the bastard that swipes you across the chops or helps himself grinning to your hard-earned wages? Oh yes, very good, and how about justice, man? No justice in the world any more, is that what you're after?"

"Listen," said Peter. "I'll tell you a story. There was this man, see, that sowed his field full of wheat. Then one day one of his enemies comes along—he was an enemy because he owed money to this man with the field and he couldn't pay it—comes along and sows this field with weeds—you know, docks, darnels and so on. Well, this

FOUR

other man's servant comes along and says: What do we do? The field's a right mess with all these weeds in it and we'd best do something. But his master says: Don't worry. Wait till harvest-time, and then you'll be able to tell the wheat from the other stuff. You can gather the wheat and shove it in the barn, and the other stuff you can burn. Just a matter of waiting, that's all. You see the meaning of this story? There's going to be a special day for justice, and you may have to wait a long time for it. But it's going to happen all right, and nobody's going to fail to get either his reward or his punishment. The Day of Judgment, that's going to be called. Who is any man to think he can dole out justice? How far do you trust these bastards that call themselves judges? How far do you trust yourself? Leave justice to God, who's the only one who knows all about it. He won't let any of the unjust swine get away, and those who are just will get a reward. You get on with loving and leave justice to God."

Bartholomew, having the healing gift, gained a fair following in Tapuach, Tachrim, Tamar, Schum and Eschkolit. In the last-named town, for instance, an epileptic started to writhe on the ground during his discourse, and he was quick to say:

"Put a bit of wood between his teeth. That stops him biting his tongue. That's right. Now just wait. Get better, get better soon. He will, you'll see." And he did. Then Bartholomew said: "How easily we see the diseases of the body—the sores, the boils, the limping, the writhing. But the diseases inside are not so easy to see—what we may call the ailments of the soul. Still, they exist, and there's only one medicine for them all. Its name is love. Laugh if you will. I have had so much experience of human diseases that potions and salves will not touch, that I respond now very wearily to such derision. I know, and the laughers do not know—it's as simple as that. Love, love. Not an easy medicine to mix, but we have to try. Loving your enemies, for instance, which we must all learn to do—how do we do it? Well, imagine your left hand is twisted and sore with cuts and boils and throbbing with pain. You hate it. *You hate it.*

But do you truly hate it? Of course not, how can you? It's you, it's part of yourself. You wish it to be cured, you wish it not to hurt you any more, but you don't wish it to be cut off. Now all mankind is one great body, and your enemy—who hurts you, who tortures you, who drenches you with hate—is part of it as you are part of it. He's of your flesh and blood and mind. He inflicts pain, but how can you hate him? He is *you*."

Judas Iscariot did not do well as a teacher. He was a man of learning and, try as he would to hide it, his erudition showed through in subtleties, qualifications, hard words. He was, however, appreciated by a certain body of men in the town of Moach, men distinguished, philosophical, concerned with the future of Israel, no lovers of foreign rule but no Zealots either. Judas Iscariot was invited to the house of Jehoash, a bookish man who had a large inherited estate which ran itself, and there met other gentlemen of his kind—Jehoram, who imported wine from Greece and Italy, and Ahaziah, a builder who had known Judas's own father. Over good wine served in fine vessels, Judas Iscariot was saying, as the sun went down over the hills and the crickets cheeped:

"He is the one. I have no doubt at all in my mind about it. I have seen and heard the evidence."

"Miracles?" said Ahaziah, stroking his piebald beard.

"They're a part of it. But it is more than miracles. As he says, miracles are no foundation for a faith which shall be sempiternal, since they belong to history and can be distorted by the historians. Cure a man of a fever, and your enthusiastic chronicler will convert that into a resurrection from the grave. Ideas, doctrines—in those the strength lies or does not lie. More than miracles. Authority, serenity, patience. Intelligence, of a very high order. But the true evidence is this—that he was born to rule and yet rejects the rule."

"You mean," said lean-limbed sharp-eyed almost beardless Jehoash, "the rule as the Zealots see it. The bloody leader storming into the palace, I mean, with the scriptures on his lips."

"That, yes," said Judas. "The Zealots are foolish enough to believe they can defy an empire."

"I'd rather say," said Jehoram, in his drawling but not unpleasant north Galilean voice, "that they don't know an empire exists. To them it's a matter of slaying a paid official or two and a few hundred mercenaries."

"Well, we know better," said Judas Iscariot. "When the power of Rome breaks, it won't be Israel that does the breaking. The collapse will come from within. That, though, is a long way off. Meanwhile we have to accept the fact of Rome and its empire but remain untouched and uncorrupted. We need a king in Judea who shall also be a king in all Israel. He is the man."

"But he rejects the rule, you say," said Jehoash.

"I've heard him reject it," said Judas, "as offered by the Zealots. But he will not reject it when it is offered by the supreme holy council of Israel. And soon, when they have a better knowledge of his doctrine—"

"And of his miracles?" said Ahaziah.

"Those too, they will be able to say to Rome: leave us alone as you left us alone in the time of the accursed Herod. For we have a king of impeccable credentials, a son of David's house. He is also a king who teaches love, who knows not the word *enemy*, who has no bitterness towards Caesar. And, in due time, the Romans will be glad to withdraw their legions."

"And their tax-collectors?" wryly smiled Jehoram.

"The Romans," said Ahaziah, shaking his head sadly, "need garrisons in Israel. The eastern flank of their empire."

"I have read things out of Rome," said Judas Iscariot. "The Romans fear the north more than the east. Things are changing. A state built on love and tolerance—that they will call a pacified state. They may keep their troops in Syria. Israel, or Palestine as they call it, will be no thorn in their side. Israel will abide the breaking of an empire built on a false premise, Israel will survive. How can it fail? The point of Jesus's teaching can be expressed as the unity of Israel under the New Law, which does not supersede the Old Law but fulfils it—at the same time wiping out its crudities, its taboos, its fears of women, its nonsense about the Sabbath—"

"You've told everybody who would listen," said Ahaziah, "that you used to be a Pharisee. That you were one is clear from your speech. You loathe what you used to be with what one might term an exaggerated loathing. But if you, and indeed all of us here, are freed from the rigid hypocrisies of the Pharisees—well, remember there are Pharisees enough on the supreme holy council."

"And Sadducees very set in their ways," said Jehoram.

"But," said Judas Iscariot, "they've all waited for the Messiah, and now the Messiah is coming to them—soon. The Messiah, as ready with signs from God as was Moses in the court of Pharaoh. They cannot resist the signs. How can they resist the teaching either—which is all of love and tolerance?"

"And of Samaritans being as Israelites, from what you tell me," said Jehoash. "The Israelites are not ready for that."

"There are thousands who are," said Judas hotly. "The throne is prepared for him who shall be a king among priests and a priest among kings. And yet not a ruler as under the Old Law. For with love there will be no need for rules."

Jehoash shook his head, though smiling kindly. "I admire this youthful idealism, my boy," he said. "I admire your innocence. If you take my advice, you'll read your history books again and see how badly innocence does in the big world. It's no good a lamb saying how much he loves the wolf and let's sit down like friends together. He gets eaten just the same."

"But," said Judas loudly, "we have the scriptures, and the scriptures tell us quite clearly to expect the prince of peace who shall take on the government of the people. Are we to turn our backs on holy writ and deny the word of the Lord?"

Ahaziah coughed, then said: "If the scriptures are fulfilled, then the scriptures are no longer needed, since they've done their work. In a sense, they cease to be holy writ. But Israel is committed to its devotion to the scriptures. Do you see my point? The fulfilment must always be sometime in the future, always tomorrow. As we know, tomorrow never comes."

"We expect the Messiah for ever," Jehoram said, "but we never get him. That's pretty well the official point of view. The Sanhedrin won't take kindly to the idea of a *real* Messiah, I can tell you. They have power over the people, which the Romans kindly allow them to have in the spiritual sphere, and they won't let it go. Innocence, innocence, a fine thing but not very fruitful of anything but disappointment. We don't want to discourage you, of course."

"When is all this kingship business going to start?" asked Jehoash.

"When we return to him," said Judas Iscariot. "When our spell of teaching is done."

"Well," said Ahaziah, "I hope you're convincing the common folk. You certainly haven't convinced me."

Judas Iscariot looked icily, then shrugged, then smiled, though sourly. He finished his wine, then said: "He'll convince you. *He* will."

In the town of Nazareth, John did well enough. He was a modest and handsome young man, polite, even diffident, with a loud voice that accorded strangely with his uncertain mode of utterance. Thus: "I know you have work to do, sheep and cattle to tend, baskets to weave, food to cook, and it would be presumptuous of me to take up even so much as a hundred heart-beats of your time. But let me give in brief the message of my master—a Nazarene like all of you. It is that we must try to love. And that this injunction to love, even your enemies, perhaps above all your enemies, comes not from some mad preacher whom the synagogues reject, but from heaven itself. I note that some of you are ready to murmur. Some of you remember Jesus well, Jesus of Nazareth. This very town—let me say it—was blessed by his conception here, and yet it rejected him and stoned him at the start of his mission. I was here. I was stoned too. But now all the other towns of Galilee have embraced him and his message...."

Mary, the mother of Jesus, a lone woman of mature beauty, one who had received offers of marriage but had rejected them all, sat spinning in the sun outside her house when Jotham the baker came to tell her that John was preaching the word. "He," he said, "didn't come himself, oh no. Jesus, that is. Not too sure of the reception he'd get. So he's sent this other harebrain to do his preaching for him. But not in the synagogue—ah no, not there." Mary got up from her spinning and said:

"Where?"

"End of the town."

When Mary arrived at the end of the town, she heard John saying: "I do not think you Nazarenes would stone him now if he returned to you. You have heard too much of the wonders he has done. For the seed is burgeoning and the tree is growing and the good news of the kingdom of heaven is swelling many hearts with a great joy. Love God—this I need not tell you to do. But also love one another, do good to those who hate you—this is the new doctrine, the hard doctrine, but the only way to joy."

When the crowd saw Mary approaching they opened up a lane for her and, with a politeness not typically Nazarene, made gestures to John to show that they appreciated his words but now had better leave since undoubtedly he and the mother of his master must have things to say to one another and here she was. When Mary and John were alone she said:

"How is he?"

"Well. Strong but thin. Burnt by the sun. I think," said John, "you must know that he is much loved."

"And also," said Mary, "much hated. I fear for him. Will we meet in Jerusalem?"

"For the Passover, yes. Don't fear for him. He has twelve strong friends."

"And uncountable enemies," Mary said. "Will you come now to the house and eat?"

I am not willing to accept the story still current, that John, a young and lusty man, was much taken by the beauty of his master's mother and paid a diffident courtship to her. This is altogether scandalous and unthinkable. The evocation of these words leads me now to the palace of Herod the tetrarch, where Jesus was being spoken of in the big bed where the king and his queen lay with a sword between them, the sword being the continuing reluctance of Herod, or inability, to consummate the marriage. She was past caring, she was concerned only with power. She said:

"It is absurd that one should have to be guarded now against one's own guards. This Jesus and his so-called Zealots—"

"No, my dear," said Herod, "you have it somewhat wrong. The Zealots are one thing, and Jesus is quite another. Although both conjoin in condemning our adulterous mode of life—ah, little do they know—which they term also incestuous. I really *must* send you back to my brother Philip, though I doubt if he'd recognise you now. I don't think he recognises anybody. Far gone in drink, very far gone. A pity. He had a certain undoubted small ability for rule."

"Back to that, are we?" said Herodias. "No, you know the answer. He comes after John, but nobody comes after *him*. This time it will really be the end."

"Another bloody head in a bag? No. I'll never forgive you for that, never. Though I must confess that it gained me a reputation for strength in certain circles. Life is full of surprises. No, my dear. As far as Jesus is concerned, it will be enough to drive him out of Galilee and into Judea. Then the Emperor's procurator can take care of him. Though why? He just preaches righteousness and loving one's enemies. And you, my dear, who are far from righteous and who don't even love your near and dear—"

"Yes, my dear lord?"

"Never mind. I think we ought to have him here. This lump in my groin—I apologise for reverting to something you find distasteful—the physicians merely shake their heads at it. This Jesus cures people, do you know that? Makes the blind see and so on. Let's have him here. Let him look at the lump at least and perhaps preach to a small group—of people, if you wish, unlikely to be touched by his teaching. You, for instance, my love. Get him to perform the odd miracle. Yes. You approve?"

What neither Herod nor his queen knew was that, that very morning, little Salome had left the palace quietly, unseen by the guards, and sought the company of a group of women she had heard of who were lodging in Tsemer, a small market-town not far from Nazareth. These women were followers of Jesus, and one of them was Mary of Magdala, a former prostitute. Salome had had a great shock, a terrible visitation of a strong sense of having sinned, and a complex knot of feelings was at work in her. She had certainly danced her last dance.

FIVE

The disciples returned from their missions worn but cheerful. Jesus was not hard to find; it was a matter only of asking where the great crowds were assembling. When the last man, Simon, formerly the Zealot (who said he should have had more time for preparation but had done, with God's help, better than he had expected), arrived to be embraced by his new master and friends (in a town called Yedid, not that the name matters), it was proposed by Matthew that all should have supper with roast meat and new bread and olives and wine and perhaps a mess of vegetables and fruit to follow—a celebration of this sort did no harm, their stomachs deserved a small reward—so this was arranged in an inn. They talked much and Jesus gravely listened. He did not ask John any questions about Nazareth or his mother there, and John was somewhat surprised. He had only one question, which he put to all of them. He said:

"You've travelled the country around, teaching the word. I have a question to ask. Did any men and women speak of me?"

"Your name was on everybody's lips," said James.

"And who," said Jesus, "do they say I am?"

"Some say John the Baptist," said Bartholomew. "They will not believe that he's really dead."

"Some know that he is dead," said Andrew. "But they think that he's risen from the grave, and that you are he. Of course, I was not having that. I tried to make it very clear that you are who you are."

"Am who I am," said Jesus. "Good."

"Jeremiah, Ezekiel," Philip was saying. "No shortage of resurrected prophets."

"And who," said Jesus, "do you, my followers, say I am?"

Now Judas Iscariot had the answer ready, but some instinct told him to leave it to another. Most hesitated, but Simon Peter stoutly spoke, saying:

"I say you are the Messiah, the Anointed, the Christ. I say you are the Son of the Living God."

Judas Iscariot smiled, pleased that the words were out, and at once was addressed by Jesus, who said:

"Judas, my son, what does that mean, if it means anything—Son of the Living God?"

"We have not yet the words, master," Judas Iscariot replied. "We have hardly the means of thinking such a thing, but, if you will not rebuke me for unhandiness, I will try to explain. God is a Spirit, and he cannot beget as men beget. But by some special miracle of begetting he has sent his own substance to the world, wholly man but also wholly God. We may speak of God the Father, but we must now also speak of God the Son. Again, forgive my—"

"There is nothing to forgive, my son. You've done well. You too believe. But let me speak now to Simon, whom we also call Peter, since, with none of your thinking gift, he has hit on the truth and, with none of your speaking gift, he has hit on the words. Son of the Living God. In saying that, Simon bar-Jonah, Simon Peter, you show yourself to be blessed among men. Flesh and blood have not revealed the truth to you: it has come from my father in heaven. And now your name is no longer Simon, no longer Simon Peter, but purely Peter, the name the world must know you by. Peter means a rock. It is upon this rock that I must build what I call my church. And the gates of hell shall not prevail against it. And to you I give the keys of the kingdom of heaven. To you all I say this: that Peter has spoken the truth, and now you know it. But you must not reveal it to any man. The time is not yet come. Now, have you anything to ask me?"

Peter had nothing to ask for the moment, being struck dumb. But Thomas said: "What is this, a church? What do you mean by a church? I think, Son of God though ye may be, ye must come down out the clouds of these words about gates of hell and keys and what not and explain yourself. With respect, of course. But I think we have a right to know what sort of a man Peter here, Simon that was, is now become. With respect, of course, always with respect."

"You're right, Thomas," Jesus said, and he ate a single grape, crunching the seeds and swallowing them. "Son of God I may be, but I am also man and must, like all men, disappear in time from the world. Now the teaching must go on. It must go on for ever. So there must be a body of men and women to hold the truth and teach the truth, and it must have a head or leader. This leader must, when he dies, pass on his authority to another leader. And so it must go on. It is easy for words to be distorted through time and ignorance and stupidity and, indeed, malice. But authority must prevail and say: *the word means this*. As all priests in the Old Law come from Aaron, so all priests in the New come from this blessed Peter. The authority shall not solely be to ensure that the message is passed on undefiled, but also to condemn and bless. Now there is a danger, long after our time yet perhaps again not so long, that men unchosen by our Peter here may believe that they and they only know the true meaning of the message, and they may set up, in good faith, churches pretending to teach the truth. But if they are not chosen by Peter or those that succeed him, they must merit condemnation. A church, you see, is no more than a body holding to the same faith, but it is false speaking to speak of a church, as it is false speaking to speak of a God, since there is only one God and only one church. That church has its beginnings with us here, and those who believe what we have taught. That church will soon be Peter's church."

"Soon, master?" said Peter. "How soon?"

"We must leave Galilee," Jesus said. "That fox Herod is plotting against me. It is not my mission to lie long in a foul prison and await the lopping off of my head. We must go to Jerusalem some time before Passover is upon us, indeed we must start our journey this very night. In Jerusalem I must suffer in a manner different from what Herod of Galilee can devise. I must be rejected by the priests and the elders of the temple. Now listen with great care. Since you believe that I am the Son of the Living God, you must take what I now tell you without shock or surprise or, Thomas, disbelief. I must be killed. On the third day after my slaying I shall be raised up. But first I must be killed."

Peter, with perhaps premature authority, cried: "This is not to happen, master. You have given me power, and now I use it to say that this shall not be. We will not permit it." And he looked towards his fellows for support. But Jesus was furious. He got up from the table and turned his back on the company and then turned to cry out:

"Is the devil working in you now? Get behind me, Satan—no longer a rock but a stone set in my path for me to stumble. You think in the way of the things of men. But it is of the things of God that I speak. And what I speak of will come to pass—soon. And no man shall stand in the way of its coming."

He said no more, but turned his back again and seemed to be breathing with difficulty. Peter opened his mouth but, warned by Judas Iscariot's look, shut it again. All the disciples had a whipped look. Bartholomew winced as with stomach pain. They were all grateful when a woman came into the supper-room—to clear the dishes, they supposed, though she carried a jar in her hand: another course? Then they saw who it was and looked forward to a deflecting outburst. But Jesus was very mild, kissed the woman, more of a girl really, though a bad girl, on the cheek and said:

"Child, God's blessing. I'm overjoyed to see you. You look

uncomfortable, Peter. Perhaps your mother would disapprove of your being in the company of— No, dear child, we will not make jokes. What have you brought me?"

"This," the girl said. "I dreamed—"only Jesus could now hear her, she spoke so low—"of washing your feet with my tears and drying them with my hair. And then a word came to me in sleep. The word *anointed*. Why that should be so I cannot say."

John heard the word and said: "Ho basileus christos."

"Scholarship has its uses," Jesus said, smiling at John. "And so," he said to Mary, "the money you earned from selling your body goes to an anointing. Very precious ointment." And so it was. She took off the lid of the alabaster jar and the odour flew gently about the room. "You may pour a little on my head," he told her. "That is right, that is in order. But keep the rest. There will be another time."

Judas Iscariot smiled somewhat sourly. Jesus noticed and nodded, as though he knew what he would say. Judas said: "Forgive me—the thought came and the thought has passed. I was thinking of the money that could have gone to the poor—"

"There speaks my submerged Pharisee," Jesus said. "The poor you have always with you, but the Son of Man for but a short space." Then he was still and silent, listening. He heard something that the others could not hear. "We must leave," he said, "now. We must make for Judea."

The moon was near the full, the night warm. The twelve, in their twos and threes, John still the companion of Jesus, took the road south. Some distance behind them a group of women followed, little Salome one of them. I had best say now, by the way, that the name *Peter* is really *Petros*, and you may wonder how a Galilean fisherman, whose only tongue was a Galilean dialect of Aramaic, should have as second name one so palpably Greek. In truth, his second name was Kepha, which is Aramaic enough, but Jonah, Simon Peter's father, preferred the Greek form, which he had learnt from an itinerant Judean seller of fishing-tackle who knew Greek. Some such story, anyway, may serve. Another story I may tell is that, the morning after the departure of the anointed Jesus, the head of his church, and the other disciples for Judea, soldiers of Herod Antipater appeared at the inn where they had supped, ready to take him.

"They'll be over the border by now, sir," the landlord said to the captain.

The captain sniffed the air in the room where supper had been served and said: "That smell. Like a whore's bedroom." But one of his men said:

"You're wrong, sir. That's a tomb smell. That's the stuff they put round bodies to keep them fresh."

It was not long before Jesus and his followers were in the town of Bethany, and it was here, according to all accounts, his biggest miracle was performed, if we except the later one, and indeed last one of our story. We must wonder why Jesus, having enjoined secrecy on his disciples as regards his divine nature, should now proceed to give proof of it to so many so near to Jerusalem. We may interpret the seeming perverseness in terms of his own control or willing of the enactments that led to his death, in which Judas Iscariot played so vital or mortal a part. It is quite certain that, observing the miracle, Judas Iscariot came to a decision which only one of his subtlety and innocence could conceive.

There were two sisters, unmarried, holy women, the one somewhat holier than the other, and their names were Martha and Mary. They had a beloved brother named Lazarus, only twenty-four years old, and he had died of a feverish condition the physicians had no skill to cure. He was interred in the family tomb which was set in a great rock, and the tomb was closed by means of a great slab of stone which had required at least the strength of fifteen men to place in position. When Martha and Mary came weeping to Jesus to ask for the restoration of their brother, he disclosed no special reason for doing them, and no others, so great a favour. He evidently regarded Mary as something of a Pharisee, overscrupulous in the fulfilment of rituals, a loud prayer in public places, not over-intelligent.

Martha he seemed to see as a sour woman, resentful of the manner in which Mary left the dull duties of running a household to herself, her own holiness joyless, her charity grudging. Nevertheless he proceeded to the tomb and seemed satisfied that so large a crowd, who had heard of his coming and of the sisters' weeping request, should be assembled to observe his fulfilment of so impossible a promise. Mary said, a little too often:

"If you had come earlier to Judea, master, I know our brother would not have died. But I know, even now, that whatever you will ask of God, God will grant you."

"Remember these words," said Jesus loudly, so that all could hear. "I am the resurrection and the life. He who believes in me, even though he were dead, yet shall live." Then, to the chief of the men servants, he said: "Remove the stone."

"Look," said the man, "I don't want any part of this. There's nothing in there but a corpse. It's been there over a week. Stink, pestilence. I don't like it."

"Nevertheless," Jesus said, "remove the stone."

Grumbling, the man signed to his fellows, and with much groaning and sweat they rolled the stone away. Jesus went to the entrance of the tomb and called:

"Lazarus. Lazarus."

Most of the servants were disposed to run away to the shelter of the cypresses when they saw the dim roll of white within start to stir. A woman, girl rather, screamed, the shaken daughter of Herodias. Jesus loudly called:

"Lazarus, come out. Lazarus, Lazarus."

But the body in its grave-clothes could only twist and writhe.

"Undo his bandages. Loose him."

It was Martha who was quickest to run to the moving mass of white cerements. She unwound the wrappings around the head to disclose the face of a blinking bewildered young man. The servants then went, with no great eagerness, to unwrap his limbs. Martha kissed him, weeping.

Thomas, watching keenly, said to Judas Iscariot: "Twice

I've seen him do that. The first time it was the girl in the family I worked for. *Talitha cumi:* I remember his words. She could have been in one of these sleeps, as I always said. But I don't think this one here was asleep."

"I must hire a horse," Judas said. "I must get to Jerusalem before the rest of you, spread the good word."

"No trouble about that, I should think. These people here would give ye a whole stable, man."

Certainly they gave a great, though cold, feast to Jesus and all his followers. The women followers too—Mary the prostitute, Salome the royal dancing-girl (in a drab robe now, her face dirty), the ladies who had made the seamless garment Jesus wore, others—were given the best of everything, though at a table apart from the men. Martha supervised the waiting on, while Mary spoke perpetual thanks to God and his Holy One, eating heartily though. Lazarus, now in fresh clothes of the living, still bewildered, blinking still, ate little but drank much water, as though death had been a thirsty experience. Thomas closely questioned him.

"Ye were dead, right, ye passed to another world, right. Do ye recall anything of it?"

"It was like a very deep sleep, and then I heard this voice calling my name, as though in my ear, and I thought: ah, time to get up, but why in the middle of the night, let me sleep longer. Then it was thunder in my ear, and I had to try to get up."

"No memory of a heaven or a hell or other of the dead floating all about ye?"

"I remember nothing."

"God, ye see," said Thomas, "gives nothing away. He keeps the riddle going."

"Like a sleep. And then my name being called."

"Aye."

Judas Iscariot had been probing in his brain for a name, the name of one with whom he had studied Greek with a very exclusive teacher in Jerusalem, and the name would not come. It was the name of a man destined for the priesthood and who, Judas knew, eventually became a priest. A man of his own age, keen-brained, given to odd quiet heresies, certainly what they termed these days *progressive*. The name would come to him on his journey perhaps. He must get to Jerusalem now, refusing another cup of wine. He had no difficulty in getting the loan of a horse, a fine grey, sumptuously saddled, the horse that had been Lazarus's favourite and would be so again. Before ceasing further to speak of Lazarus, of him I had best say what others say, though there is no evidence of a documentary nature to confirm it—namely, that what may be termed his posthumous life was wholly vicious, and that it did not last long, ending as it did at the points of knives in a tavern brawl. But perhaps this is not pertinent to our narrative, as it is certainly in no wise relevant to the fact, if it be a fact, of Jesus's resurrecting of him. Man's will is totally free and the freedom is guaranteed by the All Highest.

On his ride to Jerusalem, indeed when he was within sight of the Mount of Olives, Judas found the name of his fellow-pupil coming to him. It started with his horse's sneeze—*zzzer*-and ended with a ewe-bleat from a nearby fold—*aaaaah*. Zerah, of course. A man of good family and excellent mentality, a priest who had risen high and would rise yet higher, though young, not at all hidebound, a man who would certainly listen. Once within the gates of the city, Judas rode with difficulty—for the streets were crammed with citizens and soldiers—to the Temple. Meeting a pair of young priests strolling in its vicinity—their office recognisable from their austere but costly robes and the wide-brimmed hats that courted the wind this windy day and had to be held onto hard in the name of priestly dignity—he had but to ask to be readily told where the dwelling of the Venerable Father Zerah was: south of the Temple and north of the old market. He rode thither.

He was asked to wait on the terrace amid birdsong and the scent of bushes that had been freshened by a morning shower. At length Zerah came out—handsome, smiling, neat as he always had been, well remembering his old fellow-student, giving him both his hands, saying:

"Judas, Judas, it has been a long time, has it not?"

"Too long, I think. I must be deferential now, must I not, and call you Father Zerah?"

"Whatever you call me, first let me call for wine."

They did not talk long of the old days. Judas Iscariot was quick to arrive at the purpose of his visit. Zerah listened gravely and with close attention to the lucid account of the ministry of Jesus. At length he said:

"So. The one who is coming. The one who shall come. When?"

"Any day. Any moment. I left him and the rest of the company at the house of this Lazarus in Bethany. I would not stress this most recent act of his, except as a sign for those slow to believe. Some of us do not need these signs. It is the teaching that is all-important."

"You think he is the one." It was not a question.

"I know he is the one."

"Miracles," said Zerah. "Raising the dead. Not difficult when death is only a sleep. We have had no shortage of miracles in this very city. Healing the sick. Tell a sick man loudly enough that he's well, and he becomes well. So they say, the sceptics. My office has taught me a measure of scepticism. Now, as for his doctrine—we have, of course, heard all about it. It has, indeed, been closely studied by some of our travelling observers or audients. They have taken down some of this doctrine in character. It is new, certainly. Revolutionary even. And yet all firmly based in the Old Law. Your man seems, how shall I put it, almost pedantically—nay, fanatically—versed in the Old Law. A difficult man to confute, so I'm told. The Pharisees are not used to being trounced with their own texts."

"You've not heard him? Ah, you soon will, I trust. And see him too. A giant, great-lunged, with immense eyes. Here, I say, lies Israel's hope. A priest among kings, a king among priests. The Sanhedrin will accept him, the Sanhedrin must—"

"Must, must, must?"

"Look, Zerah, Father Zerah, you know me—I'm no fool—"

"Never a fool, Judas," Zerah smiled. "Never particularly credulous. But perhaps more than a little innocent."

"If by *innocent* you mean disposed to take the faith of the Jews seriously—Father Zerah, we know scripture, though you of course know it better than I. The scriptures foretell the coming of the Messiah. That villain who once ruled Judea believed in his coming so thoroughly that he slaughtered all the new-born of Bethlehem—"

"Slaughtering, for all we know, the Messiah among them."

"I see," said Judas, smiling somewhat nervously, "what you mean by scepticism. I have no priestly authority, and perhaps, if I may speak as an old friend, I am glad not to have it if it entails the cultivation of scepticism."

"Meaning that you *want* to believe."

"That I *have* to believe." Judas looked somewhat fiercely, then softened. "I do not matter. It is what the holy council makes of him that matters. And what the holy council will then be able to say to the occupying power."

Zerah put his left fingertips to their right counterparts, one by one, slowly, starting with the thumbs, creating a delicate airy cage into which he now looked as though his words lay there. Then he said, reading from the cage: "Look, we have a new ruler—one from the house of David, which, as your Roman lordships will know, is the royal house of Israel. In this ruler we have every confidence. He preaches non-violence, love, tolerance—even to Rome. Let Caesar withdraw his power. We have no further need of his pacifying legions."

"You put it very well."

"I would have to put it very well indeed for the Romans to wish to withdraw their legions and their procurator and their tax-gatherers."

Judas Iscariot sighed deeply. "Zerah," he said, "Father Zerah, do you believe in the imminence of the Messiah?"

"Of course. I would be a heretic if I did not. Israel has always believed in his imminence and always will."

"I see. The coming one who never comes. And yet there are many who say that the need for the Messiah is now and that God is answering our need. You will certainly hear this throughout Galilee. This, I say, is the Christ. Let him at least appear before the sacred fathers of Israel."

"I can promise you," said Zerah, "that he will so appear."

"Ah."

"Meanwhile I shall have him observed—very closely. We cannot afford to take chances. There are false prophets abroad."

"Those are his very own words."

"Bless you, Judas, bless you," said Zerah, smiling. "I see a man on fire with hope. One does not see many such these days."

"With faith, rather," Judas Iscariot said. "There is one thing, however—" His face clouded. "I may speak freely?"

"It was to speak freely that you came here."

"There's a flaw in him. He talks too much lately of failure. Of enemies. Of his own death. This morbidity must be driven out of him. This, I would say with due deference, is the task of the council. For he has much to do."

"The Sanhedrin will act," said Zerah. "Have no fear."

Jesus and the other disciples were now at Bethphage. Jesus was fondling the ears of a patient grey donkey, a mother-ass whose foal stood cropping the grass beside her. Jesus's eyes were on the Mount of Olives. Thomas said, fiercely:

"Swords and spears, spears and swords. They'll be waiting, I tell ye."

"No," said Jesus. "Neither the Romans nor the chiefs of Israel will risk the arrest of the innocent—not yet. They want me within their gates, to wait, to watch. No. The scriptures must be fulfilled. A sort of king must enter Jerusalem. The sixty-second chapter of Isaiah says these words: 'Tell ye the daughters of Zion: behold, the king cometh to thee, lowly and meek and riding on an ass—nay, upon a colt, the foal of an ass.' Not, you see, a full-grown donkey that others have ridden, but a foal—a beast that has known no rider."

"They expect much from you," said Matthew doubtfully.

"What they expect they will not get. The tearing down of the Roman eagles, the king in his palace, ruling over his own, the stranger cast out. No. They who cry hosannas will soon cast stones. Let us go then."

"If I may say so," said Simon Peter, "that foal there will hardly bear the weight of one of us, let alone you."

"There speaks my practical man. It is solely a matter of fulfilling the scriptures, Peter. A token couple of paces, and then you may take both the foal and his mother back to their owner. But I think you will find that he is able to bear my weight."

"Yes, of course, I forget these things," said Peter.

BOOK 5

ONE

There was no official opposition to the entry of Jesus into Jerusalem. The troops who stood among the small crowd awaiting him expected a fierce knot of Jewish rebels who would crack a few Roman heads before being cracked in their turn. Judas Iscariot had spread the news of the coming of the Messiah, simplified for most as the imminent appearance in their midst of the teacher and healer and raiser from the dead already so well-known in Galilee. Both Romans and Jews were alike disappointed when a big man came meekly riding in, unhandily seated on a small donkey, followed by eleven men in rags. He soon dismounted, and one of his followers (Little James, as it happened) led both the foal and its mother through the gates back to their owner. Judas Iscariot cried:

"It is he. Strew his path with flowers, with palm-leaves, with your own garments. With me now—hosanna to the son of David. Blessed is he who comes in the name of the Lord!"

The response was half-hearted. It was this matter of the donkey and the rags. Judas yelled:

"Do you not see? The prophecy is fulfilled. It is written in the Book of Isaiah: 'Tell ye the daughters of Zion: behold the king cometh to thee, lowly and meek and riding on an ass—nay, upon a colt, the foal of an ass.'"

At this some took new heart and cried "Hosanna." Some boys climbed palms and sent the fronds whistling down. The crowd grew. Pharisees, hearing the hosannas, wanted to know what all this was about.

"It's the prophet—Jesus from Nazareth."

Four of them—Eliphaz, Samuel, Jonah and Ezra—sneered and frowned and pushed forward. The disciples, accompanied by Thaddeus on the flute, were singing, led by Philip:

"Blessed is he who comes in the Lord's name. Peace in heaven, glory in the highest. Sing ye, sing ye."

Eliphaz and his friends tried to obstruct the progress of the little procession. They heard the words of the song and Eliphaz said:

"This is blasphemous. They must not use such words."

Jesus, hearing, said: "If they should hold their peace, the very stones would cry out."

Always ready for diversion, the people of Jerusalem renewed their hosannas and their throwing of palms. Judas Iscariot called and called, and the crowd grew. "I could sing another song," said a stranger to the Pharisees.

"What?" said Samuel. "Not that we care."

"'Behold, how ye prevail nothing. Lo, the whole world is gone after him.'"

"Hardly the whole world," Ezra said.

"Wait," said Eliphaz. "Just wait."

Jesus and his disciples did no work that day. Fighting off the sick and blind and palsied was work enough. Jesus at one point stood and cried out an address to the city itself which not many well understood. The words were of this order: "Jerusalem—if you had known, in this day, the things which belong to peace. But now they are hidden from your eyes. For the day shall come when your enemies shall surround you and shall dash you to the ground, and your children within you. And they shall not leave one stone upon another, because you knew not the time of your visitation." This, as so many of us now know, was true prophecy.

Judas Iscariot had arranged that Jesus and his disciples be lodged in an inn—six or seven to a room, clean floors, blankets

provided—on the Mount of Olives, and here they all sat at a
frugal supper served in the open air, looking down on the city
as evening advanced. Jesus said:

"A great city, as you can see, and your hearts must sink at
the thought of all the great cities of the world that must hear
you when your time comes and you are alone. But faith is the
great word, faith. If you have even a grain of faith within you,
you may say to a mountain: move, cast yourself into the
sea—and it shall be done."

The disciples were tired, even irritable. Thomas said: "Aye,
meaning if we believe a mountain will throw itself into the sea,
then it will happen. But I don't believe it, none of us here
believes it—nor, with respect, do ye yourself."

"Thomas," said Peter, "that's three whole cups of the wine
you've drunk. Save some for others, man."

"Thirsty. This is very thirsty weather."

"Drink water," snarled Peter. Judas Iscariot said:

"The Mount of Olives. Remember that olives stand for
peace."

"Well," said Jesus, "this is where we must find our peace at
the day's end. There will be little enough of it in the city."

"Perhaps I spoke out of turn then," said Thomas. "I forget
that ye use these parables as ye call them."

"No parables tomorrow, Thomas," said Jesus. "Nor many
words. You will see."

Jesus's first work was early the following morning, and it
was performed in the precincts of the Temple. He and his disciples stood watching a busy sale of sacrificial pigeons, stall
after stall hung with wickerwork cages, perches to which the
birds were attached by thread and a leg, moaning and cooing,
the robes of the vendors stained with pigeon-shit. "Judas,"
said Jesus. "Have we enough money to purchase a whip?"

"A whip, master?"

"Yes, the kind you would use for a refractory horse or a
sullen mastiff. Buy one. Now. Be quick."

"He's going to be asking for trouble," murmured Little

James to the other James. "He's determined to make trouble. Why?"

When Judas came back with a fine knotty thong with a hard wood handle, Jesus took it without a word and, with all his muscle, began to lay into the pigeon-vendors. He motioned to his disciples that they should open up the cages and cut the leg-leashes. The vendors were loud in protest at first—"We have to sell doves, don't we? To make the sacrifices, don't we? Who in hell's name are you anyway?" Later they had no breath except for howls of pain. Pigeons flew whirring around in freedom, settled on walls, cooed down crassly at the disorder. Jesus paused for breath before whipping out of the precincts a burly defiant vendor who defended himself with a stick. An attendant came running to say:

"Are you this Jesus of Nazareth they talk of?"

"What does my name matter?" answered Jesus. He whipped out the vendor with the stick, who cursed frightfully, and then cried out, as priests began to appear: "Does not any man have the right to do this that fears God and venerates his Temple? The Temple is for worship, not for the buying and selling of pigeons."

A priest called: "The doves are needed for sacrifice. You must stop this." It was a mild enough protest, probably from a man who had always had his doubts about the propriety of turning the Temple precincts into a livestock market. Jesus said:

"I have hardly begun." And he led his disciples to another court of the precincts, where creatures intended for more substantial sacrifice were on sale. He was whipping ferociously almost at once not the vendors alone but also the buyers, while the disciples freed oxen and sheep and sent them baaing and lowing out into the public thoroughfare. A Pharisee unfortunately cried: "This is blasphemy, blasphemy, do you hear?" since Jesus was able to reply:

"You speak a true word, my son."

He next went to violent work on the moneychangers. Now the coin in current use in the city was minted by Rome and carried the head and titles of Tiberius Caesar. Such money was not admitted into the Temple for the paying of tribute to the Lord, since it was not merely secular but also pagan, and it had to be converted to Temple money. The changers made good profits on the exchange. Jesus and the disciples heard one money-merchant, with the whine of his tribe, saying: "My colleague here and I have the monopoly of the issue of Temple money. I don't care what they tell you. You can't change your imperial money anywhere else, friend." And there was another man lending holy money at high interest: "Thirty in the hundred, payable in the coinage of the Emperor Tiberius Caesar before Passover. You understand that?"

While the disciples turned the tables over, sending gold and silver clashing and tinkling, Jesus whipped the changers and lenders, shouting: "'My house shall be called a house of prayer for all nations. But you have turned it into a den of robbers.' You fulfil the prophecy. I break it."

Jesus left the throwing out of the cursing money-men to the disciples, especially to Little James, who used all the blunt force of a wrestler at country fairs. Jesus, panting, said to Judas Iscariot:

"What does it say in the Psalms of David?"

"The zeal of thy house shall eat me up," quoted Judas promptly. Jesus nodded and nodded. Then both caught sight of a young priest standing by the main gate of the Temple— Zerah, as Judas knew. He made no sign but he looked long on Jesus. Then he whisked himself away. Judas said: "I think, master, with the utmost respect, that we ought not to—antagonise authority overmuch. We shall need their—" He did not manage to utter the word *support*. The look of loathing that Jesus cast upon him was of the kind called dumbfounding. He retreated backwards, bumping into Philip and Thaddeus, who were returning from gentle fisting of the moneychangers. "Master, I see I was wrong, master," Judas was now able to stammer, and he ran off to his task of begging, troubled with his insufficiencies, angry with his stupidity.

No official action was able to be taken against Jesus for his cleansing of the Temple precincts. The vendors and money-changers had been granted franchise of operation but were not under Temple protection. The news of the driving out ensured a large congregation for Jesus's first swathe of teaching in the main portico, further whipping undoubtedly being expected. As it was, the idle and curious had their fill of prodigies, for Jesus healed briskly—the disciples kindly and firmly sorting out the worse from the more trivial cases, as well as holding back the crowds—before proceeding to words. He was about to address the multitude when some mothers proudly brought their infants to be blessed and also to bless.

"Say it, say it."

"Oghghaghgha."

"To the son of David."

"Gaga Ghagger Ghayghigh."

Eliphaz and his fellow Pharisees were there, very ready. "How far will you go?" cried Eliphaz. "The very children are uttering blasphemies."

Jesus was, as ever, quick to reply and he used the tones of regret rather than of point-scoring triumph: "Alas that you should not have read the scriptures. 'Out of the mouths of babes and sucklings hast thou perfected praise.'" And then: "Bless you, little ones."

"Say it, dear, say it."

"Hosanna to the Son of David," said an indifferent girl of about six. The mother hugged her, undelighted, with delight. Jesus now spoke strong words:

"Beware of false prophets. They come to you in sheep's clothing, but inwardly they are ravening wolves. By their fruits you shall know them. Do men gather grapes from thorns or figs from thistles? Even so, every good tree brings forth good fruit, but the corrupt tree brings forth evil fruit. And what do you do with the tree that fails to bring forth good fruit? You hack it down and throw it into the fire. The promises of false prophets—whether they be men of the faith or men of politics—are not enough, remember that. By their fruits shall you know them."

MAN OF NAZARETH   251

Eliphaz called: "Tell us one thing, O eloquent denouncer. By what authority do you do what you do, say what you say?"

"Ah, that word *authority*," smiled Jesus grimly. "You know of John the Baptist. From where did he get the authority to baptise? From heaven? Or from men?"

Ezra started to say "From m—" but Eliphaz clapped his hand over his mouth before the word was out, saying:

"Fool. Do you want the people to tear you to pieces?"

"Did I hear someone say *from men*?" said Jesus. "Ah, of course, no one. And if then, as you must, you say *from heaven*, then I ask this question: why then did you not believe in him?"

Eliphaz growled something, but it was no articulate answer. Ezra said:

"We don't know."

"Very well," said Jesus. "You tell me nothing. Nor do I tell you by what authority I do and say these things. But let me tell you a story. There was a man who had two sons, and he said to the first: 'Son, go and work in the vineyard.' The boy said: 'No, I will not.' But shortly afterwards he relented and went to work in the vineyard. And the father said to the second son: 'Son, go and work in the vineyard.' And the son said: 'Yes, father, I will, and gladly.' But he did not go. Now, tell me—which of these two did the work of his father?"

"The answer," said a priest, in a yawning tone, "is somewhat obvious."

"Very good," said Jesus. "And what does the story mean? It means this. You people who consider yourselves so holy —you say *yes* to God, but you do not do his will. The thieves, the prostitutes, the publicans—they may say *no* to God, but who knows that they do not do his will? I say this to you, priests and Pharisees—there are many thieves and prostitutes who will get into heaven before you do. For John the Baptist came to you in the way of righteousness, and you did not believe him. Yet there were many who were sinners that believed. And even when you saw that they believed, you did not think of repentance, ah no. You went your own way. And you still go your own way. By their fruits shall ye know them."

This meeting then broke up. Jesus did not need immediate protection from the holy men who either growled unholily or pretended amused indifference; there were plenty of the common sort to cheer him, as well as men and women calling *master master* and holding up withered arms, baring cancerous bosoms, pointing to eyes as dead as stones. He was in greater need just then of protection from his friends than from his enemies. And when he went to the ablution-rooms that were attached to the Temple, pursuing a call altogether congruent with his human nature, he found three men very ready to be more than friends, brothers rather, and these he met with a heart sinking. They were well-set-up men, great-bearded and tingling with life. The tallest and brawniest of the three said:

"May I introduce Jobab and Aram? You and I, sir, share a name."

"The name is not uncommon. Jesus—?"

"Bar-Abbas. Son of his father. You may call me Barabbas. I will call you master."

"Bar-Abbas. Son of *our* father. We share that too."

"We had news of your coming," said Barabbas. "That man of yours, the one with the horse—he spread the news."

"A good man," said Jesus, with some regret.

"Born to rule, he said, and yet would not accept the rule. We understood. All must be made ready first. Passover is coming, master. What are your orders?"

"To love God and to love man," said Jesus. "You've heard me speak."

"Yes yes yes," said Barabbas, "we go forward in that together, all of us. You fire the sons of Israel to remember their God and to cling to each other in loving brotherhood. And you soothe the enemy into believing that he too is loved—or at least tolerated. But when does the work start?"

"Yes," said Jobab, or it might have been Aram, gruffly. "When does it start?"

Jesus sighed. "I fear no real news can have reached you yet from your brothers in Galilee. I preach the kingdom of heaven."

"Which we are ready to set up," said Aram or Jobab, "in the place of the kingdom of Caesar. Are you not he that was sent?"

"I am," Jesus admitted, "the one whose coming John the Baptist prophesied."

"In whom we believed," said Barabbas, "when the Pharisees and the Sadducees spat upon him. And now, as he prophesied, the high are to be dethroned and the lowly raised."

"According to his word," said Jobab or Aram. "According to yours. You raise the banner of the Messiah."

"You mistake his prophecy," said Jesus. "You mistake my mission. I must leave you. That mission is incomplete, and the time is short."

"We don't understand," said Barabbas. "You speak in riddles. If you think we are spies of the enemy, think again. You have heard plain speech from us. We demand plain speech from you. We have a right to demand."

But Jesus returned to the portico of the Temple, where his disciples awaited him, and together they left the Temple precincts. Barabbas and his fellows could not, because of the protective phalanx of the disciples, get near to him again. But, baffled, they stayed as close as they could. Riddles. Then Barabbas said, no longer baffled:

"Now then, you see? Mistake his mission, do we?"

For a Roman centurion, fully uniformed and sworded, had come up to Jesus. The protective phalanx closed in on Jesus, but the centurion said mildly:

"Master, I have something to beg of you—"

"Master?" said Jesus. "You call me *master*?"

"What else," said the centurion simply, "can I call one who comes from on high? Master, I do not wish to trouble you, for you have much to do, but I have a servant in my house—I've had him a long time, and he's good, loving, more like a son than a servant. He's very sick, I think he's dying. Master, I ask you in all humility—"

"You hear?" cried Jesus to the surrounding crowd. "Friends, disciples, all who are listening now—do you hear? I am wanted not for what I teach, but to be a bearer of signs and wonders, or else of a banner in Israel." And he shot a look of some malevolence at Barabbas and his friends. "Still," he said, more softly, to the centurion. "What I have done for ungrateful Jews I must do also for ungrateful Romans, lest men say I favour some and ignore others. I'll come to your house."

"But master, master," cried the centurion in distress. "I wish to see no signs and wonders. I'm even unworthy that you should enter under my roof. But I know that if you say the word—that, no more—then my servant will be made well again. You see, sir, I myself am a man under authority, but also I possess authority—a hundred soldiers under me. If I say to one *do this,* I know that he will do it. And to another one; *go there,* I know that he'll go. I need not *see.* It's enough that the word be given."

The centurion, who had evidently been long in the territory, spoke Aramaic well, though with Italic sharpness. Jesus, however, gave his last words back to him in Latin, savouring their meaning: "Satis est ut verbum detur." Then, with a great voice, he spoke to the multitude: "You hear this man, this officer of the Roman garrison? I say this to you all: nowhere in Israel, in Israel, *in Israel,* have I found such faith. There is a bitter surprise in store for those who think, because of their blood and race, that they are the chosen. They will see Abraham, Isaac, Jacob and all the prophets of the Lord, who are also the prophets of their own blood and race, sitting in the kingdom of heaven. But they will see many of different blood and race, from the winds' four quarters, sitting with them. And they that think, because of their blood and race, that they are of the kingdom shall be cast into the outer darkness. There shall be, I can promise, plenty of weeping and gnashing of teeth. And they that were last shall be first. And the first—need I say it?—shall be last." And with a look of great love he turned back to the centurion and said: "Go home. Your faith has cured your servant." And, not doubting for a moment this to be so, the centurion tried to kneel, but Jesus raised him. The gratitude in the face of this

Roman officer was, it was observed by the observant, more than balanced by the hate in the faces of the Pharisees and the baffled anger in the faces of Barabbas and other Zealots.

TWO

As was to be expected, the outraged Pharisees were not long in arranging a meeting for the formal expression of indignation and discussion of a plan to put Jesus down. Eliphaz, Samuel, Jonah and Ezra all, as elders of the faith, had places on the Great Religious Council, and hence they could speak to the priests, though not perhaps the highest priests of all, with a certain familiarity. Eliphaz, who had invited two of them to his house for the indignation meeting, could even, without rebuke, be patronising. The two were called Haggai and Habbakuk, good prophetic nomenclatures attached to two good trenchermen who dug deeply into the supper Eliphaz provided (grilled trout, stewed roots, roast veal, fruit, Greek wine that tanged of tar and resin). Eliphaz said, after supper:

"The council has to meet, has to. Delay encourages him, the grinner, the smiler, and that uncouth ragged lot that's with him. Strike now, I say." And he glared at Habbakuk and Haggai, who glowed amiably from Eliphaz's good victuals. Habbakuk said:

"To call the whole council together—to decide the fate of a wandering preacher—that argues our own impotence to deal with him here and now."

"I would ask you all first," fluted Haggai, "to put off personal resentment. Our grounds must be, ah, morality and public order."

"Any man," said Ezra resentfully, "has

the right to resent the diminution of his own authority. I had an apprentice in the shop who made jokes about sheep in wolves' clothing. Got rid of him, only right to do so. Now he jeers at me in the street—'whited sepulchre,' he shouts, the young—"

"Aaaah," went Eliphaz to disguise the thwarting of his un-purposed laughter (for there was something, it had to be admit-ted, of the whited sepulchre about Ezra). "Small matters. It is the faith of our fathers that is being jeered at. Well, *reverend* fa-thers, what do you suggest?"

"How far," asked Haggai, "do you wish to go?"

"All the way," growled Ezra.

"Get him out of Jerusalem," said Samuel, more moderately. "Him and his rabble of sturdy beggars. Frighten him. Catch him out in blasphemy. Remind him of the punishment for that."

"Oh, he's careful to avoid blasphemy," said Habbakuk.

"Yes," said Ezra. "All he wants to do is insult his betters."

"Is it not blasphemy," said Eliphaz, "to say that a prostitute will get into heaven before a priest of the Temple?"

"Unfortunately no," said Haggai. "Very unfortunately, but no. I was thinking of his relations with the civil power."

"He's been careful there too," said his colleague.

"That centurion," Jonah said, "will go around talking about there being at least one Jew who's a friend of Rome."

"Let him," said Habbakuk thoughtfully, "make a choice be-tween God and Caesar. A fork with two prongs."

"I don't quite see that," said Eliphaz.

"Later, later," said Haggai eagerly. "Let's try something a little simpler first."

This led to a fine exhibition of righteousness in which Ezra, who dealt in imported wheat-flour, took advantage of certain knowledge he possessed in respect of the wife of one of his em-ployees. The employee's name does not concern us, but the wife's name was Tirzah, and she had been conducting an adul-terous relationship with a rather neat handsome small man whose trade was the selling of wrought-iron lamps made by shamefully underpaid craftsmen. Ezra dragged this poor woman from her tiny house while her husband was at work, assisted in the dragging and the holy vilification by Eliphaz and Jonah, morally assisted by the silent but eyes-to-heaven presence of Fathers Habbakuk and Haggai. She was pulled, then, by her hair and her garments—which, torn in the pulling, made her seem more shameless than she was—to the precincts of the Temple at a time of day when the disciples of Jesus were taking a meal in a tavern but Jesus himself was writing or drawing something cryptic in the dust of the dusty earth (which had known no rain now for well over ten days). Some say that he was drawing a fish and writing his name JESUS in Greek all about it. This, however, is not to the point. Ezra, holding onto the hair of the shrieking Tirzah, cried out in the hearing of Jesus:

"Fellow-Israelites, it says in the commandments that the Lord gave to Moses: thou shalt not commit adultery. A foul sin, adultery, and here you see a foul sinner, an adulteress caught in the act."

"In the act?" someone said, slavering.

"Near enough. After the act. He who was her partner in the sin must be accounted the less guilty of the two, since, as the sacred scriptures tell us, it is through the wiles of the woman that the sin comes. It was so in Eden. It is so here. Stone her."

He let go of her hair, but she could not run away, surrounded as she was by willing stoners. Jesus, as all expected, now stood and cried:

"Stop!"

They stopped readily enough, expecting good entertainment. Jesus said loudly: "Is there anyone here without sin? Anyone? Well, let him throw the first stone. Why do you wait, you holy Pharisees?" And to the woman he said, raising her gently: "Go in peace. But sin no more." She ran away then, but not for good. She was soon to join the body of Jesus's women followers, an adulteress added to a prostitute and the daughter of a queen, as well as the pious seamstresses and other odd female worshippers, the Daughters of Jesus as they began to call themselves. Eliphaz now shouted:

"Who are you to flout the law of Moses?" And his friends added:

"Yes, who are you, blasphemer, breaker of the commandments?"

"It is written," said Eliphaz, "that adultery is a crime, and a foul crime, that the adulterous wife is filth that must be thrown on the midden, and as such the husband may put her away and make her face the wrath of the righteous. So it is true that you blaspheme against the law, sinner that you are, sinner in preacher's clothing, whitewashed sepulchre."

"Moses," Jesus began mildly enough, "for the sake of peace and order, had to yield to the hardness of Israelite hearts, and he suffered you or your forebears to put away your wives. But that was never the intention of the Lord God in the beginning. For, as it is written, God made them male and female, and a man shall leave his father and mother and cleave to his wife, and they shall become one flesh. What therefore God has joined together, let no man put asunder."

He maintained his mildness when the priest Haggai spoke the words he and Habbakuk had plotted together: "Jesus of Nazareth, we all know you speak the truth and teach it. Nor do you care to whom, since in your sight, as in God's, if one may say so without blasphemy, all men are the same. But there is a thing that puzzles me, and I hope you will speak out the truth on it. We sons of the faith believe that all things belong to our God. Is it then lawful to give tribute to Caesar?"

Mildly Jesus looked at the smiling priests, the narrow-eyed Pharisees, the Roman guards on the military watchtower that overlooked the Temple, Barabbas and his friends. Then he ceased to be mild. He shouted:

"Hypocrites and fools—why do you seek to draw me into the utterance of treason? Show me a piece of imperial Roman money. Come, show me, *show me,* and I will give you your answer." It was a common Roman soldier who threw a coin to Little James, who deftly caught it in his huge hands and then handed it to Jesus. Jesus held it in the air, so that the sun caught it an instant. He shouted: "Whose is this image and whose is this name?"

"Caesar's. The Emperor Tiberius Caesar's. It is Caesar's name. Caesar's name. Caesar's."

"Very well, then," said Jesus. "You must render unto Caesar the things that are Caesar's, and unto God the things that are God's." And he handed the coin to Judas Iscariot the treasurer. Every little helped.

It is generally believed that Eliphaz the Pharisee and Jesus Barabbas the Zealot yelled their denunciations simultaneously. Eliphaz cried:

"Seize him. What are you waiting for? He blasphemes against decency and law and order. He's the friend of sinners and thieves and whores. From his own mouth you have heard this. Stone him. Throw him out of the holy city."

"Throw yourself out, whited sepulchre," countercried a man, a nobody. It was the feeling of many. The very term *whited sepulchre* was becoming popular, and there was a song being sung (some say written by the disciple Philip, though there is no evidence for this) that ran in this manner:

> I'm just a whited sepulchre,
>   Lovely and fair outside,
> But look within for the filth and sin
>   And the stink of something that died.

Barabbas, as I say, also shouted, and his words are reported to have been these: "Kill him. What are you waiting for? He's a friend of Caesar, he licks the boots of the Romans, he does Egyptian tricks for them. Enemy of freedom, perverter of Israelite truth. Stone the bastard." And he and his followers started to hurl rubble and rocks, which the two Jameses wanted to hurl back. Jesus restrained them, saying:

"Do nothing. Learn from the Pharisees."

Eliphaz and his friends were leaving rapidly. The Roman policemen who had previously stood on the periphery of the crowd now moved in on the throwing of the first stone. A stone thrown by Jobab or Aram in the direction of Jesus and the disciples struck one of the police on the left cheek. Syrian soldiers began to beat innocent Jewish bystanders. Barabbas tried to throttle a small but wiry Syrian. Reinforcements were seen running, summoned by the blowing of a horn, from the near-by barracks. A standard-bearer bore aloft a standard signifying the Roman peace. A stone hit him. He lunged with the spear-tip of his standard. His standard was wrested from him. It fell. Its pole was broken. Barabbas and Jobab and Aram were seized without much difficulty. Barabbas, panting, did not revile his arresters. He reserved his hard words for Jesus:

"Traitor. You delivered me. Into the hands of." Then he was struck in the mouth by a decurion. The decurion looked, squinting in the sun, at Jesus and his men, who stood hands folded, very calm. He said to one of the troops:

"Him?"

"Nah. Love your enemies, he says. Easier said than done."

THREE

"ou should still be sleeping," Jesus said. It was before dawn on the Mount of Olives, and another hot dry day promised. Jesus knew when the weather would break. Peter said:

"We heard you get up, master. Some of us too have been finding it hard to sleep." Andrew was with him. From the inn Matthew and Thomas were coming. They had become like animals with their quickness to wake, all except Little James, who had to be kicked and thumped into getting up. "Moreover, there are things to be asked that there never seems to be time to ask."

"What things?"

"You spoke of being taken from us," Andrew said. "When? Who will do the taking?"

"Soon," said Jesus. "The taking will, in effect, be the work of everyone. Some will bear thongs and swords, some not. It makes little difference."

John, in the bull-voice that accorded so strangely with his sweetness and delicacy, was calling: "Up. Out. Fresh goat-milk. Fresh bread."

"You spoke also," Peter said, "of coming again. This means that you will be taken but freed again?"

"No, Peter. Not freed, except by my heavenly father. Taken, Peter, tried, killed. But I shall come again."

Peter and Andrew chewed that along with the breakfast bread. Soon all were drinking from the milk-crock passed from hand to hand as the dawn rose over the city. Another hot dry day.

"What," said Peter at length, "will be the sign?"

"After three days," Jesus said, "I shall be alive again. I shall be buried as Lazarus was. And, like Lazarus, I shall come out of that tomb. Alive. I shall be with you again for a brief space. Then I shall be lost to you. I shall become a memory to some, a children's tale to others; to the truly blessed, the truly believing, I shall be as a real presence. But I will return to the world, to the whole world, when the world is near to its ending."

"When," asked Bartholomew, "will that be?"

"In a thousand, a million years. Does it matter? Time is not a Roman march, time is a children's dance. Men are men. Time is nothing in the eyes of your heavenly father who made time for his world to dance in. But there will be signs of the end, and it may seem to some that the signs are always there—wars and rumours of wars, nation rising up against nation. Famines and earthquakes. Many shall stumble and deliver up one another and hate one another. Iniquity shall be multiplied, the love of many shall grow cold."

"It could be now," said Judas Iscariot.

Jesus said nothing to that. "It cannot be," he resumed, "until the gospel of the kingdom has been preached to the whole world. Under whatever name, in whatever form, the whole world must hear it, accept it, reject it. And then the end shall come. It will seem that the sun has been darkened and that the light of the moon is spent, and the stars may seem to begin to fall from heaven and the powers of the heavens be shaken. And then the Son of Man will appear. Riding on the clouds of heaven with power and great glory."

A thin shepherd's piping from the valley seemed to mock that terrible vision. "He shall," said Jesus, watching kindly the shepherd pipe his flock to pasture, "divide the sheep from the goats. And to those of the nations of the world that sit on his right hand he will say: Come, blessed of my father, possess the kingdom prepared for you from the foundation of the world. For as you showed love to your brethren, so you showed it to me. Then he shall say to those of the nations of the world that he has put on his left side: Depart from me, you accursed, into everlasting fire, for I was hungry— You know the rest, Peter."

"And you gave me no meat. Thirsty, and you gave me no drink."

"Naked," said John, "and you did not clothe me."

"And they will say these words," Jesus went on. *"When did we see you hungry and thirsty and naked and not show charity to you?* And he shall answer them, saying: You showed no charity to my brethen, *your* brethren, and so you showed none to me, and—" To Judas Iscariot he said: "Finish it, my dear son."

"And these," said Judas, "shall go away into eternal punishment, and the righteous into eternal life. Eternal life."

There was a long silence. Thomas broke it by sighing, taking a bit of bread, then chewing it somewhat loudly. He swallowed it and said, in his harsh undeferential way:

"So it will be a long time between the sinner's death and his judgment. Maybe a million years."

"A million years are nothing," Jesus said. "Enter the house of death and you leave time behind. The judgment. Neither the sinning soul nor the just soul will have long to wait. You may even say that the kingdom is now, that heaven and hell are now."

Coming up the hill was a group of children, their mothers with them. Peter grumbled: "They should go to see you in the Temple. They disturb an hour of rest. I'll send them away."

"No, Peter, let them come. Of such is the kingdom of heaven. And I say this to you all—unless you become like children yourselves, re-learning innocence and faith, you shall not enter into that kingdom." He rose and went down to meet the children. Bartholomew said to Judas Iscariot:

"Re-learning innocence. Can you do that?"

"I must try," said Judas. "It is difficult, but I must try."

Down in the city, the truly innocent—those who believed that the world could be changed for the better by changing its governors—were clamouring outside the jailhouse where

Barabbas and Jobab and Aram lay on dirty straw. "Barabbas," they shouted. "Jesus bar-Abbas. Set him free. Free Israel. Freedom for Israel. Down with the occupying tyrant." They were loud but harmless. They had no weapons. The knot of soldiers that guarded the prison had no difficulty in driving them away. Having, for the most part, nothing else to do, they kept coming back to shout: "Free Barabbas. Free Israel."

The warder Quintus brought in black bread and water for Barabbas and his friends.

"Quite a hero, eh? They want you to be set free. So you can carry on with your murdering."

"We do no murder."

"Not for lack of trying. Patriotic fervour, eh? Well, it won't be long for you now."

"It won't be a fair trial," snarled Jobab or Aram. "It never is. You may as well dispense with it."

"Trial? Trial? I wasn't talking of a trial. Self-evident guilt was the way it was put to me. It was execution I was referring to."

"When?" said Barabbas.

"As soon as his excellency the Procurator gets in from Caesarea. For your Pissover or Passover or whatever you call it, yeled. Then they'll have you up there, knees together, arms stretched, with the old nails banged in, bang bang bang. Good view you get from up there. But you soon lose interest in it."

There was now a loud noise of hissing and booing and "Kill him" from outside the jailhouse.

"Ah," said Quintus, going over to the wall-bars. "Changeable lot, you Jews. Hissing and booing you now. No, they've turned their backs. Somebody else."

It was, in fact, Jesus who was being reviled by the more ragged of the Zealots whom, however, the Roman troops were beating off with clubs and little trouble.

"Traitor, you let us down. Siding with the Romans."

"Love your enemies. Go on, love *me*, bastard." And a stone flew.

"Good Romans and good Samaritans. Go off and kiss their arses."

Jesus and his disciples passed calmly on, not hurrying, towards the Temple. Thomas said to Matthew, though quietly: "He should never have done it. Curing that centurion."

"It was his servant."

"Whoever it was. It's got around, that story. Friend of the Romans, they say. God, there's a lot of teaching to do."

While Jesus taught that morning, a select group of the Religious Council met. They met in a plain but expensively en-marbled chamber at the back of the Temple. Their table was of Lebanon wood, beautifully planed and exquisitely polished, designed in the form of a horseshoe. Their chairs were little thrones, not very comfortable. There were laymen, Eliphaz among them, as well as priests. Ten minutes after the hour at which the meeting was appointed to begin, an usher came to the door and cried:

"His eminence the Lord Caiaphas, Chief Priest of the Temple."

Everyone stood. Caiaphas was a formidable man, prow-nosed, sharp-eyed, deeply read in three tongues, quiet-spoken, polite, simply dressed in a snowy robe. He came in smiling, say-ing:

"Be seated. Please be seated. I apologise for being late. There is much to do at this season, as you know. Passover is al-most upon us. This," he said, seating himself at the middle of the horseshoe bend, "is, I gather, an emergency meeting. I regret, again because of the imminence of Passover, that it must be a brief one. There is a terrible amount to do, gentlemen. We are met to consider, so I understand, the so-called ministry of this so-called—what is he so-called? Prophet? Rabbi?"

"He is called many things, your eminence," said Haggai. "We are less concerned with what he is called than with what he does."

"He appears," said Caiaphas, "at least from what I hear, to do much that is beneficial. He cleansed the Temple precincts of those noisy vendors of pigeons and cattle. That was a good thing to do. Something we ourselves had always intended to consider doing, but apathy or something got in the way." He looked rather sharply at a priest who was believed to make money out of the franchise. "He preaches goodness, so I hear, he tells of the virtue of poverty—" The priest did not blush.

"And so," said Eliphaz boldly, "of the vices of the rich. And also of the hypocrisy of the respectable. He finds more virtue among prostitutes and cut-throats than among the keepers of the Temple."

"I see," said Caiaphas. "What is known as radical talk."

"Radical," said a layman of great age and respectability called Nicodemus. "He gets to the roots of things. I personally have nothing against his radical talk."

"I made," said Caiaphas, "no pejorative implication. My mind is open, Nicodemus. But I must hear more."

"He denies," said Habbakuk, "the validity of certain aspects of the Mosaic code. He takes it upon himself, for instance, to condemn divorce and, in effect, to condone adultery. The only sin, so he seems to imply, is not to love. He is an apostle of love," he smiled.

Caiaphas did not smile. Haggai said:

"I call it all a kind of inverted morality."

"Whatever you call it," said Caiaphas, "we have had it before. We had it from the man called John, whom Herod of Galilee very unwisely had executed. We had it from many before him, and we shall have it from many again. The return to simplicity, the crying out for justice."

"Which means," said Samuel, "the crying out against established order."

"Oh, established order can always look after itself," said Caiaphas with impatience.

"But," said Eliphaz, "we have to think, don't we, in terms of two kinds of established order. In a Judea, that is, under Roman occupation. The Romans do not molest our religion, but do they like it?"

"The Romans," Caiaphas said, "are not a religious people. They are distressingly secular. But that, of course, makes them reasonably tolerant. Our religion amuses them."

"With respect, eminence," said Habbakuk, "you have, I fear, missed Master Eliphaz's implicit argument. Which is this. Our religion is a national religion. Israel is both a people and a faith. The Zealots, who are such a nuisance to us all, the Zealots draw their whole argument for a liberated Israel out of holy scripture. The God of Israel, so to speak, presiding over the whole nation of Israel. To put it very simply, eminence, the Romans might welcome an alternative religion in Palestine."

"True," said Caiaphas, "but only one alternative religion —the worship of Caesar and the rest of the pagan pantheon— Jupiter, Mars, Venus and so on. And that is not even a faith—a mere set of convenient myths, call it, for the use of Roman poets."

"If I may make the point that my colleague Father Habbakuk is no more than implying," said Haggai, "the faith that this Jesus teaches is not a national faith. There are Syrians, even Romans, who listen to him. It seems that he effected some kind of quack cure in a Roman household—a miracle, it's called by the credulous. The point is this, eminence: it is not a faith that could ever become a sword in the hands of the Zealots. He does not teach a religion of the Jewish people. The point he makes is that it is for all people, all."

"And, let me add," said Jonah, "it grants to Caesar what Caesar considers to be his due. He was all too clear about that. The faith of this Jesus is a faith without what we may call political content. It presents to the Romans no danger whatsoever. Rather the opposite."

"But the danger to our own holy established faith," cut in Eliphaz, "is, in consequence, very considerable."

"Strange," said Caiaphas. "You all speak of the faith as though it were a new faith. And yet, I gather, the scriptures are never out of his mouth. In what way is it *new?* For if we can establish that it is new, then we may establish that it is blasphemous."

"When does a thing become *new?*" asked Nicodemus. "A moment ago we were talking of a radical thing. Roots are old, and he has been returning to the roots. Our faith is not quite the same as the faith of Moses, and yet we do not call it new. Perhaps we do not call it new because we are frightened we may have to call it blasphemous."

"Look," said Habbakuk. "This Jesus takes the holy scriptures and, as it were, pushes them in the direction of a fanatical extreme. I call such a procedure heretical. Why do we have a priesthood? Why do we have a body of elders? In order that fanaticism may be avoided, in order that learned and sensible men may interpret holy writ as it ought to be interpreted—in terms of the possible."

"In terms of the convenient," said Nicodemus. "In terms of the expedient and respectable."

"Precisely," said Haggai. "Life has to be lived."

"Look, your eminence, your reverences, gentlemen," said Eliphaz. "He's a menace to our faith. Can we not leave it at that?"

"A menace to our self-esteem," said Caiaphas. "A witness against our complacency. A very dangerous man. So what do you wish to do with him?"

"Do for him," said Jonah coarsely. "Have done with him. Do away with him."

"*Death,*" said Nicodemus, "being too radical a word."

"Well," Haggai said. "All this is literally a matter of life and death for the established faith. If his teaching prevails—and remember it is reinforced by trickery that the people are only too ready to call miraculous—the Romans may be only too happy to accept it as the main faith of the province."

"Could it," asked Caiaphas, "ever become the main faith of the province?"

"It's a faith for the poor, the sick, the downtrodden," said

Habbakuk. "Isn't that enough? The Zealots hate it, but the Zealots are a loud-mouthed minority. Besides, they'll soon be put down, all of them. The point, I think, is this—given a chance, the occupying power will disestablish our true faith as subversive and anti-Roman. He ought to die, though I shudder to utter the word. For what's the alternative? Send him to preach in exile? Put him in jail? The ways to the jail will be crammed with his followers—that's what happened with John. More riots, more troops, the eventual total Roman enslavement of the province."

"You know very little, any of you," said Caiaphas acidly, "of the true theme that struggles to rise to the surface of our discourse. 'It is meet that one man die for the people': is the expression known to you? No, I see it is not. Once in a thousand years it happens—the coming of the human scapegoat. The good man, innocent as a beast, who can carry on his back the sins of the people. Virtuous as an angel, but loaded with the nation's sins. A sacrifice on behalf of the people. Do you understand me?"

Someone now spoke who had not previously spoken, had instead kept his eyes lowered to the table, his hands clasped, his mind apparently elsewhere. He now said:

"The people may put a goat to death. But not a man."

Caiaphas smiled. "Father Zerah, I wondered when we should hear from you. You understand me well enough. And you remind us all of something we would like to forget—the limits placed upon our secular powers. Only the Romans can order an execution. They have, as it were, to be persuaded to be the hand that grasps the sacrificial knife."

"If you will excuse me, your eminence, reverend fathers," Nicodemus said, beginning to get out of his chair. "I do not think there is anything I can profitably contribute—"

"Your presence at our meetings," said Caiaphas smoothly, "is always much appreciated. You contribute much—wisdom, compassion, the mellow fruits of long experience of the world."

"Thank you," Nicodemus said, now standing. "So if you will—"

"Oh, we are all going now," said Caiaphas. "I must declare this discussion at an end—temporarily. So much to do elsewhere, so little we can profitably do here. The limits placed upon our secular powers—I repeat the phrase. Perhaps we can observe further, meet again after Passover." He rose.

"But, eminence," said Eliphaz, also rising. "It is before Passover we must act, before the city fills with Passover pilgrims. There is no knowing what corruptions, blasphemies— Also riots," he added. "Public disorder. I insist—"

"Ah, no, you do not," said Caiaphas. "Thank you all for your attendance. Perhaps, Father Zerah, if you would stay a moment— A brief word about the other matter—"

There was no other matter. Zerah and Caiaphas softly walked the conference-room together. Zerah said:

"There is an area where blasphemy and treason become one. The Romans, as we know, regularly use blasphemy to compound treason. Speak against the Emperor, and you are also speaking against God. For us, it is a question of making *our* blasphemy *their* treason. You follow me, eminence?"

"Yes yes yes."

"What is the ultimate blasphemy? I shudder to utter the words." But he was not shuddering at all. "To snatch *I am that am* from the very mouth of the divinity—"

"If he has uttered such words, he has not yet done so before the people."

"But to his immediate followers? One of his followers came to me. A highly enthusiastic young man. As a matter of fact, we knew each other from our schooldays. We studied Greek together. He seemed to take it for granted that I was—one of the *progressive* elements in the hierarchy."

Caiaphas smiled sadly. "Innocence," he said.

"He talked of miracles, of a king in Judea, of the faith which would transform all Israel. An enthusiast, a good man—"

"Innocent."

"I do not think, to be just, one can blame Jesus for the pretensions of his followers."

"If," pondered Caiaphas, "this particular follower could—

before witnesses—swear that this Jesus made the ultimate, blasphemous claim—?" And then, in some disgust: "We are plotting traps, tricks. This is unseemly. Perhaps we are taking the whole matter far too seriously, Zerah. Perhaps the flame will blow itself out. Perhaps other agencies of of of suppression could—I don't know. I gather both the Pharisees and the Zealots throw stones."

"Throwing stones is nothing. He has twelve strong men to throw stones back. And if a Zealot should take a knife to him—"

"I understand. He has stout defenders." He paused, then said: "You took my point about the scapegoat?"

"It was a just point. Well," sighed Zerah. "I must go to work. Time is very short."

Indeed, the Passover was almost upon them, and the city was filling with pious provincials. When the caravan from Nazareth arrived, Jesus, Peter, John, Judas Iscariot and the two Jameses were there to meet it. Mary, Jesus's mother, was tired and engrimed from the journey, but her mature beauty and dignity were nothing impaired. With her was the old rabbi Gomer. Jotham, sour as ever, snorted at Jesus.

"Do we spend it together?" Mary said.

"Dear mother, I think you know we cannot. You must think of me as a hen with a brood to look after. Nor may I stay much in the town. I have enemies."

"Well," barked Jotham. "You knew you'd have enemies. Didn't I always say you'd have enemies? Leaving your decent useful work behind and flying in the face of decency and normality."

"You mustn't speak so, Jotham," said the rabbi mildly. "The law has to change, and it is given to a very few, God's chosen, to change the law. Yet who wants change? There is no greater enemy than the bringer of change."

"Letters of gold," sneered Jotham, "write that in letters of— Well, you've made a name for yourself, Jesus, I'll say as much. But it's not a name any decent God-fearing man ought to care to have—"

Jesus smiled sadly as a couple of men, muscled by hard work and lined with disappointment, came up to their party. One of them said: "You pushed back the work ten years. Traitor to the cause. Traitor to John the prophet. I'd spit on you were it not for the presence of this lady. Let it be enough for now to put God's curse on you. Curse you, traitor."

Jesus sketched a mild blessing, while the two Jameses came forward, very truculent. "No, no," said Jesus. "Leave them." And, mildly, undisturbed, he shouldered the bundles of all three Nazarenes and walked away with them to look for lodgings. Nicodemus had been watching. He now came up to Judas Iscariot and said quietly:

"Forgive my addressing you. None of you knows me, but I know your work and bless it. I dare not, God help me, bless it aloud. It occurs to me that you had all best remove to a place of safety. Not even your inn on the Mount of Olives is immune from the visitations of—well, enemies."

"I see," said Judas Iscariot. "You know we are there."

"Many know. You've already had—visitors?"

"Mothers with their children. No enemies as yet. But we have been told to move out tomorrow. We cannot afford the Passover rates the landlord wants to charge—robbery, sheer barefaced—"

"My name, by the way, is Nicodemus, not that it matters. I am happy to offer you lodgings without charge. I have a garden and a small summer house over the brook Kerith. In Gethsemane."

"Gethsemane?"

"Not so loud. It's very private. Strongly walled about. A great gate and a massy key. I have the key here, look. Make sure you keep it safely. There are plenty of thieves about."

"A key would be of no use to a thief unless he knew—"

"Exactly. You must take your enemies seriously. Very seriously."

"I am overjoyed," Judas Iscariot said. "I do not know how to—"

"I am thanked enough by knowing of his safety. Forget my name. It's of no importance. God's blessing."

"Returned a thousandfold."

FOUR

It happened that Mary, the mother of Jesus, found lodging in a lodging-house which was no more than a long room with an earth floor, sacks of straw for mattresses, a well outside, and that this was the lodging-house where Mary of Magdala, little Salome, and the pious seamstresses were already installed. Thus the two Marys met, and the younger Mary heard much about the early days of Jesus and heard the great miracle confirmed of his virgin birth. Salome was not over-impressed by the story of what we may term parthenogenesis, since she had led a sheltered life, had been ill-educated, and was not able easily to separate the ordinary from the supernatural. She was also restless and somewhat bored, for there had been nothing to do in Jerusalem save observe the goings-on in the Temple precincts and hear the word of the New Law. Also what money Mary of Magdala had was near run out, and there was no decent means by which they could procure more. Salome, in her young innocence, had spoken of dancing in the taverns, but Mary quickly stamped on that. But Mary of Magdala shared an innocence with Salome that Jesus's mother found most troubling, since for a princess of Galilee to leave her palace, her mother and her royal stepfather without permission and without word was surely a high state matter, and it was a wonder that soldiers of Herod the tetrarch, perhaps as the entourage of Queen Herodias herself, were not searching in Jerusalem for her, or that letters had not been sent from Galilee to the procurator of Judea asking for aid in the finding of the missing princess. But the other Mary said:

"Their high and mightiness is of no importance. The poor child was drawn into a shameful and sinful affair and was made the cause of the death of the great prophet. She was right to leave her wicked mother and, from what I hear, her sick-minded and lecherous stepfather. Now she is my sister and, as she needs a mother, it would be right for you yourself, blessed one, to take her as a daughter."

Jesus's mother sighed at this and then said: "Gladly. But there is this matter of the law and the rights of true mothers, though wicked. And there is the matter of the force of armies and of men in power. I foresee trouble."

"There will always be trouble," said the other Mary simply. "And it is right that, in the face of trouble, the women who follow Jesus should band together and themselves be an army. To this we few who are here are pledging ourselves, and our first duty is to bid the army grow. We may know *trouble*, but are we not the daughters of him who has come and do we not hold in ourselves the strength of his spirit?"

Jesus's mother nodded, though sadly and with misgivings. It seemed to her that the mission of her blessed son was to *court* trouble. It seemed especially so to her when she heard, as she did the following morning, that Jesus had gone to supper at the house of a certain centurion named Sextus and had been jeered at and threatened by certain Zealots who called "Asslicker, friend of the enemy, Roman Jew" and threw stones. But he had gone to supper nonetheless, had eaten Roman victuals and quoted Roman poets. He had been escorted back to his new lodgings by his entire body of twelve, who had grumbled at his foolhardiness and his apparent desire *to court trouble*, but were thankful that at least he had given up preaching in the Temple and proposed remaining in his garden or summer house with his disciples, teaching them, praying, awaiting some mysterious event which he would not specify, except in words like "when I am taken away" and "when I am killed."

It was a little before the Passover feast when Judas Iscariot, begging for the poor in the Temple precincts, was accosted by the priest Zerah. Zerah began by giving a piece of silver, then he said:

"You must come with me. Important matters are afoot. Is your man safe?"

"My master is, thank God, safe. He is keeping himself in seclusion until Passover. After Passover there will be new plans."

"I share your thankfulness. Now come to my house. There is somebody important you must meet."

In Zerah's house there was a distinguished man in a grey cloak with the hood thrown back. When Judas Iscariot heard his name he at once went down on his knees and begged a blessing.

"Rise, my son. You need no blessing from me. You live, so I hear, in blessedness. Zerah, I think we might have some wine."

Wine was brought. The three men settled to it and to speech, seated round a simple table in a simple room totally without ornamentation but with many scrolls in three languages. Caiaphas said:

"I wish to hear more about his concern with death. Tell us more, my son."

"He has talked constantly of it. Of his rejection by the priests of the Temple, by the Pharisees and Sadducees, by the Zealots, by even the ordinary simple people he has cured of their diseases." Judas sipped his wine, a dry Falernian, and said: "His rejection, and then his death. He has talked of it all the time."

"A light in Israel," murmured Caiaphas, "and that light to be put out. Does he not know how much he is needed?"

"You must see it, I think, from the point of view of what I must call his *obsession*. He says that the scripture has to be fulfilled. That the Son of Man has to be killed in atonement for the sins of the world."

Caiaphas and Zerah looked at each other, and Zerah nodded.

"Scapegoat," said Caiaphas. "The ultimate scapegoat. Does he call himself the Son of Man? Or the Son of God?"

"Both," Judas Iscariot said. "He speaks of his heavenly father, however, and never his earthly one. He does not seem to believe he had an earthly father. There is, again, eminence, the prophecy about a virgin conceiving."

"Yes. What does he say will happen after his—God forbid—his death?"

"That he will rise again. After his burial. In order, again, that scripture may be fulfilled."

"What I say now," said Zerah, "is very terrible. I trust you will not," he said to Judas, "repeat these words outside. For I say now that he must be saved from fulfilling the scripture. The scripture must not be fulfilled. For," and he opened his hands and spread them, "can we doubt that this is the one, the one sent to bring the light?"

"He talks," asked Caiaphas, "of being taken soon, of being—the word sticks in my throat—?"

"He talks of enemies here and now," Judas Iscariot said. "Of the horror coming soon."

"There is only one way out, as I see it," Caiaphas said. "He must be delivered into the hands of his friends—those of his friends, I mean, who are best able to protect him. Forgive me, my son, for implying that you and your companions are powerless. Powerful in grace you may be, but grace cannot contend with stones and swords and hangman's nooses."

"Tell me, your eminence," said Judas, "what you see as the way out? How delivered? What will his—forgive me—*new* friends do?

"He must be taken to a place of *real* seclusion," Zerah said. "His eminence has in mind, I believe, his own villa, which lies very much secluded in the north of the province. There he may be persuaded to put off thoughts of impending death and to do his true work—which is to work with the guardians of the faith, to bring the New Law gently into official being to replace the Old. Israel has waited so long. So very long."

"Taken," said Caiaphas, "even against his will. Harsh, harsh, it sounds harsh, but can you, my son, think of an alternative?"

"I will not oppose this," said Judas Iscariot, "but be sure that many of his disciples will."

"We have," said Zerah, "our own armed guard. This was, as you may know, opposed by the Roman power, but they at length saw reason. The Temple must be protected, as must the servants of the Temple, and we can have no secular forces involved in this holy protection. The armed escort will be totally for his safety, and I myself will be in charge of it. He has too many enemies."

Judas said: "His worst enemy is perhaps himself." The two others nodded gravely. Zerah said:

"Where can he be found?"

"We lodge in Gethsemane. Well-protected by walls and an iron gate. I suggest very late at night. I can open to you."

"Our gratitude," said Caiaphas, "and the gratitude of the Israel that is yet to be."

"I am the grateful one," said Judas Iscariot. "When will you come?"

"It would be proper, indeed most solemn," said Caiaphas, "to do this ah salvatory work after we have all celebrated the holy rite of thanksgiving for the deliverance of our race from the bondage of Egypt. The night of Dies Jovis, to use the pagan calendar imposed on us. Again, bless you, my son."

Jesus and his twelve held their Passover supper in the upper room of an inn some hundred or so steps away from Gethsemane. It had been arranged well in advance by Matthew, who had had moreover to pay in advance, and it consisted of a whole roasted lamb, a garnishing of chicory and endives, heavy bread without leaven, a jug of wine—the meal which the Israelites had eaten when the Angel of Death passed over Egypt, a simple meal of hurry seasoned with bitterness. The disciples—all except Judas Iscariot—ate heartily, but Jesus touched little. John, who sat next to him, remarked on this. Jesus said:

"I've much on my mind, John. Troubled in spirit, if you wish me to put it more formally." Then he cleared his throat and addressed the whole table, saying: "Listen to me, all of you. In each part of our mission, in each act of my life, I have striven to fulfil the prophecies of scripture. But, unwilled by me, the prophecies must sometimes fulfil themselves. We face now, in bitterness more bitter than any herb of this Passover meal, a fulfilment that may in no wise be set aside. For it is written: he that eateth my bread lifteth up his heel against me. And so I say that I must be betrayed, sold to the enemy—and by one of you here."

Mouths at once opened, full of chewed bread. Wine sputtered and dribbled. There were shocked indrawings of breath. Matthew coughed and coughed and had to be thumped by Thomas on the back.

"I say one, and one only."

The disciples looked uncomfortably at one another. Peter said:

"I speak for us all, master, when I say—well, none here could as much as dream of betraying you, as you call it. There was that time—long past now—when there was talk, and it was me that did the talking—but that's all over and done with. Do you mean—that evil has to descend on one of us—against his will? Do you mean that the devil has to crawl into somebody just so that the scriptures can be fulfilled? If I may say so, I'm getting a bit tired of all this business about the scriptures being fulfilled, and that's a fact."

"You must wait," said Jesus, "for what must be. You will not have long to wait."

There was a great babble of talk now, and the food was ignored. John said quietly to Jesus:

"I must know who, I must. Tell me, master, as you love me."

"I name no name," said Jesus. "And only you know what I say now, and I forbid you to act on what you know. He who dips his bread in the dish of the juice of the meat when I dip mine—it shall be that one." Then he spoke aloud, stilling the babble:

"For the Son of Man goes, even as it is written of him, and woe to that man through whom the Son of Man is betrayed. But let us now think of another thing. Though, in a manner, it is the same thing. For the death of the Son of Man shall be the last of the sacrifices of flesh and blood, and it will be made to redeem mankind of all its sins. Now you must fully understand the nature of this sacrifice. It is a necessary sacrifice. God the father wills the death of his own son, who is of his own substance and essence, to pay that divine purity which sin so affronts. No smaller coin will pay for it, and thus you see the true weight of sin in the weighing hands of the eternal. Now this sacrifice must be remembered, as the Passover is remembered, till the end of time. But it must be more than remembered—it must be renewed, it must be re-enacted daily, for the continuing redemption of mankind. For the sin man commits in his own flesh and spirit, the sin he inherits from as far back as Adam, can in no wise be fully redeemed by man's own repentance and penance. As man sins daily, so daily must he be redeemed. And now I teach you the mode of the daily renewal of the sacrifice—no mere remembrance, but a true re-enactment." He took a half-cut loaf from the bread-basket and said: "This I take and give thanks for it—blessed gift of our father—and I break it, and to each of you I give a portion." He broke the bread into pieces, and the pieces were passed round. The clumsy big hands of Little James let fall his piece to the floor, and he picked it up again and dusted it on his sleeve. The disciples looked puzzled at their pieces. Then they looked shocked at his next words. Jesus said:

"Eat. This is my body. Eat." Some held their bread poised some inches away from mouths open in shock (*always full of surprises*). "Eat," commanded Jesus. So they ate. "This is my body, I say. And you that have the power which I leave with you, and they to whom you shall give the power, must do what I have done, and that till the end of time, daily for man's sins. In shape and taste this is bread, but in truth, when the words are spoken, it is also my body, my presence." In the continuing shocked silence, the gurgle of wine from the jug to a cup was to be clearly heard as Jesus poured. "And now," Jesus said, "I take this cup of wine—blessed gift of our father—and to each of you I give the wine to drink. It smells and tastes of wine, like wine it is thin and holds the light, but in truth it is my blood—the blood of the covenant, which is shed for many, for the remission of their sins. Drink." The cup passed round, and they drank. They drank gingerly, sipped rather, and there was much left in the cup when it came to the last drinker, John. "Finish it, John," Jesus said, "drain it."

To the table at large he said: "When you are alone, fulfilling your charge to spread the gospel, you must enjoin that this meal of my body and blood be taken by all who believe in me. I say *alone,* but you will never be alone. For I shall be with you, not only in the spirit, but in my flesh and blood, under these two blessed forms, to the end of time. Daily sacrificed, daily renewed." Then he sat back, as though tired. Thomas said, in his blunt way:

"There's things I don't rightly understand in all this body and blood business, if ye'll grant me the liberty of so saying. I'm leaving out this death business, because ye'll not die when we're with ye—"

"Thomas, Thomas," warned Peter.

"All right, get ye behind me Satan and all the rest of it. We'll forget the dying a minute. But ye talk of eating your flesh and drinking your blood—and that's the way of the beast, that kills and eats what it kills. Now we're men, not beasts, and I don't like it."

"Good, Thomas," Jesus said, "you show your usual courage. Let me put it this way. Sacrifice is destruction. When you take bread and wine you destroy them. But in destroying them you benefit your body. But a bit of bread and a drop of wine are a poor sacrifice for the sins of mankind. So they must be turned into something—some body—that is not a poor sacrifice. And another thing—thus, in these forms, I am with you, not as a floating spirit or a passing thought but as solidity and flow. You can only embrace the bread and the wine by taking them into yourself." He raised his voice. "It will be easy enough, too easy, so you will see, to speak of the bread and the wine as mere remembrance, as sign and symbol. But I must be truly with mankind in these forms. The simple forms of our daily life— could anything be better?"

There was a new silence, but a more settled and satisfied one. Thomas said: "Aye, aye, aye." Jesus said, swiftly, to Judas Iscariot:

"Did I put it your satisfaction, my dear son?"

Judas smiled, and some laughed, and the disciples set themselves to finishing the roast lamb, now cold, and there was a good-natured quarrel as to who should clean the bone. Peter said to Judas, kindly:

"You haven't finished your bread. Bit hard to get down, I know, when it's dry like that." He grabbed the bread that Judas held in limp fingers. "Here." And he dipped it into the meat juice at the very same moment as Jesus. John drew in his breath in shock. Jesus warned him with a look to say, show nothing. Judas took the bread from Peter and, while Peter kindly watched, ate it. "Better, Jude, my boy. We all need nourishment. Stick to your ribs, that will." Jesus was saying to John:

"You see? You see, John? I become bread and wine—fruits of the earth that is God's earth. I become the sacrifice of the New Law. But do not think it is *they—others*—that kill. You're all involved in the killing of the Son of Man." There was renewed silence, a cessation of chewing. "And though I spoke of only one, yet you are all involved in his betrayal." Peter stoutly said:

"This I will not have. I will go with you to the limit. If you are to die, I too—"

"No!" cried Jesus. "You are the living rock of the church,

the company of those that follow the word. And yet, Peter, you're man, with man's sinfulness and weakness. You will deny me and be very ready to do so. You will see."

"No, no, I'm not having that. Torture, you mean, torture, killing. No, no, they can do what they like. I swear I won't do what you say. I won't deny—"

"Three times, Peter. Three separate denials. Before the first cock of the morning crows. Remember my words."

"Never. Never. Never never never—"

He was much shaken. When the company left the inn, Judas leaving a small coin for the serving-girl amid the crumbs and wine-stains, Peter stayed alone by himself at the rear of the body that now walked towards the brook Kerith, then across the brook by a little bridge, then towards the fine walled garden of Gethsemane. He did not join in the Passover hymn that the others sang:

> "He showed the power of that mighty hand
> And out of its bondage Israel came,
> From bondage to the promised land.
> Blessed be his holy name.
> Alleluia, alleluia.
> Blessed be his holy name."

The faces of the singers showed a gravity that belied the joy of the words of their hymn. They came to the garden gate, Judas took the great key which lay hidden in his breast, Judas turned the key in the lock with a short scream of rust, Judas stood back while the others entered. But Peter would not at first enter.

"I've much on my mind, Judas. I'm sick, I cannot enter—"

But with a kindly hand on his broad fisherman's shoulder, Judas Iscariot impelled him in. They sat on the grass in the moonlight around Jesus, while Jesus said:

"The hour is coming when you shall all be scattered, every man to his own, and leave me. For it is written: I will smite the shepherd, and the sheep, and the flock shall be scattered abroad. But after I am raised up I will meet you where we first met—in

Galilee. Wait and I shall come. We will sit together, as we sat to-night, we shall eat and drink together."

"I'll die with you, master, die with you," Peter kept saying, madly hitting the earth with his fist.

"Three times, Peter. Before cockcrow." To Judas he said: "You, my son, have a thing to do."

"There is nothing to do, master, save guard the gate, though the gate guards itself well enough."

"My soul is exceedingly sorrowful," Jesus said with a quietness that made them shudder despite the heat of the night. "Even unto death. Abide with me. Be with me. While I pray." And he went over to the small fountain, now long dry, knelt, joined his hands and leaned his elbows on the low stone wall that surrounded the fountain, and passed, it seemed, into an agony of silent prayer. Not altogether silent, for John, who was nearest to him, thought he heard the words: "Father, if you are willing, remove this cup of bitterness from me. My flesh is man's flesh and fears the pain. I have the man's weakness that tells me to yield and beg forgiveness from them it is my office to forgive. But always, always, not my will, but your will be done." Thaddeus, who was only a little further distant than John, thought he saw a sweat start on the forehead of Jesus, and it seemed to him that the sweat was the colour of wine.

But the praying was long, and the moon moved down the sky, and all these men were weary with anxiety and the greater burden of thought. The warm night, without noise except for night's creatures, conduced to sleep, and all slept except Judas Iscariot, who lay on the grass by the gate, watchful and listening. Only he heard the words of Jesus, less angry than sorrowful:

"Could you not stay awake a little while with me? The spirit indeed is willing but the flesh is weak. " And when he repeated, bitterly, "The flesh is weak," it seemed to Judas Iscariot that Jesus referred to himself. Jesus gently kicked the heavy body of Peter, and Peter woke suddenly and loudly, his fists bunched. Shocked, Peter saw his companions still asleep and roughly began to wake them. Jesus said:

"Behold, the hour is at hand, and the Son of Man is betrayed into the hands of sinners."

Judas heard those words, but did not take them in, for, with a kind of guilty joy, he heard footsteps approaching up the lane that led from the bridge over the brook to the gates of the garden. He saw, in the light of a lantern, the priest Zerah. Zerah was smiling somewhat sorrowfully, also resignedly: here was the task, and the task, God help them, had to be done. Judas turned the key in the rusty lock, and the gate creaked open. Zerah handed something to Judas as he entered the garden. A bag? A bag of calf-leather?

"First," said Zerah, "this." And he led in eight men carrying drawn swords.

"This?" said Judas Iscariot, puzzled. The bag seemed to contain money.

"So it's him, him," cried Peter, and he made as to leap on Judas.

"You must do nothing," said Jesus in a loud voice. "None of you. I command it."

"And so," Zerah said, "a place of safety. Say what you have to say."

Judas went up to Jesus and, very tearfully, said: "The scriptures must not always be fulfilled, master. You have the great work still to do. It's a journey, master. God speed." He kissed Jesus on the cheek. "Salvation, master. I did what had to be done."

When the guard closed in around Jesus and, for the moment, himself, Judas could think only: They are doing their work well, they will keep him in safety from the very start of his journey. But then Zerah, in the harsh voice of a man in authority, said:

"Jesus of Nazareth, you stand under arrest on a charge of blasphemy. The charge comes from the mouth of your own disciple here. He sold you."

"Sold sold sold?" Judas gaped, found the bag still clutched in his hand. His hand shook and the money clanked.

"And has been paid," said Zerah.

Judas Iscariot babbled: "Paid—paid paid for the—it was not—paid—master, I was not—did not—" He screamed and then threw the bag away from himself as if it were on fire. It opened up on the stone surround of the dry fountain and spilled money. Judas dribbled at it.

"The finest, sweetest mode of betrayal," Zerah said. "You have taught innocence, so I hear, Jesus of Nazareth. You had a good pupil here in my old fellow-student, ever ready to learn. Good at Greek, good at innocence. The innocence of one who wished to see the salvation of the world." To Judas he rapped, very harshly: "Go on, run, man, out of it. Run."

None could dream of touching Judas the wild animal as he ran in a single circle about the garden, howling. He fell and picked himself up, howling. Then he turned to Jesus, gurgled words that made no sense, then ran to the gate. He crashed into the ironwork, then recovered, then ran, screaming in pain, down the path that led to the bridge over the brook. They heard his howls and screams receding. Then Peter said:

"Quick."

It was Little James who grabbed the sword of one of the guard but Peter who took it and hacked at the head of a man now unarmed. His ear came off in a riot of blood. It was Little James who grabbed the sword of one of the guard but Peter who took it and hacked at the head of a man unarmed. But the sword fell from his grasp at the moment of his raising it. Jesus said:

"Throw down that weapon. All they that take the sword shall perish by the sword. Do you think I could not now beseech my father in heaven to send me more than twelve legions of angels? How shall the scripture be fulfilled if you act so?"

"Out of your own mouth," said Zerah. "Your disciple spoke no lie."

"So," said Jesus, "you are come to take me as if I had plotted treason. So be it. Let us go."

"The treason will come later," Zerah said. "That is the next step. As for those who followed you and were party to your crime or crimes—" He looked at the disciples, who looked back and at Jesus and then back at the priest, aware of the sharp swords, then at Jesus for the word.

"Let the scriptures be fulfilled," said Jesus. "Go. Leave me."

They were quick to run, all except John.

"John, go," said Jesus. "I command it."

"I think," said Zerah, "we will have him." And he nodded at the man who seemed to be captain of the guard. The captain of the guard made for John and grasped his garment. It was a loose garment. In panic John ran, leaving the garment in the hand of the captain. He ran naked out of the garden, howling like Judas.

"Come, then," said Zerah. "To the house of the high priest." He gestured that Jesus be marched off, then he remembered the money scattered by the fountain, turned to look at it, and said to an ordinary soldier of the guard: "Pick that money up. Put it back in the bag. Count it. You should have exactly thirty pieces."

It was a long march to the house of Caiaphas, and feet echoed and re-echoed in the sleeping city. It was a long wait in the courtyard of Caiaphas's house. At length Zerah led Jesus into the house and dismissed the guard. Night was leaving the sky and the wind blew cold. An old man, early at his work, began to make a fire in a large metal basket in the middle of the courtyard. One of the guard helped him bring kindling and wood. Soon it blazed, and the old man, who had a squint, said:

"Ah, something like a fire, that. What you been on, then?"

"An arresting job. This Jesus. The preaching one, not the other one."

"What happened then? Any trouble?"

"Bit of a scuffle, and then one of us gets slashed, or it looked like it, but it was nothing after all. All right really. More things to hear than things to look at."

"What things?"

"Screaming and shouting and then we bring him here. The others ran off. No trouble really."

"Something like a fire, that is."

Servants began to appear, yawning. A couple of giggling serving-girls came to the fire. One of them, giggling, turned her back to it and raised her skirt to it briefly.

"Here, watch that," said the member of the guard. "Remember where you are," grinning.

"I bet even his arse gets cold. His high and mightiness. He has an arse like everybody else."

"Seen it, then, have you?"

"Naughty, naughty."

"Something like a fire, that is. But if you want more wood you'll have to fetch it."

A man in a cloak, with the hood pulled up, came into the courtyard. He rubbed cold hands. He looked about him, as if looking for someone, not here yet, hang around, he'll be here soon.

"Here, you," said the firemaker, "come and have a bit of a warm. A nice fire while it lasts. Them as wants more wood will have to get it."

"I'm warm enough."

"Suit yourself."

"Ought to be a bit of breakfast going now," said the member of the guard. "Be good, all. And don't forget: if you want more wood—" He stamped off out of the courtyard.

"You're shivering," said one of the girls. "Come on, nothing to pay."

He came over and warmed his hands, which shook. The other girl said:

"Seen you afore, haven't I? Wait—you was with him. The Temple, it was. That Jesus."

"Who? Don't know him. Seen him, of course, but I don't know him."

"Where you from, then?" said the old squinting firemaker. "Not from these parts from the sound on you."

"Up and down, you know. Now here, now there. A nice fire. Warmer already."

"Wait," said the girl, "it *was* you. You *was* with him. I seen you that time there was the throwing of the stones."

"No, I tell you, no."

"Jesus of Nazareth," said the old man. "That's in Galilee."

"Is it?"

"Don't give me that. You're a Galilee man, I can tell the Galilee twang. My wife's people come from those parts."

"No, no, never been there."

Well, if you was with him before, like she says, you ought to be with him now, in there. You know he was took? Of course, you know."

"I just came here to wait for a man to come out and pay me some money he—I don't think he's coming."

"Woodsmoke in your eyes, is it? There's some eyes can't abide woodsmoke."

But the man ran away. They watched him stumble and recover, leaving the courtyard. The old man said:

"Crying, did you see that? Come to get some money, he said. You know what that'd be for, don't you? There's a word for that. There's some men as would sell their own mothers."

FIVE

Of what now happened to Judas Iscariot I am not competent to speak. I can only bring together a few of the legends that have clustered about his end, and these belong properly to some great phantasmagoric poem, as yet unwritten, rather than to the sober chronicle of fact that this work endeavours to be. Thus, it is said that he ran wildly round the town in the small hours looking for an open rope shop but howled like a dog when he found he had no money in his purse. A little boy appeared in a doorway and crowed like a cock, flapping in wing fashion his little arms. Judas Iscariot ran from this, only to confront another prodigy in a lamplit alley, where a girl, encouraged by her parents very kindly, was vomiting up copiously writhing and talking worms. "I too can speak Greek," cried Judas Iscariot, and he ran away. There was a street in which a toothless laughing old man sold crude pictures of him, Judas himself, writhing in a fire. Judas ran yelling from the old man, who laughed loudly. Then a young man came down another street selling coils of rope, calling: "Rope, rope, fine rope, best hemp, rope."

"Yes," said Judas, "but I don't think I can pay."

"Give me that empty bag, then, and give me what you're wearing, and give me those shoes, for you won't need them where you're going. You look like a man that knows he's going to the Garden of Eden. Here you are. Get stripped."

Now a naked Judas, a rope on his shoulder, ran towards the open country and found a little mewing kitten with a hurt paw lying piteously on his path. Judas picked the poor creature up and stroked it tenderly, saying:

"How can I, how can I? Lick the paw and it will soon be better." Then he ran on, leaving the tiny cat to continue mewing.

He came at length to a wood and chose a tree called ever since a Judas tree. Climbing the tree in order to reach a convenient branch, he saw a nest with five nestlings in it, all of which opened their beaks like trumpets at him. He gently placed the nest on a higher branch. Then he fixed the rope to a strong branch a little lower and made a noose with the other end, muttering to himself:

"Oh, yes, good at Greek. Kai elabon ta triakonta arguria, teen timeen tou tetimemenon, hon etimeesanto apo huion Israel, kai edokan auta eis ton agron tou kerameos, katha sunetazen moi Kurios." And then: "That the scriptures may be fulfilled." Then he hanged himself in a deafening chorus of cockcrows.

BOOK 6

ONE

Jesus was left alone in an ante-chamber of the house of Caiaphas. It was a bare room with a marble floor and two curved chairs in the Roman style, but he had not been invited to sit, and he did not sit. Nor was he alone for long. Eliphaz and one or two other holy Pharisees came in—at whose invitation was not clear—and immediately began to sneer and revile. Eliphaz said:

"Not so ready now to revile and sneer, are you? Not so quick to curse and condemn your betters. Come on, let's hear all about the whited sepulchres and the generation of vipers and how dirty it is to wash your hands before eating. You *filth*." He spat at Jesus's face, which was much higher than his own, and the moisture merely fell onto the breast of Jesus's seamless garment, which was otherwise very clean, having been washed by John only the day before in preparation for the Passover meal. Jesus looked at the spittle but would not deign to wipe it off with his fingers. Then he looked, smilingly, at Eliphaz and his friends. Eliphaz danced with rage:

"Grinner, leerer, you'll soon stop grinning and leering. Get that superior look out of your eye, you dirt." He kicked Jesus's right shin, hurting his own toe in the process far more than he hurt the tough flesh and muscle. "Blindfold the swine," he yelled. "Get a cloth, come on." Ezra pulled from his sleeve a rag he carried for wiping off sweat, for he was a sweaty man, and, being tall enough, bound Jesus's eyes. Jesus laughed and said:

"I see you assume I must submit to your childish game. I never thought that men of your kind would end by amusing me. Go on, do what you will."

Eliphaz had to jump to deliver a weak smack at Jesus's face. He panted: "Now we'll see how clever you are with your great bright eye of the spirit." He smote again, and the others smote after him, all except Jonah, who said:

"There's a certain—well, indignity—"

"Come on, prophet," panted Eliphaz. "Prophesy who's going to hit you next, filth."

Jesus pulled the blindfold off over his head and threw it to the floor. Then, without effort, he picked up Eliphaz like a child, held him up at arm's length, and said: "Spit now, if you will. It is easier to spit down than up." Eliphaz writhed, raging, and Jesus dropped him to the floor. At once the other Pharisees began to belabour Jesus. He stood calmly smiling and let them. Then the door opened and Zerah came in. He looked coldly at Eliphaz and his friends and said:

"This is unseemly."

"You are right," Jesus said. "I apologise. It is, I suppose, a solemn moment." Eliphaz snarled.

"The assembly is ready at last," Zerah said. "You are to come with me." And he gestured that Jesus follow him through an archway that led to a bare ringing corridor that carried an ancient stale odour of bread. A kind of secretary, yawning, passed them, carrying tablets. He converted the yawn into a gape at the height and muscularity of Jesus. "Here," said Zerah, and he opened a door. "Enter."

"A priest of the Temple must take precedence over a mere criminal," said Jesus. Zerah looked stonily for a moment and then went in. Jesus followed, seeing seated at a long plain table some dozen guardians of the faith, clerical and lay. One of the priests had just completed a lengthy yawn.

"It is early," Jesus said. "I am sorry you should have been dragged from your beds on my behalf."

"The prisoner," said Zerah, taking his place at the table, "will from this moment speak only when he is addressed." A door to the left was opened by a servant and Caiaphas came in. The assembly stood. Caiaphas was wearing an old and torn and somewhat dirty robe. Jesus said:

"I foresee ceremonial rending of garments."

Zerah said: "The prisoner will speak only when addressed." Then he looked towards Caiaphas, who had taken his place in the middle of the lined assembly. Caiaphas nodded and said:

"We may now begin, I think." He looked at Jesus and said: "You are Jesus of Nazareth? That is your name?" Jesus made no answer. "That is your name?" Jesus made no answer. Zerah said:

"The prisoner is being deliberately perverse."

"You do not deny that that is your name," said Caiaphas. "Are you also the Messiah? If you consider yourself to be the Messiah, you must tell us so."

"If I tell you," said Jesus, "you will not believe. What, then, is the point of telling you?"

"The High Priest," said Zerah, "is to be addressed as Your Eminence."

"What, your eminence, is the point of telling you?"

"That," said Caiaphas, "is no answer. But there is time enough for an answer. Tell us now—what is the nature of the teaching you and your disciples have been conducting here in Judea?"

"There is no need for you to ask, your eminence," said Jesus. "I have spoken openly to all who were willing to listen. I have taught openly in the synagogues, the streets, the Temple itself. I have taught nothing in secret. If you wish to know of my teaching, ask those whom I have taught."

Caiaphas and Zerah looked at each other dumbly. The priest Haggai made a finger-gesture at Caiaphas. Caiaphas nodded. Haggai said:

"The prisoner should know that we have certain signed and

sworn depositions. An example. You are alleged to have said: I am able to destroy the Temple of God and build it again in three days. Did you say this?"

Jesus looked at him but made no answer. Haggai shrugged. Caiaphas said:

"I revert to my former question. Are you, in your view, the Messiah? Do you consider yourself to be—blasphemy, blasphemy—the Son of the Most High?"

"Your eminence," said Jesus. "The works I have done in my father's name," he then said carefully and clearly, "shall be my answer."

"Your father's name," Caiaphas said. And to his colleagues: "You have heard. He has spoken sufficient blasphemy."

"You must now," said Jesus, "ceremonially tear your garments. Your eminence."

Caiaphas, apparently unabashed, stood and made a token rent in the breast of his robe. A portion of fleshless breast and a haired nipple showed. He said: "What is the word?"

"Death is the word," said Zerah, "but it may not be *our* word. Not in the present dispensation. If it please your eminence, the defendant stands convicted out of his own mouth of blasphemy. But this our assembly is not a court of trial but a court of enquiry. The findings of the court of enquiry are that the defendant stands accused, by the nature of the blasphemy he has spoken, of the secular charge of treason. Are there any dissentients?" He looked at his colleagues. There were no dissentients. Jesus said:

"With respect to the court, the court has no authority to make such a finding. In an Israel wherein the secular and the religious are one, a crime against the law is a crime against the All Highest. A crime against the All Highest may, according to the tradition of Moses, be punished by death. While the law, as at present, is divided into the sacred and the secular, the secular authority must prefer its own charges in respect of a secular crime and exact secular punishment. You may punish me by excommunicating me from the flock of the faithful, but you have no power to convert a crime against the faith into a secular crime. I say this only that you may be properly informed. I submit, as I must, to your untenable machinations, which, if you will, I will clarify to those among you unlearned in such processes. It is simple—"

Zerah said: "The court has been indulgent to the prisoner. The court says now only: what is the word of the accused in respect to the charge? This is a mere formula of courtesy and it need not be answered any more than it need be asked."

"I will speak terrible words," said Jesus, "as you expect. All too soon you shall see the heavens opening and the angels of God ascending and descending upon the Son of Man rearisen. Rearisen to administer a justice that is God's, not man's."

"The order of the court," said Caiaphas, rising, "is that you be led away to the Procurator of Judea, representative of the occupying power, in whose hand lies the authority for trial, judgment, and execution. Father Haggai, perhaps you would be good enough to summon the Temple guards."

Haggai nodded and got up. Going to the door, he looked up at Jesus and said: "Insolence. We have never before heard such insolence." And he lifted his hand to strike. Jesus swiftly took the hand and pulled it down. He held the hand as if it were a little girl's, while he said to the court, no longer a court, merely men rising, some prepared to go back to bed:

"With respect to the assembly, the process you now initiate will not be so easy as you think. The reasoning is simple enough: a man who claims to be the Messiah claims to be a king over Israel. But a king over Israel who arises out of Israel sets himself up against the authority of Caesar. Messiah—Christos—Basileus—Rex. There is your argument. But I never claimed kingship. I spoke of the kingdom of heaven, which is neither the kingdom of Israel nor the kingdom of Caesar. I have no more to say, but I beg you, for the good of your own consciences, to remember my words." All this time, Haggai struggled without success to be unhandled. Then Jesus, as if he had forgotten, looked down at the angry priest and let him go. Then he looked at some inner vision of his own while he and Zerah awaited the coming of the guard. Zerah said nothing either, busying himself with the reading of a scroll. Haggai came back with four men carrying swords.

"Now," said Haggai, "you will see how Pontius Pilate deals with insolence." But he kept his distance.

At dawn it had been announced officially by the representatives of the Roman power (Pontius Pilate was not yet in Jerusalem; he was still travelling from Cesarea) that there would be three crucifixions that afternoon. Execution and disposal of the bodies would, it was said, be punctiliously effected before the start of the Sabbath at sundown, since the occupying power recognised the special sanctity to the occupied of the Sabbath immediately following Passover. The criminals due to be executed were Jesus bar-Abbas, commonly called Barabbas, and his accomplices Jobab and Aram. There was loud anger from the Zealots when this announcement was made at dawn and at intervals through the earlier part of the morning. When Jesus was seen being escorted towards the palace of the Procurator —formerly the palace of Herod the Great—there were cries of "Traitor—you delivered him up to the enemy" and so on, and a stone was thrown that hit Haggai on the neck. He was furious in an unpriestly way and called for Roman protection. There were plenty of Roman troops about, only too happy to hit out at unwashed Jews with the flat of the sword.

It was a very busy morning. The money rejected by Judas Iscariot was returned to the Temple treasurer, but the Temple treasurer spoke of the unseemliness and probable illegality of reimbursing what he called *blood money*. A bright young official of the Treasury suggested that here at last was a heaven-sent opportunity (his principal demurred at that epithet) to make a provision much talked of, especially at the time of Passover when the city was crammed with visitors, but never fulfilled because of alleged lack of funds—namely, the conversion of a piece of commercial real estate into a public burial ground for strangers. The bright young official knew of a man who was carrying on a pottery business in a kind of yard of about an acre and had been talking much of giving up the business if he could only find a buyer for the land. The bright young official was waved off to make an offer of purchase, pay a deposit, and then arrange for a bill of conveyance to be drawn up. He went to see the potter and said:

"The Greater Jerusalem Burial Ground for Strangers. A noble title, eh?"

"All right, thirty. But I hear rumours about this money. Blood money they won't have back in the Temple."

"Money is money, neither bloody nor unbloody. This money is buying a place of holy charity. No questions asked about how they died or where they died. All right, make your cross here."

Because of the element of blood attached to the money, the field was soon popularly called Akeldama, or the Blood Field. I think you may hazard a guess as to who was first buried there. No questions asked. A charitable work. Cats played about his nameless mound.

Much happening this morning. Pontius Pilate, irritated by the cries of Zealots, arrived hungry at his procuratorial headquarters and took breakfast—bread, honey, and a sweet light wine—while his deputy, Quintilius, gave him a rapid summary of work to be done that day. Pilate was a frowning man in hale middle age, softer than he looked, growing sick of his position and dreaming already of retirement. Quintilius was intelligent, foxy and ambitious. Quintilius said:

"So much for minor infractions not meriting the death penalty. Of the three to be executed this afternoon, the Jews who were arrested for acts of public disaffection—"

"What of them? Is this Jesus bar-Abbas one of them? His damned name was shouted at me all the way here. One of these Jewish patriots, so-called. What of him, or them?"

"Well, it's him I have chiefly in mind, your excellency. It's been urged on me by—certain citizens that it would be a profitable act of clemency to release him. Execute the others but let this Barabbas go."

"Profitable? We don't seek profit from these Jews, Quintilius. And clemency bakes no bread at Rome. Get rid of the three of them, damned nuisances, an example to the rest of the *patriots*."

"Excellency," said Quintilius, "this is the time of the Passover. The city is crammed to bursting. This Jesus bar-Abbas is a popular figure. His release will cost less than—well, the trouble of maintaining order at a time of high emotion. National feeling seems to be growing. At this season everybody seems to remember that there was a time when the Jews were a nation enslaved by the Egyptians. They got out of Egypt, you know. They set themselves up as a nation. A long time ago, but they all remember."

"Yes," said Pilate, and he drank wine. "A national religion and a little local god. When are they going to grow up?"

"A good question, your excellency."

"What's the precise nature of his crime—this Barabbas character?"

"He smashed a Roman standard. He was in a state of extreme excitability at the time. This, apparently, had been aroused by the words of a popular preacher called Jesus of Nazareth. A coincidence—the same name, you see. A common enough name, though. Another form of *Joshua*. And here's another coincidence—this Nazareth Jesus has just been arrested himself— Well, in a way arrested. It wasn't a Roman arrest."

"If it wasn't a Roman arrest it wasn't an arrest at all."

"Come, excellency, remember that we encourage the—local population to assist in the keeping of Roman order. This Nazareth Jesus faces a grave charge. There are very high-placed witnesses to attest that he spoke treason."

"Said *down with Caesar,* you mean?"

"Said that he himself was the rightful ruler of this territory, your excellency." The two Romans looked at each other, then Pilate broke a bit of bread from the loaf and swamped it with Sicilian honey. Pilate said, munching:

"Mad, then."

"Mad or not, your excellency, their religious council takes

this speaking of treason very seriously. They insist on justice being done."

"Insist, do they? It sounds to me as if they have reasons for getting rid of him which have nothing to do with what they call treason. Slimy lot, these Jews. Well, they can't have a trial yet. Not for the next month or so."

"With respect, your excellency, the Chief Priest himself considers that the trial and execution are a matter of extreme urgency."

"The Chief—Caiaphas? Caiaphas is asking for Roman justice?"

"He is asking for it this day. Now. He seems to think that you will proceed to the signing of a death warrant this very morning. When, that is, you have heard the incontrovertible evidence."

"Are they all mad?"

"There are two priests outside now, in the courtyard. They have the man himself with them. They tied his hands together. They seem to be scared that he'll fly away." Quintilius grinned. Pilate sighed. He said:

"Send them in. Let's see what it's all about."

"Oh, there's no question of sending them in," said Quintilius. "You seem to forget, your excellency, that you're unclean and your palace is unclean—according to their religion. They say they refuse to be defiled by entering the house of the heathen." Quintilius grinned further.

"These Jews. Tell them I'll be out directly. That means in about an hour. I must take a bath. Unclean, eh? Oh, my God."

The presence of Jesus in the Procurator's courtyard, hands bound, guards about him, two priests in charge, brought a very mixed crowd to the armed and eagled edge of the temple of Roman authority. The courtyard was set about, on three sides, by low walls and trees, as well as by a tough phalanx of sworded and helmeted troops. The crowd came as near as it could and yelled and raised its fists. It represented no problem to the troops, since the Jews were more inclined to fight among themselves than to attempt impotent attack on Pilate's guard. The followers of Jesus, of whom there were not many, were much beaten by the Zealots, and as the more vociferous of the supporters of the Messiah were women, the effective physical aggression was very one-sided. Most of the Roman soldiers enjoyed the spectacle of Jews fighting among themselves. One said to another:

"See that bint there?"

"Which one? The young one?"

"No, not the very young one, the other. Been with her, not here though. On the job. Right collection this Jesus yeled has around him. Whores and thieves and that. Disgusting lot, the Jews, whichever way you look at them. Hey, dear, how about a bit?" But Mary of Magdala, and Mary the mother of Jesus, and Salome, and other daughters of him who had come and was soon to go, saw the hopelessness of their case and were already pushing their way out of the crowd. None of the disciples was present. They had, through prudence, obedience, cowardice, or a great listlessness that had come upon them, gone to ground, none knew where.

Pontius Pilate came out at length, Quintilius with him, and had Jesus and the priests—the guards of the Temple, no longer needed, were dismissed by Zerah—brought round to a kind of small arbour at the back of the palace. There Pilate sat on a stone garden seat and said:

"I'm not concerned, as you know, gentlemen, with infractions of the law of your religion. My function is a purely secular one. You are priests, and you have brought a man to me, his hands bound, and an armed guard which can hardly be said to have a secular function. I think the first thing to do is to send you away and thus keep religion out of this business—whatever it is. Then my deputy and I may question this—prisoner of yours and keep this whole thing on a secular basis. You may, however, since you yourselves presumably had his hands tied, now kindly untie them. I am not frightened of him, even if you are."

The priests shrugged, and Haggai unknotted the rope which bound Jesus's wrists together. Zerah said:

"We well know, your excellency, the extent or rather the limits of your jurisdiction. But we come here with a purely secular accusation. We found this man perverting our people's views of the relationship between God and the State—"

"Keep God, meaning your god, out of it. I am not interested in your god."

"Shall I say, then, excellency, that he has been engaged in provoking civil disaffection? We have written depositions, duly signed and sealed, to that effect."

"I'm sure you have," said Pontius Pilate. "What more?"

"Your excellency," said Haggai, "he says he is the Christ, meaning the Anointed One."

"I too know some Greek."

"Yes, your excellency," said Haggai, "but the anointed state refers expressly to kingship. This Jesus entered Jerusalem as a self-appointed, self-anointed, self-crowned king of Israel."

"My deputy here tells me he entered Jerusalem on a donkey."

"That, excellency," Zerah said, "was intended as a blasphemous fulfilment of the scriptures."

"I am not concerned with your religion, I tell you. I am not concerned with what you call blasphemy."

"Not even," said Zerah, "blasphemy against the Roman faith?"

"You all blaspheme against the Roman faith, you Jews. You will not accept the divinity of the Emperor. In our perhaps stupid and civilised way we tolerate your blasphemy."

"But," said Zerah, "as he came as the self-styled king of Israel, was not that a palpable challenge to the Roman authority?"

Pilate sighed, then grinned, then frowned. "How piously you utter those words—*the Roman authority*. You hate the Roman authority as much as any of those unwashed so-called patriots yelling out there, but you want peace, meaning you don't want disestablishment. Meaning you want position and a bit of wealth and a nice little villa on the coast. Let us have no hypocrisy, your reverences, or whatever I'm to call you. So far as I know, this man here did not incite the people to overthrow Caesar's representative and accept a man on a donkey in his place. I have not had cause to have fresh legions brought in from Cesarea or to increase the armed guards round the public buildings. No, gentlemen, I have other things to do than to deal with this superstitious nonsense you call blasphemy."

All this time Jesus said nothing. He stood, chafing his hands slowly and gently, as it were listening to an inner music. Pilate looked at him and saw strength there but no madness. Zerah said:

"Your excellency, I will speak out. If we were a self-governing nation, we would have the right to exact the punishment which, under the law of Moses, is laid down for the crime of blasphemy. This Jesus calls himself the Son of God. To the occupying power this may well mean nothing, but to us children of Israel it is the ultimate affront to the deity. It deserves death. But, as an occupied people, we no longer have the power to put a sinner to death. That is why we come to you."

"That at least is honest," Pilate said. "You don't seek my judgment. You wish merely to employ me as a lethal instrument."

"We would not," said Haggai, "perhaps put it in such—down-to-earth terms."

"Of course not," Pilate said. "And if I reject your demand for this man's execution, then I may, sooner or later, be blamed for a certain failure of order and tranquillity among the people of Judea. I think I will now talk to this man. Will you talk with me?" he asked Jesus.

Jesus said nothing. Zerah indicated a leather case he was carrying. "There is no need to go further, your excellency. We have the instrument of execution already made out—in Latin as well as Aramaic. You have only to—"

"Sign," said Pilate. "I will make up my own mind as to that." He spoke now with tones of equal authority of Jesus: "Do you, sir, have any qualms about entering the house of the infidel?" He was immediately shocked by his involuntary use of the honorific. "My deputy," he said, much more curtly, "will conduct you to my private rooms." Then he strode off.

TWO

Pilate half-reclined wearily on a hard couch. The sun flooded in, the sky was the continuing merciless blue of a season of drought, but there was a fringe of thin cloud on the northern horizon. Jesus stood very still. Pilate said:

"You are a tall man and even standing I am forced to look up at you. This is, of course, not in order. Will you too sit?"

"It would be unseemly, would it not?"

"The king of the Jews," said Pilate. "Do you really consider yourself to be the king of the Jews?"

"If I have a kingdom," said Jesus, "it's not a kingdom of this world. If it were of this world I should have swords clashing on my behalf to prevent my being delivered up to judgment."

"Not of this world," said Pilate, "whatever that means. Even if your kingdom is, as you say, not of this world, yet your enemies make no mistake when they say that you claim to be a king?"

"This is not to the purpose," Jesus said. "I came into the world for one end only—to bear witness to the truth. All who are concerned with the truth will listen to my voice."

"What is truth? That is not to the purpose either. You know that the priests wish you to die? And you know that only I have the power to release you or have you crucified?"

"That power," Jesus said, with what sounded to Pilate like a faint tone of sympathy, pity even, "is circumscribed by the very people who bow to your power. There will be talk of the enemy of the faith of the Jews being no friend to Caesar. This you must know."

"Yes," said Pilate. "This I do know."

They had begun their colloquy in Aramaic, which Pilate spoke fluently enough though without nuances. When he first came to the word *king* Pilate had instinctively moved to Latin. *"Credis te esse regem verum Iudaeorum?"* and so on. Jesus had moved with him easily to the same language. *"Hoc scio,"* repeated Pilate. And then: "What can I do with you? You seem to me to have committed no crime against Rome. Do you have any feeling towards Rome?"

"Men have to be governed," said Jesus, shrugging slightly. "I think it is right that there should be a kingdom of Caesar— whoever or whatever Caesar happens to be—and a kingdom of the spirit, and that the two should rarely meet. For if the kingdom is one kingdom, then the soul will be dragged down to the world of the body and the body not at all carried up to the world of the soul. Besides, my message is for no one race but for all races. Romans have heard me as well as Jews."

"It has," said Pilate, "a sort of imperial smell about it, this—what do you call it?—mission of yours. Universality. I can see why the priests of the Jewish faith regard you as a danger. I see too why I cannot, in all justice and in all reason, carry out their bidding. I hereby release you. You are free to go."

"You may not release me," Jesus said. "This you know. *Hoc scis.*"

"I must commit an injustice?"

"You must govern."

Pilate sighed very deeply. "Let us go out and meet these priests again." He stood. "You are a very tall man," he said again, "and strong. A *filius deorum,* as the poet Cinna put it. Or *filius Dei,* as some of the daring monotheists would have it. I suppose they would take pleasure in seeing such a body bleed and die. Forgive me—very bad taste. Come, let's go together."

The two priests in the courtyard, who had now been joined by other priests and a number of Pharisees, were not pleased to see Jesus and Pilate come out together, without guards, side by side, the ruler dwarfed by the ruled. They were angry when Pilate said:

"You brought this man before me as one who perverts the people. I can find no fault in him. Rather the opposite. He speaks good sense, and in very good Latin, incidentally. To talk of his meriting death is an outrage." Quintilius, looking very busy, came up to the group, having just given detailed instructions of some kind to an ear-scratching secretary. "Quintilius," Pilate said, "you spoke of clemency. Shall I show clemency?"

"The mark of the true ruler, your excellency."

"And what is the view of your holy reverences?" Pilate asked. Zerah chewed his under-lip a moment and answered:

"Clemency is an excellent thing. I consider it would be an admirable act—to release a prisoner of our race at this season of holiness and er special reminiscence. But you have a choice of prisoners."

"No choice," Pilate said harshly. "One stands condemned on a charge of public disaffection. The other has not even been tried."

"Oh, he has been tried, your excellency, he has most certainly been tried. You have, as I say, a choice. You must hand over that choice to the people. *Decet audire vocem populi.*"

"If you mean," said Pilate, "that mob of grumbling *patriots* out there, I would hardly regard them as representative. I repudiate choice. You approve my clemency. Very well, you must doubly approve a double clemency." Pilate strode out towards the periphery of the courtyard and raised his voice.

"You have repeatedly called for the release of one of your countrymen —a certain Jesus Barabbas, condemned to crucifixion on a charge of public disaffection." At the very mention of the name there was renewed howling of it. Pilate held up his hand. "At a time like this, which you deem holy, it is fitting that mercy ride above the law. I hereby order the release of this man." The crowd yelled its joy. Pilate counter-cried: "Wait. I have not done with gratuitous acts of clemency. There is another Jesus, known as Jesus of Nazareth, who has been sent to me for trial. I have heard his case and find no guilt in him. Is it your wish that he also be released? An innocent man, I remind you. A man in whom the law of Rome finds no fault."

He spoke indiscreetly in invoking the law of Rome. The howls for blood were appropriately bestial. Cries of "Release him, let him go, Jesus is innocent" were quite overwhelmed by the yells of the Zealots, with whom such of the Pharisees as were in the crowd made a temporary alliance of vindictiveness. Pilate brusquely turned his back on the crowd and surveyed frowning the smug group in the courtyard. Jesus stood, hands gently folded before him, unmoved. Pilate strode towards the smugly smiling pious and said: "I approach a decision quite without precedent in my procuratorial career. Call it a decision not to make a decision. I declare myself innocent of the blood of the innocent. On your own heads be that blood."

"In effect, your excellency," said Quintilius somewhat pertly, "you render yourself officially absent." He was standing, so Pilate noted, rather closer to the Jews than seemed necessary: even a deputy ruler ought to keep his distance. It flashed upon Pilate that Quintilius had always lived a somewhat more luxurious life than his official salary, one would have thought, made possible. *In with the natives*—a common colonial sneer or smear. "In which case, excellency, you depute to me the duty of signing the death warrant."

Pilate said nothing. At that moment a boy servant came into view, hurrying along the nearest colonnaded way with a metal ewer of water. "You," cried Pilate. "You, boy. Bring that." Startled at the anger of the tone, the boy hurried over openmouthed, spilling the water. "Pour some on my hands," cried Pilate. "Quick, boy, stop gaping." The boy did as he was told and Pilate waved him away. He confronted the priests and Pharisees sardonically, splashing the water onto their robes from flapping hands. "No blood there," he said. "Clean, you understand." Hurrying away at a pace improper in a plenipotentiary of the Roman Empire, he looked hardly more at anyone, certainly not at Jesus. The group watched him go. Quintilius smiled and said: "If you are troubled about legality—the triple death warrant is already signed. The name Jesus was there already, fortunately without without—what do you call it?"

"Patronymic," said Zerah. "Our father in heaven disposes all for the best. We know our friends, Master Deputy Procurator."

In the cell where the other Jesus, known as Barabbas, lay on filthy straw with Aram and Jobab, there was perturbation when the key ground in the lock. Quintus the guard came in and grinned at them all. Jobab said:

"It's not time yet. I know it's not time. I can tell from the sun."

"We've had no dinner yet," cried Aram. "We were promised a good dinner. That's laid down, that's in the rules. Cheating damned Romans."

Quintus grinned at Barabbas and said:

"You. Out."

"Me first?" said Barabbas. "That's right, I suppose. What's an extra hour of life in this stinking rat-hole? But I'll have some wine from you."

"Ah no, you'll not. Buy your own if you want it, scum. I've got an order for your release. As for you two, things are as they were. I'll never understand anything in this world. Jews, where there's Jews there's madness. You, swine, out. Out, before I kick you out."

Barabbas got up lazily, affecting total lack of interest in the mad acquittal, indifferent as to whether he lived or died. Jobab frothed and yelled:

"There's a mistake, there must be. We did nothing, we just followed him here. He's the leader, not us. We just did what he told us. Let's see that order, I demand to see that order. A mistake, there has to be."

"No mistake, lads," said Quintus. "You two are going to come out a bit later on. But for you it's going to be different.

You're going"—his accent grew mock-patrician—"to provide an afternoon spectacle for the holiday populace. But you'll be in very good company. You'll see."

Aram spat at Barabbas. "So. Sold yourself to them, did you?"

"Sold us to them more like," growled Jobab. They both leapt onto Barabbas. Quintus called another guard. The two spitters and clawers were held off with some difficulty. Barabbas said:

"God's justice, friends, though the Romans don't know it. God can use anybody, even the Romans. Remember that. Don't worry—I'll carry on the work." Two more guards came in.

"Filthy traitor, treacherous swine, Roman-loving bastard pig." Barabbas waved goodbye cheerfully, his surprise still well-hidden. His two accomplices, friends, workers for the cause, were easily held off by grinning Romans.

Things were now working rapidly towards their consummation. Quintilius arranged for an official signwriter to prepare a titulus, or trilingual summary of the crime of the crucified, to be affixed to his gibbet. He was perturbed when the whitewashed wood was brought to him, the black legends still wet. IESVS NAZARENVS REX IUDAEORVM said the Latin, and the Greek: IESOUS HO BASILEUS TON IOUDAION. The Aramaic, which he could not read well, he assumed said the same. "This was not what I ordered," he said. "His crime is that he pretends to be king of the Jews. This makes him out to be really king. Take it away, do it again. Put that thing up like that and we'll have the Jews falling on us like a ton of bricks."

"With respect, sir," said the signwriter, a bow-legged man who smelt rather deliciously of size and aromatic oils. "His excellency saw us getting the board ready out in the yard. He asked us what we were going to put there, and we told him. Then he said to put what we've put. He even helped us with the Aramaic bit, terrible language that."

"His excellency the Procurator? Impossible."

"He said he knew it would offend a few people, sir, but it was about time some people got offended. Tell them, he said, if anybody complains, what I've written I've written. And then he goes off."

"Blood on his own head," muttered Quintilius.

"Beg pardon, sir?"

"Take it away. Give it to the officer in charge of crucifixion detail."

"Sir."

Jesus had now been handed over totally to the Roman arm. It was customary for crucifixion to be preceded by a flogging which, if the condemned man were a Jew, the Syrians of the occupation army were only too happy to administer. In the dirty yard of their barracks they already had him stripped naked, forced into the embrace of a stout stone pillar (his arms about it and his wrists tied), and running well with blood.

"Big bastard, not like a Jew at all. A bit lopsided that. Whip the other cheek of his arse."

"Sarnt."

"That strip of skin hanging off. Do the job properly. One slash should do it. Come on, Fido, bit of fresh meat, boy." The whipping went on. "Get the bastard yelling, can't you? How can we know they're hurt if they don't yell?"

"He won't, sarnt. Big bastard, like you said, sarnt."

"That will do," said the young officer in charge of the detail. "Get his clothes back on him."

"Hardly started, sir. The men are willing, sir. Plenty of him not yet not been touched, sir."

"That's an order, sergeant." A Syrian came up grinning with a kind of spiky wheel that he held gingerly. "What's that?"

"Well, sir, he says he's a king, doesn't he? Insult to the Emperor's majesty, sir. We ought to crown him, sir."

"Get on with it. We're running late."

They crammed the spiky wheel, which was made of twigs from a thornbush, onto the head of Jesus, standing on tiptoe because of his height.

"Needs a whatyoucall it in his grip."

"A sceptre, sarnt?"

"Give him that whip to hold. Not likely to lash out with it. Not much spunk in the Yahudies."

They put one of the soldier's red capes on Jesus's back and the whip in his hand. The blood trickled down his face from the crown. Then there was a brief game of bowing and scraping with "Hail king of the Jewboys" and "Up your royal arse, sacred Yahudi majesty" and so on.

"Can't abide the bastards, sir," confided the sergeant.

"Enough now. We have to be on our way."

"Sir."

They stripped Jesus naked again, the sergeant giving him a final token kick in the bare testicles, and then put his seamless garment back on, still clean enough except for the blood that now began to start on it. They took the whip away.

"Permission to leave the crown thing on, sir?"

"Yes yes. Come on, we're late."

Jesus was now led some distance from the Syrian barracks to a woodyard where an old man and a young boy specialised in the making of punitive crosses. The old man looked at Jesus as though to measure him for a new garment. "He's a pretty big one, sir," he said to the officer in charge of the detail. "Is he the one for the new mark?"

"The one-piece one, you mean?"

"I said at the time it wasn't such a good idea, sir. Of course, I didn't reckon on getting somebody like him. Big fellow all right he is." The yard contained a number of crosspieces to be fitted at the place of execution onto a ready-planted upright. But there was also a new very handsome cross made in a single piece with cunning mortices and tenons, though a cunning nail or two peeped out where the crosspiece met the upright. "Good wood that. Worked hard on it. Pity to get it all bloodied up, but that's life, that is. Think you can manage it?" he said, not unkindly, to Jesus. "Bloodied you up already a lot, haven't they? What's that thing on your head?"

"Cedar," said Jesus, stroking and smelling the wood. "Were you a carpenter?"

"Were? *Were?* Still am, my friend. Look at that—straight and level, good saw-work, good planing. Sin and a shame it has to be used for what it has to be used for, nobody much likely to take much notice of the work that went into it, and now it's dirty big ugly nails that has to go in. Me a carpenter? A load of insolence I call that. Each man to his trade, I say, and let the others shut up about it."

"I too was a carpenter. A good carpenter wouldn't have to nail the juncture like that. The mortice and tenon joints are very slapdash."

"Well," and the old man rubbed his chin. "As I said, there's not many as notices."

"God notices. God praises the good work, condemns the ill."

"Oh, come on," said the officer in charge of the detail. "You've done with preachifying. Get that thing picked up and then on our way. It's a fair trek yet."

As Jesus bent to heave up the cross blood dripped from his forehead onto it. The old man sighed in resignation. "A weight," he said, "even for such as you. You've got to find the point of balance, as they call it."

"The fulcrum. I know," said Jesus. Then he winced as the wood struck a skinless and bloody part of his shoulder. He found the fulcrum and the cross rocked then steadied then settled. It was the ache in his lifted and supportive arms that, he foreknew, would hurt more than the galling of the great mass of wood.

"It's good work, that," said the old man. "You can see that better now it's lifted. That that lot?" he said to the young officer. "Good, we can shut up shop, young one. *Vale* and *schalom* and *andio* and all the rest of it."

The place of execution was a hill called, from its shape, Skull Hill, and it lay, and of course still lies, just outside the walls of the city, to the south-west. The young officer said: "It's a fair march. Hurt, does it? Never mind, soon be over. Well, not all that soon, of course." And so the march began. One of the detail beat a small hand drum, of Oriental manufacture, to maintain the pace of the march. Another bore, under his arm, the blasphemous trilingual titulus. Jesus, who went before, so that he could be whipped up if he fell and on if he lagged, tried to march briskly and to keep his bloodied head erect, but the cross was a great burden. Already, approaching the main east-west street of the city, they heard the noise of a great crowd, the slap of sword-blades and orders of non-commissioned officers of the controlling cordon. This crowd had not assembled primarily to see Jesus pass to execution but to express its feelings about the impending deaths of a couple of Zealots, who had gone this way but a quarter of an hour before, carrying mere crosspieces athwart their shoulders.

A crowd is a strange animal, and it has undoubtedly a soul of its own, quite unlike the constituent souls of the mere individuals that make it up. Now its anger about the execution of Aram and Jobab was to some extent modified by the acquittal of Barabbas, very visibly in the forefront of the crowd and much hailed and congratulated. When Jesus appeared, there were many who saw what was written on the titulus and were angry about the regal claim. But they could not know whether it was Jesus's own claim that angered them or what otherwise could be only an insolent satire of the Romans. Jesus seemed huger than he had ever seemed, a great calm bull of a man all blood and loaded with a monstrous burden. That they had not seen such a cross before—the general procedure being that, as I have said already, of the detachable crosspiece and the permanent upright—was a cause of awe and puzzlement. There was a moment of silence in the crowd, and the weeping of women rose above it. It was whispered about that one of these women was the mother of the criminal, that handsome decent dignified woman there, see. A murmur of sympathy arose, and the officer in charge of the crucifixion detail, despite his comparative inexperience, felt a premonitory accession of gooseflesh, knowing that such a murmur had more of potential danger in it than any shouting and cursing and throwing of stones. It was nervousness that made him lay a feeble whip on Jesus's flanks. Jesus wheeled round, the huge cross turning in the air, to look with pity on him. "Do get on," pleaded the officer. "I don't like this any more than you do." Then Jesus turned to the side and addressed, in his known clear loud voice, the women of Jerusalem, saying:

"Don't weep for me, you daughters of Jerusalem. Weep for yourselves, weep for your children. The day is coming when they shall say: blessed is the womb that never bore, blessed are the paps that never gave suck. And they shall say to the mountains: fall on us. For if they do these things in the green tree—what shall be done in the dry?"

Very enigmatic words, and seemingly pertinent to events to come, not events already proceeding. The more terrible for that, and the terror of the words compounded by an animal uneasiness that many now began to feel, for the sky was filling with cloud and the wind had changed direction. The drought, it seemed, was soon to break. The officer nervously prodded Jesus on with the handle of his whip, and it was now that Jesus, not through faintness but through the presence of a large stone lying in the road before his feet, stumbled and nearly brought both himself and the cross crashing down. Over the intake of breath the voice of a man rang loudly:

"Roman rule, eh? Roman justice? I spit on your Roman justice."

"Who said that? Who? Where is he?" The officer in charge of the detail shook with nerves.

"There, sir. There he is."

A couple of the cordon police grabbed the man, who was thin and not young but, at this moment, fearless and literally spitting. One of the police said:

"Like a taste of it, would you? Go on, take it from him, *take it.*"

The ludicrousness of the man's attempts to take the cross from Jesus, his immediate falling to the road under its impossible burden, further fed the complex feeling in the crowd that could in no wise be expressed by hitting out at Romans and crying out against their tyranny. Whatever wrong was now in process of being done was too great and knotted to be righted by Zealot rioting. When the man dropped the cross for the third time, going down with it, Jesus himself gently raised the man and asked:

"What's your name?"

"Simon. Just up from Cyrene. For the Passover. Never expected. To have to do this."

"Take my blessing, Simon, if you will. Avoid anger. Forgive your enemies."

Those words of Jesus fired in the crowd fresh additions to the emotions that were already too complex almost to be borne. The low sound that came from the crowd was of a kind none of the most seasoned of the occupying troops had ever before heard. And now it was that the soldier who had been beating the hand drum threw it to the ground and cried out in the Latin of Iberia:

"I'll have no more. Beat me, hang me, but I'll have no more of it."* Then he howled, and he was taken away howling. Jesus said with great authority to the crowd:

"Let things proceed to their end. Do nothing. Pray. Above all, forgive as your heavenly father forgives."

So it was mostly a silent crowd that followed Jesus and the nervous soldiers to Skull Hill. There a considerable body of armed troops was assembled, word having passed quickly to the garrison of the strange behaviour of the people, and none was permitted to move up from a cordoned point about a quarter way up the hill, except, of course, the principals of the act now to be performed. The friends of Barabbas were already being fixed to their crosspieces, making a great and piteous clamour. The manner of fixing was as follows. They were thrown to the ground, a heavy soldier or two holding them there in the obscene posture of Mars Observed, and their wrists were roped to the crosspieces. Then came the nailing. A nail was driven through the wrist of each hand, with a delicate cracking of bone and a rich spurting of blood, and then the two might be regarded as well and truly semicrucified. They were made to get to their feet, which they did blind and screaming and tottering, and to stagger, whipped on their way, towards the uprights that stood like trees.

*No' prendo plu'. Fustigame, su'pendeme, no' prendo plu', digo.

They had, in turn, to climb a ladder, there was only the one ladder there, that was placed against the upright, then to turn, with the rough assistance of the professional crucifiers, so that the upright was behind them. Arms out, each finger a blood-way, they suffered the slotting of the crosspiece into a deep slit already cut into the top of the upright, and there they dangled. The ladder was removed. Then came the final act in the process, more delicate and difficult than is realised by the uninstructed. One foot was placed over the other and both were transfixed—one man holding, another nailing—to the foot-wedge which was part of the upright. The nail was exceptionally long, as you can imagine. A couple of sure hammer-strokes was enough for the true professional, but the holder of the feet together, naturally apprehensive that the nail might run through one or both of his own hands, was sometimes incontinently prone to let the feet go and the legs spread and writhe. With Jobab and Aram there was no trouble. Their screams were heart-rending, but the crucifiers were hard professional men. The two, it seems unnecessary to remind the reader, were totally naked. A peg protruded from the upright under the crotch of the crucified, to keep the body from sagging, and this made Jobab and Aram seem double-phallused. This sometimes provoked a brief smile in the executioners, but the little obscenity failed to amuse today. Nobody liked the look of the weather. It was, to judge from the clouds, going to hiss down with rain soon, and crucifying in the rain was no pleasure.

Ascending the hill, Jesus increased his pace as a burdened man sometimes will when he sees home ahead, so that the escorting officer and soldiers had to hurry to keep up with him. They panted worse than he. He dropped his cross at the crown, and then looked up with pity at the two moaning men already crucified. Death took sometimes long, sometimes not. It was often not loss of blood or fatigue that killed so much as difficulty in aerating the lungs, since the forced posture hindered the normal process of respiration. Flies were already visibly and audibly busy about the wounds in hands and feet, blessed creatures of God about their elemental affairs, above man's wickedness and tortured attempts to find an acceptable mode of social and moral order. Jesus saw, between the two wretchedly inhabited crosses, the deep brick-lined slot that was to hold the foot of his own gibbet. He looked down to see a great silent crowd at the foot of the hill, and clearly discerned his mother standing with the old baker Jotham. Jotham seemed to be shaking his head as if to deplore Jesus's insistance to the very last on making a public exhibition of himself. Jesus faintly smiled. The chief executioner said: "This is a new way of doing things, somebody's bright idea, and I'm not sure if it's any good. However, we have to try."

"So," said Jesus, "let us begin."

"Good. Don't like the look of the weather either."

Jesus began by throwing off his seamless garment, which the officer in charge of the escort took for him and hung over his own shoulder. The Romans looked at the great body with unwilling awe—its tallness, the width of the shoulders, the fine muscles of arms and legs, the insolent whip-strokes that had torn the fine skin. One man involuntarily shook his head, as to deplore waste, waste.

"Like this?" said Jesus, and he lay on his cross, feet together, arms stretched, as on a bed.

"That helps," said the chief executioner in bad Aramaic. He was a worn-looking man perhaps overdue for home leave. "If you can hold that position we can get the foot-rest fitted on just right. A lot struggles and fights. This really helps."

The foot-wedge was nailed on speedily, and the chief executioner said:

"Might as well start with the feet." He looked at Jesus as though for approval.

So the huge nail was driven in that fixed foot to foot and both to the foot-wedge. Jesus screamed and looked down in agony to see the blood pour. "I did not," he then said, "mean to scream. I meant to be—" Then he fainted but almost at once came to again.

"Oh, they all scream," said the chief executioner. "It's human nature, as they say. I'd scream myself if they was to do it to me. Now, if you could keep your hands where they are and try not to move them, there'll be no need of rope. We'll get the nails in bang bang, real quick. Soon be over, I can promise you." So the outstretched wrists were nailed to the crossbar and the fingers convulsed and reached for the nail-heads as for comfort.

"There's no wooden prick," said the assistant executioner. "I don't like this new way at all."

"Well, if he sags, he sags," said his chief. "Now comes the hard part." He waited till the wooden titulus had been nailed to the base of the foot-wedge, and then said: "Ropes."

Ten men were needed to fit the burdened cross into its slot. The foot of the upright was brought to lie over this slot, so that when the whole edifice was pulled erect it would slide in and down then thud at the brick bottom then, after an initial tremor, stand upright and unshakable except by the wind (a strong wind indeed was now blowing). The problem was the pulling of the cross to its upright position. Strong ropes were looped over the arms of the crosspiece, one rope for each arm, and five men hove on each, sweating and cursing. But once the foot had engaged its slot there was no further trouble. The great torn body with the ridiculous thorn-crown that none had thought to remove sagged and bled. The professionals, wiping their hands, looked up with pride. But the chief executioner said:

"It's not a good way. The old way's best."

THREE

Aram died quickly, perhaps of some shock to the heart. Jobab lived long enough to cease to wish to belong to the Zealots.

"You—you—you—put us here, bastard," breathed Aram. "King, eh? Son of God. Save yourself. And save us at that same time."

"You are saved," said Jesus. "But not as the world knows it."

Jobab said: "What did you do wrong? I can think of nothing you did wrong. You did nothing but right. Remember me, think of me. I'm not all bad. I worked for the kingdom. In a way."

"You shall be with me," Jesus said.

Aram made a growling noise deep in his throat, then his head sagged.

"Finished," said Jobab. "Poor bastard, he did his best."

The death of Aram was noted with little interest by the troops who formed the inner cordon about the crosses themselves. "One of them out of the way," said Quartus. They were throwing dice for the possession of Jesus's seamless garment, which their officer had contemptuously thrown to them before seeking a wineshop and a well-needed rest. "My dear children," said Quartus, in an old man's wavering voice, "I got this garment when I was serving the Emperor in Palestine. It belonged to the King of the Yahudies. A very big man he was. Very high up."

They all looked up, very high up. A word had seemed to boom out of Jesus.

"Dipsa dipsa something," said Rufo. "Greek. Did he say he was thirsty or something?"

"Give him some of that wine there," Metellus said.

"It's almost vinegar."

"He's past noticing. Dip something in it and send it up on the tip of your spear."

"Dip that unseamed garment in or whatever it's called."

"Ah no," Quartus said. "This is very special. Their priests wear them. Worth a few coin of the empire, that is. Precious relic, that is."

"I've just been having a feel of them dice of yours," said Metellus. "Loaded I'd say they were." Quartus shrugged. Rufo sighed:

"Oh, well—" And he dipped the bloody garment in the wine-jug they had, bunched it, balanced it on the tip of the spear and, tiptoe, tried to get the dripping bundle to Jesus's mouth. Jesus turned his head away from it. "All we got, mate," said Rufo. "Sorry." Then Jesus spoke again.

"What did he say then?"

"Elly elly or something. First one lingo then another. Why can't they all speak Latin like we do?"*

The priests Zerah and Haggai and Habbakuk, whose office permitted access to the place of execution, since a Hebrew dying was theoretically entitled to hear the prayers for the dying, heard Jesus, though Haggai heard wrong.

"He was calling Elijah. Asking Elijah to get him down."

"No," said Zerah. "He was quoting a psalm. Asking God why he has forsaken him. Scripture," he said more softly, "is never out of his mouth."

"Always blasphemy," said Habbakuk. Then he called coarsely: "If you are what you say you are, God forgive you, why don't you come down from that cross?"

"Unseemly," reproached Zerah. And then, thoughtfully: "He saved others. Himself he cannot save."

*Cur non omnes isti filii scortoru' Latinu' nostru' fabula't?

"So," said Haggai, "perish all blasphemers."

They heard Jesus say something about his father in heaven forgiving the innocent.

"Not long to go now, I would say," said Zerah. "He finds it hard to draw breath." And then: "He meant well, God forgive him. Alas, it is never enough to mean well. Let us go."

Mary, the mother of Jesus, Mary of Magdala, Salome the daughter of Herodias were having some difficulty in getting through the inner cordon. A decurion said:

"Sorry, missis, keep away. This is no place for *ladies*."

"I am his mother. Let me through."

"Got proof, have you?"

It was now that Salome, drab-dressed though she was, gave proof of the doctrine too often rejected that royal blood will tell, that authority is inborn and inbred, saying, and flashing out with the very look of one who had the blood of Herod the Great: "Stop this nonsense, fellow. I am the daughter of the tetrarch Philip and an adoptive princess of Galilee. Let us through at once."

"Well, lady—"

"*Your royal highness* is what you mean. Stand away."

But another under-officer saw Mary of Magdala from a distance and came up, saying:

"Out, you lot. I know you. You're one of the Yahudi whores come up for the Pissover. Go on, off."

"How dare you?" blazed the princess. "*How dare you?* This is my sister."

"Stop it, Decius," said the other. "We don't want trouble. This is the princess from from—"

"Sorry—mistakes will happen—I can see now she's not— This way, ladies."

And so the three stood weeping and helpless at the foot of the cross. Jesus looked down on them but could say nothing. His chest laboured for air.

Only two disciples came out of their hiding-hole, wherever it was. They were Little James and John. By luck they met, at the foot of the hill, the very centurion whose servant Jesus had cured. They were not at first recognised but, when they drew their cautious hoods from their heads, the centurion remembered well enough the burly wrestler. He said:

"Believe me, I had nothing to do with— I am deeply ashamed. A man under authority. Tomorrow, I think, my allegiance ends—"

"May we go up to him?" asked John.

And so there was a man at the foot of the cross not too timid to take in his arms the weeping mother and offer comfort. Jesus said, with laboured breath:

"Mother—your son." Then he cried out in great pain, as if some inner organ had ruptured. As if this were a signal to the heavens, the rain now started, and there was thunder over the distant hills.

"It begins now," Jobab said. "Now," and died.

The rain teemed. In his agony Jesus pulled his nailed wrists away from the wood, and there was a slight squeak of wood tearing. He could not achieve the total liberation of his hands. He said: "Father. Into *your* hands. I place my spirit. It is. Finished." Then his head dropped and it was clear that he had died.

Of the legends that have accumulated about this moment, there are few that a man of sense would be willing to believe. The rain and the thunder and lightning were coming anyway, the end of a long drought was due, and it was only by a kind of dramatic fitness of which nature is only too capable that the death of a man and the flushing of the grateful earth were fused into an unworthy trinket of cause and effect. There were no earthquakes, no fallings of buildings, but there was certainly a rending of the veil in the Temple. An aged priest was struck dumb by, it was alleged, an angelic visitation, and in his inevitable faintness he took hold, for support, of the curtain that divided the assembly in the Temple from the Holy of Holies. He fell, and the veil was rent. When, later, the priest was able to speak, he said that the archangel Gabriel had appeared to him and announced that his aged wife would bear a son who should be as a light in Israel. Whether this prophecy was ever fulfilled is not anywhere recorded.

A legend I blush to set down, though I have, in a sense, already anticipated it, concerns Mary the mother of Jesus and John the beloved disciple. It is said that her distress was so acute that John insisted on taking her to the secluded garden of Gethsemane and giving her comfort the long night through—which, despite the rain, was hot again—in the summer house within the sound of a fountain no longer dry. This is the kind of story put out by the enemies of the faith, but it is distressing to hear that many of the faith have faith in it.

Finally in this account of what followed on the death of Jesus, I have to interpret in the light of probability the strange legend of the transfixing of his side with a spear and the issuing from his side of blood and water. I feel that this is an obscure and timid as it were lateral mode of describing the spearlike erection of the phallus of the newly expired, and that the two fluids are a riddle of a third. He was not only the Son of God but the Son of Man, as he said so often himself.

FOUR

Pilate was looking at the rain when a secretary announced that the High Priest Caiaphas wished to see him and was, indeed, waiting in an anteroom.

"He has no fear of contaminating himself?"

"On the contrary, sir. He seems very eager to come in and speak to you."

"Usher him in."

Caiaphas was bowed in. Pilate bowed slightly. Caiaphas bowed more explicitly.

"Your excellency," said Caiaphas, accepting a chair, "I am come to deliver thanks from the Sanhedrin. Thanks for your ah cooperation."

"I did not cooperate, your eminence. I washed my hands, literally, of the whole affair. I wish now I had shown less prudence and more courage." Caiaphas listened carefully to Pilate's cold Aramaic, then replied in a subtle Latin full of *aliquantulum* and *sensim* and *haudquaquam*. He said:

"You speak with commendable frankness. But you know as well as I do that the duty of a secular ruler is little different from that of a high priest. We are not put where we are to preside over the insidious and gradual or sudden and shocking destruction of order. My life is all prudence. Courage. The encouragement of chaos. I leave courage to men like that dead man."

"Tell me," said Pilate, "*tuane condemnatio*—was the condemnation yours, or were you merely *prudent* in the face of hate and fanaticism?"

"Those are somewhat strong terms. My colleagues recognised, quite rightly I think, a threat to orthodoxy. My view has always more or less been that if orthodoxy is sufficiently sure of itself it need not fear the heretic who sways the people. But, ah—the secular aspect of the situation being what it is—"

"Meaning that Rome might disestablish you and your colleagues and favour a religion that is not shouting *Hear ye Israel* all the time?"

"One way of putting it," conceded Caiaphas. "As for the *condemnation,* I accept responsibility. But my motive was not that of my colleagues."

"Whatever your motive, the king of the Jews is dead."

"It is true about the royal blood. The house of David on both sides of the family. We may exaggerate a little now and talk of a sacrificial king. It is fitting that one man die for the sins of the people. The higher the blood, the more acceptable the sacrifice."

Pilate said, after sighing a couple of times: "I belong to a crude race. We are good at road-construction and the organisation of armies, but our intellectual achievements are not high. We leave philosophy to Greek slaves. Theologically we must consider ourselves to be far behind you Hebrews. So tell me something, eminence. What precisely would this phrase mean—the Son of God?"

"*A* son of God," said Caiaphas, "the *sons* of God. As the Almighty is our father, then we are all sons of God. But the one single Son of God—this would mean that God, a spirit, the ultimate spirit, had begotten a male child. It is a very barbarous conceit."

"But you teach that nothing is impossible to your God. Is it totally inconceivable that a deity who is all spirit should present himself to the world in a physical form?"

"Your excellency," Caiaphas smiled faintly, "you Romans have been brought up on the notion of gods coming down to earth. Taking transient physical forms—a bull, a swan, a peacock, a shower of gold—"

"Oh, come," said Pilate, "you insult my intelligence—"

"Let me say this only—that if God *did* decide to create a new aspect of himself, confining his entire spiritual essence within the body of a human being, then it would be for one purpose only: that he might sacrifice himself to himself, achieving the supreme expiation of man's sins. And human sin, in God's eyes, must be far more terrible than the human sinner is able to understand."

"But what is human sin?"

"Oh, it is not infraction of the dietary laws," said Caiaphas somewhat impatiently, "or adultery, or theft. It is some ineffable, perhaps even totally unwilled, staining by the creature of the radiance of the creator. It is as if, to give a poor and ridiculous analogy, a man were to vomit into the pure radiance of new-fallen snow and the snow should scream out with intolerable agony. This, I know, must seem ridiculous, but the ridiculous is always an aspect of the mystery. And there is another mystery to mention—that if what I say is so, then God must love man with a love so intolerable, so lacerating to the lover—"

"I'm a plain Roman," said Pilate, almost growling. He had been listening with discomfort to a straining and torturing of the plain Roman language that would hardly be tolerable in one of the new poets of Alexandria—*quasi nix clamet,* indeed—and he had a healthy western distrust of eastern subtlety. "If all this is so, or could be so," he said, "we may talk of the accomplishment of a sacrifice. And of yourself as the agent of the sacrifice."

"This is not so," said Caiaphas, "nor am I authorised by scripture to speculate on what I have merely presented to you as a conceivable, a merely conceivable notion. The Messiah—of the Jewish people—that is a very different notion. And the time of the Messiah is not yet."

"But the pagan, the non-Jew, the—"

"Gentile?"

"The Gentile remains free to believe—this inconceivable?"

"The Gentile may believe what he will. Excellency, I have already taken up too much of your time. I come with a simple request. Today is *Yom Schischi* or *dies Veneris*—day of love, interesting—and the Sabbath begins at sunset. In this holy season of the Passover the *Schabat* is considered a very high and holy day. My colleagues on the council consider it unseemly that those three Jewish bodies up on the hill should continue to pollute a time of holiness. We seek permission for the corpses to be removed."

"You may see my deputy as you leave. He will arrange it. And what of the disposal of the bodies?"

"The Zealots will bury the Zealots. As for the other man—there is a new burial ground for strangers. There is a nameless suicide already lying there. A named suicide will join him."

"A suicide? Jesus a suicide?"

"I use the term, perhaps, with a certain frivolous looseness. He was determined on death, was he not?"

Pilate did not answer that, but he said: "For *the other man* a tomb has already been provided. A prominent member of your race and faith came to me—not to you, note—full of anxiety about the proper disposal of the body of the king of the Jews. He came to me. He showed courage—or insight."

"Who was he?"

"Ah, he wished to remain anonymous. A Roman protects a Jew against his fellow Jews. A crack, the promise of a division. If I were you, I would be somewhat apprehensive about the future."

"I merely," said Caiaphas, "wished to know the where-abouts of the tomb. You understand, there has been talk of this Jesus rising from the dead. He spoke of the destruction of the Temple and its rebuilding in three days. It has dawned on some that this may be a very plain allegory. Now this sort of prognos-tication may well prevail on the superstitious. There is a general fear that the man's followers may remove the body secretly and hide it, then talk of having seen him resurrected. May the tomb be guarded?"

"There is nothing to prevent your guarding it."

"We need," said Caiaphas, "disinterested guards. With our

own people guarding, the disciples of the man Jesus will say that he truly rose again but his enemies denied it. I should be grateful therefore—"

"Very well. A Roman guard will be posted." Pilate's voice thickened. "What sort of a people are you, if I may ask, with all respect, your eminence? First you rub your hands over his death, and now the evidence of his death offends your delicate suscepti—"

The secretary had come in with a message on wax. Pilate read it while talking. Now he looked at Caiaphas, who was rising to go, with a sour grin. He said:

"Jesus bar-Abbas—the prisoner I set free out of my *clemency*. He's been quick with a renewal of his criminality. He's already killed a Roman centurion. Well, there's a crucifix awaiting him. Good afternoon, your eminence."

Caiaphas bowed *aliquantulum* awkwardly and left.

FIVE

"Joseph is the name," said the man. "A name that will not be unfamiliar to you, dear lady, God bless you. My family comes from Arimathea, but we always wished to be buried in the holy city. A large tomb, and the tomb is at your disposal. A sad time. Ah, but we must not weep, no, but do what is meet to be done. A strong tomb, very capacious, built into the rock. We must find a cart or litter to take him. I will provide bandages and oils and ointments. He will be embalmed as befits his his—"

"I have ointment here," and Mary of Magdala showed her box. "I used part of it for his—"

"Are you too of his family?" asked Joseph of Arimathea.

"I am a woman," said Mary primly, "whose trade was selling her body. And this precious ointment I bought with the money I saved from practising that trade. Does this offend you?"

"I'm quite sure," and Joseph sketched a chuckle, "that it did not offend *him*."

The rain had stopped and the earth and grass smelt deliciously, even on Skull Hill. The late afternoon sky was blue, but great white clouds sailed along it. The mauled and torn bodies were a terrible disfigurement. The companions in death of Jesus were removed with little enough trouble, though there was always some difficulty in drawing the nail that transfixed the feet. The practice of slashing the feet with a knife, to the end of easy detachment of the nail, was frowned upon as cowardly workmanship. The two wretched bodies were taken away by weeping patriots and their womenfolk, The removal of Jesus from his cross took much time, and there was apprehension on the part of some of the representatives of the orthodox faith that the task would not be completed before sunset. The great wrenching strength of the man, even when dying, had made the detachment of the hands a comparatively easy task, but there was the work of holding the body upright, with hands of men on ladders and tough cable as well. The drawing of the foot-nail entailed the successive labour of three men, each of whom fell exhausted, and the breaking of two iron wrenches. Mary, Jesus's mother, turned her eyes away throughout this sweating and cursing labour, but she cried out at the sheer sound of the body's falling to earth. Lifting it down, even with the muscles of Little James (the Romans began grudgingly to respect these strong-bodied Jews), proved more than a mere soluble problem in the absence of scaffolding and pulleys, and both James and John conceded that there was no true lack of respect entailed in allowing the huge weight of dead bone and flesh, painted all over with dried blood, to crash to the ground. Then the corpse had to be conveyed on a litter to the foot of the hill, where an ox-cart provided by Joseph of Arimathea waited to transport it to the resting-place of his own family.

At the tomb in the rock, the two disciples and the women were surprised to see three priests already waiting. There was also a section of Roman infantry, with a junior commissioned and a senior non-commissioned officer, apparently at the disposal of the burial party. Joseph of Arimathea had prudently disappeared at the moment of the whipping off of the ox-cart, but he had sent a servant with bandages and oils. The bound and aromatic body of Jesus was now ready for interment, but the rock that served as door to the tomb was of immense size, and the troops grumbled that it was not in their office to help with the shifting of it. But Zerah, inevitably one of the priests in attendance, paid money out of his own purse, and the mon-

strous stone was moved with cursing and sweat. The body of
Jesus was carried into the tomb, and the stone was, with more
sweating and the same curses, replaced. "There," said Zerah.
"We may say, I think, that it is all over."

"*You* may say that," said Little James truculently.

"And you," said Zerah, "may well have some inept trickery
in mind. Know, then, that this tomb will be guarded by these
soldiers for some little time, so that the opportunity for your
trickery may be obviated, and that I and my reverend colleagues will watch tonight and tomorrow night. I say it again: it
is all over."

The women returned to their lodging-house, and Little
James and John started the long walk to the place, just outside
Jerusalem on the Bethlehem road, where their fellow-disciples
had—shamefully, so many say, with proper prudence, others—gone to ground. The garden of Gethsemane was still
available to them, but none (though remember what I said some
pages before) was willing to return there. The kind Nicodemus
was aware that a place of sweetness and rest had turned most
sour and thorny for them, as indeed it had for him—a location
of treachery and violence—and he had recommended a run-
down farm that he owned but was trying to sell as a fair temporary spot of refuge. Nine, as the Sabbath began, sat gloomily
gnawing their knuckles or bits of bread, worrying about the absent Little James and John, mostly hating the very smell of
themselves. Thaddeus absently played a tune on his flute.
Matthew growled:

"Will you please *stop?*"

"Sorry," said Thaddeus, flicking the spit from the instrument. "It was the piece I played for the girl's funeral when
he—you know. It isn't forbidden, by the way, to play the flute
on the Sabbath. Playing is not working."

"The question is," said Matthew, "what do we do?"

"One day at a time," said Bartholomew. "We do nothing till
after the Sabbath."

"He means," the first James said, "what do we do if it's not,
you know, true? If he doesn't—"

"He will, he will," growled Peter. "Have you all forgotten how to believe?"

"We all ought to have gone," Simon said. "Not just left it to John and Little James. I'm surprised at the other James here. I thought you would have been—well, the two Jameses were almost one James. It didn't mean much, did it, when it came to—doing something, well, serious—"

"I was sick," said James sullenly. "You saw me. Everything came up. Knots in my belly. Damn, you saw me. I could hardly move."

"They should be back by now," said Thomas. "For all we know they might have—"

"We would have heard," said Peter. "Even here. One of the women, perhaps—"

"The women didn't hide, did they?" said Philip. "The women stayed."

"Ah, make a song of it," said Matthew harshly. "Our big word was *prudence*. Keeping the message safe. There's always an excuse for cowardice. But cowardice it is and was. I'm going into town now. Who'll come?"

"No journeys on the Sabbath," said Thaddeus.

"We never worried about that before," Andrew said.

"It's right enough, though," said Matthew. "Picked up by one of the guardians of the faith. Taken in for—something or other."

"He's buried now," Peter said. "He's bound to be buried. Somewhere. God knows where."

Andrew cleared his throat and said: "We behaved badly."

Peter howled: "*I* behaved—God help me, God forgive me—"

"Oh, enough of that," snapped Thomas. "We've all had enough of that."

"We all behaved badly," Bartholomew said. "But he knew how we'd behave—right from the beginning."

"What we do, I think," said Philip, "is wait for instructions. That means waiting till *Yom Rischon*. There's nothing to be done on the Sabbath."

"Where are those two?" cried Peter. "What the hell has happened to those two?"

Little James and John arrived, very weary, not long before midnight. There were embraces, tears, thank-heavens, and they told their story. The rest listened with great care. John said:

"What is there for supper? We're starved."

"Water. A bit of stale bread," said the other James.

"There are a couple of half-starved chickens pecking around outside," said Little James. "There's an old rusty pot there, I see. Why can't we have stewed chicken?"

"The Sabbath," Peter said. "The law of Moses."

John now raised the immense voice that had always assorted so ill with his well-knit but delicate-looking body. "God help you, God damn you, have you forgotten so soon? The Sabbath was made for man, not man for the Sabbath. What sort of Christians are you going to be when he's not with you any more? Have none of you any guts?"

"What was that word?" asked Bartholomew. "It sounded like a Latin word."

"It just came out," said John. "We have to be called something. Now who's going to strangle those chickens out there?"

"I'll cook them," said the other James. "Matthew here's a good hand at strangling."

It began to dawn on them that things had really changed. But Thomas, biting a soft bit of bone, said: "Well, it'll take some getting used to, lads. On our own. Funny, ye could call this the first supper of the new way."

"We're not on our own just yet," Little James insisted. "You'll see."

"Aye, I'll have to see. Seeing's believing."

Cocks crowed Sunday, or *Yom Rischon*, loudly in. Peter defied the cocks. All seemed ready, after a Sabbath sinfully spent in wood-gathering, clothes-washing, cooking of scrawny poultry, to defy a great deal of the past. It was nonsense, affirmed Thaddeus, not generally known as an advanced thinker, to say that a day began at sunset. A day ended then. Day began at dawn. Cocks crowed Sunday loudly in. Who was to go to the tomb in the rock? None was eager, none wished to be disappointed. At the end, it was John and Little James who again took the road to Jerusalem. When they arrived at the tomb, they found Mary, Jesus's mother, and Mary of Magdala there, also Zerah and the two other priests (whose names we know to have been Habbakuk and Haggai), as well as the Roman guard. Mary of Magdala turned with some hope towards the two disciples, *Christians*:

"We've asked and asked, begged indeed, but they say no."

"Who says no?" asked the truculent Little James. "Is it trickery you're frightened of?" he said to Zerah.

"When a man is entombed," Zerah said, "he is not further disturbed. He is left at peace in the sleep of death. This is the custom."

"Is it also the law?" asked John loudly. "Has the mother of the dead man no right to say a last farewell?"

"Besides," said Mary of Magdala, "there are things to leave—spices, herbs. See, I have them here."

"Look," said the officer in charge of the guard, "they had plenty of time to do all that before—"

"It was what's known as the Sabbath," said Little James. "Heard of it, have you? The Sabbath. When no man buys or sells or does anything in the nature of work."

"There's no call for insolence."

"All right, no insolence then. Just this: we're the family of the man who's in that tomb there—crucified by the Romans, remember? Handed over to the Romans by these three smart-hatted gentry here—"

"I don't think," said Habbakuk, with what was meant to be dangerous calm, "we're going to tolerate this—"

"Oh, go on, then," cried Little James. "Let's have another mock trial and another couple of crucifixions. I'm going to open that tomb there."

"You can't," said the non-commissioned officer. "You know you can't."

"Are you going to stop me?"

"Well—" The non-commissioned looked at the commissioned, and both at Zerah. Zerah shrugged.

"We'll give you a hand, mate," said one of the private soldiers.

"You'll wait for orders," said the non-commissioned officer.

"Oh, let's have it open," said the commissioned officer. "We've heard so much about trickery, let's see what sort of trickery you mean." He looked at Zerah again, and Zerah shrugged again. With little sweat and no cursing the great stone was rolled away. Zerah said to Little James:

"There's a thing you hope, isn't there? Believe, even. But this is the end. In there you will find a dead body." He made as to go into the tomb, first, a priestly right. But Little James said:

"This, friend, is not for you." And he motioned that Mary, Jesus's mother, enter first. Then he himself entered. They closed their eyes and then opened them again, trying to pierce the dark. There was no dead body there. There was no body there in its grave-wrappings. There was a smell of oil and ointment, true, but there was no dead body. Mary opened her mouth, listening. Little James motioned to Mary of Magdala and John to enter, saying: "Well, if you can find anything in here—"

"Hush," said Mary. "The voice. I know the voice." She listened. They all listened. John shook his head. Then Mary said: "I knew that voice. Listen. This is what it said. It said: 'Why do you seek the living in a place of the dead, foolish one? Jesus is risen. Go and tell his disciples that he has gone before them into Galilee. They will see him there.'"

Little James nodded in satisfaction. Then he smiled at the three priests and all the Roman troops. "In," he said, "if you like. Everybody welcome. Then we'll have a good long talk about trickery."

There were, for the moment, no words from the three priests, who looked at each other white-faced. Nobody in there. Nothing in there. Empty except for the smell of spices. The Romans had a look and came out glum and puzzled and ready to be frightened. The officer said:

"Are you sure? Are you absolutely sure? This must have happened when I had my two hours off."

"Nothing happened, sir, I swear. I swear by Hercules and Castor and Pollux—"

"Yes yes yes, that you've been awake all night and haven't stirred from that spot over there."

"That's right, sir. After all, we was given very strict instructions. Nobody's been here. I swear by Minerva and Venus and the lot, sir."

"Then who moved that stone? Somebody must have moved that stone—twice." There was a silence. "I don't like this at all." He eyed some of the troops. "Sure some of you didn't fancy playing a bit of a game to pass the time?"

"Look, sir, would we?" said a scarred veteran. "We was

given our instructions, like he said. And these three Jewish priests here was with us all the time. They don't look like the sort as would play games."

"It's what I'd call a mystery," said the commissioned officer.

"Could I have a word?" said Zerah, and he motioned to the officer that he withdraw a little way with him.

"Ah, got an explanation, have you, sir? All right." The two removed themselves to the shade of a fig tree that, having been blasted by lightning, or something, gave little shade.

"I think you'll agree," said Zerah, "that we want no idle speculations running round the town."

"I'm inclined to go in for a few idle ones myself, sir. But I see your point. No good encouraging the superstitious."

"Exactly. So there's only one explanation. His followers came during the night, removed the stone, carried the body away, put the stone back again."

"Why would they want to put it back again, sir? I mean, like a horse and a stable-door—"

"To allay suspicion. To give them time to get away without a hue and cry after them. Do you follow me?"

"Wait a minute, though," said the officer, who was none of the brightest. "Nobody came. I always had sentries posted on both sides. Ah, no, I'm not having that, sir, if you'll pardon me."

"The sentries on duty were assaulted. In the dark. By soft-footed men, twelve of them, no, eleven. And very strong. Assaulted and rendered insensible."

"Now I follow you," said the officer, rubbing his chin with its morning bristles. "It'll cost a bit, you know."

"It will cost a lot. It will cost a very great deal. But I think the treasury of the Temple can meet whatever it will cost. It will mean, of course, a signed deposition, no wagging tongues, a warning about the consequences of perjury, and some genuine—"

"Hitting about? Well, now," and the young man turned

round, grinning, to look at John and Little James. "We could make a start there. A bit of a fight—a couple of ours against those two. And, of course, we have to arrest those two, don't we? Interfering with Roman law and order. Say that the rest got away, but those two—"

"Don't make it too complicated," said Zerah. "Anyway, they're all going now. I don't think we'll be troubled with them again." And the two watched the four go away, puzzled, in a daze that would soon permit joy to strike.

"We all have our duty to do, sir," said the officer. "And I consider that the er protection of the people from the horrible consequences of unbridled superstition is a very serious duty indeed, sir." He said this standing to attention.

"Good," said Zerah. "So—shall we talk to your men?"

"Horses?" said Peter. "Horsemen. Well, they've come for us at last. What do we do? Fight or give in? Ah, what a waste."

"There's a woman riding sidewise on one of them," said Thaddeus, squinting. "No, it's a girl. Wait, it's that girl that—"

Eight horsemen and a horsewoman. Four horsemen helped her down. She was wearing a red cloak and her hair loose. They all, except the girl, looked with distaste at the disorder of the farmyard—dung unshovelled, a forlorn cock too hoarse for more than a parody of crowing (easily defied by Peter), rotting wood intended for fences never built, weeds, bones, mud.

SEVEN

"You know me, I think," when she entered the farmhouse. "I was one of the women who followed him. Now I'm taken back, but I too take back. The word, the good news."

"We never," said Peter, "quite got to know you. You all kept your distance. Men separate from women, that's the way it was."

"The princess Salome, daughter of the tetrarch Philip, step-daughter of the tetrarch Herod. Ordered by the Procurator of Judea to return to her home and rank. Galilee, but he too will be in Galilee."

"I'll believe that when I see it," said Thomas wearily. "These then are not come to arrest us?"

"No, but you had best leave Judea. He said you must leave now."

"He?" frowned Little James. "What do you mean, he?"

"I saw him," she said.

The men writhed politely, spread disbelieving hands, raised shoulders, said: "Ah." Women, girls, visions, dreams, fancy, excitability.

"Disbelieve if you will," she said. "He came to me in the place where we lodged. At dawn, this morning. An hour before I was taken. I was the only one awake, I had, you see, a feeling, a—"

"Premonition?" said Bartholomew, his eyes tiredly hooded.

"I don't know the word. It was him—his face, his voice. Also—his hands and feet—as they were in the—when they took him down from the—"

"You're sure of this?" said Peter.

Salome nodded. "I think I understand. The news should come from his mother—but his mother has already started back for Nazareth. Or from my sister, for so I call her, who was a common prostitute and crowned him king. Not, you will say, from the girl who danced for her step-father and gained a reward for her mother. Who ended her dance naked and later saw the bloody head thrown in the fire."

"So," said Simon. "You were the one. So." And he nodded and nodded.

"If you don't believe," she said, "meaning you don't want to—you'll still have to go back to Galilee. To start fishing again, or whatever it was you did."

"We don't all come from Galilee," said Thomas. "I come from over the water, Gadarene country. So does Thad there."

"I can say no more than what I've said," said the princess. "He appeared before me before the cocks crew, and said someone was to go to you and—"

"Tell us to go to Galilee, aye. Did he say where in Galilee?"

"No. But wherever you are in Galilee, he'll be there too."

"Well, then," said Philip somewhat dispiritedly, "we'd better start for Galilee."

"I too must go to Galilee," said the princess. "I have told you what I was told to tell you. I wish you—what do we say?

Go safe in Jesus? The Lord be with you?"

"All these things," said Matthew with great seriousness, "have to be worked out. How we eat, what we say— Thank you," he said. "We all thank you. *Sister,* I think we may say."

"That will do," she said. She smiled and made a brief gesture, the gesture of a girl to friends. Then she turned and went out, mounted her horse with the help of four horsemen, and nodded that the cavalcade might move off. They were all silent, her eleven brothers, till the clop of the horses had been eaten by the air. Then Peter sighed and said: "To Galilee, then."

"All together?" said Thomas. "We might be picked up by the authorities. Eleven men, most of them speaking the Galilee twang."

"Which authorities?" asked Andrew.

"Either or both. I don't trust any of them," said Thomas, "not to pick us up for teaching false doctrine. Following a false prophet." And then: "Well well, so it was that little girl. Poor child, well no, she's got over it. Prophet after prophet, though. Betrayed by the innocent. All done in. All axed and felled and eaten."

"But one rose again," said Little James with weary loudness. "How many times do I have to tell you what we saw? And now she says she saw him, him, real, wounds and all. When are you going to believe?"

"I'll tell ye when," said Thomas, quietly fierce. "There aren't going to be any more betrayals. There'll be a lot of false Jesuses going around soon, you mark my words. Ye'll be glad of my *doubts,* as one of ye called them—you I think it was, Bart—and it's my opinion that he himself wanted me because of he knew the good of having a man who doesn't believe the first thing he's told. Anyhow, I'll believe when I can see those wounds of his in hands and feet. Close to, not at a distance and not in the dark. I'll believe when I can shove my fingers into the damned holes. I tell ye again, this is a time for being careful."

There was a thoughtful silence. Thaddeus even nodded.

Peter then said: "Well, one thing at a time, lads. We'll deal with what to believe later on. For now we'll talk about the move. Thomas is right about one thing. Small groups. Twos and threes. And we'll all meet in Capernaum. At the house, right, Andrew? You two first, Thomas and Matthew. No need to tell you to be careful. Wear your hoods. Don't speak to strangers."

"They're all strangers now," said Matthew. "Everybody's a stranger."

"Aye, we'll be careful. And we'll have a little money if there is any."

"There's not much," said John, who had become a kind of theoretical treasurer.

Awkwardly Peter sketched a blessing with his right hand. The shape of the gesture came to him without thought—hand down, hand across, hand across, a figure of four made out of a movement of three, a kind of mystery. "God and his blessed Son be with you. And the soul that belongs to both of them."

Sixty furlongs out of Jerusalem—or threescore as many have started saying again, having becoming newly delighted to rediscover that they have twenty digits, if they are lucky— Thomas, weary, limping, leaning on the staff he had cut from an olive tree, said to Matthew, who was very red and feeling the fat he still had:

"I don't think any will follow us now. I think we're safe."

"You're sure we're safe?"

"I didn't say that. Think, I said. It's not wise to be sure of anything. " They plodded another twenty or so steps. Birds sang what they had learned in the earlier part of the Book of Genesis, unmodified by fall, prophets, redemption. The sun, a great hunk of fire very many score of furlongs off, was going round the earth with an obedience that seemed not to accord well with its bloody ferocity. "Faith is a fine word, aye, and I hope I have as much as the next man. But God gave us eyes and ears. Aye, and fingers too. Tell me that's the moon up there, and do I believe you?"

"You believe nobody's following us?"

"Aye, perhaps ye could say I believe that."

"I trust," said the voice, "you'll let me travel in your company. We go the same road."

"That's not possible," cried Thomas, turning in fear. "Where did you come from? Get away, Satan or whoever ye are." The man was deep-hooded, his face in shadow, his feet shod in new leather, his hands buried in long sleeves. Matthew said:

"You come from Jerusalem?"

"Yes, Jerusalem. May we talk? You were talking when I joined you. May I ask what you were talking about?"

"Joined us, aye. Where did ye spring from, tell us that." And Thomas rather self-consciously made a cross-sign at him. "Ah, that tree. Resting behind that tree, were ye?"

The stranger chuckled not unpleasantly. Matthew said:

"There's only one thing to talk about if you're coming from Jerusalem."

"Careful, careful, Matt," growled Thomas.

"What thing?" said the man.

"Why, Jesus of Nazareth, his crucifixion, the story of his—"

"For Christ's sake, be careful." Then Thomas could have bitten his tongue out.

"For Christ's sake," said the stranger. "You speak like some of the Romans. I have heard them at their dicing. They swear by Jupiter and Juno and Mercury. Some are finding it smart and new to swear by Christ. What is this Christ—a new god?"

"This Christ," said Matthew, "is Jesus of Nazareth."

"Ah," said the stranger, "and who or what is he, was he?"

"Where have ye been all these years?" growled Thomas, no longer cautious. "The man sent from God, as they say—I'm not saying," caution scurrying back, "that I say it, mind ye—"

"Dead and buried," said Matthew, "and on the third day he said he'd rise again from the dead. And this is something they say has happened, but nobody can be sure."

"Sent from God?" said the man. "If he was sent from God, why should anyone be unsure? If he said he could rise again—why then, he has risen. You seem to me to be foolish men unread in the scriptures."

"Look ye," said Thomas, shaking his fist, "we may be no scholars, but we're no fools either, and we're not going to be called fools by any stranger that joins us on the road and is frightened of showing his face. Anyway, it's ye that are the fool, for ye know nothing of what the Greeks call logic. If they say a man's sent from God that's not the same thing as *knowing* he was sent by—"

"We know the scriptures," said Matthew. "We believe the scriptures."

"Believe that the prophecies would be fulfilled—the prophecies concerning the coming of the Son of God?"

"Of course we believe," said Matthew.

"Believe," said the man, "that the prophecies *have* been fulfilled?"

"Look ye," said Thomas, and he stopped walking to stand in front of the stranger, so that the stranger too had to stop. "Whoever ye are, man, all I ask is a very simple thing. That I can see him standing in front of me, for seeing is believing. And to touch the wounds they made on him with my five fingers here and my five fingers there and—"

"If you wish to touch with ten fingers, Thomas," said the man, "you had best drop your stick."

"How do ye know my name? Who told ye my—" And then he saw and was down on his knees.

"Up, Thomas. Up, Matthew. Blessed are they who believe *without* seeing. Touch, Thomas."

EIGHT

Some weeks later, at nightfall, the eleven disciples were seated about a table in the upper room of an inn near the Galilean lake. The waiter, a pert young man with a tiny sliver of wood wedged between his gat-teeth, a sort of mouth-toy that he agitated with his tongue, said:

"Shall I serve now?"

"Is it hot or cold?" said Simon.

"It'll be hot when it comes to you. Whether you eat it hot is your own business."

"Serve, then," said Peter. "And we shall need another plate and another cup."

"Somebody else coming then?"

"We don't know yet," said Thomas. "We think so."

"Well, you'd better leave him a bit of room, hadn't you?" said the waiter. And he went off to fetch a jug of wine and a bread-basket. The disciples who sat on the bench nearest the wall awkwardly began shuffling, not knowing where to leave the bit of room.

"Ye can have him next to you," said Thomas to John. "The way it was before."

"Pretty well as we were last time," Andrew said. "A month or so ago. It seems years."

"Eleven of us now," said Peter. "We'll have to wait for somebody else."

"Perhaps he'll choose," said Matthew. "Perhaps he'll bring somebody with him."

"No," said Peter. "I think it's all up to us now."

"Up to you," said Bartholomew. "Do we start calling you *master*?"

"No, Peter will do. Just plain Peter." And then: "This dream of yours, Philip. I'm getting to be a bit like Thomas here, not trusting. We were more trusting in the old days. Did he say what day, did he say what time?"

"I've told you," said Philip somewhat irritable, "till I'm sick of telling you. He sang a little song."

"Sing it again," said Thaddeus.

"Aye, let him, but we don't want any twiddly bits on yon flute," said Thomas.

Philip merely recited the little verse, keeping his voice flat:

> "At the hour of the last
> On the day of the last
> Order your meat
> And sit and eat."

"The last what, that's the point of it," Matthew said. "Dreams were just the same in the old time, Joseph and so on. They never speak out."

"Last supper," said Simon. "That seems clear. But it wasn't the last supper."

"If we don't see him again it was," Andrew said.

"You're sure it was him?" said Peter, looking first at Thomas and then, on his other side, at Matthew.

"It was him," said Matthew, while Thomas snorted.

"And he just disappeared?"

"Like a bird. Turned and went and wasn't there. Right, Thomas?"

"But it was *him*?" repeated Peter.

"See here," said Thomas, "you know me. I've always been—what's the word?"

"Sceptical," said Bartholomew.

"I touched him, and then he gave me this mouthful about it being better to believe without seeing—I still have my reservations about that, but never mind. Anyway, there was no doubt at all about it. Right, Matt?"

"What I couldn't understand was this, though. If he was on

his way to Galilee, why didn't he continue the journey with us?"

"He might have had to visit people," said Simon. "We're not the only ones in the world."

There was a long silence. They could hear the clash of metal dishes below, a cook's curse. Thaddeus said:

"They say that his mother came looking for his body. It was too late, though. Couldn't move it. But there's a sort of inscription on it now. Just his name."

"Who?" said Andrew.

"You know damn well who," said Simon. "He's here now, in a way. Just by not being here, if you see what I mean. Poor bastard. There didn't seem to be any real villainy in him. He believed. I'll never understand."

"Innocence," said Peter, "can be a kind of treachery." It was the first gnomic statement he had ever made. They all looked at him with respect. "Somebody had to do it. We were lucky, I suppose." He had driven out of his mind totally the memory of his own denial, chiefly by brooding on the parable of the son who said no but did, the son who said yes but didn't.

The waiter came up with a steaming dish. "Nice bit of broiled fish, fresh-caught today."

"Order your meat, was it?" said Simon.

"A general term," said Bartholomew. "Meat means cooked food."

"There's one downstairs just come," said the waiter, setting the dish down. "Would he be the one? Big man in a cloak. If he's the one, you don't have to eat it cold."

He left, and his feet could be heard running down while graver slower feet could be heard walking up. They looked at each other. Matthew made a terrible throat-clearing noise. Then awkwardly they started to stand up, difficult for those nearest the wall, since the table was so close to it. A tall burly man came in, cloaked, hooded. He briskly threw the covering onto the floor and smiled. Jesus. The hand-wounds were healing well. John did the right thing. He pushed the table away, sending a metal plate to the floor, where it span and sang, wobbled and then lay still. He put his arms about Jesus. Jesus smote him many times on the back, smiling. "Lake fish," he said. "Good. We'll eat."

They ate, none heartily save he. This man had died, been in the grave. Where had he been, the reality, the spirit, during that day of the body's death? Nobody liked to ask. Jesus talked cheerfully. He said:

"Totally fulfilled, everything. Even to the throwing of the dice for my garment. I liked that garment." The robe he was now wearing was not seamless. Where had he found or bought it? Who had given it to him? The only friend with money they could think of was a reformed prostitute. Where was she, by the way? Had Jesus been to see his mother yet? If not, would he? There were many questions they would have liked to ask but dared not.

"'They parted my garments among them, and upon my vesture did they cast lots.' We no longer have anyone with us who can say: That, master, is in the twenty-second of the Psalms of David."

Everyone was now very uncomfortable except, of course, Jesus.

"And everything that happens from now on, from the time that I leave you—that too is foretold. The preaching of repentance and the remission of sins, in my name, to all the nations—beginning from Jerusalem."

"When will you leave us, master?" asked Peter. "And where will you go?"

"Where?" repeated Jesus, chewing bread. "Eventually I will go whence I came. When? For now, do not ask. I leave you, a resurrected man not unhappy to be back in the flesh again and live in the flesh—where, you ask. Do not ask that either, for I do not know. My mission is at an end, and yours must begin. What men must learn they must learn from men unresurrected. You may know, however, that I shall be on the earth, though never again with you—except in the sense I spoke of before my death."

"Before your death," began Peter, and then the words

struck him like a crack on the jaw. "You died and you've come back. Hard to take in." He shivered. Jesus smote him on the back as though he had choked on a fish-bone.

"Hard to take in," said Jesus. "Dying is painful, but death itself is a mere nothing. Remember that—dying exists but there is no death. Remember what I said and did before my dying. The bread and the wine, God's gifts, and the word as palpable as bread and wine. The word now is yours, and the power, and the triumph will be yours, and also the agony. The way, as you have already seen, will not be easy." Nature glibly came in at that point with the noise of a wild thing not far off, caught and screaming. "You'll start in Jerusalem. But the word is not for Israel only. You will be driven as seed is driven by the winds of autumn—to other cities, other lands. To the islands of the Greeks and to Ethiopia, to the islands of the sea that the Romans call their sea, to Rome itself, for the word is for all men."

"How soon do we start?" asked Peter.

"Tomorrow," said Jesus promptly. "Or, if you will, tonight. There is little more for me to say to you. Love men, but beware of them—for they will deliver you up and scourge you, and for my sake you will be brought even before kings and governors, to be tried, to be punished for preaching love. But in the hour when you are called upon to testify for the Son of Man, have no fear. For it will not be you who speak but the spirit of your heavenly father that speaks within you. You shall be hated— for my sake. But he that endures to the end shall be saved. And the word shall prevail. Go then, and make disciples of all the nations, baptising them in three names—that of the father, that of the son, and that of the holy spirit which binds us all in one. And remember this—I am with you always, even unto the end of the world."

There was silence. Then the feet of the waiter could be heard coming up the stairs. He stood at the entrance, the sliver of wood, a mouth-toy, wagging between his gat-teeh.

"Everything all right? More wine? Who do I give the reckoning to?"

"To me," said Jesus.

NINE

And so I end my narrative. The events I have described, and the characters I have tried to delineate, already belong to a past that is in danger of fading into myth, so that Jesus may grow another cubit and become a true giant, and Judas Iscariot may dwindle into a man who needed thirty pieces of silver. Soon, I doubt not, there will be as it were official versions of Jesus and his life and his good news, made authoritative by men who claim authority, and enforced in every detail upon the faithful. This story of mine makes no claim to be a sacred text, but it does not abase itself either to the level of a pure diversion. Though I am no Christian, I believe that Jesus of Nazareth was a great man and his life worthy of that disinterested recording which only a non-believer is able to give. When I say *no Christian* and *non-believer* I mean that I am not greatly concerned one way or the other with the supposed evidence of Jesus's divine origin, with his virgin birth, with his resurrection, with his so-called miracles. "By their fruits shall ye know them," he said. It is with his fruits I am concerned, and not as colourful objects in a wooden dish but as esculent matter full of nourishing and tasty juice.

It is said by some that the creator of the universe made it in sport and maintains it as a diversion. If this is so, and I am half-inclined to believe it, then man's life may be little more than a game, in the sense that he is not able to be responsible for its maintenance, as this is in the hands of nature, and hence his time must be taken up with inessentials which, lest he die of boredom, he must consider as of great moment and large ultimate significance. He decks his house and body, he seasons the fruits of the earth, he hears music and reads stories. Sometimes his diversions are bloody and tyrannical and are termed politics and the art of governance or even the duty and necessity of imperial expansion. Man is a social animal who gladly builds loose human societies which bad men love to rigidify with laws and superstitious sanctions and dignify with the name of a State. That men are forced into having a duty towards each other I think none may deny.

Jesus of Nazareth taught the importance of the duty and clarified its nature in the word love—ahavah or agape but not properly amor. In all languages the word is treacherous and hard to define, but Jesus showed by story and example what meaning he attached to the term. He propounded an impossibility—the love of our enemies—but the impossibility must seem less so when it is seen in those what I must call ludic terms which have been applied to the creation of the world and its maintenance. The duty is also a game—fiendishly hard to play but still playable. The game of forbearance, the game of turning the other cheek, the game of overcoming our natural revulsion to a pocked or leprous skin and covering it with loving kisses. You win the game, and you receive a prize, and the prize is known as the kingdom of heaven. The kingdom is of men and women who play the game well and wish to play it even better. You can always recognise members of the kingdom: by their fruits shall ye know them. The game makes life uncommonly interesting. Why then do so many not merely not wish to play the game but persecute with what must seem disproportionate ferocity those who do?

It is because they take life too seriously. Jesus and his men did not take life seriously at all. Matthew had to be rescued from taking it seriously, as we have seen, but the rest of the followers were men who possessed nothing, and hence had nothing they could take seriously. Owning things is dangerous; the peril of owning an empire is the final madness of taking things seriously. When you own a thing you will always fight for it and, perhaps, find that fighting is a fine solvent of boredom. But fighting is destructive of self as well as of enemy, is immensely tiring, and too often ends in loss of the thing fought for. It is far better to play the game of the kingdom.

I could say more of this, but I am no moral philosopher (meaning arbiter of the game of social behaviour). I can speak only of my own life and the satisfaction I have gained from developing the skills of tolerance, forbearance and affection. It is, of course, necessary to love oneself before one loves others (else what would be the ludic virtue of loving one's neighbour as one loves oneself?), but the nature of this love is hard to explain to Pharisees and Sadducees. It is not a love of action but a love of essence: love yourself as a being remarkably made and (I would avoid the word if I could but I see I cannot) somewhat miraculously maintained. If it was good enough for God (so the Christians will say) then it is good enough for you.

Despite Jesus's appearance on the earth to preach the doctrine of love, and despite the stout work of his disciples (all put to death in curiously ludic ways by the serious), it cannot be said that the kingdom of heaven he promised as a reward for love is as yet likely to overtake the kingdom of the serious, which we also may call the kingdom of Caesar. Consider what has happened since Jesus died (I refer to the recorded death on the cross and not the death that followed the renewal of life, which I am not sure anyway whether I can accept). The Romans invaded Britain under Aulus Plautius. Caractacus was taken in chains as a slave to Rome. Boudicca revolted in Britain and was put down. The man Saul who became Paul was executed for preaching love. Rome was set alight, and it was all blamed on the Christians. The Jews of Palestine revolted at last against Roman rule, and the rebellion was most viciously repressed by Titus. Bar-Cochba (whose first name was said to be Jesus) revolted, and this revolt ended in the dispersion of the

Jews. Jesus of Nazareth saw clearly what would happen, and he implored men to be frivolous like the lilies of the field and to try (what the lilies cannot do) playing the game of forbearance and charity.

Some day perhaps all men will learn to join the kingdom, so that the kingdom of heaven will be coterminous with the kingdom of Caesar, in which event the very name and laurel crown of Caesar will only be the stuff of the games of children. But I somehow doubt this, as Jesus himself seems to have doubted it—else why so much talk about the gathering in of the harvest and the burning of the weeds? However, since Jesus insisted that God was not much concerned with time, it may be inferred that he is not much concerned with any kind of quantitative measurement, and that the kingdom does not have to pride itself on mere size.

I take my leave of you, bidding the captious not to be too hard on the literary shortcomings of one who has pretended to little but the zest of telling a plain story. The inimical I ask to love me, as I try to love them. To him who may, in time to come, translate this chronicle into a language not one of mine, I ask that he consult the claims of the spirit and not be too niggling about the mere letter. To all I say: work hard at the game of love that you may join me, and him, in the kingdom. *Schalom. Ila al-laqaa. Andi'o. Kwaheri.* Farewell.

EDWARD WHITTEMORE

Sinai Tapestry

'An epic hashish dream . . . cosmic . . . fabulous . . .
droll and moving' NEW YORK TIMES BOOK REVIEW

With the first book in his epic Jerusalem quartet,
Edward Whittemore embarks upon a powerful
re-working of the fabric of history. His fantastic
characters' separate journey of discovery begin in the
Sinai in the nineteenth century and move towards a
dramatic climax in the years leading up to World War
II. Rich, varied, outrageous and crazy, his extraordinary
narrative moves through a mad universe, his characters
propelled by a cosmic imagination.

'Sit back and enjoy an outrageously wild and disparate
cast . . . range over the Holy Land and other parts . . .
highly original . . . Sophisticated, surreal fun with a
cutting edge' PUBLISHERS WEEKLY

'Whittemore is to Vonnegut what a tapestry is to a
cat's cradle' Rhoda Lerman

EDWARD WHITTEMORE

Jerusalem Poker

'A fabulous adventure . . . a terrific read by one of
America's best writers' HARPER'S MAGAZINE

On the last day of December 1921 three men sat down to
a game of poker in the back room of an antiquities shop
in Jerusalem: Cairo Martyr, a Moslem with blue eyes
who made a fortune dealing in aphrodisiac mummy
dust; O'Sullivan Beare, the Irishman; and Monk Szondi,
a scion of the famous matriarchal banking house of
Budapest. The Great Jerusalem Poker Game, as it came
to be called, continued for twelve years, the stakes
nothing less than the control of the Holy City itself.

'A fantastic odyssey' THE GUARDIAN

More top fiction from Magnum Books

	Donald Lindquist	
417 0388	Berlin Tunnel 21	£1.50
	Ronald Lockley	
454 0004	Seal Woman	90p
	Jerry Ludwig	
417 0314	Little Boy Lost	95p
	Baron Moss	
417 0380	Chains	£1.50
	Timeri Murari	
417 0385	The Oblivion Tapes	£1.10
417 0333	Lovers are not People	95p
	C. Northcote Parkinson	
417 0549	The Fireship	90p
417 0548	Devil to Pay	95p
417 0246	Touch and Go	95p
417 0361	Dead Reckoning	£1.10
	Derry Quinn	
417 0187	The Limbo Connection	90p
417 0237	The Solstice Man	90p
417 0338	The Fear of God	95p
	Howell Raines	
417 0332	Whiskey Man	£1.25
	Bob Randall	
417 0245	The Fan	90p
	David Rogers	
417 0540	The In-Laws	95p
	David St George	
417 0492	The Right Honourable Chimpanzee	£1.25
	Oscar Saul	
417 0331	The Dark Side of Love	80p
	J I M Stewart	
413 3677	The Gaudy	85p
413 3678	Young Pattullo	85p
417 0189	A Memorial Service	85p
417 0219	The Madonna of the Astrolabe	£1.25
417 0378	Full Term	£1.25
	Peter Way	
417 0218	Super-Celeste	90p
	Ken Welsh	
417 0329	Hail the Hero!	95p
	Edward Whittemore	
417 0340	Sinai Tapestry	£1.50

These and other Magnum Books are available at your bookshop or newsagent. In case of difficulties orders may be sent to:

Magnum Books
Cash Sales Department
P.O. Box 11
Falmouth
Cornwall TR10 109EN

Please send cheque or postal order, no currency, for purchase price quoted and allow the following for postage and packing:

U.K.	30p for the first book plus 15p for the second book and 12p for each additional book ordered to a maximum charge of £1.29.
B.F.P.O. & Eire	30p for the first book plus 15p for the second book plus 12p per copy for the next 7 books, thereafter 6p per book.
Overseas Customers	50p for the first book plus 15p per copy for each additional book.

While every effort is made to keep prices low, it is sometimes necessary to increase prices at short notice. Magnum Books reserves the right to show new retail prices on covers which may differ from those previously advertised in the text or elsewhere